"I wish a word with my husband—alone."

The angry red imprint of her fingers against his hard jaw deeply embarrassed her. Only through sheer will and determination was she able to meet his eyes. What she saw there caught her by surprise.

The devil was enjoying this!

She was creating a scene that would make them the talk of London for a fortnight, yet in the clear, sharp depths of his eyes she saw humor. For an instant the memory of their wedding night so many years ago rippled through her like wind across water. The hopes, the dreams, the fears . . .

He placed his hand on her shoulder . . . a stranger's hand, she realized with a start—large, well-formed, capable. Mallory felt as if she'd swallowed a bubble and couldn't breathe. She remembered so much, suddenly, in that touch—

Her senses screamed a warning.

And then her feet left the ground! Before she knew what he was about, John Barron swung her easily up into his arms amid a flurry of skirts and petticoats.

The crowd roared its approval.

Avon Books by
Cathy Maxwell

His Christmas Pleasure
The Marriage Ring
The Earl Claims His Wife
A Seduction at Christmas
In the Highlander's Bed
Bedding the Heiress
In the Bed of a Duke
The Price of Indiscretion
Temptation of a Proper Governess
The Seduction of an English Lady
Adventures of a Scottish Heiress
The Wedding Wager
The Lady Is Tempted
The Marriage Contract
A Scandalous Marriage
Married in Haste
Because of You
When Dreams Come True
Falling in Love Again
You and No Other
Treasured Vows
All Things Beautiful

Cathy Maxwell

FALLING IN LOVE AGAIN

AVON
An Imprint of HarperCollins*Publishers*

This is a work of fiction. Names, characters, places, and incidents are products of the author's imagination or are used fictitiously and are not to be construed as real. Any resemblance to actual events, locales, organizations, or persons, living or dead, is entirely coincidental.

AVON BOOKS
An Imprint of HarperCollins*Publishers*
10 East 53rd Street
New York, New York 10022-5299

ISBN 978-0-380-78718-0
www.avonromance.com

First Avon Books mass market printing: August 1997

Printed in the U.S.A.

10 9

To my sister, Cindy Wollen, with love.

And to Trudy Bateman, Kay Bendall, and
Maude Kerby, with appreciation.

Thank you for being there
from the very beginning.

Acknowledgments

My thanks to Alex Tillen and his staff of historical interpreters at the Museum of American Frontier Culture in Staunton, Virginia, for their patience in answering my questions concerning English country life.

I also wish to express my appreciation to Chelsea Maxwell, Chris Peirson, Mary Burton, Pamela Gagné, and Donna Whitfield for their assistance, and to Damaris Rowland for her always wise counsel. Nor do I want to leave out any of my traveling companions on Lady Barrow's Tour of London, 1996. *Such a lovely day in the country, ladies, a lovely day!*

The verses on the title pages of each chapter are from English folk songs.

Chapter 1

Here is health unto the man, said he,
The man they call the groom;
Here's health unto the man, said he,
Who may enjoy his bride.

"The Green Wedding"

Craige Castle
East Anglia, England
1806

"He didn't want to marry me," Mallory Edwards Barron said in a low, troubled voice. "I could tell."

Sitting on the bench in front of the vanity table, she took a steadying breath and met her mother's gaze in the mirror, daring—no, hoping—Lady Craige would contradict her.

For the space of a heartbeat, Mallory saw her fears reflected in her mother's eyes before they were quickly blinked away. Lady Craige lowered the brush from Mallory's hair in mid-stroke and gave her daughter's shoulders a reassuring hug. "Of course John Barron wanted to marry you."

They spoke in whispers, conscious of the two maids cleaning up after Mallory's bath. The door leading to the hallway opening and closing behind them let in the hum of conversation, punctuated by laughter, from the wedding guests in the dining room.

"I overheard him arguing with his father last night in the library, Mother. It sounded as if John didn't even know he was going to be married until he arrived here. Can that be possible? Would a man not tell his son he'd contracted a marriage for him until the night before the wedding?"

"Mallory, you are allowing your imagination to run away with your common sense! What does it matter *when* John discovered he was to be married? What is important is our home, Craige Castle, and that this marriage will make you its future mistress. But first you must consummate your union with John Barron."

Mallory's stomach tightened at the thought. "He barely said two words to me this evening during the wedding feast. . . ."

Her mother's gentle squeeze on her shoulder reminded Mallory that they were not alone. Sally, a young village girl who'd been hired to serve as Mallory's maid for the evening, had returned and was busily turning down the sheets on the ornately carved Elizabethan tester bed that dominated the room.

Mallory's own parents had consummated their marriage on this bed, and their parents before them, and the generation before that. *And now she was expected to lie with a man she barely knew and fulfill the tradition, the tradition that would give her the right to be known as the Lady of Craige Castle.*

Since the days of William the Conqueror, when William had given this castle to Mallard, his most trusted friend and confidant, each Craige bride had spent her wedding night in this room. Tomorrow morning, the parish priest, Mallory's mother, and her new father-in-law, Sir Richard Barron, who had inherited her father's title, Viscount Craige, would come to this room and inspect the sheets for the bride's blood, proof that Mallory Craige had been a virgin. From that moment on, she and her husband, John Barron, would be truly married in the sight of God and man.

The sheet would then be hung from the window of this chamber and a day of feasting for the parish surrounding the castle would begin.

Mallory's hand shook as she reached for the crystal wine glass on the vanity table. She avoided her image in the mirror. The virginal white of her graceful nightdress drained all color from her face, emphasizing the dark circles under her eyes. One month had passed since her father's death following a long illness—a month that had turned her life inside out. "My nightdress should be black," she whispered.

"Sally, leave us," Lady Craige told the maid. "I'll see to my daughter from here."

"Yes, ma'am," the maid murmured before curtseying and moving toward the door. She paused a moment. "If I may be so bold, Miss Mallory, my mother and I wish you happiness in this marriage and want you to know that everyone in the village is resting easier knowing that you will be the lady of the castle."

Mallory forced a wan smile. "Thank you, Sally."

Sally turned the handle on the door. "We're also glad you're marrying such a hale and handsome man, Miss Mallory." Her cheeks turning pink, the maid slipped through the door.

"It seems the wedding party is a great success," Mallory said quietly. The wedding had been kept small out of respect for the family's mourning, but judging from the sounds coming from the dining hall, the guests were having a good time.

Lady Craige didn't answer. Instead, she sat beside Mallory on the bench and took the wine glass from her. She set it on the vanity before rubbing her palm over the top of Mallory's hands. "Your fingers are so cold." Lady Craige pressed her hands around her daughter's. "You must believe me when I promise that you have nothing to be afraid of."

"I wish it were over. I wish I hadn't married him. Not now. It's too soon after Father's death."

Lady Craige's expression softened. She lightly pushed back a curling tendril of hair from Mallory's face and tucked it behind her ear. "All brides are nervous. Marriage is a big step. Believe it or not, I was afraid of my first night with your father."

"Why couldn't I have inherited Craige Castle? It's unfair that in order to keep my birthright I must marry the son of this distant cousin who has inherited it from my father." Mallory pulled her hand away from her mother and stood. Her gaze fell on the bed, its rose-scented sheets turned down expectantly. Suddenly the room felt hot, close, and she purposely walked over to the window and pushed it open to let in the spring air with its promise of rain.

No moon or stars broke the night's darkness. For a moment Mallory could believe all the world was a void save for this candlelit room. She turned to face her mother, falling back on blunt honesty. "I was born to run this castle. What does John Barron know of it or the people who depend upon the Craige family for their livelihood? Does he know that Sally is the only support for her crippled mother? Can he calculate the return of a bushel of grain per acre, or understand the need to rotate the crops?"

"I doubt John knows anything except his studies," Lady Craige answered. "It will rest on your shoulders to teach him these matters. And don't ever forget that through this marriage, we are fulfilling your father's most fervent wish—that your children inherit the castle someday."

Mallory slid a glance toward the bed. "Mother, I'm not yet seventeen."

"You will be in a month." She came to her feet. "My dearest child, you are our only hope. If I could have saved you from marrying at such an early age and still kept Craige Castle, I would have. Either way, this is a spectacular match. The Barron family is fabulously wealthy, and someday John will inherit it all. He already has a substantial income from his mother's side of the family. Mallory, you have become a very rich woman."

"But I had dreams. I thought I would have a season in London, like Louise," she said, referring to Louise Haddon, her best friend, who planned to leave for London in the middle of June. *I wanted to go to dances . . . and to be courted,* she added silently. *To have the opportunity to fall in love. . . .*

"You could have had a thousand seasons and never have made a match as fine as this one. Furthermore, you'll live your dreams, but now you'll be living them with the freedom of a married woman. Of course, you can't go to London immediately because of our mourning, but Lord Barron has promised to have you presented at court a year from now."

Mallory looked down at the sapphire-and-diamond ring John had placed on her finger that morning. The sapphires mirrored the deep blue of his eyes.

When she had first met John yesterday afternoon, it was as if her imagination had conjured him from her dreams of the perfect man. Considering the haste with which the new Viscount Craige had insisted his son be wed, a haste Lady Craige and Mallory had been forced to agree with, since her father's death had left them penniless, Mallory had assumed something was wrong with John. She had anticipated that he would be ugly or fat or stupid, even lame! Instead, she'd been presented with a tall, dark-haired, brooding man only three years her senior whose looks were the stuff of romantic novels.

Almost as if reading her thoughts, Lady Craige said, "Besides, John is exceedingly handsome."

Mallory lifted her gaze from the ring. "Actually, he's far more attractive than I am."

"Mallory! How can you say such a thing? You are a lovely young woman."

"Oh, Mother." Mallory moved back toward the mirror, giving her reflection a critical eye. "My chin is too pointed, my mouth too full, and my eyes too small."

"You have lovely eyes."

"They disappear into slits when I laugh. And then there is my hair." Mallory pushed her fingers through it. "It refuses to obey and is of such a nondescript brown it's boring."

"That is not true. Your hair is your best feature—"

"Exactly!"

Lady Craige ignored her sarcasm. "It's not boring. It's thick and full of blonde tendrils."

"Mother, my hair is not blonde."

"You look exactly like your father's sister, Jennifer. She was a lovely woman. You have her beauty, her grace, and her spirit, too."

"I'm not a beauty, Mama . . . and I have freckles."

Lady Craige put her arm around Mallory's shoulders. "Yes, you are a beauty, freckles and all. You're still growing and changing, my love. Wait a few more years. The women on your father's side of the family always took their time maturing into their looks, and you will, too." She leaned her head forward so that they touched foreheads. "I know this marriage is hard. It would have been nice if you and John could have had time to get to know each other better—but Mallory, sometimes life doesn't work out as we wish."

"What I wish is that he wasn't so—" Embarrassed, she broke off.

"Handsome?" Lady Craige finished for her. "Mallory, John Barron may be a very handsome man, but he has his faults. Don't ever forget it. Don't allow his looks to intimidate you." She paused before adding thoughtfully, "I do like the sound of his voice. Very distinctive, don't you agree?"

Yes, Mallory agreed silently. Though he was still young, he had the voice of a man. Raspy and deep, it touched her in ways she'd never thought possible. Standing by his side before the Reverend Sweeney this morning, listening to him repeat his vows, was the first time since her beloved father's death that Mallory hadn't felt so alone.

Her gaze lingered on the bed a moment, and she felt a touch of anticipation. Still, something about this marriage wasn't quite right.

"What are those faults, Mother? Why is he marrying me? After all, someday he'll inherit Craige Castle. He could have married any woman of his choice, yet his father insisted that the two of us marry."

Lady Craige's mouth flattened. She played with the blue and gold ribbons of her lace cap a moment before admitting, "Well, it's just gossip actually."

Mallory was disappointed to realize that her suspicions were correct. "What is it?"

A knock on the door joining the master bedroom to a very large sitting and dressing room startled the two women.

John! He would have left the wedding party shortly after her own departure and repaired to the adjoining room to prepare for their wedding night.

He couldn't be ready yet. No, please, not yet!

While Mallory's heart beat in panic, Lady Craige walked serenely to the door and opened it a crack. "Yes?"

Mallory caught a glimpse of the man who served as her husband's valet. "The master wishes to know if his bride is ready."

Mallory feared her knees would buckle beneath her. She started to sit down on the bed, then shot back up again. The bed was the last place she wanted to be at this moment. She crossed to the window and stared out into the night.

In the background, she heard her mother calmly say, "The bride wishes a few more minutes."

A few more minutes! Mallory wished she had another year.

She wasn't aware that Lady Craige had returned until her mother gently forced the wine glass into her hand. "Take a sip. It will calm your fears." She smoothed Mallory's hair. "The marriage bed is not something to be abhorred."

Sipping the heady red wine, Mallory wasn't sure she agreed. Only two nights ago, Lady Craige had sat her down and explained her wifely duties. Even for Mallory, who'd spent her whole life around the care and breeding of animals, this information about what happened between a man and a woman was shocking. She'd led a sheltered, protected life, and the thought that humans were little different from animals startled her. She still wasn't certain how it was all supposed to work, but she had been too embarrassed to question her mother any further.

Nor was she going to question her now. Instead, she grasped for anything to delay the inevitable. "What is the gossip surrounding John Barron?"

Lady Craige shook her head. "You can't delay your fate, my child."

"I can defer it for a few moments," Mallory retorted. She paused, suddenly vulnerable. "Besides, not knowing him is hard. Is it wrong to ask questions, especially now that I've met him?"

Lady Craige led Mallory back to the bench, sat her in front of the mirror, and began brushing her hair before she said simply, "He's a bastard."

Mallory blinked in surprise, uncertain she'd heard correctly.

Lady Craige nodded to the unspoken question and replied in a whisper. "He is the illicit offspring of an affair his lady mother had with . . . well, one can only speculate, but the gossip is that his father was a stablemaster."

"A stablemaster—? But he has the Barron name!"

Her mother heaved a world-weary sigh. "Something one learns as one grows older, Mallory, is that life is seldom uncomplicated. Knowing Sir Richard as I do now, I can only speculate that pride led him to recognize John as his own son . . . and, of course, no one would accuse John of being a bastard to Sir Richard's face. He's far too powerful. It's rumored Sir Richard would have nothing to do with his wife once the child was born."

"If he was so angry, why did he recognize John?"

"Because every man wants an heir." There was a wistfulness in Lady Craige's voice that reminded Mallory she had once had a younger brother who had died in infancy. Mallory remembered little except the milk smells of the nursery and the sad, quiet conversation of the adults gathered around the crib.

She reached for her mother's hand. For a moment, the two women took comfort from each other. Then Lady Craige said, "Sir Richard and his wife were married for years without producing any children. The truth is, Sir Richard was out of the country and his wife in London when John was conceived. Everyone in society who can count on his fingers knows that. I believe Sir Richard fervently hopes he can buy a measure of acceptance for John through your marriage. After all, our family lines are impeccable. And, of course, he will someday be Viscount Craige."

Mallory was not that naive. "Certainly there will be sticklers for the proprieties who will never open their door to John."

"Or you either, I'm afraid."

Her comment stunned Mallory.

Lady Craige immediately attempted to soften her words. "But those people are the few members of the *haut ton* who look down their noses at everyone. And who cares about vouchers to Almack's? Mallory, your husband is a very wealthy man, and we shall keep our home."

"Why did you not tell me this when we were negotiating the marriage contract?" Mallory asked.

"Would it have made a difference?"

Slowly Mallory shook her head. Their financial circumstances had been too dire for her to let John's questionable lineage stand in the way of the marriage. She hadn't even been able to observe a decent interval of mourning, since Sir Richard would be leaving soon for a governorship in India and had not wanted the marriage delayed.

She took another sip of wine. The tension in her shoulders eased slightly. The candlelit room took on a muted glow.

Lady Craige sat down beside her on the bench. "Look for the good things in John, and your marriage will be a success."

"I barely know him."

"You were impressed when you learned he was a fellow at All Souls College, weren't you?"

Mallory couldn't deny it.

Reaching for the decanter on the vanity, Lady Craige poured a bit more wine into Mallory's glass before adding, "Sir Richard is ambitious for John. With his father's connections, the Craige title, and his own intelligence, there is no telling how much John may achieve, in spite of his rumored origins. Sir Richard seems to believe John is suited for a career in the Church. And admit it now, Mallory, it doesn't hurt the eyes to look at him."

Mallory found herself smiling. "No," she admitted self-consciously.

"Couldn't you learn to love him just a tiny bit?"

The heat of a blush crept up Mallory's cheeks.

"See?" her mother said, with a touch of triumph. "I thought you found him attractive. You shall both give me beautiful grandchildren, and together you and I will raise them at Craige Castle."

On that note, Mallory all but drained her glass of wine.

"Easy," her mother warned her. "You are not accustomed to strong drink. Besides, I have a confession to make."

Mallory lowered the glass. "In addition to everything else we've discussed?" She was suddenly finding it difficult to keep hold of the glass, even using both hands. What was wrong with her? "What is it?"

"I put a sleeping draught in your wine."

"What?" Mallory cried.

Lady Craige took the glass from Mallory before she spilled the little wine left in it. "I feared you would be upset."

"This is no jest?"

Lady Craige shook her head and kneaded Mallory's shoulders. "But see? You have grown tense again."

Mallory shrugged her off and came to her feet. "Why did you drug me?"

Lady Craige also rose from the bench, her

brows coming together in concern. "I knew you would be upset, but I did it for your own good. You were so obviously disturbed by our talk the other night about what to expect in the marriage bed that I—well . . . I thought this would make matters easier. It's what my mother did for me."

Mallory brought her hands up to her cheeks. She now realized their heat had nothing to do with embarrassment. In fact, they felt slightly numb.

A knock sounded at the adjoining door. Mallory looked to it and back to her mother, horror welling inside her. *"How could you?"*

"I only meant to relax you. I didn't anticipate you would guzzle the wine." Lady Craige took a step, but Mallory stopped her with a raised hand.

Someone rapped on the door again.

Mallory dropped her hand, her anger at her mother evaporating. "We have to let him in," she whispered.

Lady Craige raised her voice. "One moment, please." She turned back to Mallory. "No, *you* will let him in. I must leave. Now, quickly, climb onto the bed."

Mallory balked. "I'm not ready!" Apprehension shook her growing lassitude. "I should braid my hair. I always braid my hair at night."

"But it looks so pretty down past your shoulders."

"I want it braided," Mallory said, with steel in her voice. It had suddenly become important to her to pretend this night was no different from the others.

For once, her mother had the good sense not to argue. Mallory quickly plaited her long hair into a straight braid down her back and tied it off with a piece of gold cord.

Lady Craige crossed to close the window, but Mallory's voice stayed her. "I prefer it open." It might help keep her awake.

Her mother considered her for a moment and then lifted her shoulders in a dismissive shrug. Instead, she stoked the fire in the stone hearth and began snuffing the candles.

"What are you doing?" Mallory asked.

"Making the room more inviting." Her mother left one candle burning on the night table beside the bed. "Now, come. Don't be afraid."

Mallory had no choice but to climb up on the bed, the mattress bending under her weight. The rose scent of the sheets seemed stronger, mingling with the fresh air. As if in a dream, she sank back against the pillows.

Lady Craige bent forward and kissed her daughter's forehead. "Be a good wife to your husband and he shall be a good husband to you. Trust in your destiny, Mallory, and believe me when I say everything will look better on the morrow." With those words, she crossed to the door adjoining the two rooms. She rapped once, apparently a signal that all was well, and then left through the door leading out to the hallway.

Mallory was alone.

Outside the castle walls, a spring rain came down with a sudden intensity that drowned out all other sounds. Rain on her wedding day.

The flickering light from the candle cast an eerie glow that didn't reach the darkness of the room beyond the large bed. But that wan light did catch and reflect off the smooth old gold and sparkling jewels of her wedding ring.

A sharp knock, different from the others, on the heavy oak door adjoining her room startled her.

Her husband.

For one wild moment, Mallory panicked. She actually stood up on the bed, wanting to run, to hide.

But she couldn't. She understood duty, honor . . . necessity. She would not disgrace her family name.

Slowly Mallory sank back down on the bed, her night dress billowing around her. Now she was thankful for the drugged wine. The hard edges of reality blurred.

Clasping her hands in her lap as if in prayer, she called, "Come in."

The handle of the door stuck as he turned it. Mallory held her breath.

With a strong jerk, the latch lifted, the sound of metal against wood loud in the still room. The hinges creaked.

The small light of the candle beside her bed didn't reach across the room, but Mallory knew he was there, this tall, quiet man she'd married. She felt his presence.

His footsteps were silent as he crossed the worn carpet. He stepped out of the darkness and into the circle of light, and Mallory's breath caught in her throat, part in fear, part in wonder.

John's features weren't classically perfect.

There was a hint of ruggedness, of independence, that didn't seem bred for society drawing rooms—and was immensely attractive. His thick, silky dark hair conformed to no style but his own. He wore it straight and back from his face, but a boyish cowlick at the hairline, his one imperfection, bent a lock of it over one eye. His mouth was wide, even generous, and his cobalt eyes reflected the candle's flame.

With his broad shoulders and long, lean figure, Mallory couldn't imagine him in cleric's robes. The role of theologian seemed too tame. Despite his youth, this man commanded attention.

She raised a hesitant hand to touch her long braid lying against her chest. She should have left her hair loose. Now, with him in the room, the braid made her feel childish, foolish.

He'd removed the black jacket and silver waistcoat he'd worn to the wedding banquet. His stockless white lawn shirt hung loose outside his black breeches. He wore no shoes.

The sight of his stocking feet suggested intimacy.

He studied her solemnly for a moment before asking quietly in his low, raspy voice, "Do you know what is to happen between us?"

Her face flooding with hot color, she whispered, "I've been told. I'm to do whatever you ask of me."

His shoulders dropped slightly, as if she'd placed a great weight upon them, and she remembered that he'd not touched a drop to drink and barely eaten during the wedding breakfast or this evening's supper. But then neither had she.

Slowly, with a sense of grim resolution, he straightened his shoulders. "You are so young."

"I'll be seventeen next month. Besides, you are not so old yourself."

He didn't answer, but watched her with wary eyes.

She shifted uncomfortably in the silence. "Please, I'd like to have this deed done." Done and over.

He took a step away from the bed. "Mallory, we don't have to do this now. We can wait until we know each other better."

Her name sounded strange, unusual on his lips, almost like music. Then the meaning of his words hit her.

He didn't want her.

He found her unattractive. Mallory knew it as clearly as if she could read his mind. The wine and tension turned on her, robbing her of the self-restraint and composure so many people expected of her. Tears burned her eyes.

His heavy eyebrows drew together in alarm. "Please." The word sounded almost desperate.

"You don't want me."

"I'm suggesting it would be better if we waited. Until you've grown up a bit more."

"No!" The word echoed through the room. "Tomorrow, when my mother, your father, and the Reverend Sweeney come to this room, our marriage must have been consummated. It's the tradition."

"But we've only just met each other."

"I'm your wife." Feeling the effects of the

drugged wine, Mallory slurred the last word. A strange sense of well-being, almost as if she lived in a dream, invaded her senses. She no longer felt the panic she'd experienced only moments before. "We must do this."

He laughed, a bitter sound, and muttered something about his father being more of a bastard than he was.

Mallory didn't care. "I can't face the morrow if the deed is not done. It's a matter of honor," she added, her voice low, hushed.

For a second she thought he was going to argue with her, and it made her angry. The blood of warrior kings drummed through her veins. She would not back down from her duty. Boldly, deliberately, she stood upon the bed, reached down and pulled the white batiste nightdress up over her head, and tossed it aside.

The air between them crackled with tension. Mortified by her own brazen action, Mallory forced herself to face him.

He stared at her, his expression unfathomable. A dull red stain spread across his features. Mallory thought she could hear his heart hammering in his chest. Or was it her own?

She gathered her pride around her. "We must do this—now, tonight."

To her relief he nodded. She came to her knees and reached for the bedclothes to cover her nakedness. She slipped beneath the rose-scented sheets, their texture silky and cool.

John began pulling the hem of his shirt up and over his head. She watched with fascination. He was gorgeous, all strong, lithe muscle glowing with vibrant warmth. He seemed more man than boy, more soldier than scholar.

He folded the shirt and laid it on the end of the bed. His gaze met hers. His mouth tightened as if he found her interest unseemly. "Do you want the candle burning or not?"

A hard lump formed in her throat. "Perhaps it would be best with the candle out."

He walked to the bedside table and blew out the candle, plunging the room into darkness, save for the soft glow from the fire in the hearth. The smell of hot beeswax mingled with the cool, rain-drenched air flowing from the window. A log in the fire popped.

Mallory listened to his movements in the dark, the slide of his breeches down his legs, the soft sound of the material being folded and then tossed on a wooden chair. He lifted the sheet to join her. The mattress gave under his weight.

They lay separate and apart for several long seconds, then his legs brushed against hers, their rough texture emphasizing the differences between them. He pulled back, as if the brief body contact startled him as much as it had her. Protectively, she pressed the bedclothes around her body and stifled a yawn.

They lay still, side by side. Mallory's eyelids felt heavy. "What do we do now?" she whispered, afraid she might fall asleep.

He reached for her as if to hug her. Mallory stiffened.

His voice came low in her ear. "Could you relax a bit?"

"No." Her voice sounded small.

With a groan, he lay back on the bed, the space between them seemingly wider than the Channel between England and France.

Mallory drew in a steadying breath. If she wished to hold the title of Lady of Craige Castle one day, she had to do this with him. "You can try now." Could he hear how frightened she was? "I'll relax."

John placed a hand on her shoulder. His fingers felt warm against her skin. Slowly, gently, he ran his palm down under the sheet and over her breast. Mallory flinched. "I'm sorry," she whispered.

"Don't apologize." He was angry.

She didn't answer. Hot tears stung the backs of her eyelids and she couldn't say a word without sounding stiff and resentful.

And then he kissed her.

It was her first kiss, other than the chaste peck he'd given her cheek that morning before the altar at his father's hearty insistence.

The softness of his lips against her closed mouth surprised her. His arm slipped beneath her and gathered her close. Their nakedness no longer seemed to matter. He'd shaved. She rubbed her cheek against his smooth, hard jaw. The light citrus scent of his shaving soap mingled with the smell of roses . . . and suddenly everything started to feel right. Slowly, Mallory relaxed, curving her body next to his. Here she felt warm, safe. Her nakedness was no longer an embarrassment—and then he pulled away.

She frowned, wishing he would kiss her again,

when to her horror he reached out and brushed a tear from her cheek. "Mallory—"

"Now. Please." The strain of the last few minutes made her tremble. If he didn't act soon, she would disgrace herself completely.

He murmured something under his breath, the words soft, concerned, but Mallory didn't pay attention. Instead, she did as her mother had instructed—rolled on her back, and spread her legs in the position necessary for her husband to claim her.

He came up on one elbow. He seemed to hesitate, a dark shadow looming above her. Mallory stared up at the ceiling, her body pressed into the mattress. Now she was glad her mother had given her the sleeping draught. She wanted to forget the humiliation of what she was doing. She'd never grow accustomed to submitting to her husband like this, not ever.

He lifted himself up so that he could settle over her body, one knee parting her legs further to better accommodate him. His weight on top of her was not uncomfortable.

And yes, she could feel something else. His man part. Like any purebred stallion in her father's breeding yard, he was ready and able. The deed would be done, tradition fulfilled.

Mallory dug her fingers into the soft feather mattress, closed her eyes, and promised herself she wouldn't cry out. No matter how it hurt, she couldn't cry out. Her limbs felt heavier, her movements grew slower, and with a soft, thankful sigh, she escaped into oblivion.

John attempted to kiss her again before realizing his new wife had fallen asleep in his arms. He shifted his weight off her and leaned back on one elbow, not sure what to do.

"Mallory," he whispered. "Mallory?"

She murmured something unintelligible and curled up like a kitten beside him, her skin warm and smooth.

John touched her lightly, placing his hand on the feminine curve of her hip. Before coming into this room, his intention had been to talk her out of consummating their marriage this night. However, once she'd brazenly removed the voluminous nightdress, all such thoughts had fled his mind. Even now he was hard.

But his new wife was sound asleep.

He rolled out of the bed and onto his feet, uncertain of his next move. The night air sent a shiver across his flesh. He slipped on his breeches and walked around the bed to the hearth. He lit a taper off the fire and used it to light the candle on the vanity.

The glowing light barely illuminated the bed where his wife lay sleeping. Dear Lord, she looked so young and innocent.

Even now, his traitorous body reacted to her slim, long-legged beauty and her effortless grace.

In spite of his almost violent anger with his father, John couldn't help but admire this young woman he'd been ordered to wed. She'd managed the myriad details of the wedding ceremony and guests with the cool calm of a young queen. Her mother had always been bustling about, but had actually accomplished nothing. No, he was certain Mallory had made all the plans. In fact, he'd seen no hint of her anxiety over this marriage until just now, when she'd cried in his arms.

Those tears had gone straight to his heart.

John had few illusions concerning his status in life. He was the result of an indiscretion of his willful mother's. She'd paid for that lapse of judgment by being banished by her husband to an extreme and lonely part of England. John could count on one hand the number of times he'd seen his mother—and he'd cherished each and every one of those visits.

But he knew he was a bastard. He'd known the truth from the first moment he'd been cruelly taunted by the other boys at school. His father might wish to pretend otherwise, but John was tired of pretending.

He shot a glance at the woman on the bed. Did she know? Was that why she'd cried?

Wearily, John sat down on the bench. His gaze settled on the decanter of wine and an empty glass. He poured some and took a healthy swallow. With a sputter, he just as quickly spat the wine back into the glass.

It tasted funny, cloyingly sweet. He stuck a finger into the decanter, tilting it until he wetted the tip, and raised his finger to his nose.

Beneath the wine's natural fruitiness was the elusive scent of something else. He knew enough to realize this wine had been drugged.

John frowned thoughtfully, scanning the top of the vanity until his gaze rested on a half-full glass of wine. Had his wife been drinking it?

He shot a look at Mallory. She hadn't moved from where he'd left her. Her breathing was deep and regular, too deep, considering the circumstances.

She'd been drugged!

Or had she taken the drug willingly?

Or was this another of his father's machinations? Was there no area of John's life where he could be his own man?

With a fierce shout of frustration, he threw the decanter at the stone mantel, where it smashed into a thousand shards of crystal, a dark stain spreading there. His sweet young wife slept on, lost in the oblivion of drug-induced sleep.

John pushed his hair back from his head. His father had told him about the barbaric sheet ritual when he'd informed John that he was to be married. Of course, that had been the night before the wedding. Until that moment, John hadn't had any idea why he'd been ordered down from school and told to meet his father at a place called Craige Castle.

Worse, on the morrow, his father expected John to return to his tutors and studies for the Church, to bury himself in learning scholarly rites and dogma. Years ago, his father had decided the time had come for the Barron family to increase its influence in England by allying itself with the Church. He'd decided his son should fulfill the role, and John's feelings over the matter were of little importance—just as John's desire not to marry someone he didn't know had been unimportant.

His gaze drifted toward his sleeping bride. Had his father had a hand in drugging her? Would the man really go so far?

And did he believe John could commit such a cold-blooded, dishonorable act of lust and take his child-bride while she was unconscious?

For what seemed like hours, John sat as if turned to stone. He relived past events and situations in his mind. He'd spent his life trying to fulfill his father's need to prove John was his true son and not merely symbol of his mother's infidelity. John's whole life—even this, the sacrament of marriage—was nothing more than a sham to hide the secret of his birth.

The answer to his prayers came in the wee hours right before dawn. His wife wanted to be the mistress of Craige Castle. She'd been born here and had sold herself into a loveless marriage to stay and serve as its mistress. John took in the cold walls and ancient furniture and wished her happiness with it.

Meanwhile, his father wanted his son to be accepted by society, to be acknowledged as a legitimate heir without the whisper of scandal.

John could understand a man needing a son, even though, in truth, he and his father had never been close. Affairs of state had often kept Sir Richard away from England, and John had spent his life in a succession of public schools being "prepared" for his future.

Exactly how much did John owe this man? The question had plagued him ever since their argument last night.

In a vanity drawer, John found a small knife. It was a lady's tool, carved from fine silver, but with a sharp, wicked tip.

He sliced the pad of his thumb and watched with fascination as a bead of blood appeared. Silently he walked to the bed.

Mallory slept as if the very demons of hell would never wake her. All the loneliness John had known in life welled up inside him. Gently he reached over her sleeping form and wiped his blood upon the sheet.

Minutes later, he slipped unnoticed from the room.

In the early hours of a clear dawn, John Barron stood on a fallen log beyond the castle's aged walls and looked up at the window of the room where he'd spent his wedding night. The torrents of rain from the night before had washed the world fresh and new. For the first time in his life, he felt hope.

At that moment, in a ritual followed by the Craige family for centuries, the bridal sheet was hung out the window of the stone tower for all the tenants to witness. From this distance, no one could see the bloodstain on the sheet—but they would understand it was there, proof that John Barron, the future Lord Craige, had done his duty. He had claimed his wife.

Suddenly, John began running through the woods, faster and faster. His lungs filled with air. His feet threw up clods of wet, newly turned earth as he crossed a farmer's field. He ran until pain and cold air ripped through him and he couldn't draw another breath. He ran until he finally collapsed at the roots of a huge oak tree. For long moments, there was no sound in his ears but the mad beating of his heart and the ragged unevenness of his breathing.

The world swirled over his head and then ever so slowly steadied. A squirrel leaped from one branch to another, its claws scratching against the bark as it worked to build a nest. The sky beyond the oak's strong, long limbs was a light, clear blue. A mourning dove called, its plaintive call disquieting, questioning.

He rose to his feet and looked toward Craige Castle, its gray stone tower still visible above the trees. For a moment he hesitated, thinking of an innocent young girl, her honey-gold eyes so full of apprehension that she had made him feel like a monster. Worse, he remembered the feel of her breast beneath his hand, the pounding of her heart against her throat, and the smooth warmth of her skin.

John shut the memory from his mind. She belonged to this castle. Here she would be safe and protected. For all intents and purposes, she was Lady Craige. That was how her people thought of her and how she would remain. She could have the ten thousand a year he received from his mother's estate and live happily ever after, as in one of the German fables so popular with children.

John had other plans. He turned away from the castle tower and, finding a path through the forest, made his way toward the coast. He wasn't a churchman, a husband, or a lover.

What he wanted was to be a soldier, a warrior-saint like St. George, who had led England to glory and destroyed her enemies. With God's help, he would live that dream.

And so it happened that the day after a wedding that had linked two important ancestral families and delivered a great estate into his father's hands, John Barron escaped to create his own destiny.

Chapter 2

First he kiss'd me,
Then he left me
Bid me always answer No.
O No, John! No, John! No, John! No!

"O No, John!"

London
Seven years later

He was determined to be a hell-raiser of a nobleman.

John Barron, the new Viscount Craige, took off his hat and handed it to Titus, the butler of his latest mistress, Lady Sarah Ramsgate. Sarah's drawing rooms were filled with the extravagant, self-indulgent members of the *ton* who enjoyed the sort of wicked entertainments that could be found at her soirées. The smell of spirits and smoke hung in the air. The doors and windows of the house were open to the summer night, and the sounds of laughter and conversation drifted out to the line of carriages and horses waiting in the street.

The daughter of an actress, Sarah had purchased respectability by marrying a very rich, very ancient lord who turned a blind eye to his wife's indiscretions and spent most of his time in the country. It was a good thing he did. John couldn't imagine Lord Ramsgate would be pleased to see three actresses dancing on his dining room table while musicians played in hand-clapping time. One sweet young thing was already naked, while the other two were working their way to that state, urged on by the shouting admiration of male and female guests alike.

The Prince Regent, or Prinny, as he was called by his friends, held court in the main salon, laughing with other members of the dissipated Carleton House set—Brummell, Alvanley, and a portly lord named Applegate, an avid gambler who depended on John to cover his debts. The men were laying wagers on who of their party could roll a marble across the fireplace mantel and knock off a very expensive vase sitting on the edge. They took to the task with the enthusiasm of small boys and broke out into gales of laughter when Alvanley's marble sent the vase crashing. Wine was called for as another vase was found and set on the mantel edge. Applegate caught sight of John and called him over, hiccupping after every word.

John pretended not to hear. With the restless energy of a caged animal, he wove his way through the glittering crowd, his tall presence commanding respect.

He wasn't dressed for a night on the town but wore his riding clothes, doeskin breeches, a dark blue coat cut of the finest stuff, and polished boots sporting a single spur. He'd spent the day at Tattersall's auction house buying new bits of horseflesh that he neither needed nor wanted. It had been something to do, something to spend money on, something to break the terrible monotony of his days, now that he'd been "retired" from the active military life he'd loved.

"John!" Sarah's husky voice came to him over the noisy crowd.

Her extraordinary blonde beauty stood out in the circle of people around her. She was the reigning queen of this extravagant, self-indulgent group and loved the drama of her role. She moved toward him slowly, her walk a study in seduction. The gauzy muslin of her dress left nothing to the imagination. Sapphires sparkled in her hair, on her hands, and around her neck, while skillfully applied cosmetics ensured that she retained her youthful bloom.

What all that artifice couldn't hide was her possessiveness. John had started their affair because he'd expected her to make no demands upon his time or person. He'd discovered the opposite to be true and found her almost insane jealousy boring. He'd come this evening with the express purpose of breaking off their liaison.

He'd have to postpone their discussion until tomorrow, since he anticipated her throwing one of her infamous tantrums over his rejection. A diamond collar worth a king's ransom rested in a velvet-lined box inside the pocket of his coat jacket to ward off any unpleasantness.

He forced himself to smile, a smile that turned genuine when he recognized the man who was coming toward him behind Sarah.

Major Victor Peterson was one of his oldest friends. The two had served as ensigns together in India before both were ordered to Portugal. Blond and elegantly handsome, Victor wore the blue and red uniform of the Royal Artillery, the same company John had led before he'd been ordered home. Ignoring Sarah, John clasped his friend's hand warmly. "When did you arrive in London?"

"Only this afternoon. I stopped by your house earlier but you weren't there. Then I ran into Applegate at the club and he said you'd be here." For a second, Peterson's gaze lingered on the generous expanse of cleavage over Sarah's bodice. "You lucky dog."

Sarah laughed, her voice deep and throaty, and started to take John's arm, but he managed to slip away. "Come," he said to Peterson, "let's go where we can talk."

Sarah stepped into their path. "And leave me?" Her lower lip pulled out in a pout, but there was a hint of warning in her voice. "You just arrived, John. You can't leave—not yet." She lifted her eyes to Peterson. "My John has been hard to domesticate. I fear he still prefers the battlefield and hard living to soft beds and his late father's fortune."

"Prefers them even to your bed?" Peterson murmured gallantly, lifting Sarah's hand to his lips.

John rolled his eyes while Sarah basked in the glory of a new conquest. "Can you imagine it?" she asked, lightly touching one of the gold tassels decorating the chest of Peterson's uniform.

"No, my lady," Peterson answered warmly. "A man would be a fool to prefer French bullets to you. However, you must remember that John is one of our more decorated heroes of the war. He saved my life more times than I care to admit."

"Yes, yes, yes," she said. "Everyone knows he was not happy when Prinny ordered him to return to London after his father's death. I have done my best to make him happy, but see? He shows up late even for *my* soirées."

Peterson "tsked" over John's perfidy. Sarah moved closer to him, shooting a look over her shoulder to see if her attention to Peterson was making John jealous.

John shook his head. He'd never be jealous of Peterson. He loved the man like a brother, and he could have Sarah and her expensive tastes with John's best wishes.

As if reading his thoughts, Sarah took a step back. The smile on her face turned brittle. "Major Peterson, I pray that you may convince him to relax and enjoy his good fortune. I fear I have little influence."

Sarah was apparently more astute than John had given her credit for being. Perhaps ending their affair wouldn't be so difficult, after all.

"Did you know we call him the Dark Prince?" she asked Peterson.

"No, I hadn't heard," Peterson said. "On the

battlefield, we had a host of other, more colorful names for him. How did you earn such a romantic sobriquet, John?"

Sarah answered, "Because he is so different from his father. Richard Barron was the confidant of kings, a complete politician with unparalleled power. Our John prefers to entertain the court jesters." She nodded toward Prinny, terribly fat and overstuffed in his tight clothes. At that moment another vase fell to the floor. The men drained their glasses in one gulp, laughing uproariously.

"I didn't know you paid attention to politics, Sarah," John said softly.

"I pay attention to everything that concerns you, my Lord Craige." She tilted her head up at Peterson. "John has held the title for six months. In that time he has established a reputation as a lion of society and a rake of the first order. Did you know, there are women who send him things, personal things like their gloves, ear bobs. . . ." She paused before adding in a considering tone, "And perhaps even more intimate items?"

"Whyever would they do that?" Peterson asked.

"To gain Lord Craige's attention," she answered matter-of-factly. "He has captured the imagination of the female populace. There are women who idolize him more than they do the current poets." She leaned closer to John, the cloying scent of her heavy perfume stinging his nostrils, and added in a voice only the two of them could hear, "And not without good cause." Her ungloved hand ran down his arm, feeling the muscle beneath the cloth.

Peterson laughed. "It has ever been that way, Lady Ramsgate. In Spain, the other officers and I used John and his handsome face to shamelessly attract women. My wife was the only woman I've met who looked at me before John—and for that I dropped to one knee and proposed."

"Oh, so you are married, Major Peterson?"

The laughter in Peterson's eyes vanished. "I was. She died."

John shared his friend's sorrow. Liana Peterson had been his only female friend, the first woman he'd trusted. In fact, she'd died in childbirth in his arms. Peterson had been away on special duty at the time. It had fallen on John's shoulders to sit beside her, praying for a miracle that had never come. One of the hardest tasks he'd ever performed had been breaking the news to Peterson. The man had been inconsolable for months.

"How sad," Sarah said, in a voice that expressed no sympathy.

John had had enough of Sarah. "Come, Victor, let us go and have a drink. I'm hungry for news from the war. Has Horton turned out to be as great an ass as we feared?" he asked, referring to the man who had taken over John's command.

"Worse," Peterson answered, and he would have elaborated, except that at that moment a man's voice bellowed John's name from the hallway.

John thought he was hearing things until the

man shouted again. "Craige! Where are you? Come out and face me!"

The music stopped abruptly and voices hushed. Conscious that all eyes in the room had turned to stare at him, John calmly nodded to Sarah and Peterson. "You'll excuse me for a moment, won't you?"

As Sarah's guests stepped aside to clear a path, John walked out into the hallway. Sir Everett Carpenter, an older man, stood weaving unsteadily near the front door. Titus had his hand on the man's arm, as if he were prepared to physically eject him from the house. The party guests gathered around the dining room and drawing room doorways, avidly watching the confrontation.

"Yes, Sir Everett, what can I do for you?" John asked, nodding for Titus to take a step back.

Sir Everett's face beneath his balding pate was flushed from drink—John could almost smell the fumes of the man's breath from where he stood—but his eyes burned with intensity. "I want my wife back. I want you to release her."

John lifted an eyebrow. "I'm sorry, sir, I don't understand what you mean." He searched his mind. "I don't remember having had the honor of meeting your wife, let alone holding her in some way from which she needs to be *released.*"

"You lie!" Sir Everett cried, and raised the hand he'd been hiding inside his coat. He pointed a small pistol squarely at John. Their audience pulled back from the doors with a collective gasp of surprise.

"You danced with my wife at Lady Cogswell's

rout a week ago last Tuesday," Sir Everett accused. "Since that day she thinks of nothing but you."

Conscious that the man could blow off his head at any moment and was endangering the lives of those around them, John calmly brushed an imaginary piece of lint from his dark superfine jacket before repeating politely, "I am sorry, Sir Everett, but I don't remember having the pleasure of meeting her."

"She writes you every day. She goes to the park hoping to see you, hoping you will notice her, and when you don't, when you ride past without so much as a nod in her direction, she is brokenhearted. She no longer speaks to me. She's unhappy. I'm unhappy." His hand holding the pistol shook as he declared, "Tonight she told me she's leaving me."

John started walking toward the man, his steps measured and deliberate. "I'm sorry she is unhappy. But she belongs with her husband."

Sir Everett nodded. "That's what I told her, but she won't listen to me. The only way I can have her back is if you are dead!"

John heard a movement behind him and knew Peterson was coming forward in his defense. Keeping his gaze locked on Sir Everett's, John held up his hand, a signal for Peterson to stay back. "Let us go outside, sir, and talk this over as gentlemen."

Sir Everett shook his head sadly. "I won't. You would kill me. I'm afraid I have no choice, Lord Craige, but to shoot you dead."

John stopped. The man was bloody mad. "Then shoot and be damned," he said softly.

Beads of sweat broke out on Sir Everett's forehead. John focused on the bore of the dueling pistol. He resumed walking toward Sir Everett.

"I will shoot," the man said, his voice shrill.

John didn't stop.

Sir Everett moved back, his knees practically knocking together in fright, and John thought the game was won, until the pistol went off.

The heat of the bullet whizzed past his cheek, searing his skin. It smashed safely into the clock standing against the wall behind John.

For one long heartbeat, the two men stared at each other in surprise. The incredible control John exercised over himself warred with his very real anger at almost having had his head blown off.

Sir Everett dropped the smoking pistol. It hit the wood floor with a dull thud. "You don't understand," he said, his voice hoarse with emotion. "If you had a wife, you'd understand."

The corners of John's mouth turned down cynically. "Oh, but you're wrong, sir. I do have a wife, and I would never sacrifice my reputation for her."

The color drained from Sir Everett's face and the man fell to his knees.

John pitied him. London was full of women who cared for nothing more than a man's bank balance or his status in society. Men like Lord Ramsgate and Sir Everett were little more than puppets in the hands of such women. "Set your wife aside, sir," he said, in a voice so low no one but Sir Everett could hear him. "She'll break your heart."

"She already has," Sir Everett answered. He lowered his head and began weeping without shame.

John turned to Titus and ordered him to see Sir Everett home. The butler signaled for a footman. John was now more impatient than ever to leave the party. The smell of burnt powder mixed with that of perfumed bodies and candle wax was beginning to give him a headache. He turned on his heel, ready to suggest to Peterson that they leave—but his words died in his throat.

He'd forgotten he had an audience. Peterson, Sarah, and all the guests at the party, including Prinny, were staring at him in wide-eyed amazement. Not a man or woman moved.

It was plump, good-natured Applegate who found his voice first. "You're married, Craige?"

John pulled back, suddenly realizing what he'd admitted in a flash of anger. He looked from Applegate to Peterson, who had a dumbfounded expression on his handsome face.

"Is that so remarkable?" John asked, noncommittally.

It was Prinny who answered. "Remarkable? Astounding!"

Applegate blinked. "I've known you since the moment you came to town—"

"I fought by your side," Peterson interrupted. "We've shared rations, ammunition, women. . . ." His voice trailed off self-consciously as he realized what he'd said.

Applegate shot Peterson a cross look before

finishing his own thoughts. "I believed myself your closest friend here in London. Of anyone, *I* should have known you were married."

John frowned. This was not a conversation he wanted to have. He started walking up the hallway. He needed a drink. Something, anything to turn attention away from himself. Prinny and Applegate emerged from the drawing room and followed.

"Who is she?" Prinny asked, keeping pace with John's long strides. "Do we know her? Know her family?"

"She lives in the country," John tossed over his shoulder.

"Does she ever come to town?" Applegate asked.

"Is it any of your business?" John countered.

"No, but we're full of curiosity," Applegate returned, with his usual good humor. "After all, John, since you inherited the title, you're considered one of London's most eligible bachelors. You can't blame *us* for our interest."

John stopped, rolling his eyes in exasperation. "I never said I was a bachelor, eligible or otherwise."

"You've never said anything—that's why we are so surprised," Prinny said, pointing out the obvious. "Although I must admit in your defense, you have avoided matchmaking mamas. But I never dreamed you did so because you were *married.*"

"It's no wonder then that Craige doesn't honor another man's wife," Sir Everett said in an overloud voice. "He doesn't even honor his own."

John turned and faced his recent opponent. Sir Everett had gotten to his feet and now, apparently, desired to recover some of his lost pride. "Do you wish to repeat yourself, sir?" John asked coldly.

Sir Everett's features flushed red, but he stood his ground. "You may have inherited a gentleman's title, Craige, but everyone knows you are a disgrace. You don't even pay your gambling debts."

John took a step in his direction. "What is that you say, sir?"

Everett seemed to realize what his intemperate tongue had expressed. His face turned deathly pale and he started to shuffle backward, but John stalked him with easy grace. "I've met every debt of *honor* in my life," he said tightly.

The crowd of people who had spilled into the hallway after the first confrontation quickly stepped back again. But Peterson moved protectively in front of Everett, who was already being escorted out the door by Titus. "No one would ever say you are without honor, John—no one. Now, come, let us go and find a drink."

In answer, John looked to Applegate. "What does he mean by that, William?"

Applegate's ruddy cheeks turned ruddier. "It's unimportant."

John knew better. He rarely gambled; it was one vice that didn't tempt him. But it tempted Applegate, and John had assumed his spendthrift friend's debts, which he turned over to his uncle, Louis Barron, who also served as his man of business.

Nor was Applegate the only man John supported. He provided the living for a motley assortment of ex-soldiers who'd fought with him on the Peninsula, men who'd made sacrifices in the service of their country and then been abandoned. He also loaned generous amounts to his new *tonnish* friends, including Prinny and Brummell, both of whom were far too extravagant for their own pockets. Recently, in the past week or so, certain friends had cautioned John to keep a better accounting of his money, but he hadn't placed much significance in their warnings, attributing them to well-intentioned meddling. Now he wondered. . . .

Peterson clapped a hand on his shoulder and changed the subject. "This wife of yours must be a paragon, to put up with you. You must tell us everything about her. Come."

John turned away from Applegate, making a mental note to discuss the unpaid gambling debts. Or perhaps it would be better to go directly to Louis, who had handled John's affairs since the day he'd purchased his commission.

Sarah signaled for the musicians to resume playing. A servant appeared at John's side with a tray of champagne glasses. John took one before saying, "What is it you wish to know?"

"Well, let's start with her name," Peterson said.

"Yes, her name," Prinny and Applegate echoed in unison.

John took a sip of champagne before replying succinctly, "I don't recall."

His response left his friends in open-mouthed surprise, which quickly turned into laughter. John didn't laugh. He considered himself a very private man, and his marriage was not a subject he wished to discuss with anyone. Not even Peterson.

His wife. Lady Craige, mistress of Craige Castle. Other than the short notes he wrote her twice a year, one at Christmas, the other in the spring, around the time of their anniversary, he rarely thought of her. Louis handled all of the financial details between them. Louis probably remembered his wife's name.

Mallory.

That was her name. And with the name came memories of an ornately carved bed and a young girl, her eyes wide with fear. . . .

John lightly touched the scar on his thumb.

Sarah interrupted his thoughts by taking hold of his arm. She rubbed her breasts against him. "You were very brave, my love, and a touch insane. Sir Everett seems a mad man." Her green eyes smoldered with desire.

John stifled a yawn and wished he could go home. Unfortunately, Prinny had cornered Peterson and was giving the officer his opinions concerning Wellington's handling of the war. John would have to think of a clever way to extricate Peterson from such a conversation . . . and then he had the uncomfortable feeling that someone was staring at him.

Slowly he turned. There, in the open front door, stood a young woman dressed in serviceable brown cambric and a plain straw bonnet. She held her reticule in front of her with both gloved hands, her tight grip suggesting she feared someone would snatch it from her.

Their eyes met, and John saw a flash of recognition. She stepped forward just as Titus came from the drawing room.

"May I help you, miss?" the butler asked politely.

The woman kept her gaze on John. "I'm here to see Lord Craige."

Titus looked up questioningly at John, but Sarah, overhearing John's name, turned to meet this new guest. She smiled, cool and slightly distracted, as she sized the young woman up from head to toe and then dismissed her. "The servant's entrance is in the back."

Anger flared in the woman's intelligent dark eyes. She lifted her chin to a determined tilt and John felt an unexpected flash of desire. This woman standing arrow straight and proud in her modest brown dress wasn't his usual style, but there was something about her that caught his interest.

"I am not a servant," the woman said in clear, clipped tones. The authority in her voice attracted attention. Prinny stopped speaking. Both he and Peterson turned to see who this new intruder was. Even Applegate, who had cornered an actress and had been trying to nibble on her ear, looked up.

Sarah's smile didn't quite reach her eyes as she said in her soft, musical voice, "Then are you one of the dancers?" Sly snickers met her words.

The young woman frowned at Sarah's impertinence. "I am here to see Lord Craige."

"I'm his hostess," Sarah said, drawing out the last word with unmistakable innuendo. "You can state your business with me."

"I'll state it with Lord Craige."

Sarah laughed. "My dear, what possible business could you have with my John? I assure you, his taste doesn't run toward the common. With those freckles all over your face, you look like you have been working in the fields."

The crowd rippled with low murmurs and guffaws at her cruel words. The woman suddenly seemed to become aware of the amount of attention she had drawn. Bright splashes of hot color stained her cheeks—and brought John to her rescue.

"As a matter of fact, I do like freckles, Sarah." His mistress stiffened and her eyes turned cold.

John ignored her and walked toward the young woman. "I'm Lord Craige," he said, his voice one of authority. He was probably doing something foolish. For all he knew she could be Sir Everett's wife or one of the other silly females who had developed an infatuation for him.

The young woman took a step toward him, where the light was better. Now John could see that her hair framed by the bonnet wasn't completely brown, that there were streaks of gold shot through it like beams of sunlight, and the smattering of freckles across her nose was very attractive. Unfortunately, the expression in her honey brown eyes had turned fierce. Their color stirred a memory inside him. "We've met before, haven't we?"

His words offended her. He could tell by the

way she pulled back, her shoulders straightening. He had no idea why until she spoke and erased all mystery: "I'm Mallory Barron . . . your wife."

Chapter 3

Lie there, lie there, you false-hearted man,
Lie there instead of me.

"The Outlandish Knight"

Stunned silence met Mallory's announcement. Ever so slowly, other guests at the party realized something was amiss and stopped speaking. They craned their necks in her direction. Even the musicians paused mid-note and brought their instruments down.

It gave Mallory tremendous satisfaction.

She'd dreamed of this moment, practiced for it. *"I'm your wife—you useless philanderer,"* she'd whispered countless times to her mirror, whenever the hurt, anger, and loneliness had got the better of her. *"I am mistress of Craige Castle,"* she'd reminded herself, when a crisis with a tenant or the crop made her want to break down in tears—or run away as her husband had. *"I'm the Viscountess Craige,"* she had raged at the unsympathetic bailiff and army of bill collectors last week when they had stormed Craige Castle and taken over her beloved home.

This moment of confrontation was all she'd imagined. Except. . . .

In her mind's eye, John had remained just as he'd been on their wedding night, a tall, solemn youth with bright blue eyes. She barely recognized this dark-haired Corinthian with the devil's own looks and glittering, dangerous eyes.

He still combed his unfashionably long hair straight back from his face, but she didn't recall his features being so hard, so strong—so masculine. Everything about him, from his finely tailored jacket in Spanish blue cloth to the high gloss of his black top boots, spoke of money and privilege, while the thigh-hugging buff leather of his pantaloons proclaimed strength and power.

Rumor had it that when White Hall had ordered the heroic Colonel Barron home to assume the responsibilities of Viscount Craige, the French had cheered and the Spanish *señoritas* had cried. Mallory decided the rumors must be true. Not even she was immune to his fabled magnetism.

Their eyes met. She was conscious of a strange flutter of excitement rising from somewhere deep inside her. Her knees threatened to go weak. Her pulse beat faster.

But not even her wildest dreams of their meeting after so many years of absence had prepared her for the drunken lord who looked up at her from nuzzling a half-naked woman's neck and said in wine-slurred speech, "So glad to meet you, my lady. I'm Applegate, a friend of your husband's. Only a few minutes ago, I'd asked Craige what your name was and he said he'd forgot."

Applegate turned toward her husband and chastised mildly, "Her name's Mallory. You really should be more careful, Craige. A man don't have to remember much in this life, but he should remember his wife's name."

Mallory, and everyone else in the room, stared at her husband. She expected him to deny that he'd forgotten her name, or at least appear slightly embarrassed. Instead, he raised his eyes heavenward and muttered something that sounded like, "What else can go wrong this day?"

The stark truth struck her: *the man didn't even remember her name!*

No wonder he'd shamefully neglected Craige Castle and his responsibilities to Mallory and her mother over the past seven years. Suddenly, Mallory hated being the center of attention. Her face flushed with hot embarrassment. Stand proud, stand tall, she ordered herself, and wished she didn't feel as if the earth had disappeared beneath her feet. His wedding ring felt like a lead weight in her skirt pocket.

Then John did something even more outrageous. He laughed.

It started off as a chuckle and then rose into warm, full-bodied masculine laughter. The crowd around Mallory stared at him in open-mouthed surprise . . . and then, slowly at first, they joined him—until before she knew it, she was surrounded by the sound of giggles, snickers, and hearty guffaws.

A man's voice boomed, "Only Craige could get away with this!"

"Craige needs to hire a secretary to ensure his appointments with his wife don't overlap the ones with his mistress!"

"Or that he remembers his wife's name!" The laughter grew louder.

Humiliation and anger shot through every fiber of Mallory's being. Five hundred years of proud Craige blood sang in her veins. She struggled for control. But when Lady Ramsgate tilted her head back in a high feminine trill and put her arms around John's waist, rubbing her breasts against him right there in front of Mallory—*and he allowed it*—something snapped.

In three quick steps, Mallory placed herself directly in front of her husband. She could feel her fury blazing from her eyes. She no longer had control over her emotions. If she'd held one of the huge broadswords that hung over the mantel in Craige Castle, she'd have found the strength to circle it high over her head and cut John Barron in half. She might even have done a jig over his body parts.

Instead, she settled for delivering a stinging slap to his face, hard enough to force him to take a step back.

The crowd's laughter stopped abruptly on a shocked gasp.

John raised a hand to his jaw while Lady Ramsgate stepped protectively in front of him. In a voice full of dramatic outrage, she announced, "I must ask you to leave immediately."

This was not how Mallory had imagined her first meeting with John.

But she wasn't about to cry, "Quarter." Not now.

Of course, she realized, she might have gone too far. Perhaps her mother had been right. She should have stayed at the inn and waited until John answered the notes she'd sent requesting an audience.

But he was her husband! She shouldn't have to wait for his summons like an indentured servant. Besides, she didn't have time for this nonsense. She wanted Craige Castle returned to her! She had fields of wheat to make ready for the harvest. She couldn't spend precious days cooling her heels in an inn, waiting for her lord.

Her impervious glare, which had put many a saucy milkmaid in her place, sent the lush Lady Ramsgate back a step. "I wish a word with my husband—alone," Mallory said, proud that her voice didn't shake.

The angry red imprint of her fingers against his hard jaw deeply embarrassed her. Only through sheer will and determination was she able to meet his eyes. What she saw there caught her by surprise.

The devil was enjoying this!

She was creating a scene that would make them the talk of London for a fortnight, yet in the clear, sharp depths of his eyes she saw humor. For an instant the memory of their wedding night so many years ago rippled through her like wind across water. The hopes, the dreams, the fears. . . .

And then, just as quickly, those memories vanished as the corners of his mouth twisted cynically. His eyes never left Mallory's as he said, "You'll excuse us, won't you, Sarah? My—" He hesitated slightly as if to savor the next word, "*wife* and I want to be alone."

Mallory panicked.

When had his voice turned so deep, so resonant, so authoritative? And he must have grown a foot in height, even from a moment ago, when her anger had propelled her forward.

He moved closer to her now, too close, almost as if he were challenging her. Mallory stood her ground but discovered she was reluctant to meet those too-perceptive eyes. Instead, she stared at the fine weave of his jacket, the crisp, snowy folds of his neck cloth. She could even smell the starch in the fine lawn of his shirt and a warm, spicy, masculine scent that was like a breath of fresh air in the smoky room.

This was something she definitely remembered from her wedding day—this intense *awareness* of him.

He placed his hand on her shoulder . . . a stranger's hand, she realized with a start—large, well-formed, capable. Mallory felt as if she'd swallowed a bubble and couldn't breathe. She remembered so much, suddenly, in that touch—

Her senses screamed a warning.

And then her feet left the ground! Before she

knew what he was about, John Barron swung her easily up into his arms amid a flurry of skirts and petticoats.

The crowd roared its approval.

"Hadley," John said to a dark-haired man standing close to Lady Ramsgate, "lend me your carriage."

"Of course, Craige. I'd be honored," Hadley answered, and with a click of his fingers, signaled a servant to hurry from the parlor to fetch the conveyance.

"What do you think you are doing?" Mallory demanded, the very second she could catch her breath long enough to speak.

John looked down at her with laughing eyes. "Did you not say you wanted us to be alone?"

"I didn't tell you to pick me up. Put me down this second!" She pushed against him, but he only tightened his hold.

"Perhaps you'd better do as she says, Craige," Hadley warned with a laugh. "I want my coach back in one piece!"

"I'll have it returned tomorrow morning—polished, shined, and completely intact," John promised, and started toward the door. Mallory arched her back, trying to roll out of his arms.

"I lay five-to-one odds Craige doesn't make it to Mayfair without getting his eyes scratched out!" a voice shouted, and then, to Mallory's mortification, the man's bet was met with many laughing offers—some even from women!

She struggled harder, wanting to put her feet securely on the ground, but her actions led to further indignity when he easily shifted her up and onto his shoulder, as if she weighed little more than a sack of wool. Flabbergasted, Mallory pushed herself upright, her fingers still clutching her reticule. The pins fell from her neat chignon, and she realized that she'd lost her best bonnet in the mélée. From this vantage point, she had a clear view of all the drunken faces looking up at her and laughing.

"Let me down," she commanded through clenched teeth, loud enough for only the two of them to hear.

"In a moment, my dear," he responded perfunctorily.

Furious, Mallory was about to let her breeding be damned and box his ears when a woman's screech interrupted them. *"John!"*

He turned to face the speaker. Looking over her shoulder, Mallory could see that the crowd, in delicious anticipation, had cleared a path for the lovely Lady Ramsgate to confront her lover.

The woman smiled a practiced look of enticement before asking softly, "You'll be coming back, won't you, John?"

Everyone in the room, including Mallory, looked to John for his reply.

Raising his eyebrows in an expression of complete indifference, he drawled, "Don't wait up, Sarah."

The crowd howled even as Lady Ramsgate shrieked with outrage, grabbed a vase from a side table, and hurled it at John and Mallory. The vase flew wide of its mark and hit Applegate without breaking, although it did knock him back into the arms of the half-dressed woman. The two of them fell to the floor while the crowd shouted catcalls.

"Duck," John said.

"What?" Mallory asked, still caught up in the sight of the plump Applegate rolling around on the floor with the woman. Fortunately, Mallory had looked down, or else she would have whacked her head a good one on the door frame. The next time he said "Duck" she ducked, and he carried her through the front door and out into the summer night.

Lady Ramsgate's butler handed John his top hat before closing the door behind them. John lowered her feet to the porch step with an undignified thud. Two large oil lamps illuminated the step.

It took Mallory a second to find her balance before she came back spitting with suppressed fury. "How dare you!"

"It's good to see you again, too," he replied pleasantly. He pushed a stray lock of straight dark hair back from his brow, set his hat on his head, and started to take her arm.

Mallory jerked away and backed to the other side of the small stoop. Her whole body shook with outrage. "Don't you touch me. Don't *ever* touch me."

He frowned as if he found her anger unjustified. "Mallory—"

The pent-up emotion, the frustration and lost hopes, exploded inside her. "I want a divorce!" Through the red haze of anger, she felt the words more keenly than a knife's point. "Before I came here and was so thoroughly abused and humiliated, I was afraid to say those words. But now I'm not! In fact, I'm glad to say them. I'm *proud* to say them! Do you hear me? I want a divorce!"

There were only a few feet between them, but Mallory and John might just as well have been in separate countries. While her emotions roiled inside her, he faced her, perfectly calm and at ease.

For the first time, Mallory knew her decision was the right one. This man didn't care for her. He hadn't even batted an eye at her outburst. Scandal be damned; she'd divorce John Barron and build a new life with a good, stable man like Hal Thomas, a man she'd known from childhood, a man who wouldn't abandon, betray, or humiliate her.

Only the sound of her breathing stretched between them, and slowly Mallory was able to gather up the tattered remnants of her dignity. Her hair was a tangled mess. Self-consciously, she pulled the unruly mass to the nape of her neck.

The masklike calm never left her husband's face.

"You have no response?" She let her hand drop to her side and straightened her shoulders. "Didn't you hear what I said?"

"Yes, I did," he drawled. "And so did everyone else."

Everyone else? Surprised, Mallory turned and her eyes opened wide in horror when she saw all the party guests leaning out the windows along the front of Lady Ramsgate's townhouse, enthusiastically watching the scene being played out on the stoop. As Mallory's mouth dropped open in dumbfounded shock, they burst into hoots of laughter.

Mallory chose the only course open to her. She walked down the steps and to the curb, praying she'd never see any of these people again. A team and ornate closed coach with windows on all four sides stood in front of the townhouse. A liveried footman held open the door. Assuming the coach was for them, and not truly caring one way or the other, Mallory climbed in. "Drive," she announced grandly to the coachman.

The driver waited until John removed his top hat and climbed beside her. The chaise shifted with his weight. When her body started to slide across the velvet squabs toward him, Mallory scooted quickly toward the opposite door to avoid contact with him. "I don't want you here," she said.

"I didn't ask," he replied, before giving the coachman his Mayfair address.

Mallory opened her mouth to protest, but with a snap of the whip they were off. The coach lurched around the other coaches lined up for the party and started down the street. John's friends shouted and called encouragement from the windows. Mallory, happily, couldn't make out exactly what they said. From the corner of her eye, she noticed that John good-naturedly waved goodbye. She clung closer to the opposite door and stared out into the night.

John leaned back in the seat. Mallory felt him staring at her, the hairs at the nape of her neck tingling, but when she slid a look in his direction, he was checking his fob watch for the time. He closed the timepiece with a soft click and she looked away quickly, not wanting to be caught staring.

In fact, she could hardly wait to rid herself of him. She should tell him so, and also that she had no intention of returning to his house, that she wanted to be delivered to the Red Horse Inn, where her mother waited. In fact, if she had to spend another second in the company of this man—

"No," he said.

"No what?" She looked over her shoulder. All she could see of his face, hidden in the shadows, was the grim set of his mouth.

"No divorce," he answered.

Mallory turned to face him fully. Conscious of the listening ears of the coachman and the footman, she leaned close and whispered, "Why not? Certainly from what I've seen tonight, I have plenty of justification!"

"What are you talking about?" he whispered back, as if they were playing a game.

"Your mistress," she hissed.

He waved a dismissive hand and sat back before answering in a normal voice, heedless of the servants, "If having a mistress were grounds for divorce, then half of Parliament would be unattached."

"Adultery certainly *is* grounds for a divorce!" Mallory whispered back, sending a pointed look at the coachman.

John ignored her. "For a wife, but not for a husband." He studied her in the darkness for a moment before asking, "I don't have a fear on that count, do I?"

Surprised that he would even voice such a concern, hot indignation and guilt flashed through her. What if the rumors about the many duels he'd fought were true and he decided to call Hal Thomas out? "I am as you left me," she hurried to assure him.

John pursed his lips, the coach lights illuminating his even features. Mallory held her breath. Could he read her mind? Did he sense she was hiding something? At last he said dryly, "Well, that's comforting."

She bristled at his sarcasm. "Of course, I don't run in the same circles you do. We country folk—" she laced these words with disdain—"take our wedding vows seriously."

"You have a very attractive lower lip when you pout."

She immediately pressed her lips together, angered by her reaction to his off-hand compliment. "Haven't you heard a word I've been saying?"

"Of course, I've heard every word. How else would I notice the shape of your lower lip?" He moved closer to her, his arm coming around the seat back. "In fact, perhaps having a wife isn't such a bad idea." His rough voice sounded very intimate in such close quarters. His finger lightly touched her cheek, and Mallory couldn't suppress a shiver of awareness. He smiled, as if her reaction were exactly what he'd hoped.

He removed his arm and sat back. "Fine. I'll give up my mistress. No more adultery. No more discussion about divorce."

Mallory opened her eyes wide in feigned surprise. "I have farm animals I speak of with more attachment than you do of a woman whose bed you share." Her cheeks burned. Such plain speaking embarrassed her.

"You're blushing, aren't you?" He stretched out his long legs and shoved his hands in his pocket. "I can't remember a time when anything embarrassed me—least of all words." He shot her a smile, one that had charmed women from duchesses to dairy maids, if her friend Louise Haddon's gossipy letters from London could be believed. "Would it make you feel better if I professed an undying love for her?"

"No," she said firmly.

"Then there's no sense in pretending, is there? Mallory, there *is* no attachment. Sarah and I had an affair. I've tired of it and it's over. There's no need for excess emotion. I'll contact my uncle Louis Barron tomorrow and have him finish it with her."

Mallory stared at him as his words sank in. He really believed what he said. He believed that the beautiful, elegant woman who served as his mistress considered him little more than a pastime—in spite of the fact that Lady Ramsgate had just made a fool of herself before society by begging John to come back to her. Her mother was right—men and women had completely different views of the world. She gave a short, humorless laugh.

"What's so funny?"

"You. Us." Mallory pressed a pleat into the material of her dress with two fingers before admitting, "Imagine, we've been married for over seven years, yet we're strangers. You're nothing like what I remember." And she suddenly realized that in spite of Hal and with all evidence to the contrary, a part of her had naively believed they might still have managed to make something out of this soulless union.

"Or how I remember you." He paused before adding, "You've grown up, Mallory."

For a second her heart stopped. What could he mean? And why did his words and the deep, appreciative timbre of his voice start a dizzy little humming deep inside her?

Mallory clutched her hands together in fists, questioning her sanity. John had had his chance. She'd waited over six years, playing the role of dutiful wife to her roving soldier husband. She'd expected a note, a visit, *something* when he'd returned from the war. Being ignored with such finality hurt. Trusting him in spite of all evidence to the contrary and losing her home had made her incensed with fury.

"I want a divorce, John. I do *not* want to go to your home, especially in light of what happened at—" she discovered she didn't want to say Lady Ramsgate's name, "—back there. Please convey me to the Red Horse Inn. My mother is waiting for me there, and since I've been gone several hours, she will be anxious." There. She'd said it—and very well, too, she thought. This was as she'd pictured the meeting between them, a moment of dignity and grace, in spite of the somewhat scandalous circumstances.

He made an impatient sound. "There will be no divorce."

Mutinously, Mallory refused to answer. There most certainly *would* be a divorce . . . or a separation. She'd sue for private separation in the ecclesiastical courts. It was what Hal had encouraged her to do from the start.

John frowned. "You're upset over what happened this evening. I'm sorry I embarrassed you, but after you stormed into my mistress's house, publicly announced yourself, and slapped me, I felt that removing us in the most expedient manner was the best solution—and no, I don't give a damn what anyone thinks."

All her outrage welled up again. "I've never been manhandled in such a manner. . . ." Her voice trailed off as words failed her. Unfortunately, she also felt an annoying sense that he was right in some measure.

Her mother had begged her to stay at the inn and wait for John to respond to one of the many notes Mallory had sent him that day. However, when she hadn't heard from him after hours of waiting, Mallory's temper had got the better of her. She'd marched over to John's house and badgered the one-legged brute named Richards, her husband's butler, for John's whereabouts. The real insult had been that Richards hadn't believed his lord was married.

"Couldn't we just have walked out the door?" she asked. "Or do you make it a practice to pick up any woman you see and carry her off whenever you are bored?"

John answered her with a smile that was so

wickedly tempting it had the power to charm even her, a woman who believed herself impervious to the fatal appeal of scamps and bounders.

And that was what she'd married, she reminded herself—a rake. An infamous rake.

"We can't divorce," he said, almost apologetically. "First, there's the scandal a divorce would create. A stigma on both our family names."

She gave an unladylike snort. "Since when have you worried about our family names?"

"Do you mean, when have I worried how my actions affect the family name or about propagating the family name?" His grin turned wolfish.

"Your actions!" Mallory snapped. "I'll not let you close enough to think of the other."

"Oh, I'm thinking of the other already," he assured her, and there was something in the warmth of his voice that turned her stomach to jelly. But his voice was businesslike. "Besides, I can't see you leaving your precious Craige Castle. After all, you are the last of the *true* Craiges."

His words washed all good humor out of Mallory. "Craige Castle is gone. Your creditors evicted my mother and me last week."

"You're joking!" He sat up.

"Do you believe I would joke about such a thing? I've been told there is already a new owner. And when did you ever give a care to scandal or Craige Castle and its tenants? I admit you were fine in the beginning, albeit somewhat stingy, but the last several years we've been lucky to see a shilling for anything in the way of improvements to the castle itself!"

He leaned forward. "Lucky to see a shilling?

Mallory, how can you call an allowance of ten thousand a year a pittance?"

"What ten thousand a year?"

He looked squarely at her, his expression completely serious for the first time since she'd met him this evening. "The money I've been putting into your accounts ever since we parted company seven years ago. It was the living I inherited from my mother's side of the family. I lived off my pay as an officer and gave the rest completely over to you. Are you telling me you've never received the money?"

"John, we've been fortunate if we've had a thousand pounds from you in a year, and that stopped coming two years ago while you claimed half the harvest to support your grand way of life and your *women.*" She spat the last word out.

"This is astounding," he said. "You've had nothing from me at all for two years?"

"Well, there was the brick walkway you insisted on building. I was forced to let go of servants who had been with my family for years and you were sending workmen to build walkways! Oh, yes, and I mustn't forget your occasional letters." She couldn't resist making that jab. "Especially the one that read, 'Dear Wife, I hope all is well with you. I am well. Sincerely, John Barron.'" She paused a moment before asking, "Had you really forgotten my name, John?"

He shot her an irritated frown. "I've been sending money. Granted, I've been negligent in many aspects of my life, but I have always honored my financial obligations. I'm not a complete villain, Mallory."

She and the good people of Craige Castle, who had gone so long without the basic necessities, disagreed.

"Mallory, I don't know what happened to Craige Castle, but tomorrow we will both go to see my Uncle Louis and straighten this matter out. In the meantime, you will come home with me. I will send for your mother to join us."

Mallory opened her mouth to protest, but John cut her off. "You are my wife and will stay under my roof. The Red Horse is a mediocre establishment and certainly not in the safest section of the city for two women alone."

"What makes you so certain we are alone?" she asked stiffly, irritated by his high-handed, if completely sensible, manner.

"Oh, I have no doubt that if you'd had a host of yeomen at your back, you would have threatened me with them by now."

Mallory wished she'd thought of that. One of her reasons for forcing a meeting with John this evening was to avoid the likelihood of his encountering her mother. It had taken the loss of Craige Castle for her mother to see reason and consider a divorce. However, if their eviction had been a mistake and John actually *did* start providing Craige Castle an allowance of ten thousand a year, her mother would fight a divorce with every breath she drew.

Mallory looked out the coach window and saw that they were already in Mayfair and approaching his street.

Hal had wanted to come with her, but she had insisted on his staying back in East Anglia. She'd assured Hal that she would remain true to her dreams. She didn't want to live out her days as a married woman in name only. She wanted a family. A husband who cared about her, who shared his thoughts and helped shoulder the responsibility of Craige Castle and its tenants.

At the very least, she wanted someone who remembered her name!

"What the devil!"

Startled by John's oath, Mallory turned to him in time to watch him throw open the door of the still moving coach and stand on the step. She craned her neck to look past him.

His house appeared to be ablaze with light and a host of men and women moved from the small circular park across from John's home and out into the street. For a moment, Mallory feared that the party from Lady Ramsgate's had managed to race them to Mayfair and now waited to poke more cruel fun. But peering out the window, she didn't recognize anyone. This group of men and women was dressed too plainly, and they were too sober to be more of John's friends.

The coach rolled to a stop. A man's rough face, framed by an officious-looking leather top hat, glared at them in the torch light. "Lord Craige?" he demanded.

John stepped down to confront the man, who took a step back as if awed by the height and breadth of her infamous husband. "I am he."

At that moment, another man in the crowd, his expression ugly, pounded on the window on Mallory's side of the coach. She jumped, startled by the man's anger. Suddenly deciding she had no desire to be trapped inside the small coach, she tried to push her way out on John's side, but he protectively refused to let her leave, guarding the door with his body.

"What is going on here?" John demanded.

Before the officious-looking man could answer, a voice shouted from the crowd, "I'll tell you what's going on!" The man pushed his way to the front and Mallory recognized him as the one who had pounded on her coach window. "His high-and-mighty lordship owes me money, and now it looks like I won't ever get paid because the magistrate is going to have him taken away."

"The magistrate!" Mallory repeated, even as John stiffened at the threat.

"This is absolute nonsense," her husband said. "I owe no man."

"You owe me," another man cried. "Fourteen hundred pounds for feed and boarding."

"Louis Barron is my man of business," John said with indifference, as if such matters were beneath his notice. "Submit your bills to him and you'll be paid, with interest. I'll draft a note to him on the morrow with my instructions—"

"Bah! I've had it up to here with your Mr. Barron," the first creditor answered. "We've sent all your bills to Mr. Barron, and we're sick of his excuses. We want what's right and ours. That's why we've sent for the bailiff." Heads in the crowd nodded; fists were raised threateningly.

"And I'll see that you receive payment," John announced, in a voice of steady command. Mallory marveled at his control. Her knees had turned to pudding. Fourteen hundred pounds in debt for feed!

John continued calmly, "Give me a moment to escort my wife to our door and we will settle this matter like gentlemen."

Angry shouts met his words. "You ain't goin' anywhere, guv!" a voice called.

Another said, "The gaol's the only settlement you'll get!"

Terrified, Mallory touched John's arm, just as the man in the top hat who had first confronted them stepped forward. For the first time, Mallory noticed the man's blue coat and vivid waistcoat. A Bow Street Runner!

"I'm afraid they have the right of it, Lord Craige," the Runner said. "The Magistrate of Bow Street has ordered me to bring you before him."

"Now?" John asked. "At this hour of the night?"

"Yes, my lord."

"And for what reason?"

"Bankruptcy, my lord," the Runner replied respectfully.

The first creditor practically danced with glee as he delivered the news. "That's right, Lord Craige, you're bloody broke!"

Chapter 4

O true-love, have you my gold?
And can you set me free?
Or are you come to see me hung
All on the gallows tree?

"The Briery Bush"

"That's impossible!" The steel edge in John's voice could have commanded battalions on a battlefield, but it had little effect on the Runner. Mallory understood John's anger. Such a public humiliation was practically unheard of—unless the charges were true and John was bankrupt.

"That's not what they say, my lord." The Runner nodded toward the people closing in around the coach. "Now, if you will come with me, I've been hired to take you to the Magistrate."

From the back of the crowd, a man's deep bass voice boomed, "Wait there—just one minute!"

Every head turned. A heavy-set man in a caped great coat and wide cocked hat, and carrying a tall walking stick with an air of authority, pushed through the crowd. "Clear the way! Bailiff of the Court with court orders."

A host of people followed him like tiny boats in the wake of a big ship. These newcomers were a better attired class of people, although they'd obviously dressed in haste. One man still wore his nightcap under his top hat.

Confronting the bailiff, the Runner spread his jacket to show off his red waistcoat. "You may not have Lord Craige right now. He is to appear before Bow Street."

The bailiff waved a dismissive hand. "You may have the man. I've come for the house and contents. We'll be auctioning them to pay off Lord Craige's debts to these men."

With a quiet, "Stay here," to Mallory, John stepped down from the coach's footboard and closed the coach door. "I couldn't possibly owe them money," he said, aristocratic disdain etched in every line of his face. "I've never set eyes on a one of them."

The bailiff's eyes narrowed to piggish slits. "They're moneylenders, my lord. They know their business."

John had borrowed from moneylenders? Mallory sat up on the seat in shock. Only a fool would pay their exorbitant interest—or a man desperate for money.

"The devil you say!" John exclaimed. "I would never leave my mark with sharks."

The moneylenders muttered angrily among themselves. The man in his nightcap shoved his way forward to stand in front of the bailiff. "You may turn up your high-and-mighty nose at our business, my lord, but you used our money and you knew the terms."

"I have never used a moneylender," John said, his voice tight with anger.

The moneylender shook his head. "Your agent, Mr. Barron, handled the loans. I have papers to prove it, including copies of your signature giving him authority to act on your behalf." The man matched John's proud look with pride of his own. "Isaiah Benjamin conducts himself honorably and fairly in business and expects you to pay the debts!" A chorus of agreement met the man's words.

John's anger melted to surprise. "Louis Barron worked with moneylenders?"

"For years, my lord, and we've been happy to extend you the credit," another moneylender replied. "Now we've come for our money."

"Aye. We want our money," came several shouts of agreement.

"Starting with this fine and fancy coach," someone cried.

John raised his arms, his height commanding attention. "I will pay my creditors," he announced firmly.

That statement sent the bailiff's eyebrows up to his hairline. "You can do that, my lord?"

"Certainly," John said with authority. "What is the amount?"

"Ninety-eight thousand pounds, with the interest calculated in."

Mallory fell back on the leather seat. The enormity of the figure confounded her imagination. Ninety-eight thousand pounds! Dear Lord, certainly even the Regent himself didn't have that kind of money. Debtor's Court would claim everything John owned to meet the debt. Craige Castle was lost. She'd never find a way to win back her beloved home.

"That's impossible! I can't possibly owe that much money," John was saying, arguing loudly with the bailiff while the crowd around him hooted in derision.

Mallory wished she'd never come to London. Never, never, never . . . and then the thought struck her. As John's wife, she, too, would be held responsible for such an enormous debt.

Shame and horror turned her cold with fear. She should leave now. While everyone was shouting and arguing, she should crack open the opposite coach door and slip away unnoticed into the night—

A blast exploded, the sound reverberating off the fine brick houses of Mayfair.

Mallory fell to her knees on the coach floor and threw her arms over her head.

Several heartbeats later, finding herself still alive, she gathered what was left of her courage and scrambled to look out the window. The world had fallen into chaos.

Torches lay burning right where they'd fallen and everyone cowered close to the ground in fear. Even the bailiff and the Runner huddled together.

Someone moved near the open door of John's

house. It was the one-legged butler in the act of reloading a huge blunderbuss. "She still packs a punch, doesn't she, Colonel?" he shouted.

It took Mallory a moment to realize that the "Colonel" was John, who no longer stood in the coach door but sat hatless astride the lead horse. Before she could gather her scattered wits, the butler lifted the musket to his shoulder and fired another shot into the air. John kicked the horses and they sprang forward, throwing Mallory back against the seat.

Someone shouted, "He's bolting!"

Women screamed and moneylenders swore as John drove the terrified horses through the crowd. Mallory prayed he wouldn't trample anyone. She looked out the back window. To her amazement, no one appeared injured because they all started chasing after the coach, shaking their fists and swearing. The coach hit a bump that bounced Mallory so high her head hit the roof. The coach landed to the ground with a fearsome hop that tested its springs and sent the door opposite Mallory flying open.

The door banged against the side of the coach and swung back. She grabbed for the handle and slammed it shut. She rubbed her bruised head, holding onto the velvet squabs with the other hand. John rode the lead horse neck or nothing.

And then Mallory gave a small cry of alarm. Up the street ahead of them, a small army of torch-bearing Bow Street Runners was spreading out, determined to stop them.

This was it. This was the end. John would have to halt—and the moneylenders would hang him right on the spot. And they'd string her up next to this philandering, lying, spendthrift—

She hadn't run out of names to call John when he reached over to the bridle of the other lead horse and turned both animals sharply down a narrow side street. The coach heeled up, running on only two wheels as Mallory screamed and quickly threw her body weight to the opposite side.

The coach seemed to hang suspended in mid-air. Sparks flew from the wheels as they grated against the cobblestones.

And then the coach righted itself, jumping and lurching on its springs so that Mallory bounced around inside like a child's India rubber ball. She landed, wedged between the seat and the floor. Every bone in her body felt as if it were broken.

Still John drove the horses on. The coach lanterns reflected off the buildings lining the narrow street as they charged past. Over the clattering of hooves and the screech of coach wheels, Mallory could hear the clacking of the Watchman's rattles.

John heard her scream, but he couldn't stop. He wouldn't let them catch him.

Not since the war had he felt such freedom! The lethargy that had weighed him down since his return to London dissipated. In its place drummed a lust for adventure, of anticipation and excitement!

He felt alive again.

He took two more turns down winding side roads before he was convinced he had an excellent lead over the Runners. He had to get rid of the coach. Both animals were spent, their muscles quivering. Hadley would have his head for using his cattle in such a manner, but there wasn't a moment to waste. The Runners might call out the Horse Patrol.

And he had to check on his wife. He hadn't heard a sound from her since that last scream.

Bringing her along had not been one of his more sane impulses.

John reined the horses to a halt, slid to the ground, and hurried back to the coach, only to stop dead in his tracks. One of the coach lamps had been knocked off in the chase, but the remaining one lit the interior.

His wife sat on the coach seat as regal as a princess waiting for her Sunday ride—although her hair looked as if it had been captured in a windstorm.

She faced him as he yanked open the door, her eyes flashing with fiery indignation. The only signs of her fear were the white knuckles on the hand still gripping the passenger strap and the steel in her voice as she said, "Are you quite done?"

John almost grinned at her, but caught himself in time. "I don't know if we're still being chased by the Runners or if we are safe. It all depends on how tenacious they are. You may stay here or come with me."

"What is the advantage of staying here?"

"You can tell them what a blackguard I am."

"It's tempting."

Her response earned a short laugh from him.

His child-bride was growing more entertaining by the moment. "I wouldn't advise it."

She nodded her head. "I'd probably be locked up for your debts."

"Once they know you are my wife," he agreed amicably.

"I don't think I like you." She said each word clearly and separately.

"You're in good company." Struck by a new thought, he added, "But then, you're the one who came looking for me." Sparks shot from her eyes at that statement, but now was not the time to match verbal swords, no matter how much he enjoyed the challenge. He held out his hand. "Come, we must hurry."

Mallory didn't release her hold on the strap. "Why? Don't you believe we have escaped them?"

"Not if they've been hired to catch me."

"Someone would pay them to hunt you down?"

Just then, a man shouted, "Here they are! I've spotted them."

Mallory had barely let go of the hand strap before John grabbed her arm and practically dragged her out of the coach. "Run, Mallory, run," he said, helping her gain her balance while still moving.

"What about the coach?"

"Hadley will be disappointed in its condition when it's returned," he answered, then shouted at the horses.

The already frenzied animals bolted, charging

down the street into the night, pulling the coach behind them. John joined Mallory. "Run!"

A group of mounted riders charged around the corner up the street. John pushed Mallory toward an alley. She ran. Behind her she heard the riders give chase to the runaway coach.

The alley opened onto another street. John didn't let them slow their pace, but led her down another side street and then another and another until she had no idea where they were.

With each corner they turned, the streets became darker and seedier. He shoved past pedestrians, drunks, and sailors, heedless of the curses and shouts thrown at them. A stitch needled her side. Her breathing grew labored and painful in her chest. Oblivious to all, John took them deeper and deeper into a part of the city that was strange and foreign to her country eyes.

At last, just when she thought her lungs would burst, he pulled her down another side alley and stopped.

Mallory jerked her arm free even as he let go, and placing her hands on her hips, walked the parameters of the alley, trying to catch her breath. Immediately, the smells of rotting food and human waste struck her full force. She gagged.

"Come over here," his voice ordered from the shadows. "It smells a little better."

She followed his advice, covering her mouth and nose with her hand and stumbling over some sort of slippery debris on the ground. The moon barely reached the alley's depths and she didn't see the cat until it hissed and growled in outrage, knocking over a wooden crate in its flight.

Startled, Mallory jumped back—and bumped into John's hard, strong body. His hands came down on her arms to steady her. For one blessed second, she let herself rest there. He smelled so clean and fresh compared to the sordid odors of the alley. From a distance, over their heads, she heard a child cry and then a woman laughing. Or was she sobbing?

But there were no shouts of alarm. No sounds of the wooden watch rattles the Runners and the Watch used clacking in the night.

Mallory pulled away from his reassuring warmth. "So, you're . . ." She searched for a word, the right word. "Ruined."

"Apparently." John moved out of the shadows. His teeth flashed white in a sudden dare devil grin. "But not until they catch us."

Us?

Not if she could help it.

She confronted him head on. "I think now I could build a strong case for divorce."

A cloud that had covered the moon passed. Silver illumination highlighted the planes of his face, giving him an almost mythical beauty. "No." His eyes glittered in the darkness. "I said no divorce."

"You can't stop me—"

"I can and I will." He reached her in two long strides, his broad-shouldered form blocking out the light. "Mallory, I am fighting for my life right now. I don't believe it's a coincidence that tonight of all nights my fortune came toppling down around me. Someone is paying Bow Street to send out the Runners and paying them enough that they are being damned tenacious about it, too. Furthermore, whether you like it or not, as my wife, you're in this as deeply as I am. Now is not the time to discuss divorce." He made the last word sound like the foulest epithet.

But Mallory was no longer paying attention. She'd been struck by a new, more urgent thought. "Mother."

"What?"

"My mother will be sick with worry when she hears all of this." Mallory raised a hand to her forehead. "Now we'll never recover the castle. It's lost to us for good." Hot tears threatened. "How could you have involved yourself with moneylenders?"

"Mallory—"

"Ninety-eight thousand pounds!"

"I didn't—"

"But your man of business did. Your uncle, Louis Barron! I can't tell you how many times over the past years I came close to throttling him myself! The man is worthless. I'd write him letters requesting he pay attention to improvements needed for Craige Castle or outstanding debts that begged to be paid, and he would respond with empty promises!"

"Mallory, he never told me you had written—"

"You should have known about his involvement with moneylenders. Didn't you ever check on him, John, or question his activities? A debt so large doesn't accumulate overnight. It was irresponsible of you to give him such license!"

Anger flared in his eyes, hard and bright. "No, I

didn't question him. I trusted him. He's my uncle—"

"Never trust anyone with your money," she said briskly.

"You sound just like a bloody wife."

If he'd meant to hurt her, he could have chosen no better insult. Everyone in the shire surrounding Craige Castle agreed that Mallory had a bright mind, a keen wit, and a too-sharp tongue. They were among the many reasons used to explain her husband's absence. Other, far less kind reasons were bandied about as well to justify why he had abandoned her after their wedding night. . . .

Mallory refused to let the old hurt touch her.

She faced her husband. "I am no longer a 'little girl,' John. I am a woman, a woman deeply in debt, so pray indulge me a moment and answer my questions."

Silence stretched between them, during which the loudest sound seemed to be the pounding of her own heart. "No," he finally said. "I didn't question Louis's activities. Nor did I even think to."

"And you never instructed him to deal with money lenders?"

"Why would I borrow money when my coffers were filled to overflowing?"

"Why would you let him have full discretionary power over your money?" To Mallory, who handled every penny that passed through Craige Castle, the idea didn't make sense.

John's boots crunched on the stones and dirt in the alley as he stepped back into the shadows.

"When I purchased my commission in the army, I had no choice but to hire an agent, a man of business. I'd purchased my colors with part of the estate my mother left me, but there was a sizable income coming in . . . and I had to take care of you."

"John, why didn't you take care of your money yourself?"

"I was fighting the French, Mallory—not making a Grand Tour. Napoleon didn't give us time to sit around some coffeehouse reading the financial papers." He ran an exasperated hand through his hair before he continued. "Louis seemed the logical choice. He was my father's brother, and he and I got along quite well. After all, I couldn't very well have asked my father to do it, not after I'd run out on all his well-laid schemes for my future. Furthermore, Father left England shortly after the wedding for his governorship in India."

"But what about six months ago, John, after you inherited and returned from the war? Didn't you ask your uncle for an accounting then?"

"When Wellington ordered me home to see to my responsibilities as Viscount Craige, I was so angry I didn't care about the money, the properties, or any of it. I was content to let Louis manage it all. You may not believe this, Mallory, but I was happy with my life in the military. I don't fit in here." He encompassed the whole of London with a sweep of his arm. "I don't belong."

Mallory listened to not only his words, but also to the way he said them. She doubted he'd ever explained himself to anyone.

Of course, she understood the wish to keep

some details private. *No, my husband isn't home. He's with Wellington. Yes, he fought at Oporto. Albuera. Salamanca. No, I have no idea when he'll return. Perhaps when the fighting is finished in Spain* . . . until one day he'd returned and everyone in England had known it—except Mallory.

He turned on her, his eyes silver bright. "You could have said something. All these years I never received a word from you, not even a complaint, and say what you will against me, I did write. Granted, I'm not a poet, but at least you got a letter from time to time, which is more than I ever received from you. That is, until tonight, when you walked into my life and demanded a divorce."

A sudden rush of guilt burned her cheeks. She still had his letters, a short stack of curt notes he'd sent over the years. She kept them in a drawer of her wardrobe, tied with ribbon and a sprig of lavender.

But she hadn't written back. She couldn't. The hurt ran too deep. Her pride would never let him know how deep.

Another reason to keep as far away from John Barron as possible.

John made a short, angry sound. He took her arm, his grip firm, and started walking. "Come, I'm going to resolve this right now, tonight, so that you and your mother can return to the country and your precious castle." Bitter resentment colored his words.

In the face of his sudden anger, Mallory wondered if she would be better off staying in the alley. "Where are we going?"

"To pay a call on my uncle, Louis Barron."

John guided them to a better section of London without incident and hailed a hack, cool as you please. It seemed so simple that for a moment she could almost believe the earlier events had been a bad dream—until she found herself standing on the front step of Louis Barron's modest house in the wee hours of the night with a man she knew only as a bankrupt and wayward husband.

John knocked on the paneled door. The sound echoed.

There was no answer.

Mallory whispered, "Perhaps he is not at home."

"Perhaps," John agreed, his voice pensive. "Uncle Louis has his nights out."

"Where does he go?"

John shrugged. "His club, usually. He enjoys cards. But he's a bachelor. He could be anywhere." He knocked again.

"If he's not there, why are you knocking?"

Her husband shot her a frown. "Louis lives on the first floor. His landlady lives in an upstairs apartment. She's a bit loose in the noggin, but I'm sure she's there and will let us in. That is, unless you wish to stand out on the street all night."

Mallory ignored his sarcasm by giving him her back. He knocked again, more forcibly.

Still no answer.

Finally, John stepped down from the stoop and peered through the windows.

"Do you see anything?" Mallory asked.

"No. The draperies are closed."

Mallory knocked, while John began removing his jacket.

"What are you doing?" she asked.

"I'm going to break in." He handed the jacket to her.

"You can't possibly do that! It's against the law."

"Watch me." To her horror, he disappeared down a very narrow alleyway between the houses. A split second later, she heard the sound of breaking glass.

Mallory moved to the corner of the stoop, feeling very vulnerable and exposed. She brushed a hand over the weave of his jacket. She was mad to be here, in league with John Barron. She thought of Hal waiting patiently in East Anglia for her return. He'd always considered her the soul of practicality and good sense, and now here she was, housebreaking.

Something crashed, and then a loud male grunt came from inside the house. Mallory placed her ear to the door. "John? Are you all right?"

No answer.

Seconds ticked by like hours. Then she heard the sound of a bolt slide from its setting and the front door opened. John held the door ajar and she gratefully slipped inside.

"It's damned dark in here," he whispered, closing the door behind her. "But I think it looks deserted."

Mallory's eyes slowly adjusted to the lack of light. They were standing in a short, narrow hall with a staircase. John led her into a side room and opened the front window drapes. Moonlight illuminated the shapes of tables, chairs, and a desk. The room smelled of stale tobacco smoke and furniture wax. "He worked out of this room," John explained.

"What makes you think no one is here?"

"Because the window I came through is in his bedroom. There's no clothing in the wardrobe. Furthermore, Louis is a bit of a pack rat. His desk has always been covered with papers and books. It's completely bare now."

Mallory turned toward the desk. The smooth, clear surface reflected moonlight. "Then what—"

A woman's shaky voice interrupted them. "Hello? Is someone here?"

Quickly, John closed the draperies and pulled Mallory down with him to hide between two chairs. Mallory heard footsteps. They moved slowly, hesitantly, one step at a time down the staircase.

"It's the landlady," John said in her ear. The reflection of a candle warned of the woman's approach.

John pulled Mallory closer as an older woman wearing her dressing gown, an Indian shawl of dark blue worsted, and a muslin nightcap came into view at the bottom of the stairs. Cautiously the woman moved to the doorway of the office.

Mallory sank deeper into the shadows next to John. "What do we do?" she whispered.

In answer, John did what she least expected. He stood up.

"Good evening to you, Mrs. Daniels," he said pleasantly.

The old woman practically dropped the candle in her shock, and John hurried to her side to steady her. She looked up at him with wide, rheumy eyes. "Lord Craige?" she asked, with doubtful recognition. She blinked as if she quite expected him to disappear.

"Yes, it is, Mrs. Daniels. I'm sorry. Did I give you a terrible fright?" John acted as if it were completely natural for him to be marauding about her house in the middle of the night.

"Well, it's just that I wasn't expecting to see you here."

Mallory felt stupid crouching on the floor and also rose to her feet. Mrs. Daniels turned in surprise. "Who are you?"

"She's my wife, Lady Craige," John said casually. "Mallory, dear, this is Mrs. Daniels." He took his jacket from her and shrugged it on.

Conscious of her windblown hair hanging below her shoulders, Mallory widened her eyes when Mrs. Daniels curtseyed. But then the woman started to lose her balance.

John caught her. He took the candle holder from her and set it on a table. "Here, I can see we've given you quite a start. Please, rest here a moment." He helped her to a chair.

Still confused, Mrs. Daniels muttered, "Isn't it rather late for a call, my lord?"

John raised his eyebrows in consideration, then gave her a rakish smile. The landlady blushed and Mallory noted that even an aged woman like Mrs.

Daniels wasn't immune to his charm. He sat on a footstool next to her. "Yes, well, actually, my wife and I had a question for Uncle Louis that couldn't wait until morning and we hoped he'd have a moment to spare tonight."

"Oh, that's impossible," Mrs. Daniels confirmed with a shake of her head. "He isn't here. He's left London."

"When did he leave?" John asked with mild surprise. "And did he tell you where he went?

Mrs. Daniels shook her head. "He left this morning. Packed all his worldly goods, just like that. I told him I thought this was very sudden and that he should give me proper notice. He said it was doctor's orders. Said the air here in London was bad for him—" Her voice broke off as she turned to John. "But you know, my lord, I think he was toying with me."

"And why is that?" John asked.

"Because he appeared in robust health and was smoking one of those foul cigars he always has in his mouth. I asked him if he was going to take the furniture, but he told me to keep it. Said he wouldn't need it." She looked around the room. "Furniture is expensive. Why would a man give up so much because of his health? Won't he need something to sit on, wherever he is?"

John didn't answer her. Instead, he lifted his gaze to meet Mallory's. She drew in a deep breath. She knew what he was thinking—his uncle had stolen his fortune.

He turned back to the landlady. "Are you certain, Mrs. Daniels, that my Uncle Louis didn't say where he was going? It's imperative that I talk to him. Family business, you know."

Mrs. Daniels pursed her lips before saying tightly, "He didn't want to tell me a thing. He wanted to walk out my front door after twenty years of living under my roof without so much as a fare-thee-well." She folded her hands in her lap. "But I'm not a stupid woman, my lord. He may think he can fool me, but I can ferret out what I want to know."

"And did you happen to ferret out where Louis went?" John asked, a gold guinea appearing in his hand from his pocket as if by magic.

Mrs. Daniels smiled and took the coin. "I overheard him talking to the driver of the coach he'd hired. He ordered him to take the Post Road north."

"North?" Mallory said. She'd assumed Louis would head for the coast with the money.

"Aye," Mrs. Daniels said. "North."

Mallory and John exchanged a look and she knew he was thinking what she was: three-quarters of England was north of London.

Someone pounded on the front door. Mallory jumped, startled by the sound, and took a step closer to John as a deep male voice shouted, "Open this door, in the name of the Magistrate of Bow Street!"

"Heavens!" Mrs. Daniels whispered, her eyes as round as saucers. "What could that be about?"

"I'm certain I don't know," John answered, his voice mild, his expression as innocent as an altar boy's. "Mallory, my dear, why don't you answer the door and find out? And please advise them to keep their voices low. They'll wake Mrs. Daniels's neighbors."

Chapter 5

I heard a maid in Bedlam
so sweetly she did sing,
Her chains she rattled in her hands,
and always so sang she.
I love my love because I know
he first loved me.

"Bedlam"

Mallory stared at John, certain he'd gone completely mad. She couldn't possibly answer the door and talk to the Runners; he knew that. Nor could she voice her doubts in front of the landlady. He seemed to know that, too.

John returned her stare with a calm, determined one of his own.

And then a form of silent communication flowed between them—and Mallory understood as clearly as if he'd said the words out loud. The Runners had no idea who Mallory was. She'd been in the coach during the earlier confrontation at John's house, and of course, few people even knew he was married. She could answer the door without the Runners being the wiser and send them on their way.

"Mallory?" he prompted, a hint of challenge in his voice.

Did he think she lacked the courage?

Well, she didn't. She'd run Craige Castle and made her own decisions. She'd faced fear, and even though her heart was in her throat now, she'd face the Runners. Leaving the candle for Mrs. Daniels and John, Mallory walked out into the small, dark entrance hallway.

She turned the door handle and cracked open the door. Three Bow Street Runners stood on the small front step, moonlight shining off the hard leather of their polished black hats. In the night shadows, they seemed larger than life.

"Yes?" she asked.

The lead Runner doffed his hat. "Bow Street, ma'am. We're sorry to disturb you at this hour, but we must see Mr. Barron. Please tell him Bertie Goodman is here and it is most urgent."

"Mr. Barron isn't here," Mallory said.

"He isn't?" Bertie scratched his head. He looked to his comrades for advice while placing his hat back on. They shrugged their shoulders. Bertie turned back to her. "Tell Mr. Barron that Lord Craige got away from us. He might even come here. He was an angry one tonight when we went to arrest him, and if Mr. Barron is wise, he'll take precautions. Are you here by yourself, ma'am?"

From the darkness behind her, she heard a

muffled sound and realized Mrs. Daniels had heard the Runner's warning and was frightened. Mallory refused to consider what John was doing to keep the woman quiet. "No, I'm not alone," she assured the Runner, thankful it was the truth, since she wasn't a very good liar.

"Good," Bertie said. "Lord Craige has led us a merry chase, that he has. But you have no fear. We'll capture him. We three," he nodded at his companions, "are going to stand watch in this area. I'll be in the shadows, over yonder." He pointed to a street corner. "If you need me, you have only to shout."

"Yes, I will," Mallory assured him. "Thank you."

"Goodnight to you, ma'am."

As Mallory shut the door, her knees almost buckled beneath her. She moved quickly into the parlor, then stopped at the candlelit scene in front of her.

John still knelt on the floor, his arm around Mrs. Daniels's shoulders, his other hand over her mouth. The lady's eyes were wide with fright and she leaned back in her chair, her arms stiff at her sides, as if she didn't want to get closer to John.

"Did she hear all of it?" Mallory asked, understanding now that her fate was completely tied to John's. The realization made her angry. "John, please, you are frightening her. Let her go."

He didn't move, his expression serious. "If I release my hand, she'll scream."

Mallory made an exasperated sound. "Well, you can't sit there all night with your hand over her mouth." She bent down to Mrs. Daniels's eye level. "I know you are upset about what you may have heard, but you must understand, Lord Craige and I have done nothing wrong. We mean you no harm. Now, please, promise not to scream, and Lord Craige will remove his hand. May I have your promise?"

Mrs. Daniels nodded her head.

Mallory looked at John. "Remove your hand."

"Mallory—"

"Remove your hand. She's a frail, old woman who shouldn't be treated this way. Furthermore, she's given her word of honor."

John started to disagree with her, but Mallory silenced him with a glare. She could be as stubborn as he.

For a second, they fought a silent war of wills, then, with a small sigh of resignation, he removed his hand from Mrs. Daniels's mouth.

The woman burst out screaming, demonstrating a very healthy set of lungs for her advanced years.

Shocked, Mallory was about to tell Mrs. Daniels she'd broken her promise, when John jumped up from the floor, grabbed Mallory's hand, and pulled her toward the door. Mrs. Daniels rose, too, still screaming.

Together, the three of them ran out into the hall. Mrs. Daniels ran for the front door; John charged down the narrow hallway toward the back quarters of the house, half-dragging Mallory with him. He led them into one room, then another, before finally reaching a door that opened onto a small porch.

Fresh night air signaled freedom as they burst out of the door, then ran down a set of wooden steps and into a small yard, enclosed on all sides by a six-foot wooden fence.

"Where's the gate?" John whispered in annoyance, just as the Runners' watch rattles started shaking. Apparently Mrs. Daniels had managed to capture Bertie's attention.

John didn't worry about a gate. Instead, his long arms reached for the top of the fence and he pulled himself up, the sleeves of his jacket ripping in the process. Seated precariously on the edge, he reached down for Mallory. "Grab hold and I'll pull you up."

"No," Mallory said. She couldn't climb a fence; she couldn't.

Then the back door slammed open and from the stoop, Bertie shouted, "Stop, in the name of the Magistrate of Bow Street!" and she did the impossible.

She reached for John's hand, and before she could draw a second breath, he pulled her up beside him. For one wild second, she felt as if she were sitting on top of the world, until he gathered her in his arms and jumped down to the hard dirt of the alleyway on the other side.

John grunted as he broke the force of her fall with his body. "Are you all right?" he said in her ear. He didn't wait for an answer but rolled easily to his feet, bringing her with him.

On the opposite side of the fence, Bertie was shouting at Mrs. Daniels to open the gate. But the landlady was so busy screaming, her voice loud enough to wake the dead, that she didn't hear him. Her cries of, "The wicked Lord Craige has broken into my house!" set neighborhood dogs to barking.

A man's gruff voice yelled from a neighboring window, "Be quiet out there!" Several lights appeared in various windows as homeowners investigated.

"Come," John commanded. He took Mallory's hand and started in one direction, just as Mallory pulled in the opposite one.

Their clasp broke. John stopped abruptly, his expression almost comical.

"This way," she urged him. "Bertie posted a Runner in that direction."

"And this is the closest way out of the alley," he shot back. "The Runner has moved to the front of the house or else we would see him by now." He caught her hand and through sheer masculine domination propelled them in the direction he wanted—only to stop abruptly when a man wearing a glossy, hard hat appeared in the alley entrance.

"Damn, you were right," John said. They ran back the way Mallory had chosen.

Under her breath, Mallory mimicked his words, "I'm certain the Runner has moved to the front of the house." For her impertinence, he squeezed her hand.

They ran with the Runner hard on their heels. *We aren't going to make it,* Mallory thought. Her feet barely seemed to touch the ground. Her heart pounded against her chest.

"Hard-headed lads, aren't they?" John asked,

and Mallory wondered how he could tease at such a moment.

Just as they left the alley and emerged onto the street, Mallory heard the distant clacking sounds of more watch rattles coming from another direction. More Runners!

"John," Mallory called, trying to get his attention. He had to see that it was no use. They couldn't run all night. They must give themselves up.

She started to call again, to pull on his hand and force him to stop, when a team of horses pulling an enclosed wagon charged around a corner. The driver practically stood in his seat to pull the wild-eyed team to a halt.

"Craige!" the driver yelled. "Get in, man! Hurry!"

"It's Peterson!" John shouted, and pushed Mallory toward the wagon while he turned to confront the Runners.

Mallory ran to the back of the wagon. Her trembling fingers felt along the lacquered wood for the door handle. From the other side of the wagon, she heard the sound of a fist hitting flesh. Then another.

She threw open the door, but, suddenly uncertain, didn't move. What if John needed help? Holding the door open for protection, she peeked around the corner.

John swung one fist and knocked a Runner into the arms of his other three comrades. He ran to join her, skidding before she climbed inside.

Without ceremony, he gave her a boost up with

a hand to her rump, practically throwing her into the wagon. Peterson didn't wait for them to slam the door shut before he set the horses in motion with a crack of his whip. Mallory started to rise, lost her balance, and tumbled back against the side. Over her head in the dark were hooks with different tools hanging from them. A peculiar odor permeated the interior.

Peterson's driving was far worse than John's as they charged down empty streets. She and John were bounced every which way until Bertie's cries for them to halt and the watch rattles faded in the distance. Eventually, Peterson slowed the horses.

Mallory's heartbeat gradually returned to normal. She sat up from her place on the floor. Then John sat up, reached for her in the dark, pulled her to him, and gave her a big, smacking kiss right on the lips!

"You were wonderful!" he exclaimed.

Mallory blinked, dazed by his enthusiasm. Her lips tingled, warmth radiating throughout her body. She'd been kissed only three times before—twice by John on their wedding day; once by Hal, when she'd said she'd consider his marriage proposal as soon as she'd obtained a divorce.

But this one was different from all the others.

Before she could gather her addled wits, John dropped his hands and scrambled over her to pound his fist against the wall next to the driver's seat. "Peterson! Peterson, hold up."

The wagon came to a complete halt. John made his way to the back of the wagon and opened the door.

The fresh air smelled wonderful. Mallory wondered again what the peculiar odor was. It smelled of chemicals, like the sort used in a druggist's shop.

John jumped to the ground. "Lord, Peterson, what a bruising ride." He started to shut the doors—in Mallory's face! He'd forgotten her presence already!

"John," she said with fierce control.

"Oh, Mallory, here, let me help you." He held out his hand.

Mallory ignored it. How *dare* he give her a push on the rump, kiss her, and then forget her? She hopped down from the wagon on her own.

John frowned at the hand he still held out to her, his expression puzzled. "Have I done something wrong?"

"What would make you think that?" Mallory asked crisply. She straightened her skirts and used her fingers to try to restore some semblance of order to her hair. Even in the dark, she knew she looked a fright.

John shut the doors. The man he called Peterson had climbed down from the driver's seat and now rushed back to them. "Are you two all right?" The nervousness in his voice suggested he truly regretted driving like a lunatic.

"We're whole and in one piece, thanks to you," John replied. "Oh, please meet my wife, Mallory, Lady Craige. Mallory, this is Major Victor Peterson, one of my most trusted friends."

Major Peterson made a short, proper bow in Mallory's direction before saying, "Actually, John, I may be the *only* friend you have left. At

Lady Ramsgate's, someone ran in with the news that your house was surrounded by a battalion of Runners and bill collectors."

"I imagine that cleared the party."

"In an amazing fashion."

"Even Applegate?"

"Applegate was with me when I rushed over to your home, but he turned tail when I decided you needed to be rescued. By the way, Hadley won't be happy with you. His coach flipped over and is smashed."

"Are the horses all right?"

"Yes, they're fine, but Hadley will want your head on a platter."

"He deserves it," John agreed soberly. "By the way, Peterson, where did you get this wagon? It smells damned funny inside."

"It was standing behind one of your neighbor's houses, John. It's an undertaker's rig. Guess one of the servants died. You know how it is, no one wants a dead body in the house. I'm just relieved the body hadn't already been loaded into it. Could have been a mess during the chase."

Mallory looked in horror at the black lacquered wagon where she could now make out in the gloom gold letters on the side proclaiming "Frederick Breward, Undertaker." She turned on Major Peterson. "You *stole* this wagon?"

"I didn't steal it, Lady Craige. I borrowed it," he said politely.

He turned to John as if to continue the conversation, but Mallory was fed up to her eyeballs with their cavalier attitude. "You *stole* this wagon, and the horses, and you call that *borrowing?*"

Major Peterson's eyebrows rose in surprise. "It was an emergency, Lady Craige. I had to rescue you and your husband."

"Rescue us for what?" Mallory demanded. "Our hanging?"

"Lady Craige—"

"Before, we were guilty only of being bankrupt," Mallory said reasonably. "*Now,* we've moved on to crimes such as evading the law, breaking and entering, assaulting a Runner, and stealing horses!"

"Mallory," John said in a low voice, "you are getting worked up over very little—"

"Very little? Do you gentlemen still believe you are on the battlefield? That you can just take command of whatever you wish? This is London, sir, not some remote village in Portugal!"

Major Peterson took a step back. "I thought it was an emergency, Lady—"

She whirled to face John. "And you should turn yourself over to the Magistrate. Now, before any more crimes are added to the list."

His eyebrows shot up. "Have you gone mad?"

"I believe I'm close to it," Mallory said with perfect frankness. "Please, we can't spend the rest of our lives running all over England. Go to the Magistrate, explain that you will need some time to sort out your affairs . . . and that we didn't mean to take the undertaker's rig and horses."

"He'll order me slapped in irons before I get the first sentence out of my mouth. Mallory, in the eyes of the law, my uncle's actions were as good as my own. He had a legal right to act as my agent, and I'm responsible, even if the man stole all my money. Based upon what you've said about the accounts at Craige Castle, I believe the man has been stealing from me for years, starting from the day I entered the army."

Mallory felt a rush of relief. "This is even better! The Magistrate will have your uncle arrested—"

"No. If anyone finds Louis, it's going to be me, and it will be *me* he answers to."

"You?" Mallory echoed. "You don't even know where he is!"

John's mouth flattened and his eyes glittered. "I'll find him."

She turned on her heel, needing to put space between them, and found herself face to face with Major Peterson, who dropped his gaze as if suddenly very interested in the toe of his boot. All of a sudden she realized how shrewish she must sound to him.

She whirled around on one heel and started walking away from the two men.

"Mallory." John was following her.

"Go away! Please."

"No." He caught up with her, took hold of her arm and pulled her around to face him.

She refused to look at him. A terrible sadness suddenly weighed her down. Reaching into her pocket, she pulled out her wedding ring. She held it out to him, the sapphire black in the moonlight, the diamonds twinkling like stars. "Here." Her voice sounded dry, hoarse. "Take this and apply it to your debt."

"Mallory—"

"This marriage is not going to work, John. We are too different."

John ignored her outstretched hand. "Mallory, believe in me; I will get Craige Castle back for you."

"It's not the castle!" She turned away from him. "The castle is gone."

"Then what is it, Mallory?"

"I said take the ring."

"The ring is yours. I gave it to you."

"I don't want it. Can't you understand—?"

"No! I don't." He stepped in front of her, forcing her to look at him, and it proved her undoing.

Tears burned in her eyes. She fought to hold them back. "I'm not the person you married." Her voice was hoarse with pent-up emotion. "Not anymore."

"Neither of us is."

"Take it, John." She pushed the ring toward him.

"Mallory, it is not over between us—"

"John, it never started—"

"You're all I have left. You and the title."

"I am not a possession, John. I'm a person. A person you don't even know."

"I'll learn to know you," he said with confidence.

Mallory frowned at him. He truly believed what he said, that he could erase years of neglect for no other reason than because she was all he had left. "I've met someone else. He wants to marry me after I've obtained a divorce from you."

Her words seemed to hang in the air between them.

John didn't move. He stared at her as if he was

uncertain he'd heard correctly. Surprised by his stunned reaction, Mallory felt a wave of guilt. "John, I . . . I didn't mean to burst out with it—"

He held a hand up for silence. His jaw tightened and he turned away. For long moments he appeared to study the building across the way.

You're all I have left.

Dear Lord, what had she done? Nothing, she told herself . . . she'd only spoken the truth.

Finally he faced her, the hard planes of his face unreadable in the moonlight. "Will he be good to you, Mallory?"

The question caught her by surprise. She drew a deep breath. "I believe so."

"Better than a husband who runs out on you?"

She didn't answer. What could she say?

John seemed to come to a decision. "All I ask is that you stand beside me until I find my uncle and clear my name. Do this . . ." He paused a moment. "Do this, and I will not challenge you if you wish to divorce me."

Mallory opened her mouth in surprise. "You'd agree to a divorce?" she asked, still not certain she'd heard him correctly.

He nodded, his eyes watchful.

Mallory took a step back, dazed by the sudden turn of events—and by her own confused reaction. John was willing to give her a divorce. Wasn't that what she wanted?

After what they'd experienced together this night, he seemed a far cry from the jaded Corinthian she had confronted earlier at Lady Ramsgate's party—but no less devastatingly handsome.

In fact, if anything, she found him more appealing than the cold, distant person she had thought was her husband.

John's voice interrupted her thoughts. "What is his name?"

"Whose name?"

"The man who has taken my wife from me."

Mallory was glad for the derision in his voice. This was familiar ground. She shook her head. "I was never a wife to you."

"I disagree, Mallory. According to the laws of man and the church, we are truly married. We have witnesses to that fact."

Mallory felt her cheeks grow warm at the reminder of their wedding night. "John, there's more to marriage than one night. We haven't been with each other for years."

"Ah, but during those years, I've been serving my country. In the eyes of the law—"

"In *my* eyes, John. We're talking about what I think. I already *know* what you want. I've been living that life for the last seven years. Well, I want children. I want companionship and someone I can talk to. I want what my parents had."

He looked confused. "What your parents had?"

Mallory made an exasperated sound. "I want to be loved. Is that so hard to understand?" There, she'd said it, the innermost desire of her heart. And now that the words were out in the open, they didn't sound trite or silly.

They sounded like the truth.

She drew a deep, steadying breath. "I will accept your terms. I will stay with you until your name is clear. I really have no choice. But I want you to understand that I've made a commitment to another man, one who wants me. Our marriage has been in name only for seven years, and it will remain that way until we are divorced."

Her words seemed to blaze a path across John's soul. But he had absolutely no intention of relinquishing his hold over her, though every word she spoke was true.

Nor did this proud woman standing before him with her hand fisted tight over her wedding ring bear any resemblance to the frightened young girl he'd left in their marriage bed. Moonlight turned Mallory's wild, wind-tossed hair to silver and highlighted the defiance in her pert, fine-boned features. She looked like a night-sprite, but she was strong and brave. John felt an inordinate pride in this wife of his. A man could do far worse.

"Then we're agreed," he said curtly. "But I insist upon one more condition."

Her expressive eyes grew cautious. Did she realize they revealed every emotion passing through her mind? he wondered. "And what condition is that?" she asked warily.

"That you wear my ring."

She raised the hand holding the ring up to her chest protectively. "What of my conditions? You won't expect me to . . ." Her voice trailed off, but John knew what she meant.

"Share my bed?"

She blushed so furiously he could almost feel the heat. She nodded.

A surge of anger rose inside him. "I'm not some monster. I won't force myself on you." He took a step away from her. "Nor am I asking such a very large thing. After all, you've been wearing it for years. A few more weeks won't matter."

"Weeks?"

"Or days. However long it takes to track Louis down."

"And how will you do that?"

"I don't know, Mallory, but I will," he said, letting his irritation show. "And I promise that the minute I find him, you may give me the ring back and you will be free to go."

She opened her fist and looked at the ring in her palm.

"It's a small gesture, Mallory. Not really significant."

She lifted her gaze to meet his. "Yes, it is," she denied quickly and then looked away, as if embarrassed, before adding softly, "Or it was at one time. I waited for you, John. I wanted to be a wife to you, until finally, I grew tired of waiting."

A wealth of meaning was contained in those words.

Then, slowly, with deliberate movements, Mallory placed the ring on her finger.

John wanted to give a shout of victory, but he kept his expression solemn. He held out his hand for her.

Mallory looked at his outstretched fingers. Tentatively, she placed her hand in his.

For a swift second, John took solace in this small triumph on a night of many reversals. He tucked her hand in the crook of his arm and led her back to the wagon, where Peterson stood waiting.

For the first time, he noticed the graceful length of her fingers and the calluses. His wife was accustomed to hard work. Furthermore, she wasn't soft and round, like so many other women he had known. She was lithely muscular, with tight, high breasts and strong, smooth arms.

He had no intention of letting her divorce him.

Remembering their wedding night, John gently rubbed his finger against the scar on his thumb. He now had a mission, a goal. He silently vowed he would recover his fortune and save his marriage. He would woo and win his wife. His pride demanded it.

Of course, the one thing that could make Mallory angrier than she was now over the loss of her precious Craige Castle would be to learn that after seven years of marriage, she was still a virgin.

John realized he'd set an impossible task for himself, and he wasn't anticipating that one particular moment of truth when she found out what had really happened on their wedding night. Turning himself over to the Magistrate and debtor's prison might prove easier.

Chapter 6

Last night you slept on a goosefeather bed,
With the sheet turn'd down so bravely, O!
And tonight you'll sleep in a cold open field,
Along with the wraggle taggle gipsies O!

"The Wraggle Taggle Gipsies, O!"

Major Peterson drove them a good distance out of London until they came to a small posting inn. By then, it was two in the morning and Mallory was hungry and exhausted. To please her, John roused a groom and paid him good coin to return the undertaker's wagon to one "Frederick Breward, Undertaker."

While Major Peterson made those arrangements, John escorted Mallory to the inn. "Are you sure Major Peterson won't come to harm because he helped us?" she asked John.

He shook his head. "Peterson's father is the Duke of Tyndale. It's difficult to hang a duke's son, even a disowned one like Victor. The undertaker will be more than pleased to have his wagon and horses back and will spend the rest of his days telling of his near brush with the wicked Lord and Lady Craige."

"Either that, or he'll contact the magistrate and add another crime to your growing list."

He shot her a quick grin before his expression turned to one of concern. "You're limping."

"I've rubbed a blister on my foot," Mallory confessed. "Tell me, why did Major Peterson's father disown him?"

"Why?" John repeated blankly.

Mallory looked over her shoulder at the silhouette of the noble major talking to the stablehand. "He seems everything a nobleman should be."

"And what exactly is that?"

Mallory glanced at her husband. Was it her imagination, or did he sound testy—jealous, even? She smiled, ready to give him a bit of his own back for all his dalliances with women. "Why, he's brave, loyal, manly—"

"*Manly?* Why? Because he stole an undertaker's rig? Believe me, Mallory, any fool can nab an undertaker's wagon. The dead don't run fast."

She laughed, and he laughed with her. "In all honesty, John, it took a remarkable man to come to our rescue. Why would a father disown such a son?"

"Because Peterson married the wrong person, in his father's eyes."

"The wrong person?"

"Peterson's wife was a young Spanish woman. Her family was noble but penniless. Upon hearing of the impending nuptials, Peterson's father delivered an ultimatum which Victor wisely ignored."

John's voice held a warmth Mallory hadn't heard in it before. "Did you know his wife?"

"Yes."

"And you believe he did the right thing by defying his father?"

John didn't hesitate. "Yes."

It was on the tip of Mallory's tongue to ask if he wished he had defied *his* father over their marriage, but they'd entered the inn and the moment for such confidences had passed.

A servant met them at the door. "We need a light supper, and I'd like it served in a private room," John said, his tone lordly.

The servant scowled, his glance taking in Mallory's windblown hair and the ripped sleeves in John's jacket. A flash of gold coin between John's fingers brought about an astounding change in the man's attitude.

"It will have to be a cold supper, sir," the servant said, pocketing the coin. "Will that be all right with ye?"

"That will be fine," John answered.

A moment later, they were escorted to a private room with a small hearth and a low ceiling. The servant lit two candles while John had a few quiet words with him. Mallory took stock of their surroundings. The room appeared clean enough, although the whitewashed walls were stained with age and the smoke of many fires. A table and four chairs occupied the center area.

She sank gratefully down on a hard seat, her back to the door. She was exhausted. With a sigh of relief, she slipped off her shoes.

John sat in the chair directly next to hers. "Let me see the blister."

Mallory tucked her toes under the hem of her skirt. "No, I'm not going to let you look at my feet."

"Why not?"

"Because they are my feet and I don't want you touching them."

He raised a questioning eyebrow.

Mallory elaborated. "Touching someone's feet is very . . . well, very *familiar.*"

"Oh." He drew the syllable out, then smiled, the kind of smile that could rob a woman of all common sense—that was, if she wasn't a practical woman like her. "Mallory, if I wanted to be *familiar*"—he gave the word the same indignant inflection she had used—"it wouldn't be your *feet* I would be trying to touch."

There was blatant sensuality in his husky tone. He rested his hands on either side of her chair.

Mallory leaned back. She'd never heard the like, or at least, directed toward her. It set her pulse to racing.

"Besides," he said, "I've practically walked the length of Europe with the army. I know a little something about feet, and I know that if a blister isn't attended to, it can fester—" He made an ominous face before adding sinisterly, "Or worse."

"Worse?" she managed to croak out.

"Worse," he said solemnly. "How do you think my butler Sergeant Richards lost his leg?"

"Not from a blister."

His eyes opened wide, as if he were offended by her doubts. "It started small." He pinched two fingers in the air to indicate an inch. "But before Richards knew it, the blister grew wider and wider—" He spread both palms apart to signal the size. "—Until it ate up his leg." His hands reached down for Mallory's foot, pulled it up, and set it in his lap, almost tumbling her off her chair in the process.

Mallory grabbed hold of the seat with both hands to keep her balance. To her horror, the bottom of her foot rested against his well-muscled thigh, her big toe peeking out a hole in her stocking. Her cheeks flamed with color.

He ran a hand over the top of her foot, pressing it against his thigh, then lightly touched her exposed toe. "It seems I need to buy my wife new stockings." The muscles in his leg tightened beneath her heel.

Her errant pulse beat even faster.

"You don't need to buy me anything," she denied, her own voice as breathlessly husky as his. She tried to yank her foot back, but his grip was too firm.

"Tsk, tsk," he cautioned her. "And I need to buy you shoes. Kid slippers are not the best shoes for running through London."

"I hadn't planned on *running through London* when I put them on." She forced herself to overcome her initial embarrassment. John would grow tired of nursing her, just as he had grown tired of her on their wedding night—

Her tart thoughts melted into a sigh of unimaginable bliss. John was massaging her foot. Her hands gripping the chair seat relaxed their hold. Who would have thought such a simple thing as a foot rub could do this to a woman? Or was the magic in John's hands? Her bones seemed to be turning to jelly.

He raised his eyes to meet hers. "Does it feel better?"

Everything felt better, Mallory wanted to tell him, but she couldn't speak. She could barely breathe.

"We need to put a plaster on you, too."

"Plaster?" she repeated dumbly.

"For your blister."

"Oh, yes." She found herself smiling at him. "That would be nice."

The golden glow of the candles created a circle of light around them against the darkness of the room. A lock of his hair had fallen over one eye and he looked relaxed and roguishly disheveled. "I also asked the servant to see if he could arrange a hairbrush and piece of ribbon for your hair. He thought he might."

"A hairbrush?" Mallory reached a hand up to the tangled mess, genuinely touched by his thoughtfulness. She'd always considered herself immune to male charm—but she was feeling far from unaffected now. However, John's appeal had less to do with his rugged masculinity and startling blue eyes than with his protective nature and the small considerations of a hairbrush, a piece of ribbon, and this incredible foot massage.

She was quite tired. The day had been the most stressful of her life. For the first time since she'd been evicted from Craige Castle, she allowed herself to relax. She eased down in the chair and closed her eyes—

John's palm ran up her calf, moving up under her skirts to her thigh.

Her eyes flew open. She shot to her feet, snatching her skirts from him. "What are you doing?"

John met her indignant stare with an expression of complete innocence. "I was going to remove your stocking to have a better look at the blister."

"I'm not about to let you untie my—" She stopped, too modest to mention the word aloud.

"Garters?" he supplied helpfully.

Mallory's face turned hot with outrage. "Oh, don't attempt your rakish ways with me, John. My garters were only the beginning." Mallory placed her hands on her hips, lifting her chin with pride. "Let me inform you that I'm not like your *other* women. I will not be treated like some milkmaid and tumbled on the floor with little more than a wink from you. Do you understand me?"

"Yes, I do," John said readily. "And I imagine Peterson and the servant do, too. Isn't that right, gentlemen?"

Mallory whirled around to find Major Peterson and the servant, holding a tray of food, standing in the doorway. She turned on John, furious with him and her own culpability. "Is there no place around you that is private?" she said between clenched teeth. "Everything, *everything,* between us seems to be played out in front of an audience!"

"I've been the soul of discretion," John countered amiably. "You're the one who keeps blurting things out."

Mallory feared she would explode, she was so angry.

"I should have knocked . . . louder," Major Peterson said self-consciously.

"Nonsense," John told him, ignoring the tension radiating from Mallory. "Come in and have a seat. And you," he said to the servant, "were you able to get the brush and ribbon for my lady?"

"Aye, my lord." The portly man set the tray on the table and reached around his back where he'd stuck the handle of a brush and a length of black ribbon in his belt. "I hope these will do," he said, holding them out.

John nodded to Mallory, who stood apart from the men, her fists clenched at her side. "Mallory?"

"Fine, thank you." She meant the words, too. In spite of her anger, she couldn't wait to straighten her hair.

The servant gave her a short bow. "Then perhaps my lady would like to come with me? There's a small private room for the ladies just down this hall. Or perhaps you would rather eat first?"

"I don't have an appetite," Mallory said. She shot an angry glance at John to let him know he was the cause. "Let us go now." She slipped on her shoes and followed the man from the room, limping from the blister with every other step.

John and Peterson came to their feet as she left the room and watched the door shut behind her. Peterson poured two glasses of ale.

"You know, she's right about one thing," Peterson said, offering a glass to John.

"And what is that?"

"She is different from any other woman you've known."

"In what way?" John sat, taking a thoughtful sip of the amber-colored ale.

"She'll not come running just because you crook your finger." He shook his head. "No, you're going to have to work for this one, John, and I'm going to enjoy every moment of it."

John pulled a leg off a cold roasted chicken. "I never knew you to be a sadist, Victor."

Peterson laughed. "Hours ago, I was astounded to learn you were married. Now, after hearing the two of you together, I believe it. Your Mallory reminds me of my Liana."

John was surprised. Peterson rarely mentioned Liana by name.

Peterson smiled, the expression not reaching his eyes. "I miss her, John. I feel as if I've lost my soul."

John didn't know what to say in the face of such raw pain. He'd never felt that way for another person, ever.

At that moment, Mallory returned to the room. The gentlemen rose.

The plaster had done the trick and she walked

without limping. She'd also washed the dirt and muck off her face and hands, and her unruly hair was brushed to a high gloss and pulled back into a thick, neat braid tied off by the ribbon.

No one could mistake her breeding now, even in that dowdy dress, John thought. His chest swelled with pride.

He filled a plate for her, selecting the choicest pieces of meat and a thick slice of fresh bread. Peterson offered his chair and sat down on the one next to John.

John envied the easy grace with which Peterson performed the small gallantry. Because of his own history—years of male boarding schools and living with the whispers concerning the scandal of his birth—John felt he lacked the social graces needed to be a true gentleman. He wondered how Mallory would rank him and Peterson if she had to choose between them.

Mallory daintily spread a drop of mustard on a piece of chicken. "Have you decided what we are to do now?" she asked John.

He admired her direct approach. "That's what we must discuss. I've been thinking of what the landlady said. Louis isn't leaving the country."

"How can you be sure?" she asked. "If I had stolen someone's money, especially someone like yourself, my first action would be to go as far away as possible."

"No, not my Uncle Louis," John said. "He detests foreigners and anything that isn't English. He can barely abide even the Scots! He would no sooner bask under an Italian sun than pluck out his right eye." He leaned his arm on the table.

"What I suspect is that he hoped to force *me* to leave the country."

"But he's your uncle," Mallory protested. "Why would he wish to see you ruined?"

"So he could keep my money. I'm certain he has it all. Or at least, I hope he does." John sat back. "Louis was my father's junior by almost fifteen years. He's a flamboyant man, completely different from my father. I remember overhearing the two of them arguing over Louis's expenses. But Louis and I got along well. I trusted him, especially since the two of us were often at odds with Father, and I paid him a handsome wage to be my man of business. I've been played for a fool."

Peterson spoke. "Don't blame yourself, John. You aren't the first man who has been betrayed by his own family, and you won't be the last. The question is, are you going to let Louis get away with it?"

"Absolutely not." John ran through his options in his mind. "But I am going to let him believe that he has. I'm going to pretend to leave the country."

Mallory placed her napkin beside her plate. "But how does that help us find Louis and your money?"

"It will make him careless," John told her. "My uncle is not the smartest man. If he thinks he has won, then he's going to do what he's always done."

"And what is that?" she asked.

"Spend money," John said with a smile. "You met Louis once, Mallory, at our wedding. He's shorter than my father and that day he wore a lime green silk jacket and red heeled shoes. The collar points on his shirt were starched so high, he could barely turn his head. Fortunately, he has developed better taste over the years."

She shook her head. A very attractive blush stained her cheeks as she admitted, "I don't recall meeting him. But then, my mind was on other matters that day."

Suddenly John was curious to know exactly what "matters" had occupied her thoughts on their wedding day. Had she been against the marriage? Is that why she'd been drugged? Once he'd set his course, he hadn't stopped to evaluate his action. He was certain she hadn't taken his desertion in a flattering light.

"And how do you plan to pretend to leave the country?" Peterson asked, bringing John's thought back to the moment.

"Mallory and I are going to hide."

"Hide?" Mallory cried.

"It would be best," Peterson told her. "If anyone sees either of you, you'll be thrown into debtor's prison."

John continued outlining his plan. "You, Victor, will return to London and tell everyone that I've left for the Continent. No, wait! It would be best if you rode to Dover and purchased two tickets to Italy or Greece. That way, if anyone checks behind you, there will be evidence of our flight."

"And then what?" Mallory asked.

"Then we wait for Louis to surface, nab him, and take him before a Magistrate," John said.

"Just that simple, hmmm?" she asked.

"Just that simple," John agreed with a smile.

Mallory held his eye. "I think it's a ridiculous idea."

John's smile became a frown. "Why?"

"What if he doesn't 'surface'? We could be hiding for years!"

"He'll surface."

"And if he doesn't in a reasonable amount of time?"

"Mallory, we won't just be waiting. I'll have Peterson organize a search. We'll find Louis one way or another."

"And with what will we manage all that?" she asked. "We barely have money for our dinner, let alone tickets from Dover to Italy, or paying men to search for your uncle."

It gave John great pleasure to pull the velvet lined case out of the pocket of his coat jacket. He flipped up the lid, and the diamond neck collar spilled out onto the table. "Do you think this will cover our expenses?"

Peterson whistled under his breath. Mallory appeared speechless. She reached out and gently lifted the collar off the table. Her fingers held the stones up to the candlelight. "It's beautiful," she whispered.

"And worth a fortune," Peterson added.

"Unfortunately, nowhere close to ninety-eight thousand pounds," John said.

Mallory tilted her head in his direction. "Do you always walk around with necklaces in your pocket?"

Now, John questioned the wisdom of showing her the bauble.

She held it out to him. "It would have looked lovely around Lady Ramsgate's neck," she said coolly.

"What makes you think it was for Lady Ramsgate?" he asked stiffly.

She smiled in reply, and John felt uncomfortable under the scrutiny of her intelligent, all-too-knowing gaze.

Peterson cleared his voice. "If I may interrupt, I have an idea of where the two of you could hide."

John turned to him, grateful for his intervention. He didn't know how much longer he could have continued to hold out in a staring contest with his wife. "What is your idea?"

"I called on my mother yesterday before I rode down to London. She's upset over the estrangement between me and my father and wants us to make our peace."

"Will you?" John asked.

"No. I won't forgive him for the things he said about Liana. My conversation with Mother was somewhat strained after I told her that. However, in the course of fishing around for a topic of discussion, she said they were still having trouble with my Uncle Bartholomew Woodruff and his management of an estate Father inherited six or seven years ago called Cardiff Hall. It's in Sussex, and since our family seat and most of our holdings are in Hertfordshire, the place is a bit of a nuisance."

"Go on," John said.

"It's not a very large estate," Peterson said. "Uncle Bartholomew is a bit eccentric—nothing as sad as your Uncle Louis, of course. Bart tried the church, but he'd rather write bad poetry than preach sermons. Of course, he is no better a farmer than he is a poet. The estate is in terrible shape."

Peterson pushed his chair away from the table. "Mother says, because of where the estate is located, our land agent wants nothing to do with it, but we can't get rid of it. Otherwise, Bart will move in with my parents, something my father won't tolerate. Mother believes the best solution is to hire a steward to manage the estate. She asked me to deliver this advertisement to the papers for such a position, but I didn't get around to it."

"I could be the new steward," John said.

"Yes," Peterson answered. "No one would search for you on a farm, John. Nor would it seem odd for the steward to have a wife."

"You're right," John agreed, feeling a hum of excitement. "Furthermore, Sussex is close enough to London that once Louis makes an appearance, you can contact me immediately."

"That's what I thought," Peterson agreed.

"There's only one problem," Mallory said, interrupting their discussion.

John threw himself back in his chair, letting his impatience show. "Of course," he said under his breath.

She glared at him, but didn't back down. "You don't know anything about farming. Or do you?"

He smiled. Very deliberately, he took her hand, raised it to his lips, and kissed the back of her fingers before saying softly, "But I imagine you know a thing or two."

She blinked. "You would take instruction from me?"

John felt a flash of irritation. "But of course."

He had the satisfaction of seeing the expression on Mallory's face change from haughty skepticism to dumbfounded amazement. She sat back in her chair. "Well. I suppose the plan might work."

"Of course it will," John assured her.

The three of them spent the next few minutes discussing details. John told Peterson to get in touch with his butler Richards. The former sergeant would fence the diamonds in the necklace for the best price. Peterson called the servant for paper and they set to work on drafting a suitable letter of introduction to Lord Bartholomew Woodruff.

John and Mallory would become Mr. and Mrs. John Dawson. The letter told the story of their confrontation with robbers, who'd stolen all their worldly goods, and of the Duke of Tyndale's determination to help the young couple by offering them the position at Cardiff Hall.

"Smooth," John said with satisfaction. "Your uncle won't even think to question us."

Peterson signed his own name, reasoning that his mother had given him permission to act on his parents' behalf. He then left to buy John and Mallory a ticket on the morning post to Sussex, a two-and-a-half-hour journey.

John was thankful for his friend's help. After he paid for the private room and supper, he would have only two gold guineas to his name until Peterson sold the necklace. Enough, but by no means the fortune he was accustomed to.

"Is it possible I could write a letter to my mother and assure her that I will be all right?" Mallory asked.

"Of course," John said. He handed her the ink bottle, pen, and paper. "Peterson will deliver it to her at the Red Horse Inn."

While Mallory wrote, John rose from his chair and stretched his legs. He discovered that if he moved around the room a bit, he could stop and read over her shoulder without her being the wiser.

Her letter began in the standard manner. She urged her mother not to be alarmed and told her all was well. She then begged her mother to turn to Hal Thomas for protection.

Hal Thomas.

"Who's Hal Thomas?" John asked, before he could stop himself.

She looked up with a puzzled frown that turned thunderous when she realized he'd been reading over her shoulder. She covered the letter with a protective arm. "He's a friend of the family."

"Is he the man who wants to marry you?"

She glared at him before saying a curt, "Yes."

John grunted. She *would* be bold enough to admit it out loud. He ignored the fact that he'd asked her point blank. "Does he know anything about farming?"

"Of course. He's the squire in our shire."

"A squire?" John said the words as if he could taste them, and they tasted terrible. "You would leave me for a mere squire?"

"Yes."

John threw himself down in the chair beside her. "And do you ever lose your temper with him?

She fidgeted with the pen. "John, what an odd question. Of course not."

"Not even once?"

"No, and I've known Hal since childhood. He's a very reasonable man." She added sweetly, "I'm certain he will not walk around with necklaces in his pocket."

With a frown, John got up from his chair and crossed to the room's only window. He stared out into the night.

Mallory continued to work on the letter. She was probably adding some postscript to Hal, he thought with derision. *Dear Hal, please rescue me from the rakehell I married.*

In the reflection of the windowpane, he watched her carefully sand the letter, fold it and affix a wax seal. She looked so serene and graceful sitting in the golden candlelight that the thought struck him. *She's lovely.*

More than just lovely. His child-bride was now a woman grown. He was tempted to cross the room to her, brush aside the heavy braid lying against the smooth column of her neck, and place a kiss right on the sensitive spot below her shell-shaped ear. But he stood, rooted to the earth.

He had a rival. Hal Thomas.

He'd never had a rival before.

And Peterson was right—he'd never pursued a woman. They'd always come to him.

Finished with her letter, Mallory pushed her

chair back, the legs scraping the bare wood floor, and froze.

John stood by the window watching her, and for one moment, the hunger in his eyes held her mesmerized. No man had ever looked at her that way before.

Peterson's entrance into the room broke the spell between them. "I have the tickets. The first post should be arriving within the hour. You're lucky. Yours will be the first stage of the day."

"Thank you," John said. He walked over to the table and picked up her letter. "Will you see that this is delivered to Lady Craige at the Red Lion? It's off Blackman Street."

"I'd be more than happy to," the major replied.

Mallory looked for her reticule, wishing to give him a coin with which to use to tip the porter at the Red Horse, and then groaned.

"What is the matter?" John asked.

She sank down in the chair. "My reticule. It's gone. I must have left it in your friend Hadley's coach. I set it on the seat beside me when I took off my gloves." She covered her face with her hand, heartsick at the loss.

"Don't worry about it," John told her. "In fact, don't look back. It's a lesson I learned the hard way."

"Do you need any money?" Peterson asked.

"I've got two fat gold ones," John answered. "They'll keep us fine until we hear from you."

Mallory stepped forward. "Major Peterson, thank you for all your help."

He took her hand and kissed it. "Think nothing

of it, Lady Craige." He squeezed her hand lightly and added in a low voice, "Believe it or not, you married a good man."

Mallory shifted, uncertain how to take his words. She was still mulling them over an hour later when she and John climbed onto the post to Sussex, beginning their new life together as "man and wife."

Chapter 7

The trees they do grow high,
and the leaves they do grow green;
But the time is gone and past, my Love,
that you and I have seen.
It's a cold winter's night, my Love,
when you and I must abide alone.

"The Trees They Do Grow High"

Mallory woke to the sound of someone whistling a jaunty tune. She groaned. It was too early to wake up.

She curled over on her side and hugged the pillow—but it wasn't a pillow she was hugging; it was a man's doeskin-clad thigh.

A very hard, muscular thigh.

Startled, Mallory started to sit up and almost toppled off the back of the farmer's hay wagon.

John caught her just in time, easily pulling her into his arms. "Did you have pleasant dreams?"

Memories came rushing back to her. After they'd been dropped off at the inn by the Sussex post, they'd begged a ride on the back of a farmer's hay cart to Cardiff Hall. They could walk faster than the ox could pull the wagon, but John had reasoned that they needed to rest. He'd been right.

She pushed away. "Why couldn't it all have been just an unpleasant dream?" Uncomfortably aware of how close she still sat to him, she scooted across the wagon bed to put a little more space between them, but it was very little. He had her trapped against the bowed rear of the wagon and the load of hay.

"Good morning, or afternoon, to you, too."

Mallory shot him a discontented look before stretching to work the kinks out of her muscles.

It was a bright, sunny afternoon. Around them were low, rolling fields bordered by hedgerows.

Wiping the sleep from her eyes, Mallory reflected that the harvest in this part of the country would be a good one. Already, the fields of wheat were turning. Her fields at Craige Castle wouldn't be ready to harvest for another six weeks.

Jacketless, John leaned back against the hay pile, one booted leg against the high side of the wagon, the other bent at the knee. His face, shadowed with the beginnings of a beard, was already turning a healthy color from the afternoon sun.

It wasn't fair that he should appear so completely handsome while she felt as dirty and used as a dishcloth.

Mallory raised her hands to her face. "I wish I had my bonnet. I'm going to get more freckles."

"I like freckles."

"My mother assures me you are in the minority. May I have the brush?"

He pulled it from a pocket in his jacket lying beside him and Mallory unbraided her hair and brushed it out.

"You have pretty hair."

Mallory shook her head. "It's too brown."

John pulled the piece of straw he'd been chewing out of his mouth. "Ah, but when the sunlight hits it, it is the color of rich toffee."

"Toffee?" The word triggered a memory. "You like toffee, don't you?"

He smiled, his teeth flashing white. "Yes, I do. How did you know that?"

Because for our wedding, your father told my mother that toffee was your favorite. Mallory and the cook had spent hours making toffee for him. It was also one of the few things he'd eaten that day. She wondered if he had any memories of their wedding day.

"No reason," she said. "You just look like you have a sweet tooth." She rebraided her hair.

He started whistling again, the same tune he'd been whistling when she'd first awakened.

"Do you sing, too?" she asked archly.

He laughed. "No, I can't carry a tune in a bucket with this gravelly voice of mine, but I like music. Do you?"

She tossed her braid over her shoulders. "I like to listen to good music." She emphasized the last two words. It was childish of her, but she felt like being childish. What she'd really like would be hot water and a change of clothes.

He didn't acknowledge her sarcasm. "I'll bet you sing. Every young Lady of Quality must have some musical talent," he said, as if quoting a source. "I imagine you have a lovely singing voice."

"Mother insisted I learn the harp and take voice lessons, but I never enjoyed them. Besides, I never had time for nonsense like singing or painting," she added righteously. "I had an estate to run."

"There is always time for music."

She focused her eyes on the toe of his expensively shod foot. His boots no longer sparkled with the shine of champagne blacking. "Not when you have responsibilities."

He let his breath out slowly and she realized she'd struck a blow. She also heard how shrewish she sounded. She glanced at the farmer driving the wagon. He wasn't paying any attention to their conversation but stared at the ox's rump, lost in his own thoughts.

"I'm sorry," she said. "I shouldn't have said that. I'm not at my best when I first wake."

"No. You were right to say it. I just wonder what I can do to earn your forgiveness. Walk over hot coals? Cut off one of my arms? Bleed to death from the sharpness of your tongue?"

Mallory frowned, feeling a stab of guilt in the face of his justifiable anger. But she refused to back down. "See that Craige Castle is returned to me," she answered coolly. "Its return will be penance enough."

He gave her a fixed smile.

The farmer pulled his wagon to a halt and

turned to them. "Cardiff Hall lies down that road a stretch of the leg. The village of Tunleah Mews is on up this way ahead." He spoke with the round vowels of a Sussex man. "Follow this road and you should meet the drive. It's shaded by huge oaks and there are two stone pillars at the end. You can't miss it."

"Thank you," John said, and jumped off the wagon. He reached up to help Mallory down from the high wagon bed. His hands came to her waist.

For a moment their eyes met. It had been on the tip of Mallory's tongue to tell him she didn't need his help, but the words died in her throat.

He grinned as if he understood the battle warring inside her and swung her easily down to the ground. Mallory quickly stepped away, needing to put distance between them.

"Are you ready?" he asked.

She nodded.

John waved to the farmer. "Thank you for the ride."

"No bother," the farmer replied. "Give my respects to Lord Woodruff."

"Do you know him?" John asked, shrugging into his jacket.

The farmer gave a bark of laughter. "I know *of* him. He don't come around much. Spends most of his time in his garden, talking to himself. He couldn't raise pole beans. You should have an interesting time of it, young man." With those words, he flicked his switch at the ox and started the cart moving up the road.

John laced his fingers with Mallory's, the gesture natural and unaffected. Mallory knew she should remove her hand from his, but she didn't. As they walked toward Cardiff Hall, the contact was comforting.

It was a perfect day for a walk in the country. Primroses and buttercups bloomed in the ditches on either side of the road.

John broke the silence between them once again by whistling.

"What's that song called?" Mallory asked.

"No name. Just a melody I like. So, I know you don't sing, but do you whistle?"

Mallory looked at him as if he were ready for Bedlam. "You should know a lady never whistles." She lowered her voice and confided, "But sometimes I do, when I'm alone, even though Mother doesn't like it."

"Would you whistle now?"

"Of course not."

"Because of those rules, or because of me?"

She shot him a look from beneath her lashes. "Both. Besides, it is one thing to whistle in your own scullery while churning butter and quite another to be walking hatless and gloveless on a public road, whistling away. My mother would suffer heart palpitations if she saw me now."

John winced. "Is this the same mother who said women shouldn't have freckles?"

"Yes."

"Well," John's tone was dry, "we've had one piece of luck."

"What is that?"

"Your mother is not with us."

"I'm glad she's not here, too," she admitted with equal candor.

When her father had been alive, he had catered to her mother's every whim. Now it was Mallory who struggled to see that all her mother's needs were met.

"Does your mother like Squire Hal?"

John's question caught her by surprise. "Do you mean Squire Thomas?" she asked pointedly.

He shrugged, turning his head to look over the fields on the other side of the road.

Mallory decided to take his question seriously. "They get along. We've been friends with Hal for years. Mother believes he is beneath me socially but admits he is a good man."

"But no grand passion?" he asked.

Mallory rolled her eyes. "What does passion have to do with marriage?"

"Everything," he told her stoutly.

She couldn't stop herself from laughing. "Now I know what went wrong in *our* marriage. A lack of passion."

"Mallory—"

"Are you going to pretend you felt passion for me, John? We were complete strangers and obviously mismatched from the start. At least I know Hal. I know his morals and his beliefs. We shall do well together."

John pretended to yawn.

"I'd be better off speaking to a stone wall than you, John Barron," Mallory said, ignoring him by focusing on the road ahead.

John easily kept pace beside her. "How does your mother feel about the divorce?"

"She's against it, or was."

"Was?"

"Losing Craige Castle upset her, although she was still arguing with me to give you another chance when we came to London."

"A wise woman."

Mallory drew a regretful sigh. "However, now that you've lost *everything,* I'm certain she will agree to a divorce without delay."

John stopped dead in his tracks. "For no other reason than that I'm bankrupt? What happened to our wedding vows, Mallory?"

She turned to him. "The ones we both took *forsaking* all others?" she asked archly.

John frowned. Her point made, Mallory continued walking.

A second later, he followed. "Is your blister bothering you?"

"No. The plaster helped."

"You should have more sturdy shoes."

Mallory opened her mouth to warn him to let her feet alone, but he held up his hands as if begging for mercy. "I know, we are talking about your feet again. However, I do think we should get you a new pair of shoes. Those slippers won't last a week on the farm."

"Spending what little coin we have on shoes is not a wise idea. We must practice economy, John. Do you have any idea what shoes cost? You must remember, you are not a rich man anymore. You can't purchase whatever strikes your fancy."

John reached out, took her arm, and swung her around to a halt. "A man has to make sure his wife has a decent pair of shoes. That's not some fancy."

"If you don't have the money, you can't buy anything," Mallory said. "Furthermore, I'm not your wife. Not truly."

John's eyes burned bright with angry pride. "You are until the divorce. You may not believe this, Mallory, but I am not a spendthrift. I've lived on close to nothing for years, believing during that time that all my money was going to you and Craige Castle. *I will buy you shoes.*"

Mallory chose not to argue further. She shrugged her shoulders and almost smiled as he practically ground his teeth in frustration. "Having a wife isn't as easy as you thought, is it?" she asked, before striding away, her pace brisk.

He easily caught up with her. "By the way, while we are alone, you should start teaching me about farming."

"All right. Tell me what you know and I'll fill in the spaces," Mallory said, not slowing her pace.

"It can't be difficult. Everyone in England does it."

"Is that a fact?" Mallory said, feigning wide-eyed wonder.

"Didn't anyone ever tell you sarcasm is the lowest form of humor?"

"No."

John changed the subject. "Well, look over there. That field of whatever doesn't look so bad."

Mallory gazed in the direction he was pointing

beyond the oak trees to a field of ripening wheat. "No, you are right. The field looks very good. By the way, John, what crop is that?"

"Crop?"

"What is growing in that field?"

John's gaze slid from her to the wheat and back again. He quirked his mouth to one side, a small dimple Mallory had never noticed before at the lower corner of his mouth. "Oats?"

She shook her head. "Wheat." She crossed to the side of the road for a better look. "It will be ready to be harvested in three to four weeks. Your job as steward will be to hire and oversee the workers for the harvest. Then you will be responsible for the threshing and seeing the grain to the mill." She bent down to look at the hedgerow circling the field. "Of course, here it appears there is a hole in the hedgerow." John hopped over the ditch to join her and she stepped back so he could see the underweaving of the hedgerow. "It isn't a worry now, but when this field is turned over for grazing—"

"It's a field of wheat. Why would I let anything graze on it?"

"To clean the stubble and fertilize the field."

"Fertilize?"

Mallory was beginning to enjoy herself. "The refuse from the animals enriches the field. Of course, you don't have to let animals graze on the field. If Cardiff Hall has a good-sized stable, you can shovel the muck from the stalls over to the field and work it into the soil." She stood, brushing off her hands, and drew a deep breath. "Can you smell it?"

"What? The muck?" His nose wrinkled.

She smiled and shook her head. "No, the ripening wheat. This is my favorite time of year. I love the sunlight, fresh air, and the smell of growing things. And listen—can you hear them?"

John listened a moment before saying, "Hear who?"

"The insects, the birds . . . this whole field is teeming with life. Listen again."

John cocked his head. "I hear birds. I hear a bee." He looked toward the sound, and a huge bumblebee buzzed dizzily toward them and away. He shook his head. "But I don't think it's anything special."

"You don't?" Mallory said with genuine surprise. She took his hand and led him back across the ditch to the road. "I've never grown tired of life in the country. Mother would like to move to London, but not me. The two days I spent in London were enough."

"This was your first trip to London?" John asked.

"My first and only time . . . and I didn't like it. It's too smelly and crowded."

"Oh, but you didn't really see London. You should visit the theaters, the parks, the opera—"

"Instead of the home of your mistress?" she asked innocently.

He ignored her. "I can't believe your parents never took you there."

"My parents had planned on *you* taking me there after our wedding."

John stopped, his hand pulling her back. "Mallory," he started, then stopped as if words failed him. A myriad of emotions—regret, anger, uncertainty—flickered in his eyes.

And suddenly, Mallory wasn't sure she wanted him to explain himself. She didn't *want* to hear the truth. "It's passed, John. It no longer matters."

He lightly touched the braid lying over her shoulder. "It still matters to *you.*"

She conceded his point. "All right, I've been a bit snippy." A cloud passed over the sun, softening the bright sunlight. "Would it help if I confessed that I'm no longer quite so angry as I was when we first met at Lady Ramsgate's?"

"I'm not certain I should be let off the proverbial hook so easily. I truly am sorry for all you went through because of my own neglect."

"I realize now it wasn't all your fault."

"It was my responsibility." He took her hand and turned it over, palm up. He ran his hand over hers. "I never dreamed a wife of mine would ever have to work so hard as to form calluses."

Mallory drew her hand back and hid it in the folds of her dress. "It's in the past, John."

"Aye. It's in the past." But neither believed it.

They stood side by side, lost in their own thoughts. Mallory discovered she actually liked him. He was more easygoing than Hal and therefore a more tolerant companion. Hal could never admit he'd been wrong—not even once in his life. It was a quality that irritated her.

She started walking and John fell in step beside her.

Neither touched the other.

At the stone gateposts leading to Cardiff Hall, John said, "We need to ensure that our stories are the same."

"I'm Mrs. Dawson, you are Mr. Dawson."

John brought his brows together in an expression of great concentration. "Good. I think we're ready to fool anyone now."

Mallory smiled up at him, pleased he understood her dry humor. Hal didn't always understand her small jokes and often answered her literally.

John led them through the gates. Huge, ancient oaks lined the dirt drive, creating a canopy of boughs overhead. "Where did we last work?"

"In East Anglia?" she offered. "We can pretend you are a soldier home from the war and I am the patient wife who waited seven years for you."

He chuckled. "Fair enough. That will be our story, then. It's always good to weave a touch of the truth into a lie. Makes it more believable."

"And do you lie often?"

"Obviously not as often as you do," he shot back, and she laughed.

They followed a bend in the drive and came upon the house. Cardiff Hall was a lovely, sprawling country manor, two stories high, surrounded by lush, blooming flowerbeds. Roses climbed the brick around the heavy oak front door. Trellises of sweet peas separated beds of daisies, roses, and lilies.

John began tying his neck cloth. "Are you ready?" he asked her.

Mallory nodded with an assurance she was far

from feeling. John took her hand, lacing his fingers with hers. "Should we go to the servant's entrance?" he asked. "I've never been one so I don't know how one goes about it."

Mallory shook her head. "You use the servant's entrance after you've been hired."

"Well, then," he said, "let's raise the curtain on the second act of our little farce. Come." He led her to the front step and rang the bell.

A second later, the door was opened by a tall, slim woman in dark clothes, a white apron, and an unwelcoming face beneath her mob cap. "Yes?" she asked abruptly, and then her expression softened, color coming to her cheeks, as the full impact of John's handsome appearance registered.

"My name is John Dawson," John said, with just the right touch of courteous respect. He pulled from his pocket the letter Peterson had penned. "My wife and I are here to see Lord Woodruff."

She drew back with a frown. "Lord Woodruff doesn't like unexpected visitors," she told him, and made no move to let them in.

"He'll like us," John said, putting his foot in the door to prevent her from closing it.

"I don't think so," the woman said. "I've been with him going on five years now, and I've never seen him happy to receive guests."

"This letter is from the Duke of Tyndale's son," John said, with more steel in his voice. "He's acting on his father's behalf."

The woman whispered, "Tyndale," her eyes

widening in surprise, and she held the door open. "Perhaps you'd best come in and wait while I deliver the letter to Lord Woodruff."

"Perhaps," John echoed softly. He and Mallory entered the huge foyer. It was a welcoming room done up in green and rose. Family portraits and gilt-framed mirrors lined the walls. A staircase and three rooms led off the foyer. A huge, carved walnut table stood in the middle of the room for guests' hats and the like. At the moment it boasted a dramatic arrangement of flowers.

John handed the letter to the woman, who said, "I'm Mrs. Irongate, Lord Woodruff's housekeeper." She fluffed the edges of her mob cap with her fingers, a girlish gesture Mallory was certain was for John's benefit. "I don't mean to appear rude, but Lord Woodruff is a touch funny about guests." She leaned toward John and confided in a low voice, "He's artistic, you know."

"Yes, we've heard," John answered.

Satisfied, Mrs. Irongate bustled over to the closed door on the far right of the foyer. "Stay here," she ordered, before rapping three times on the door, waiting a beat, and then rapping a fourth time.

"What the devil do you want, Mrs. Irongate?" a man's voice boomed from beyond the door.

Mrs. Irongate flashed them an apologetic smile, turned the handle, and went in, shutting the door behind her. They heard the sound of muffled shouting followed by Mrs. Irongate's calm, unruffled voice. Mallory moved closer to John. "What is it he does again?"

"Peterson said he is a poet. A bad one."

A second later, the door opened and Mrs. Irongate said, "Lord Woodruff will see you now." She batted her eyelashes at John as he entered, his hand protectively on Mallory's elbow.

Lord Woodruff's study was a stark contrast to the neat, tidy appearance of the rest of the house. It was obviously a man's room, with leather chairs and walls lined from floor to ceiling with books. A huge desk placed before a large window dominated the room.

There all semblance of order ended. The room looked as if it had been ransacked. Balls of wadded paper littered the floor so that Mallory and John had to kick them out of the way as they crossed to the desk. Books spilled from the shelves and covered every available surface. Many were open and stacked one on top of the other. On the desk, the piles of open books were six to seven deep. Lord Woodruff sat behind the desk, a huge stack of blank paper before him. He held Major Peterson's letter.

Lord Woodruff looked like a bird—a raven, to be exact—with a great hooked nose, a balding pate he covered with hair combed from the back of his head to the front, and black, burning eyes. He stood up. "How am I supposed to work with all these interruptions?"

He came around the desk and marched over to a tray of liquor set on a side table. He wore an overlong purple robe, black breeches and socks, and slippers. A yellow silk scarf was wrapped around his neck, the ends trailing down his back.

"You're from Tyndale, you say?" he asked, as if

not expecting an answer. He shot them a malevolent glance as he poured a generous drink from one of the decanters. "I don't give a damn for Tyndale. I have only one goal in my life, and that is to finish my book." He honed his black gaze on John. "Do you realize how difficult it is to write a book?"

"No, sir," John replied respectfully, "but I imagine it is a prodigious feat."

"Prodigious?" Lord Woodruff raised an eyebrow. "Prodigious. I'd forgotten that word." He drained his glass in one gulp and crossed to the desk. "I have to remember it," he whispered. Tossing Major Peterson's letter to the floor, he picked up a pen, dipped it in ink, and began scribbling. He muttered as he wrote, his pen scratching back and forth across the page.

Mallory looked to John, who shrugged. They stood before Lord Woodruff's desk for a good three minutes before John cleared his throat.

Lord Woodruff looked up, his eyes bulging in surprise. He fired out questions in rapid succession. "What are you doing here? Why are you bothering me?" His arm came down protectively over his writing. "What is it you want?"

John gently pushed Mallory behind him. "I'm your new steward, John Dawson, and this woman is my wife."

Mallory bobbed a quick curtsey. Lord Woodruff frowned, as if seeing them for the first time. "Steward? I don't remember hiring a steward."

"You didn't. Major Peterson, the Duke of Tyndale's son, hired me," John told him.

Lord Woodruff's great bushy brows came together. "Why do I need more hired help? I have Terrell. I have the dairy maids. What do I need with more interruptions?"

"I'm here to ensure you are not interrupted," John explained, his voice reasonable even as he began backing toward the door, taking Mallory with him. "Tyndale wants me to run the farm. He thought you would appreciate my help."

Lord Woodruff pressed his lips together until his face looked like a dried apple with black eyes. "I can't think about the farm now. I have a book to write. I have work to do. I can't take time for anything else!"

John pushed Mallory out the door into the foyer as he said, "I understand that, Lord Woodruff. Please, continue with your work. I'll see to everything else." He shut the door and rolled his eyes heavenward.

"Do you really think he's working on a book?" she asked, picking up several of the balls of paper they'd kicked on their way out of the room. Tiny, cramped writing covered both sides of the sheets. She smoothed the papers out and laid them on the foyer table. "Or is he just mad as a hatter?"

"Who knows?" John answered. "Since I've been back to London, I've met a score of people who claim to be writers and, I have to admit, they are a very odd lot. The question is, is he like this all the time, or only when he's preparing a book for his publisher? Because if this is his usual state, I understand why Tyndale is so worried—and why he'd like to keep Woodruff as far away from him as possible."

At that moment, Mrs. Irongate entered the

foyer from the opposite direction. "Is everything settled with Lord Woodruff?"

John straightened. "Yes, he's very pleased to have us on the staff."

"Excellent," Mrs. Irongate said, and again batted her wispy eyelashes at John. "Did he tell you where you would sleep?"

Mallory stepped forward. "Isn't there a house for the steward?"

"Yes, there is," Mrs. Irongate said. "But it was let to one of the tenants by his grace's land manager."

"Where else can we sleep?" Mallory asked.

"You could stay here in the house with us," Mrs. Irongate offered, her gaze sliding toward John.

John and Mallory both said, "No," at the same time. Their eyes met, and she couldn't help smiling at him. For once, they were in perfect accord.

"I didn't think so," Mrs. Irongate said with a sad sigh. "There is a small cottage beyond the barn. I don't know what shape it is in, but I imagine we could make it homey quick enough."

"I'd love to see it," Mallory said, anxious to get settled.

"Then follow me," Mrs. Irongate said. She led them through the back of the house, stopping to introduce them to Mrs. Watkins, the cook, and Lucy, the serving girl. Both the servants preened with girlish delight upon meeting John, especially when he gallantly bowed over their hands.

Mrs. Irongate led them out of the house. "That's all the help we have in the house and all we need," she said proudly. They crossed the back lawn to a carriage path. Flowers bloomed in glorious display from several beds. "Lord Woodruff loves his flowers. Takes care of them himself, he does. Says they help him think. Did he tell you about Terrell?"

"He didn't have an opportunity to say much beyond mentioning the name," John said dryly.

"Terrell comes from the village and helps around the barn. He's a wee bit slow, but a nice lad. We don't actually do much farming here. Two village lasses help him out with the dairy, but I think you'll see there is a good deal of work that isn't getting done." She led them down a stone path that turned to dirt. "This path takes us to the barn. Lord Woodruff won't bother you much," she assured them. "He rarely goes out. He's working on a book, you know."

"He told us," Mallory said.

"He's been working on it ever since I arrived here five years ago. He calls it his 'epic.' 'Course, I don't know what an 'epic' is. I don't read myself. Seems a waste of time to me for a man to spend all his time writing something most people can't read, but it keeps Lord Woodruff busy. One thing I should tell you—he will insist on using the coach every Sunday to take him to church. Ten thirty sharp. And he expects us to go with him too. We sit in the pew behind his. Whatever you do, don't be late. He hates to be late. Our Lord Woodruff is a creature of habit, that he is. Do you know the seams on your sleeves are torn, Mr. Dawson?"

Mallory had grown lost in Mrs. Irongate's whirlwind monologue, but John answered easily,

"Yes, I do." He then told the story of their being robbed. He wove such an animated tale, even Mallory started to believe it.

She watched as John easily charmed Mrs. Irongate. In short order, the woman promised to provide them with necessities such as a needle and thread, and pots and pans. For a moment, Mallory thought Mrs. Irongate would offer to sew up the seams of his jacket, too, but she took one look at Mallory's face and pressed her lips together.

Mallory wondered if her irritation at the fawning woman showed that clearly.

Around a clump of trees stood the barn. It was a pleasing old Norman structure of stone and timber with a tile roof. Nearby was a pond with ducks swimming across it. Several chickens scratched in the yard.

"What do you think?" John asked her.

Mallory sniffed the air experimentally. "I think the bedding for the animals hasn't been changed for ages." She flashed a teasing look at him. "You may have plenty of fertilizer to use on the fields."

He sent her a dark look before laughing. "You'd like to see me mucking out stalls, wouldn't you?

"It could be entertaining."

Mrs. Irongate led them down a hill and through a small wooded area before they came upon a clearing. There, beside a small gurgling stream and sheltered by the branches of two spreading oaks, stood a small thatched cottage.

"It's lovely," Mallory said. "The setting is charming."

"Yes, it is," Mrs. Irongate agreed. "The stream

flows to another pond about a quarter mile that way. You might wish to use it for your washing and such."

But when Mallory entered the cottage, she immediately wanted to turn on her heel and leave. The room was little better than a pig sty. The hard dirt floor hadn't seen a broom in decades, and spiderwebs hung from the wooden ceiling beams.

A bed large enough for two people had been pushed against one wall close to a hearth full of cold ashes. No mattress or bed ropes were laced on the frame. Several pieces of broken pottery lay on the floor. A table and one chair looked to be in good condition, although another chair lay on its side, a leg broken.

"Oh, dear," Mrs. Irongate said. "I haven't been down here for quite some time."

Mallory turned to John, who was frowning. He took a deep breath before saying, "We'll just have to make it better."

"Make it better?" Mallory repeated skeptically.

"Mrs. Irongate, you have bedding up at the house?"

"Oh, yes. We do."

"Then why don't we give my wife a moment to relax while you and I fetch some things down."

"Yes, we can do that," the housekeeper said, and they left Mallory alone.

Mallory wondered how he'd known she needed these few moments alone. She sank down onto the only good chair, an almost overwhelming sadness threatening to engulf her. She had gone from being the proud lady of Craige Castle to the hunted mistress of this little hovel. She clasped her hands together, feeling her wedding ring bite into her finger. She wouldn't give in to her emotions. She wouldn't. But the struggle to maintain her composure was hard.

By the time John returned with rope and a rolled-up mattress, she had herself firmly in control again and was picking broken pottery up off the floor.

He stopped in the doorway. "Are you going to be all right?"

She looked up at him. "I'll be fine. I'm always fine. One thing I know how to do is survive."

He reached a hand out to her, his gaze dark and full of concern. "I'll make it up to you, Mallory. I promise I will."

"It's not all your fault, John. I know that now." Impetuously, she lifted her hand and brushed it against the hard line of his jaw. His day's growth of whiskers scraped her skin. "We need to get you a razor. You're starting to look like a felon." Her teasing eased the concern in his eyes. He set to work on weaving bed ropes for the mattress. A few moments later, Mrs. Irongate, Lucy, and Mrs. Watkins arrived, their arms loaded with dishes, bedding, a broom, and other household items—including a razor.

Mrs. Watkins also brought a hamper of food. She was a chubby lady with rosy cheeks. "Come to the kitchen on the morrow and I'll supply you from the food stores," she promised Mallory. "You're also welcome to help yourself from our nice vegetable garden. Lord Woodruff doesn't eat much."

The first fireflies of the evening lit the path up to the barn by the time the three women had left. In an amazingly short time, they'd helped make the cottage habitable.

John finished tying the bed ropes and tucked sheets around the mattress. Mallory laid out food from the hamper—a cold chicken, cheese, buns, and a jug of cider. "I'm surprised you know how to make a bed," she told him, and her cheeks flushed as she realized the unintentional double meaning of her words.

He shot her a lopsided grin, acknowledging that he had also heard the double entendre. "I can cook, too."

Mallory stepped back, feeling awkward. She searched for a safe topic. "Shall we eat?"

The simple meal was delicious, but Mallory could barely finish what was on her plate. She was exhausted and the bed looked far too inviting. She slipped outside for a private moment.

Night had fallen. Croaking bullfrogs called from the stream, joined by a chorus of other night sounds. Some of the tension left her shoulders. She took her time washing her face and hands. Tomorrow matters would look better. Problems always appeared easier to handle in the morning. What she needed right now was a good night's sleep.

One thing was certain, John had turned out to be the complete opposite of what she'd expected. He no longer seemed the irresponsible scoundrel she'd first thought him. In fact, he was as much a victim of Louis Barron's treachery as she was—maybe more so since Louis was his uncle. Considering some of the harsh things she'd said to John earlier, she owed him an apology. It would help her sleep better.

Her mind made up, Mallory returned to the cottage. As she crossed the threshold, the first thing she noticed was that John had cleared the table.

The second was that John stood in the middle of the room, getting undressed. He tugged his shirt from his breeches and lifted the hem.

"What are you doing?" she asked.

He paused in his actions, one eye peeking out at her through the neck of his shirt. "Getting undressed."

He tugged the shirt off over his head. His broad-shouldered presence filled the room. Except for her wedding night, she'd never been with a half-naked man before—and in those days, John hadn't had as many muscles as he did now.

Memories flooded through her, vague, half-focused memories of a night she'd thought she'd all but forgotten. "I can see that. Where do you plan to sleep?" she said.

He tossed the shirt on the bed and unfastened the top button of his breeches, completely at ease as he replied, "Right there on the bed with you."

Chapter 8

As he was ariding, and ariding one day,
He met with sweet Kitty all on the highway;
I gave her a wink and she roll'd her black eye;
Thinks I to myself I'll be there by and by.

"Sweet Kitty"

Mallory slammed the door shut behind her. "I knew it!" Fire flashed in her eyes. Angry color rose in her cheeks.

John didn't think she'd ever looked more stunning—and suddenly sleep was the last thing on his mind. Challenged, he sat down on the bed, willing to play the game with her. "Knew what?" he asked innocently.

"Stay back, John." She took a step away from him, holding up her hand to ward him off.

He grinned. "Mallory, I haven't come near you."

The golden light from the single candle shut out the world beyond its small glow. An insect flew too close to the flame, causing it to sputter, and shadows danced upon the whitewashed walls.

"No, but you want to."

He laughed. He wouldn't deny it. Right now his wife held him completely captivated. Her braid lay over one shoulder, her hands fisted at her hips as if she dared him to doubt her.

John leaned one elbow on the bed. "Mallory, we're married."

"We're going to be divorced."

He wagged a chiding finger at her. "But we want everyone to *think* we are married. We should sleep together, to keep up appearances."

Her defensive posture relaxed ever so slightly.

He patted the bed next to him. "Come, Mallory, let us be friends." *Let us be lovers.*

He saw her hesitate and knew she'd heard his unspoken invitation. He wasn't a fool. Whether she admitted it or not, there was a part of her that was deeply attracted to him. It's what made her so prickly.

And he wanted her.

His feelings went beyond the merely physical. He admired her. He liked her intelligence, dry wit, and courage. In the twenty-four hours they'd been together, he'd begun to think of them as a couple.

It seemed only natural that they sleep together.

Of course, he reminded himself, his wife was still a virgin. But he suspected that what she lacked in experience she'd make up for in creativity. And he was just the man to initiate her. Every muscle in his body vibrated with a heavy, pulsing desire.

Her wary golden brown eyes watched him.

John rose from the bed. He would erase all thoughts of divorce from her mind forever. All thoughts of this Hal person. He had no doubt he could do it.

He walked across to her and reached for her hand, his movements slow, unhurried. Almost reverently, he lifted her hand to his lips and lightly kissed the tips of her fingers. She gave a start as his lips touched her skin. A shiver of excitement flowed through her to him. He went still, giving her time to adjust, and then kissed the top of each and every finger, first one, then another . . . the third, he tasted with the tip of his tongue.

Her lips parted in surprise, but she didn't pull away. John took another sample, letting her feel his teeth against the delicate skin at her wrist, and discovered he was the one being seduced. Dear Lord, she tasted sweet, like honey. Warm, sweet, wild honey. It shot straight to his soul with the power of an aphrodisiac.

A new sparkle appeared in her eyes. If that wasn't an open invitation to kiss her, then John had never received one.

He leaned toward her, closing his eyes, ready to savor the moment—

She covered his mouth with the tips of her fingers.

He opened his eyes. Their faces were mere inches apart.

"What is the matter?" he asked, his lips brushing against her.

"We can't . . ." she whispered.

"Yes, we can," he answered, his voice hoarse with lust. He pulled her hand from his lips.

She turned her head away. Her eyelashes fluttered. "I can't. I feel so travel stained. Let me bathe. And then we can."

John let his lips curl in a smile of delicious anticipation. "Let me bathe you."

His suggestion shocked her. A bright spot of color appeared on each cheek. He laughed, his low voice full of pride, full of lust. "Sweet little innocent." He brushed his lips against her hair, her neck, and finally the lobe of her ear, reveling in the warm, heady scent of her. He couldn't wait to have her naked. "I'll get water."

John scooped up the bucket from its place by the table, lifted the bar on the door, and opened it. "I'll be back in a moment," he promised.

She nodded, her eyes demurely downcast, her color high.

The heady drum of lust pounded in his ears. Having a wife was a wonderful thing, especially one this modestly enchanting. Eager to return, he slipped out the door, leaving it open.

The night air felt like velvet. The light of a full moon lit his way to the stream. He'd taken only a few steps when the door slammed shut.

Surprised, he turned. The wind must have blown it closed. Funny, but he hadn't thought there was much wind this evening.

He tried the latch. It lifted but when he pushed the door, it was barred fast.

"Mallory? Mallory, the bar's down on the door."

"That's right," came her muffled voice from inside. "And it's going to stay barred."

"But what about me?" John leaned against the door, dropping his voice in case someone should happen by. "You've shut *me* out."

"Yes, I have, haven't I?"

"You can't leave me out here. Where will I sleep?"

"You can sleep in the barn," came her incisive reply. "And you can kiss your own fingers!"

John stepped back, refusing to believe his ears. "Mallory, what happened? What caused you to change your mind? You were warm and willing only moments ago."

"No, *you* were warm and willing. I stood my ground and bided my time."

She'd tricked him?

John stared at the door. No, that couldn't be true.

No woman had ever rejected him before. Not one. She must be suffering from maidenly modesty. Every text he'd ever read in his life, from Homer to Milton, had assured him that virtuous women were shy. They had to coaxed.

In fact, he had it on great authority—from the other officers in the army—that virtuous women didn't like sex. Only those of bad moral character, of whom John had known plenty, enjoyed carnal passions.

Mallory was probably suffering from an attack of nerves. He should be pleased his wife was so innocent . . . although virginal shyness was a damned nuisance when he wanted to make mindless love to her all night.

He leaned his shoulder against the door. He kept his voice gently even. "Mallory, open the door and let's talk about it. I know you may be shy and a little frightened, but your fears are misplaced. You can trust me."

At first, John didn't think she'd answer. Maybe she hadn't heard him. And then, he thought he heard something that sounded like . . . he had to strain to hear, putting his ear against the good solid door . . . *laughter!*

She was laughing at him!

John pushed away from the door, his body tight with surprised humiliation. "Mallory, let me in," he said, with all the authority at his command.

"No!"

"Mallory!"

She didn't answer.

In frustrated anger, he threw the wooden bucket at the door. It shattered. "Now, look!" he shouted. "I broke the bucket!"

"Then you'll have to replace it."

Had the woman no sensibility? No soul? John pounded the door with his fist hard enough to make the wood bounce. "Open up this door, Mallory."

"Go sleep in the barn, John. You'll not be sleeping in my bed this night—or any other night."

John took a step back from the door. "Is that a challenge?"

"No, that's not a challenge," she said, and he could tell by the sound of her voice that she was standing directly opposite him. "It's a promise."

"You're my wife—"

"Wife? You didn't want me, remember? You left me. And I waited for you, John. Fool that I was, I waited. Waited for a very long time, but I'm not waiting anymore."

John let her words sink in, hearing the truth of them. He also heard something he didn't think she wanted him to hear. He heard loneliness and pain, the kind of pain that only another person who has been deserted could understand.

A pain he understood all too well because he'd been raised with it. He'd felt that pain almost every day of his childhood, knowing his mother had been sent away because of him. Knowing that no matter how hard he worked to excel, he would always be considered by his tutors and classmates as an impostor, the Barron bastard.

The lust throbbing through his loins died a sudden death, and John knew they couldn't avoid discussing his desertion any longer. "I never meant to hurt you, Mallory. Never."

No answer came from the other side.

John pressed both hands against the door, wishing he could see her face. "Mallory?"

She still didn't answer, but she was there, listening. Every instinct told him so.

He spoke slowly at first, cautiously feeling his way. "I didn't leave to hurt you. I left—" He paused. "I was young . . . confused." That much was very true. "And angry."

John pressed his cheek against the cool, smooth wood of the door. "Yes, I left, but I didn't run away from *you*. I ran away to find myself." He paused, wishing she would say something, anything.

But the woman on the other side of the door was silent.

"Mallory, I admit it was wrong of me not to stop and think about how my departure would hurt you. I thought you'd be taken care of, and that was what you wanted, wasn't it? To be taken care of and to keep your castle? Never, not even in my wildest dreams, did I expect our marriage to come to this pass."

He thought back to their wedding and those fateful moments between them. "Do you remember our wedding night? You were frightened, Mallory, even though you pretended to be bold."

No response.

He straightened, determined to see the air cleared between them. Until he did so, he knew she wouldn't give up this nonsense talk of a divorce.

"I have a confession, Mallory, one I don't think you'll like hearing—but I never felt as if I were married." He paused, frowning. The words didn't sound good when spoken out loud. For a second, he was tempted to confess that he hadn't consummated the marriage so she would understand his feelings, but he quickly erased that idea from his mind. Mallory was angry enough without him giving her more ammunition. Later, perhaps when she trusted him more, he could tell her the full truth. Right now, he had to convince her to open the door.

He thought of Liana and Victor Peterson, of what he'd learned from watching them defy all odds in their marriage. He spoke from his heart. "I believe marriage should mean something more than fulfilling the wishes of parents or adding gold to a family's coffers. Marriage can't be good unless both people are committed, and neither one of us was committed to each other when we married, no matter what vows we took before God. Mallory, we still don't know each other very well, but we're older and wiser now. We can give our marriage a chance. We can make it work—but not if you lock me out."

He pushed away from the door, straightened his shoulders, and faced it. "I'm asking you to forgive me, Mallory. Please."

No words had ever been harder to say.

And no man had ever felt the need for forgiveness more. The irony was, he hadn't realized it until this moment, when he'd found himself standing in the dark outside a cottage door, waiting. . . .

For an absolution that never came.

She wasn't going to forgive him. Minutes passed while he put his astonished thoughts in order.

He'd spoken from his soul, and the woman wasn't going to forgive him! The realization made him irrationally angry.

He stomped away from the door and then charged back to confront her again, only this time his words were far from conciliatory. "I feel like a bloody idiot. You have a heart of stone, Mallory Barron, to listen to me talk on and on and say not one word yourself. I'm a fool! A fool to think you'd ever forgive me, and a fool to want to lie with you. Well, keep the cottage and the bed. I'm a man. I don't need to beg."

No answer.

He doubled his fist and punched the air in anger. "You are an obstinate woman. I'll sleep in the barn, but I wish you no joy in your cold bed."

He waited, willing her to answer, demanding her to answer. Needing her to answer.

John waited until the crickets felt it was safe to begin their chorus and the air was full of their melody. But Mallory remained silent.

Finally, he turned on his heel and walked up the narrow path heading toward the barn.

Inside the cottage, Mallory sat on the floor, her head pressed back against the door, tears streaming down her face.

No, John, she wanted to say, *I'm the fool.*

Out of a misplaced sense of duty, or pride, she'd waited for him, postponing her own dreams and desires. His words brutally confirmed what she'd always known in her heart about her wedding—he hadn't wanted her.

What was worse, over the past twenty-four hours she'd found much to admire in him. John Barron would be a very easy man to love, and the honest truth in his words about marriage, a *real* marriage, had touched her deeply.

She would have to be very careful and guard her heart . . . or she would quickly lose it to John Barron.

* * *

"Wake up, Mr. Man. Wake up," cooed a woman's soft voice. Something brushed against his ear.

Years of military conditioning had honed John's reflexes, even when he was dead asleep. He reached up and grabbed the hand holding a piece of straw over his head.

The woman on the other end of the hand gave a squeal of surprise. John rolled on top of her and pinned her with his body before he'd fully awakened.

He found himself looking into a stranger's face. "Who are you?" he asked gruffly.

The woman in his arms was at least twenty. She had curly red hair and an inviting smile. "Who are you?" she echoed, and then boldly wiggled her body beneath his in a suggestive manner. "And do you always wake up this way?"

John rolled off her immediately, coming to his feet in one easy motion. "Who are you?" he repeated.

"I'm Evie Linton," a soft voice said behind him. "And she's my cousin, Ruth Tarlin."

John whirled to face the new person, another young woman with red hair, only this one was very obviously pregnant. "What are you doing here, Mrs. Linton?" he said formally.

"Oh, isn't he fine, Evie?" Ruth cooed. "Manners and all." She rose to her feet.

Evie ignored her cousin. "We're the dairy maids—and you must be Mr. Dawson, Lord Woodruff's new steward."

"That's right, I am. How did you know?"

Ruth rubbed against his shoulder like a cat.

"Tunleah Mews is a small place. We heard last night, straight from Lucy." She drew a deep breath of appreciation. "For once, Lucy wasn't telling tales when she said you were a fine man, Mr. Dawson. A *fine* man."

John took a step back from the very forward maid and bumped into her cousin. He turned to face Evie, pointedly ignoring Ruth, who practically leered at him.

"You work in the dairy? Isn't that difficult in your, ah, delicate condition?"

Evie rested a hand on the small of her back, her eyes brimming with laughter. "Delicate condition? My ma had nine children, and I've never thought of her as delicate."

Since Liana's death, John hadn't take pregnancy and childbirth for granted. "Working in the dairy is too hard for an expectant woman."

Evie's eyes opened wide with alarm. "You are saying you would cut me off, are you, sir? I need my job. You'll be taking bread from the mouths of my family if you send me home."

John frowned. He didn't like his choices, but all he could hear in his mind were Liana and her cries during labor.

"It's not right, Mr. Dawson," Evie said, her blue eyes brimming with tears. "I have three months until this babe is due. I can work. I've worked through my last two pregnancies."

"You can stay," he finally conceded against his better judgment, "but the moment you start to feel the strain, I want you to tell me. I don't want you to hurt yourself."

Evie heaved a sigh of relief. "I'm having a child,

Mr. Dawson, not dying of the plague. Now come, Ruth, those cows won't milk themselves."

Ruth puffed out her lower lip in a pout. "I'd much rather stay here and help Mr. Dawson."

"Ruth," Evie said in warning, and Ruth moved toward her cousin. The two of them disappeared through a doorway. A second later he heard the clatter of wooden pails.

Now John was glad he'd let Evie stay. He'd never been in charge of women before. He didn't think he could treat them like soldiers, and he'd need Evie to keep Ruth in line.

He reached down for his jacket, picked it up and groaned. The jacket was covered with manure. He'd made a sleeping place for himself out of grain sacks thrown over straw. Now, he realized the straw was foul with clumps of muck, and his boots and leather breeches had patches of crud on them.

He even smelled of manure—which made him question Ruth's intelligence in getting close to him.

Disgusted, John picked up one of the grain bags and had started to clean his boots with it when he glanced up and found a wizened man, some thirty years his senior and as filthy as the barn, staring at him from the stall's entrance. Four dogs in all shapes and sizes sat at his feet, scratching fleas.

"Who are you?" John asked.

"Terrell." The man scratched behind his ear.

"The hired man?"

"Aye." Terrell was missing his two front teeth. He used the hole in his mouth to spit through.

John came out of the stall. "Well, Terrell," he said with good humored authority, "I'm John Dawson, Lord Woodruff's new steward."

"Steward? Lord Woodruff hired a steward? Why'd he do that when he has me?"

John looked down at the straw and muck on his boots and answered dryly, "I have no idea." He threw the grain sack down and hung his jacket over the side of the stall. "But I do know that our first order of the day is for you to muck out every stall in this barn."

Terrell's eyes grew wide with disbelief. "This is a big barn."

"Yes, and a filthy one." John took in the scope and magnitude of the task. The barn was much larger on the inside than it appeared from the outside. The exterior walls were of good, solid English brick with oak pillars spaced evenly to hold up a shingle-and-thatch roof. Stalls lined the wall where John stood, although only three held horses. He walked down and peered in each stall. Lord Woodruff would never garner a reputation for knowing good horseflesh. Two of the animals were swaybacked carriage horses; the third was a mottled gray pony in need of exercise, but with more spirit than the other two combined.

Against a far wall were a farm wagon, a green-and-yellow pony cart, and a black lacquered coach, the one Lord Woodruff obviously took out once a week for church.

A rooster crowed outside. John hadn't been up before dawn since he'd left the army. He frowned, wondering when he'd turned so indolent. Of course, many nights when he'd been out carousing with Prinny, Applegate, and the others he hadn't returned home until after dawn.

"Where are the cows?" John looked around, expecting cows to materialize from someplace.

"The cows are out in the field," Terrell said, the wind whistling through his missing teeth, "where they should be. We milk them out there."

"Of course," John answered, irritated by his show of ignorance. He'd never stopped to think before about where cows were milked or why. He didn't even like milk.

"We've got pigs out there, too," Terrell said helpfully. "Don't like to bring them inside. They dirty up the barn."

"Yes, I can imagine," John answered, trying not to let his lip curl in disgust.

"Keep them penned out there, we do," Terrell said with a nod toward the back of the barn. "Do you want to go out and look at them?"

"I'll wait." John rubbed a hand over his chin. The stubble on his face felt thick. He should have shaved last night. He turned, ready to get started with the day, and then stopped.

Mallory stood in the barn entrance. She appeared clean and fresh in comparison to his grubbiness. Her braid lay over one shoulder. Her brown dress didn't look as if she'd slept in it. In her hands she carried the food hamper.

"Good morning," she said.

He crossed his arms and was surprised by the anger and resentment welling up inside him, while another part of him seemed almost overjoyed to see her. "Good morning," he replied civilly. He wondered if she'd had a good night's sleep.

Had probably slept like a lamb.

She stepped inside the barn. "It's a beautiful morning."

He grunted. He had a different opinion of the day so far.

"This barn is huge," she said, her eyes bright with curiosity.

"Oh, you mean the one at Craige Castle wasn't this large?" He couldn't stop the jibe and immediately regretted it.

A wall seemed to come down between them. Her manner turned cool. "I brought your breakfast," she said, setting the hamper down. "I'll have your dinner for you this evening." She turned to go.

He watched her walk almost out the door before he said, "Wait."

She stopped. "What do you wish?"

I wish we could start over—from the very beginning, he thought. Instead, he grabbed the first excuse that entered his mind. "You haven't met Terrell and the others."

"Terrell?" she repeated blankly. She suddenly seemed to realize they were not alone. "Oh, yes, the hired man." She came back into the barn.

John nodded. "This is Terrell. Terrell, my wife, Mrs. Dawson."

Terrell pulled a forelock and gave Mallory a big grin, showing the gap in his teeth. "Is she the one wot made you sleep in the barn last night?"

"Yes, Terrell, she is," John replied ruthlessly. Terrell cackled at his admission.

John motioned Mallory toward the scullery.

"You didn't have to be so honest," she said, under her breath.

"I'm not going to shirk the truth."

"Well, I guess that will be a first."

"I see you're in good form today," he replied.

"Just on my guard," she answered sweetly, as they walked through a stone archway into a brick room that served as a scullery. It smelled of milk and cheese. Evie and Ruth, empty pails hanging from yokes across their shoulders, were preparing to go out a side door.

"Evie, Ruth, I want you to meet my wife, Mrs. Dawson."

Evie bobbed a respectful curtsey, but Ruth looked Mallory up and down with an interest that bordered on insolence.

Mallory returned her stare with a quelling look of her own. John had enough good sense not to chuckle, but he could imagine Mallory running Craige Castle. She seemed born to the role.

Evie broke the silence. "Ruth, we have to get to the cows. It was good to meet you, Mrs. Dawson."

"And you," Mallory replied pleasantly. "When is your baby due?"

Evie's face immediately lit with pleasure. "Not for another three months. If you'll excuse us?" Ruth boldly gave a little wave and a wink over her shoulder at John. Evie grabbed her cousin's arm and pulled her out the door. As they walked off, they could hear Evie lecturing Ruth on how they needed these jobs and to stop flirting.

Mallory turned to John. "You shouldn't let her get away with being so cheeky."

"I can handle her."

"Yes, well, it seems everytime I come upon you, some woman is flirting with you."

"Now wait, Mallory. You can't blame that forward little dairy maid's behavior on me."

She glared at him, and he saw she certainly could. "Women do not deliberately throw themselves at a man without encouragement," she said, with smug superiority. "We are not like men."

John practically snorted his disagreement. "Is this something carved in the Mallory Barron Book of Stone? You may not believe this, Mallory, but you have a thing or two to learn about life."

"And I wager *you* are just the man to teach me?"

"I could," he countered.

"Teach me what? How to flirt?" She started to walk away when John blocked her path by placing his hand against the brick wall.

"Yes," he said, drawing out the word. "That and a few other things. That is, if you are *woman* enough to be interested."

That barb hit its mark. Her eyes locked with his, and he smiled. She was a challenging adversary. She could draw blood, but then, so could he . . . His triumphant thoughts faded and his elation turned to a slower, more heated excitement as he realized they stood close enough for their toes to touch. In fact, if he leaned toward her, his lips could almost brush the top of her hair. He dropped his gaze to the pattern of freckles across her pert nose. "We need to talk, you know," he said, his voice warm, husky.

"Everyone expects us to behave as man and wife."

She raised her eyes to meet his. She wet her lips, the glimpse of her tongue pulling him closer. Then her nose wrinkled. She sniffed the air and made a face. "John, is that you?

The mood was broken.

He straightened his shoulders. "Yes, I stink," he said, his tone clipped. All the emotion and resentment of the night before returned with a rush. He raised an explanatory hand. "The barn needs mucking out."

"I should say so." She turned her head away from him, her mouth twitching suspiciously, and he realized she was struggling not to laugh at him. Again!

Pressing his lips together, he pushed away from the wall and with a mocking bow stepped out of her way.

She slid him an appraising look from the corner of her eye. "You're upset with me again."

"Upset? Why?" he asked with false sweetness. "Because you barred me from my own cottage—?"

"*Our* cottage."

"Made me sleep in the barn—"

"That had to be uncomfortable for you."

"And now you tell me I stink!"

"Actually, *you* said you stink," she corrected him.

John wanted to roar with outrage. He'd never met such a headstrong, fault-finding, mote-magnifying, hard-to-please—

Mallory came up on her tiptoes and placed a

kiss on the end of his nose. "You're right," she said. "We do need to talk. Come by the cottage this evening when you finish here. I'll have your supper ready."

And then she left.

Stunned, John stared after her. She'd kissed him, mucky smell and all.

He followed her out through the archway, whistling.

Chapter 9

There's carrotty Kit so jolly and fat,
With her girt flippety, floppety hat;
A hole in her stocking as big as a crown,
And the hoops of her skirt hanging down
to the ground.
O Master John, do you beware!
And don't go kissing the girls
at Bridgewater Fair.

"Bridgewater Fair"

Mallory practically danced her way home to the cottage. She'd surprised herself by kissing John on the nose . . . but she was glad she'd done it. He'd looked so completely startled.

Only a few fat clouds marred the dawn sky of what promised to be a bright summer day—a perfect day. She started whistling John's tune.

Last night, she'd tossed and turned, replaying John's confession in her mind. Finally, sometime after midnight, she'd come to terms with what she'd dismissed as her "infatuation" for him.

Granted, she'd had a glimpse of the true man behind the handsome looks and reckless reputation, a man who had regrets, a man who could admit he'd made mistakes, a man who inspired loyalty in his friends—but that didn't mean he was a good husband. Or ever would be.

He'd lost Craige Castle. She'd be a fool, or as silly as that redheaded dairy maid, to allow John's good looks and powers of seduction to cloud her common sense.

Still, she was looking forward to being with John this evening. As she kneaded the bread dough, she wondered what excuses he would use to try and talk his way into her bed this time. She smiled. She rather enjoyed matching wits with him.

Mallory had learned to cook two years ago when finances at Craige Castle had become so tight she'd been forced to make a choice between keeping the cook and buying new seed for the fields. Her mother had been appalled at her daughter's willingness to do menial tasks, but Mallory had always found a certain joy in working. She couldn't sit and do needlework all day, as her mother and her mother's friends did. She was interested in all the details concerning the running of Craige Castle, from the best method for repairing the roof, to harvesting crops, to airing out mattresses.

She divided the dough into loaves, leaving a portion aside to be pounded out and filled for meat pies. She set the dough to rise and turned to her next task—giving the cottage a good scrubbing.

By the middle of the afternoon, the cottage was free of cobwebs. Three baked loaves of bread and five meat pies set on the table, cooling. She was repairing the broken chair with a sturdy branch and some twine when the cramps came. At first, she hoped they were from overexertion. An hour later, she knew they were not. The pain doubled her over.

Why did it have to come now? Every month, a week before her menses, she suffered terrible, horrible cramps that made her feel as if she were being pulled inside out. The tension in her body set off a pounding headache.

There was nothing she could do to stop them. For now, they had control of her life. She stumbled to the bed and lay down on her side. Pulling her knees up to her chest, she tried to lose the pain in a tense sleep.

She wasn't going to cook dinner for John, after all.

"Mallory? Are you all right?" A cool hand rested on her forehead.

John. Through slitted eyes, she looked up at him. He'd bathed. His hair was still wet and slicked back from his face. He'd also shaved. He must have found the razor she'd thought to place in the hamper she'd delivered to him that morning. She closed her eyes tight.

Had she really been looking forward to seeing him earlier that day?

"Go away."

"You don't look well."

No? Really? she thought sarcastically, refusing to

open her eyes. Another spasm of pain struck and she frowned. The cramps always got worse before they got better.

"You're in pain," John said.

She ignored him, silently willing him to leave. This was not how she had planned the evening, and she kept her eyes closed, embarrassed that he should see her this way.

"Tell me where you hurt." His low voice sounded anxious.

"It's nothing," she muttered. "Go away." She pressed her arms against her lower abdomen and wished she could die.

He rose from the bed. She heard his footsteps cross the hard dirt floor. A beat later the door opened and closed.

Good; he was gone. Mallory curled herself up tighter, giving free rein to the pain washing through her, and wished she could fall back to sleep. It would pass, she kept telling herself. It always passed . . .

Several minutes later, the cottage door opened.

Mallory went very still. She opened one eye.

John had returned. He held a smooth, oval rock about twice the size of his hand. Kneeling down by the hearth, he threw another log on top of the burning embers. Sparks shot up the chimney. He placed the rock at the edge of the fire.

"What are you doing?" she asked. It hurt her to lift her head.

Still crouched before the fire, he turned to her. He lifted an eyebrow, as if surprised to learn she was awake. "Helping you."

"I don't need help. I need to be left *alone.*"

He nodded but stayed where he was.

Mallory rolled away from him and closed her eyes. John Barron was the most stubborn man she'd ever met. People usually jumped to do her bidding when she used that tone of voice—but of course, not John.

Her breath caught in her throat as another spasm started to build. Soon. The pain would leave soon. The cramping never lasted more than twenty-four hours.

Sometimes, she didn't like being a woman.

John sat down on the edge of the bed. "Here, try this."

She refused to turn over to see what he was talking about. "Try what?"

"I've heated a rock and wrapped it in a clean rag." He reached over her and pressed it against her abdomen. In seconds, warmth radiated through the flannel. Almost against her will, her arms came down to pull it closer. The heat permeated the layers of her clothes. The tight knot of cramps eased slightly.

"Better?" he asked.

She nodded, still too involved in pain to speak.

He leaned over her. "Mallory, there are some pains that can be very serious if they are not treated by a physician."

She did not want to discuss *this* pain with *him.* She was even too modest to talk about such things with her mother. She maintained her silence.

He waited, and then, to her horror, said, "I'll

fetch a physician." He rose from the bed and was almost to the door before she stopped him.

"The pain isn't serious."

"You look wretched. And the location worries me."

"I know, but . . ." She took a deep breath. "I have it once a month. It's bad, but it goes away."

"Once a month?" he repeated blankly. "And you've never seen a physician for it?"

Mallory wanted to groan in frustration. "I don't need to see a doctor, John. It's not a sick kind of pain."

"Then what kind of pain *is* it?"

"John, please, let's not go into it," she begged. She gave him her back and hugged the rock tighter.

A moment later, John walked to the edge of the bed. "Can I get you something to eat?"

Mallory shook her head.

"No, I guess not," he murmured.

She closed her eyes again, praying she could relax enough to go to sleep. Another tightening cramp erased the idea from her head.

John sat down next to her. Mallory ignored him. This spasm was so strong, tears came to her eyes, a signal that the worst was about to begin.

John stretched out beside her on the bed. He'd removed his boots. She hadn't even heard him do it. He cradled her against his body. Mallory opened her eyes wide. "What are you doing *now?*"

"Lying down with you."

No, she wanted to say, but he was already there, his long body curving around her. He slipped one arm under her head; the other, he put around her waist. Mallory stiffened and started to rise.

"Relax," he said. "I only want to help you through this."

"There *is* no help for it," she shot back, and paused. Actually, that wasn't true. She was starting to feel better. The heat of his body and the warmth from the stone eased the pain. She lay back down, her head resting in the crook of his arm.

"Mallory, I want to send for a doctor."

She wished he weren't so persistent. Drawing in a deep breath, she said, "John," then hesitated. She searched her mind for the right words—words that wouldn't unduly embarrass her. "It's a female problem," she muttered quickly, and buried her head against the pillow.

"A female—?" He stopped, and his understanding came with a simple, "Oh."

"But it is *not* something I want to talk about," Mallory added.

"Then we won't," he assured her. "We'll speak of other things."

"Like what? The weather?" Another cramp started, this one stronger than the one before, and her words ended with a groan.

"Give in to the pain," he said in her ear.

"Oh, what do you know about it?" she managed to gasp out rudely.

"I've fought pain like this," he said simply. "When I was wounded at Salamanca—"

"You were wounded?" she asked, her discomfort momentarily forgotten out of concern for him.

"In the thigh."

Mallory stared at the wall before admitting, "I didn't know."

He shrugged. "It doesn't matter. Not now."

Not now. She heard the loneliness in his words, a loneliness she'd often felt over the years. "Do you have a scar?"

"Of course." His voice held a hint of laughter. "Do you want to see it?"

Another cramp started building inside her. She tensed.

"Take deep, even breaths," he said in a hushed tone. "Don't fight, Mallory. Give in to it."

She didn't want to listen to him. She wanted to fight. But his voice was hypnotic, and she found herself trying to breathe deeply.

He kept her in the comfort of his arms, her head resting against his chest. By the time the next round of cramps started, she was better able to cope with them.

"Are they always this bad?" he asked. The interior of the cottage was dark, only the fire's glow providing light.

Mallory nodded. "I spoke with a physician several years ago. He said it might always be this way for me. For some women, the cramps leave after the birth of their first child."

John's head rested against the top of hers, and she felt his lips curve into a smile.

"What's so funny?" she asked.

"Nothing. Did I laugh?" he answered innocently, and Mallory found enough energy to give him a playful elbow in the side. He snuggled her closer to her. "The mysteries of womanhood," he whispered, with a touch of what sounded like respect.

Mallory discovered that her previous embarrassment had evaporated. Even being in his arms now felt right. He laced the fingers of one hand with hers.

A wave of pain came and went. Mallory followed his calm instructions, the sound of his voice more soothing than any balm. Before she knew it, the worst of the cramps had passed in less time than it normally took—and even then, she didn't want to move. She liked lying beside him like this.

They'd been quiet for some time, both lost in their own thoughts, before Mallory'd gathered her courage and asked, "Why did you leave me, John?"

He went very still.

She touched his hand, tracing his thumb with her finger. "Last night, you said you never felt married. Is that why you left, because you hadn't had time to reconcile yourself to the marriage?"

"Oh, Mallory." He propped himself up on one elbow so he could look down over her shoulder. Mallory stared at his thumbnail, unwilling to face him just yet.

"I was rebelling against my father," John said. "You were just an unfortunate bystander in our battle."

"What battle?"

"He wasn't an easy man to please. He spent most of his life overseas in different diplomatic posts while I lived at various schools. I can't remember him ever once asking me what I thought or what I wanted. But I tried to please him. Especially after I learned that I really wasn't his son."

"So the stories are true."

"Yes, although no one would say it to my face, since my father forced everyone from the king to the admiralty to recognize me as his legitimate heir. Does it bother you?"

Mallory mulled over his question and finally shook her head. "No, I guess it doesn't. Does it bother you?"

"Oh, yes . . . though it bothered me more when I was in school and the other boys taunted me. I was never accepted by their parents as a suitable companion for their noble sons, you know."

"But you are titled now—and accepted."

"In some circles," he said carefully, "but not all. I've never received vouchers for Almack's."

"In spite of being a war hero?"

"And very wealthy."

"Well, I don't think you can anticipate the patronesses letting down their guard any time soon," she said dryly, gesturing around the mean interior of the cottage.

He laughed. "I believe you're right." He laced his fingers with hers again and gave her hand a squeeze. "I have a question. Did you ever think of me while I was away?"

Mallory's mouth went dry. She wasn't about to tell him the truth—that no matter how hard she'd tried over the years, he'd never been far from her thoughts. "I said a prayer for you every Sunday."

"Every Sunday, hmmm? And what of the rest of the week?"

"I thought of you as often as you thought of me."

He laughed. "You have the mind of a barrister, wife."

"I shall take that as a compliment."

"It is," he agreed warmly.

"So," Mallory said, rolling on her back to face him, "why did you leave me?"

John's clear blue eyes met and held hers. "I didn't leave you. I ran away from my father. I was furious with him for ordering me into marriage. Mallory, the first I knew of it was when I arrived at Craige Castle the evening before the ceremony. I'd never even contemplated getting married. I thought he'd invited me to discuss my letter asking his permission to buy my commission."

"I heard you arguing with him in the library."

"Yes, we said bitter words to each other. I said more than he did, and more than I should have. He told me I should be grateful, that he could have turned me out to an orphanage and the workhouse. I shouted back that I wished he had."

"Then you married me because you felt you had no choice?"

"I married you because Father told me you and your mother would lose your home and be left destitute if I didn't. He was the sort of man who would have done it, too, if that's what it took to get his way. But what of you, Mallory? Were your motives to marry me so pure?"

She shifted uncomfortably. "What your father

threatened was true. If we hadn't married, Mother and I would have been sent away from Craige Castle, which has been in my family for centuries, and forced to live with my aunt in Cornwall."

"Not Cornwall!" he said with mock distaste.

"My sentiments exactly," she agreed.

They lay beside each other quietly. Mallory began to feel sleepy.

John spoke. "So there you have it. We're not exactly a love match." He paused a moment before adding soberly, "Although I wasn't happy to discover you had to be drugged for our wedding night. Something inside me snapped when I tasted the wine. It was that moment when I decided to take control of my life. I wanted to be a man, Mallory, not my father's puppet or a bastard coward who couldn't stand up for himself. Nor did I want to be a bridegroom who had to buy his wife."

Mallory felt her cheeks flame with embarrassment. "John, I didn't know about the drugged wine. My mother prepared it without my knowledge. She knew I was nervous and wanted to make matters easier for me . . . but I drank too much."

His hand brushed a tendril of hair from her face, tucking it behind her ear. "And did it make things easier?" he asked quietly.

Mallory looked away, unwilling to admit aloud that she remembered very little of their wedding night and nothing of the consummation.

"Don't frown so," he chided softly. "It's in the past. Remember?"

She nodded before lowering her head and curling up by his side. She felt drained, exhausted. "I would have been a wife to you. I meant my wedding vows." She closed her eyes.

John studied the fire for a moment, his thoughts on the past. Then he said, "You know, we could try to make this marriage work."

He waited for Mallory's response.

Nothing.

Coming up on one elbow, he peered down at her. Even in sleep, she appeared worn out, and he felt a stab of guilt. He brushed her cheek with the back of his hand. It was his fault she was gallivanting around the countryside instead of safe inside her precious castle.

Then, to his surprise, she murmured, "I don't think it will work, John. You aren't good husband material." She snuggled her nose into the pillow.

Stung by her words, he demanded, "Why not? Because I no longer have any money?"

He never received an answer. His wife had fallen fast asleep.

Mallory woke the next morning shortly before dawn to find John sleeping on the floor. He could have slept by her side all night; she wouldn't have known or cared.

But he hadn't.

She wondered why. His actions weren't consistent with his rakish reputation.

She called his name softly and he woke instantly. His gaze met hers, and he gave her a sleepy smile. "Feel better?"

She nodded.

"Good." He stretched and stood up on bare feet. She didn't remember him taking off his socks. He'd removed his shirt, too. Seeing him in hardly anything but the doeskin breeches left little to the imagination—and she had a very active imagination.

She quickly raised her gaze to his face. His hair was sleep tousled, his blue eyes lazy and dark. He helped himself to a glass of cider. "Do you want some?" he offered over his shoulder.

"No, thank you." She got out of bed. Her brown dress was hopelessly wrinkled. Her braid was half undone, hanging in a tangle down her back.

John drained the glass and reached for his shirt. "I want to be at the barn before Terrell and the others arrive. If I don't, he'll try and slide out of the work I've planned for the day." He pulled on the shirt and tucked the hem in his breeches. Already the fine lawn of his dress shirt was showing wear. He sat in a chair and reached for his boots. "Mucking out stalls isn't his favorite activity, and we still have a good portion of the barn to clean out."

"What about the fields? Have you taken a look at the crops?"

John shook his head while stamping his foot into a boot. "Tomorrow. Will you go out with me?"

"Of course."

"And stop by the barn today if you get a chance. I'd like to hear your opinion of what I'm doing. I think the hog pen needs to be cleaned out, but Terrell disagrees. Do you know anything about hogs?"

She smiled. "A little." At one time, Craige Castle had boasted several swine herds.

He returned her smile. "I thought you might." He stopped in front of her, the light in his eyes warm as he said softly, "You're an uncommon woman, Mallory Barron."

Before she knew what he was about, he kissed her forehead, and said with a wink, "We're a fine pair, aren't we?"

Her nose tingled where he'd touched it. She raised her hand to it.

"I'll see you later," he said. He picked up a meat pie off the table, raised the bar, and went outside.

Mallory rushed over to the doorway and watched him as far as she could until he disappeared around a bend in the path. Thoughtfully, she closed the door.

Something had happened between them. Something she hadn't expected.

She and John were starting to become friends.

John had left his jacket hanging on a peg in the wall. Mallory sewed up the sleeves. With Mrs. Watkins's permission, she borrowed Terrell long enough to kill one of the chickens, which she plucked and stewed for their supper.

Later, in the early part of the afternoon, Mrs. Irongate sent Lucy to fetch her. Apparently it was felt that as the steward's wife, Mallory should help with some of the chores around the manor house. Mallory didn't mind. She delivered John's lunch to him, meat pies and a jug of cider, and after taking a moment to offer a few suggestions on his work in the barn, went to help Mrs. Irongate.

The housekeeper wanted the silver polished. The job was easy enough; however, Mallory discovered she would have lots of help while she was at it in the kitchen. Mrs. Irongate and Mrs. Watkins were both widows—Mrs. Watkins three times over—and they were interested in John. He'd made a dashing impression on them the few times he'd been up to the kitchen, and they couldn't help comparing him to other men they had known.

They'd known a good number of men.

As mistress of Craige Castle, Mallory had been friendly but had never fraternized with the servants on such a personal level. She found Mrs. Irongate and Mrs. Watkins and their earthy conversation disconcerting. She answered their questions awkwardly, wishing John would arrive and rescue her with his charm and easy lies.

"Why haven't you and the mister had children?" Mrs. Irongate asked baldly.

Before Mallory could frame an answer, Mrs. Watkins leaned against the kitchen table, a flour-covered hand on her hip, and said, "Don't tell us he has a problem with Dickie Diddle. He's such a handsome figure of a man, it will break my heart if he does."

Mallory frowned. She wasn't certain what Mrs. Watkins meant. "I don't believe John knows Dickie Diddle," she answered seriously.

The two women howled with laughter. Mrs. Irongate almost fell off the high kitchen stool, she was laughing so hard. Even Lucy giggled.

And then Mallory understood what they meant. She blushed so furiously that the tips of her ears burned hot.

She lifted her chin. "This conversation is inappropriate."

"Inappropriate?" Mrs. Irongate repeated, dabbing the tears of laughter from her eyes with her apron. "We're not the ones who said her husband doesn't know Dick!"

Her words sent everyone back into screams of laughter. Mrs. Watkins even pounded the table with her fist in her merriment.

Mallory threw down the polishing cloth. "Stop it! Stop laughing at me! That's not what I meant."

Mrs. Watkins moved to place her hand on Mallory's shoulder. "Ah, now, we're just having a little jest."

Mallory pulled away, brushing the flour print of Mrs. Watkins's fingers off her brown dress. "I don't think it's funny." Her tone could have frozen water.

For a long second, silence reigned in the kitchen.

"Well," Mrs. Irongate said. "I guess you've told us, haven't you, *Mrs.* Dawson."

Mallory realized they had considered her their peer, and now she had spoiled any bonds of friendship she might have formed with these women. Picking up the polishing cloth, Mallory reminded herself that she wasn't hired help, not really. She was Lady Craige. It shouldn't matter what a cook and a housekeeper thought of her.

But it did.

They spoke among themselves now, pointedly ignoring her. Mallory felt awkward. The worst part was that she had no idea how to make amends. Not only was she naturally reserved, but she'd never had any really close female friends. Her whole life had been spent at Craige Castle surrounded by people who treated her deferentially.

The revelation that she might have been self-absorbed while growing up shocked Mallory. She stared at her reflection in the silver serving tray. She'd always thought herself very equal minded where servants were concerned—and polite. She was unfailingly polite. But she'd never thought of them as her peers.

Nor did she have any idea how to smooth over her unintentional rudeness with Mrs. Irongate and Mrs. Watkins.

Mrs. Irongate came over to her. "I know you didn't mean to come across so high and mighty," she said in a low voice.

Thankful for the opening, Mallory murmured, "In East Anglia, people don't talk as openly about personal matters as they do here."

Mrs. Irongate shot a look over her shoulder at Mrs. Watkins before answering, "Well, Emma and I enjoy a good joke, and we like our men, too. If we offended you, then we're sorry for it."

"I'm not," Mrs. Watkins said. "I don't like stiff-necked people."

"Oh, Emma," Mrs. Irongate started, but a bell tinkling over the kitchen door interrupted her. The housekeeper gave a start. "That's the master. Ready for his tea, he is."

"Lucy," Mrs. Watkins called. "Do you have the tray ready?"

"Right away," the kitchen maid said.

While Mrs. Watkins and Lucy worked on the tray, Mallory asked Mrs. Irongate if she'd ever seen the book Lord Woodruff was writing.

"Heavens, no! And I don't want to see it, either."

"Has he been working on it long?"

"Years!" Mrs. Irongate set a vase with a single rose on the tray. "About five years ago, a man came from London to talk to Lord Woodruff about his book, and since then he's been scribbling away frantically. I left him after lunch, drawing lines through everything he'd written this morning and muttering, 'It's not right. It's not right.'" She wiggled her head back and forth while she mimicked Lord Woodruff's frenetic talk. Everyone in the kitchen laughed. "Makes a person wonder why anyone would subject himself to that type of nonsense," she added, picking up the tray and bustling from the kitchen.

Mrs. Watkins and Lucy gave Mallory their backs once Mrs. Irongate had left. Mallory finished the silver quickly. She was about to return to the cottage when Mrs. Irongate returned carrying a heavy leatherbound ledger.

"I'm glad you haven't left yet, Mrs. Dawson," Mrs. Irongate said. "Lord Woodruff wants you to give this to your husband."

Mallory took the book. "What is it?"

"It's the rent record. Lord Woodruff wants his new steward to collect the rents, and good luck to him, I say. No one has succeeded yet in getting what is owed from the tenants. Stubborn lot they all are, and sly to boot."

Mrs. Watkins spoke for the first time to Mallory. "An unpleasant job if ever there was one. Here, take this round of cheese and a jug of ale for *Mr.* Dawson's supper. He's been working hard and deserves a good woman's care."

Mallory ignored the slight. Instead, she turned to Mrs. Irongate. "I noticed that cabinet over there in the corner." She nodded to a small cupboard about waist high. "I noticed it was empty, and if you don't need it, I could use it in the cottage."

Mrs. Watkins scowled and started to say no, just as Mrs. Irongate answered, "Of course, dear, and Lucy will help you carry it home."

Lucy pulled a face to let Mallory know she didn't want to help her, but Mallory didn't care. She appreciated Mrs. Irongate's generosity. Picking up the cheese and ale, Mallory would have started out the door, but Mrs. Watkins's voice called her back.

"Wait a minute. Why should Lucy be carrying the cupboard while you take the lighter load?"

Mallory felt the heat of a blush rise to her cheeks. She hadn't stopped to think how her actions would be interpreted. She'd just naturally assumed the kitchen maid would be on a lower pecking order than the steward's wife. Apparently, Mrs. Watkins disagreed.

Her back straight with pride, Mallory handed

the cheese and jug to Lucy. She picked up the heavy little cupboard. "Thank you for the cupboard," she said to Mrs. Irongate. Deliberately, she turned to Mrs. Watkins. "I thank you for the cheese and the ale. My husband will enjoy them this evening." And Mallory would make a point of not letting a single bite or sip pass her lips! She and Lucy left.

They had taken two steps down the path for home when Mrs. Watkins's carrying voice announced to Mrs. Irongate, "I don't like her. She acts like the lady of the manor."

"She's shy," Mrs. Irongate replied.

Mrs. Watkins snorted. "She's thinks she's better than us."

Mallory noticed Lucy staring at her. Embarrassed to be caught eavesdropping, she headed for the path.

The cupboard wasn't easy to carry. Once they reached the barnyard, Mallory set it down to catch her breath. A fat black-and-white barn cat came up and rubbed her leg. She bent down and gave it a pet.

Her attention was claimed by the sound of John's voice calling her name. He waved to her from a high window in the barn. "What are you doing?" she called back.

"Mucking out the loft," he shouted.

She laughed. "Lofts don't need mucking."

"This one does. I'll see you later." He shot her a crooked grin and pulled his head back inside.

For a second, Mallory stared after him, her mind on her marriage. She'd felt as shy and inexperienced as a young girl—but she wasn't young any longer . . . and she was no longer a girl. For the first time since waking up seven years ago and realizing John had deserted her, Mallory tried to remember her wedding night. What had happened between them?

She recalled little of the events after John had entered the room.

Lucy cleared her throat, bringing Mallory back to the present. Suddenly eager to see John this evening, Mallory hurried down the path.

At the cottage, she thanked Lucy and sent the girl on her way. The chicken was done. She fluttered around, straightening a few things and setting the cupboard by the hearth, then took a few moments to brush out her hair. Wanting to do something different than braid it but lacking pins, Mallory decided to leave it down around her shoulders. She hadn't worn it in this style since before she'd married, and it made her feel almost girlish and carefree.

She looked around the cottage. It needed something special. Flowers. She picked up a knife and headed out the door.

The best wildflowers were close to the pond a short distance from the cottage. She stepped off the path and headed for an area sheltered by an overgrowth of hedges and small trees.

As Mallory approached, she saw Ruth crouched behind some bushes, watching something happening on the other side. She didn't even hear Mallory's footsteps. And then Ruth did something altogether strange. She started taking off her clothes.

Mallory dropped her mouth wide open in

shock. It was daylight! Didn't the woman have any modesty at all?

Ruth was naked in a flash and moving through the bushes toward the pond.

And then Mallory heard a familiar whistling . . . and knew who Ruth had been spying on.

Chapter 10

As they were riding on alone,
They saw some pooks of hay.
O is not this a very pretty place
For boys and girls to play?

"Blow Away the Morning Dew"

Whistling, John lathered up with Mrs. Irongate's homemade soap. The coarse bar didn't smell of spice, but it overcame the odors of manure, sweat, and animals. He'd already washed his shirt, which lay on a bush, drying in the sun.

He was in a great mood. He'd cleaned the barn. The whole barn. He couldn't remember when he'd experienced such a sense of accomplishment. Since the day he'd stepped off the military frigate, he hadn't finished one bloody thing . . . but today he'd mucked out a barn.

Furthermore, matters were progressing satisfactorily with Mallory. Last night for the first time he'd lain beside a woman and just held her. The fact that she'd found comfort in his arms made him feel almost heroic. He couldn't wait to see her this evening to offer a different sort of comfort, and the anticipation made him scrub his hair faster.

In his haste he sent soapsuds into his eyes, the lye stinging painfully. He drew a deep breath and ducked under water.

A splash sounded from the far side of the pond. Surprised, John put his feet on the muddy bottom and came up for air just as a pair of hands ran up his legs.

He shook the water from his eyes, reached down, and pulled up a wet and naked Ruth by one arm, catching her hands as she reached for his more intimate parts.

He frowned down at her.

She smiled up at him, her full, bare breasts bobbing like corks below the water's murky surface. "Would you like me to wash your back?" Reaching out with one finger, she drew a heart in his wet chest hairs.

John pushed her away as if he were scalded. "Are you daft? Get out of here!"

"I can't," she answered with a pout. "I don't have any clothes on." She reached for him underwater. "Do you?"

John jumped back. Her groping hands just missed him. With a low, angry growl, he turned and would have stomped out of the pond—except that Mallory stood there at the edge, glaring.

"Are you having problems, John?" she asked.

He was stunned speechless. Mallory was wearing her hair down. The only other time he'd seen it down was during their escape from London, when it had been windblown and tangled. Now, it hung in loose waves almost to her waist. He'd always admired the color, but he hadn't realized how long or thick it was. He ached to touch it, to wrap it around his hand and wind it round and round, pulling her closer. And the first thing he would do when he got Mallory close enough would be remove that dowdy brown dress.

Immediately, his mind's eye conjured Mallory covered by nothing but her beautiful hair, and his body's reaction, even in the cool pond water, was stiff and strong.

He'd all but forgotten Ruth, who chose that moment to plaster herself against his back. Her legs came around his waist, brushing against his erection. She drew in a deep gasp of appreciation and laughed. "Oh yes! You're a randy one, aren't you, John?"

Her boldness embarrassed him, and for one of the few times in his life, he felt the heat of a blush. But before he could say anything, Mallory looked him directly in the eye and repeated, "John? She calls you John?"

"I didn't give her permission, Mallory!" He shrugged Ruth off his back. She fell back into the water with a small splash. "Mallory, please, this isn't what you think."

Ruth surfaced and blew a stream of water out of her mouth at him before mimicking, "Mallory, this isn't what you think." Giggling, she turned to his wife. "I'm sorry, Mrs. Dawson, but your husband can't come out right now. He's a bit too excited to expose himself. Perhaps you can join us? That is, if'n you don't believe you are too la-di-da for us."

John couldn't believe the maid's impertinence. Mallory's body tensed at Ruth's taunt, and two spots of angry color appeared on her cheeks. Ruth laughed. Then, to his surprise, Mallory turned on one foot and charged back the way she'd come.

John swore volubly. "You'll have me sleeping out in the barn again!"

"Do you need company?" Ruth asked, puckering up her lips and offering herself to him.

Furious, John reached out to throttle the woman, then realized there was no safe place for him to put his hands on her without making the situation worse.

He stomped out of the pond.

Ruth playfully slapped the water. "You have a firm fanny, Johnny."

He didn't answer. He'd deal with her later.

He'd just reached for his breeches when there was a rustling behind him. He looked up and found himself staring at Mallory. She'd come back, her arms full of what appeared to be the wash. He froze, all too aware of his nakedness and the capricious male member that was again rising to the occasion. He covered himself with his pants. "You're back," he said inanely.

Mallory's mouth had dropped open at the sight of him. She closed it with a snap, her face blazing.

"What are you doing with my clothes?" Ruth

asked. She started to walk out of the pond, water sluicing off her bouncing bosom.

"I thought you might be needing them," Mallory said tightly. She dropped the pile of clothing to the ground and then began throwing it piece by piece into the pond.

"What are you doing?" Ruth screamed, scrambling to save what she could from getting wet.

"I'm giving you back your clothes," Mallory replied reasonably. She turned to John. "I can't believe you prefer her!"

"Mallory, you're jumping to the wrong conclusion—" His words were cut off when Mallory threw the last article of clothing, Ruth's wool skirt, at him. Temporarily blinded, John wasn't prepared for the shove that sent him back into the pond. He fell against Ruth, taking her with him.

Ruth came up spitting mad. The skirt floated away. John saw that Mallory was gone.

"Damn."

"I'll say damn!" Ruth exclaimed. "She's ruined the only thing I have to wear, and all because you and I were having a little fun—"

John dunked her under the water, then strode from the pond, his wet breeches in one hand. If Mallory thought she'd seen the last of him this evening she was wrong.

Mallory didn't stop to think until she'd safely reached the cottage, shut the door, thrown the bar, and sat down in the mended chair now placed beside the table.

Her face felt hot and flushed. Her pulse raced madly—and not from running.

Dear Lord! Who would have thought that a naked man could appear so masculine, so powerful, so . . . virile.

It wasn't just his handsome face. Every inch of him—and bless her soul, she'd seen it all, including the scar on the inside of his right thigh—appeared to have been molded by the hand of God.

Seeing John naked had appealed to something very deep and needy inside Mallory. Something she hadn't realized existed until today. For the first time, she considered herself more akin to the lusty Mrs. Irongate and Mrs. Watkins than to her aristocratic mother.

And the stab of jealousy she'd felt at his obvious attraction to Ruth had sent her world spinning like a top. She hadn't known she was capable of such a strong emotion—or such outrageous behavior.

She came to her feet and paced slowly around the room, trying to put her jumbled thoughts in order. She'd left Hal's house for London confident that she could deal with her husband alone, that she had absolutely no feeling for him. Instead, to her shock, the opposite appeared to be true. She'd never felt this heady rush of desire for Hal. Or such insane jealousy . . .

She sat back down in the chair. She had to think, to decide what to do next.

A knock sounded at the door.

Mallory jumped to her feet, one hand over her heart, the other on the back of the chair. She stared at the door.

"Mallory?" John's raspy, deep voice called from the other side.

Wiping her palms against her dress, she approached the door but stopped without reaching for the handle. She had to erase from her mind how he'd been last night: caring and considerate. Instead, she struggled to remember her opinion of him before she'd left for London: uncaring, irresponsible, philandering—now, *there* was an image she could grasp!

But amazingly, the old hurts didn't seem as sharp as before. Furthermore, she knew Ruth had attempted to seduce him. She'd listened to him tell her to go away.

She heard his booted steps move over to the half-shuttered window and she pulled back even though she doubted he could see her from there. "I didn't invite Ruth to join me in the pond, Mallory. She took it on herself." He waited for an answer.

She had to let him in.

He walked back to the door and knocked again. "Mallory, please let me in. Let's talk about it."

She stood paralyzed, too unsure of herself to take action.

He muttered something under his breath, his words too indistinct for her to understand.

Are you going to let him walk away?

The question motivated her to action. She pinched color into her cheeks, threw back the bar, and opened the door.

John had started to walk up the path, but turned at the sound of the opening door. For the space of several heartbeats, the two of them stood stock still.

He'd brushed his hair straight back, the style emphasizing the masculine hardness of his features. His damp shirt molded to his shoulders. And in his hand, he held a bunch of wilting flowers.

Mallory said the first words that popped into her mind, "Did you get your pants dry?" Immediately, she wanted to call the words back. What an inane thing to say!

John shifted uncomfortably. "No, I put them on damp. Otherwise, I was afraid they'd shrink."

Mallory dropped her gaze. His breeches appeared indecently tight. She averted her eyes quickly.

"They'll stretch," he assured her.

She felt the heat of a blush. At the same time, she had to smile.

He smiled back at her. "May I come in?"

Not trusting herself to speak, she opened the door wider, silently inviting him in.

John ducked his head under the low doorway. Mallory stepped back. His presence seemed to fill the small room . . . and immediately her mind conjured the image of him naked, an image she ruthlessly squashed.

There was an uneasy pause.

"You did more work around the cottage," he said. "That cabinet by the hearth is new, isn't it?"

She was surprised he'd noticed. "Yes—well, actually, all I really did was dust out the cobwebs."

"It looks nice."

Another lull in the conversation. "Thank you," she said to fill it.

He pushed the bouquet toward her. "I brought these for you."

She took the wildflowers—Queen Anne's lace, black-eyed Susans, daisies, with grapevines for greenery. Several of the stems appeared mashed, as if he'd had trouble separating them from the plants.

She'd never received flowers before. To her surprise, hot tears welled in her eyes. She fought them back. "They're lovely." She looked up at him. "Thank you."

He seemed to relax slightly. "I wasn't certain of my reception."

"Is that why you brought flowers?"

"My mother always liked flowers."

"Your mother? I didn't think you . . ." Her voice trailed off, and she could have cut out her tongue for her blundering words.

John finished her sentence. "You've heard that my parents had nothing to do with each other."

"I should put these flowers in water." She didn't want to discuss anything so fraught with emotion. Not now, when her own emotions were so confused. She would have brushed past him, but John held up his hand to stop her.

"Mallory, please, as my wife you have the right to ask me any question you wish."

As my wife. A dizzy humming seemed to start inside her at his words. This was *exactly* the sort of issue she wanted to avoid. "I shouldn't have broached the subject," she said stiffly.

The lines of his mouth flattened. "We aren't in

some London drawing room where we must follow a list of unwritten rules, Mallory."

She didn't answer him, almost wanting that list of rules to help keep a distance between them.

He reached out with one long finger and lightly touched a black-eyed Susan. "At least once a year, my father sent me to visit Mother. He always gave me a bouquet of flowers to take to her." His gaze met hers. "She'd cry when I gave it to her because she knew they weren't really from me, but from him."

"Did they never see each other?"

"No, not after he sent her away. The year before she died—I must have been twelve—I asked her why he could accept me and reject her. She told me it was because he had rules that he lived by. Rejecting her was one of the rules he believed he had to follow. But when she died, he mourned deeply."

Mallory looked down at the flowers in her hands. "It's a sad story. He never remarried, did he?"

John shook his head. "My father was a difficult man to understand. I don't think I started to see him fully as another human being until I'd been in the army for several years. He set very high standards—for himself and for me. Of course, now I understand why my parents never talked. This type of conversation isn't easy, is it?"

Suddenly feeling on dangerous ground, especially with him standing so close, Mallory backed away. "I should put these in water," she said again, and withdrew to find a container. She took her time arranging the flowers in a pottery pitcher.

John stood waiting.

Her hands shook as she set the pitcher in the center of the table. Did he notice?

"We need to talk, Mallory."

Oh no, we don't. Not if he's going to slip past my defenses so easily.

She kept her face deliberately blank. "About what?" Desperate to be busy, she tied an apron around her waist, preparing to serve the evening meal.

John sat at the table in the rickety chair she'd mended. A lock of his heavy hair fell over one eye, and he pushed it back before saying, "We need to talk about us."

She transferred the stewed chicken from the pot to a round platter and set it on the table. "I'm not certain I want to talk right now."

His hand came out and captured her wrist. He held her in place with a direct, unwavering gaze. "We must talk. I've made enough mistakes with you without making the same one my father did. We must clear the air."

Mallory slowly sat down across from him, knowing she could not avoid this confrontation.

He released her hand. She folded her arms protectively across her chest.

"Mallory, I didn't have an assignation with Ruth at the pond. She completely surprised me."

Mallory almost breathed a sigh of relief. They were only going to talk about Ruth. "I know that, John."

He raised his eyebrows. "You do?"

"Yes." She smiled, pleased they weren't going to have a deeper conversation. She would have gotten up and gone to the hearth, but John reached across the table and held her in place.

"There have been other women, but no one serious."

Even though she knew such a reaction was silly, the pain of his admission staggered her. She'd always known there were other women. She'd met Lady Ramsgate. There had to have been more besides her. "What is *serious,* John? What does the word mean to you?"

He sat back in the chair, his hand still on the table, but no longer touching her. He thought for a moment before saying, "It means my affections were not attached."

"Affections?" She heard the chill in her voice but couldn't help it.

He looked resentful. "You aren't going to make this easy, are you?"

"Should I?"

He drummed his fingers on the table, the sound loud in the silence. "I've never given my heart to a woman."

Mallory lowered her head and stared at her hands. Why did she feel disappointed? What had she expected him to say? That he'd fallen in love with her? "What a ridiculous notion."

She hadn't realized she'd spoken aloud until John said, "I beg your pardon?"

Mallory felt like a fool. She also feared she was going to cry. She never cried. Leastwise, not for John. . . .

She rose from the table, wiping her hands on the apron around her waist, and would have returned to the hearth except that John again captured her hand.

He stood. She stared at their joined hands. He had what her father would have described as a swordsman's hand, his fingers callused by a hard day's work.

She looked up to find him studying her, the intensity in his bright, blue eyes disconcerting. If she wasn't careful, they would see too much . . . emotions too new and awkward for her to understand herself.

And then John slipped beneath her guard by saying, "I'd like us to have a real marriage."

For one wild, heady moment, Mallory's heart stopped.

"You can't mean that," she whispered.

"Yes, I do." He rubbed his thumb, the one with the small scar on it, over the wedding ring on her finger. "I was thinking about us today while I was working, and I believe it would be reasonable of us to honor our union."

"Reasonable?"

"Desirable, even."

"Desirable in what way, John?" she asked carefully.

He inched closer. "I feel a certain attraction for you." His hand slipped around her waist.

Mallory heard the pounding of her heart in her ears. She raised her eyes and found him so close she could see the shadow of his whiskers along his lean jaw and her image reflected in his eyes. Their lips were only inches apart.

Her common sense warred with her fantasies. Common sense won. "Are you attempting to seduce me?" she asked bluntly.

He blinked as if her words had caught him off guard, then smiled. "Yes."

Mallory pushed away from him. "Of all the cheap, underhanded things for a man to do—"

"Mallory, you're my wife. I'm *supposed* to seduce you."

She pointed a righteous finger in his direction, warning him back. "We had an agreement! I help you; I get a divorce."

John shrugged. "Agreements can be changed."

Mallory wanted to scream with vexation. She paced the length of the cottage before facing him. "I am going to marry Hal Thomas—"

"Oh, yes, your potbellied, balding little squire." John sat down and crossed his legs, his expression disgruntled.

Mallory was momentarily diverted. "What makes you say he's potbellied?"

"Because all squires are," John said reasonably. He pulled a piece off the chicken and popped it in his mouth. "He'll probably suffer gout, too, when he's older—if he doesn't already."

There was truth in his words. Hal did complain of various ailments—but she wasn't going to admit that to John! She raised her chin proudly. "Hal Thomas is a good man."

"Good men are bores."

"Good men honor their wedding vows."

John stood, brushing off his hands. "I'm willing to honor mine." He bowed.

Mallory raised a hand to her forehead. "Something is not quite right here. I seem to recall that you've had seven years to honor your vows, *which you haven't.* Is that not correct?"

"But I'm ready now."

She rolled her eyes heavenward and would have turned away, but John stepped in her path. "Mallory, haven't you heard that rakes make the best husbands?"

"I never believed it," she snapped. She walked to the hearth. John followed.

"Give me a chance. That's all I'm asking. Let me into your life—"

"And my bed?" she added sarcastically.

"Well, if you insist," he said, and gave her a smile so charming it made her feel light-headed. As if sensing her vulnerability, John pressed on. "Mallory, I need you in my life. I know my past behavior was thoughtless—"

"Thoughtless!" The word burst out of her.

"Unforgivable," he corrected. "But I'm asking for your forgiveness."

He sounded so sincere, every alarm inside Mallory cried out a warning. She crossed to the other side of the cottage, away from him. "Hal is solid and dependable," she said, more to remind herself than to answer John. "I've known him all my life. It will not be difficult to be his wife." The back of her legs bumped the bed. She jumped forward in surprise. John smiled—even as she quickly moved away.

"Mallory, it won't be difficult to be my wife, either. I hope that in the last two days you've discovered I'm not an ogre. I'm a man, a man who makes mistakes. I know I can be a better man if I have a wife. But not just any wife. I need one who can set me to rights, keep me in line—"

"Are you looking for a wife or a conscience?"

"A wife," he said firmly without missing a beat. "Besides, solid and dependable can be boring."

"How would you know? You've never understood the meaning of the words. You're like the sun, John, a blazing star too bright for my predictable little corner of the world. You know Wellington. You've dined with the Prince Regent. You've traveled the world." She waved her hand at the stewed chicken. "More nights than naught, that is what Mother and I ate, and afterward we went to bed. *I'm* dependable and boring."

"Then you need me!"

Mallory stared at him, dumbfounded he'd taken her words that way. "John, that's not what I meant."

"It's what you said." He placed his hands on his hips, challenging her.

She groaned her frustration aloud. "Yes, but it wasn't the point I was trying to make. Please stop putting words in my mouth."

A spark of temper flared in his eye. "I'm not putting words in your mouth. You said I was like the sun."

"I didn't mean it as a compliment. I was pointing out how different we are."

"Well, you compared me to something powerful and inspiring. I'm flattered."

"You wouldn't be flattered if you were listening to me," she said through clenched teeth.

"Mallory, I've been hanging on your every word since I walked in the door."

"But you don't understand what I've been trying to say. And that is the problem between us." Mallory took a step away from him. "John, I'm not beautiful enough or confident enough or clever enough to be the wife of a man such as yourself."

He snorted. "That's nonsense! You're a very handsome woman—"

"John, please! You heard Lady Ramsgate and the others laugh at me. I'm a country woman raised in a crumbling castle on the East Anglia coast. In the few days we've been together, every time I turn around, one woman after another is flirting with you or tearing her clothes off."

His lips formed a grim line. "That won't happen again—"

"It's more than just the women. Marriage should *mean* something. It should mean companionship—"

"I'm trying to be a good companion—"

"—Commitment, understanding, *children,*" Mallory continued, as if he hadn't spoken.

"If it's children you want, Mallory, I can give you children."

Mallory stopped, struck by a new thought. "You don't already have children, do you, John?"

"Absolutely none," he said, "and I'm certain of that. I'd never condemn another child to the stigma I've had to deal with most of my life. What I was suggesting is that we could, ah . . . create our own children." He gave her a positively wicked grin and nodded hopefully to the bed. "We could start tonight."

His suggestion startled Mallory and turned her

insides to softened taffy. Almost of their own volition, her feet took a step toward the bed—until her good sense and reason prevailed.

"That's all you think about, isn't it?"

John shook his head. "Is *what* all I think about?"

She couldn't put a word to it. She didn't know any! So she waved her hands toward the bed.

"Making love?" he suggested helpfully, his tongue lingering over the words. He began walking toward her, his steps slow and deliberate. To save her soul, Mallory couldn't move. He stopped in front of her. His teeth flashed white in his smile. "You, Mallory," he said softly, "you're the one who keeps talking about having children. I'm just trying to be accommodating."

He leaned down, lowering his lips to hers. Fascinated, Mallory watched him come closer, her heart pounding. She wanted him to kiss her with all the force of her being. But then, at the last moment . . . she ducked.

His lips grazed the top of her head. Mallory kept moving. She marched over to the door. Her fingers closed over the latch as if grasping a lifeline. She pulled the door open. "I think it would be best if you left now, John."

She didn't look at him. She couldn't. If she did, he might soften her resolve, and she couldn't let him do that. Instead, she kept her focus inward, reminding herself of Lady Ramsgate, Ruth, and the others.

"Mallory, I didn't mean to offend," he said tensely.

"You didn't," she replied. Her voice shook

slightly. "It's just that I think it would be best if we didn't spend the night under the same roof."

"You want me to sleep in the barn again?" he asked incredulously.

"I think it best."

"I won't go."

Mallory drew a deep breath and came to a decision. She lifted her gaze to meet his. "All right, I will."

John's eyes narrowed in fury. "This is ridiculous!"

"Not to me." No, to her it was self-defense. She was protecting herself, protecting her heart. She had to keep a safe distance from him. She turned to walk out the door.

"No, wait," he said. "I'll go."

Mallory felt no surge of triumph. If anything, she felt a small frisson of disappointment that he was willing to leave so easily. What was the matter with her? She usually knew her own mind . . .

She stepped back from the door.

John started out, but stopped in front of her. Unable to meet his gaze, Mallory gazed at the scuffed toe of his boot. "You promised me supper," he said. "We're civilized. We should be able to sit down and share a meal together."

She went to the table, picked up the platter of chicken, and placed it in his hands. "Here, take this with you."

Then, as an afterthought, she lifted the ledger off the table and shoved it into his hands under the platter.

"What's that?" he asked.

"The rent ledger. Lord Woodruff wants you to collect back rents tomorrow."

"I have to be a rent collector?" John said in angry disbelief.

She nodded.

John muttered, "Good night," the words sounding constricted in his throat. He didn't move, apparently waiting for her to respond.

Mallory didn't say a word. She didn't trust herself to speak.

At last John charged out the door and into the night. As he climbed the path up to the barn, she heard him shout, "Louis! Wherever you are, you are damned well going to pay for this!"

Mallory closed the door behind him and put down the bar. She leaned her head against the door.

Her gaze rested on the pitcher of wildflowers. Instead of peaceful, the cottage seemed lonelier than ever.

She went to bed.

John stayed up late. He and several of the hounds that hung around the barn made quick work of the chicken. Of course, he had a bit of trouble getting rid of his newfound flea-ridden friends after such a delicious meal, but he managed.

He stretched out on a bed of new hay and stared up at the rafters, his thoughts on Mallory.

She wanted him. He knew the signs of desire, and his little wife showed every one of them, no matter what she said. The tension in her this evening had been incredible. Every time he'd come near her, she'd practically quivered.

Lord! There had been fire in her eyes when she'd dumped the dairy maid's clothes in the pond.

What would she have done if he'd marched into the cottage, swept her up, carried her to the bed, and kissed her into submission?

The image his thoughts envisioned made him restless and aroused.

Mallory was like no other woman he'd known—a combination of aching vulnerability, pride, intelligence, and stubbornness.

It was as if she wanted more than the money in a man's pockets or the grandeur of his title. She wanted companionship, children . . . someone to share her life.

Her balding little squire didn't deserve her. She was a woman with the strength of character to challenge a man, to hold his interest, and to love him with equal passion.

John wanted to be that man.

Chapter 11

Then she became a duck,
A duck all on the stream;
And he became a waterdog
And fetch'd her back again.
Then she became a hare,
A hare upon the plain;
And he became a greyhound dog
And fetch'd her back again;
Then she became a fly,
A fly all in the air;
And he became a spider
And fetch'd her to his lair.

"The Two Magicians"

Mallory didn't learn that John had dismissed Ruth until early the next morning, when she was confronted by Mrs. Irongate and Mrs. Watkins, who paid her an angry call at the cottage.

"We all know Ruthie is a forward puss," Mrs. Irongate said, "but she needs her job."

"Her job? Isn't she still working in the dairy?" Mallory asked, still groggy after having spent another restless night with little sleep. For the first time in her life, she'd dreamed of kissing and touching. She refused to believe her dream lover had been John.

"No!" Mrs. Watkins said, waving a wooden spoon in Mallory's face. "Your husband turned her out. Now, not only does Evie have to work twice as hard, but Ruth is living with her!"

"Why does she have to live with Evie?" Mallory asked, confused.

"Why, *everyone* knows what happened at the pond yesterday afternoon," Mrs. Irongate said. "How else could Ruth explain her wet clothes. She has nothing else to wear, poor thing."

"And once her husband found out she lost her job," Mrs. Watkins put in, "he beat her soundly and sent her to live with Evie. All because she was caught doing a bit of flirting."

Mrs. Irongate placed a hand on the cook's shoulder. "Mrs. Dawson, we all know what Ruth is like, but we take her in stride. You ruined her only set of clothes. That was lesson enough to warn her from your husband. You didn't need to take the food from her mouth and the roof over her head, too."

"I'm not the one who dismissed her," Mallory said.

Mrs. Watkins harrumped, while Mrs. Irongate pressed her lips together in disbelieving silence.

"All right," Mallory said at last, well aware that no matter what she said, she'd be held responsible. "I'll talk to Mr. Dawson."

"Thank you," Mrs. Irongate said civilly. Mrs. Watkins just continued to glare.

Mrs. Irongate pulled on her friend's arm. "Come, Emma, we must get back up to the house." The two women left, but as they were walking to the path, Mallory overheard the cook say, "So cool and hoity-toity she is. Makes her husband sleep in the barn and then begrudges another woman for treating a man the way he should be treated."

Mallory didn't waste any time searching out John. She found him in the barnyard, dealing with a well-muscled man wearing sooty clothes.

John greeted her with a huge smile. If he'd been angry with her last night, it didn't show this morning. "Mallory, come here and meet Mr. Nichols, the blacksmith."

Mallory nodded to the man, who rudely gave her a cold eye. No doubt he lived in Tunleah Mews and had heard Ruth's story. It was interesting that no one seemed to hold Ruth's dismissal against John . . . but then, that was the way of small communities.

Mallory pulled on the sleeve of John's shirt. "I need to talk to you, privately."

"Of course," he said. "You'll excuse us, Mr. Nichols?" He didn't wait for an answer but led her over to the shade of a big oak tree.

Mallory came right to the point. "You must give Ruth back her job."

His smile faded. "I won't do that. She deserved to be booted."

"The people here don't see it that way."

"The people here?"

"John, Cardiff Hall and Tunleah Mews are a very small world. Everyone knows everyone else's business. The people are upset that Ruth was dismissed. It's created a hardship for her. Last night her husband beat her and kicked her out of the house."

The expression in John's eyes turned somber. "Mallory, I don't think I can take her back. After you threw her clothes in the pond, she said some unforgivable things about you. I will not have her speak of my wife in that manner, nor am I going to spend my time worrying if she is going to jump out of the bushes at me. The woman is damn bold."

Mallory tilted her head up at him, surprised by the firmness in his voice. She'd never had a champion before. But she also knew he wasn't right in letting Ruth go.

She placed her hand on his arm. "John, if you had a soldier under your command who didn't always follow orders, would you send him home to England?"

"Of course not. I would order him to get in line."

"And what if that didn't work? Let's say he was an incorrigible fellow."

"Incorrigible?" He smiled at her choice of words.

"You know what I mean."

He crossed his arms, seriously considering her question. "I'd probably take him aside and beat some sense into him."

"That's right," Mallory agreed, "and that is exactly what I did to Ruth when I threw her clothes into the pond. John, this isn't London. In such a close-knit community, you don't dismiss a worker unless she has done something truly terrible, such as stealing. You must give Ruth her job back."

"I can't believe you're defending her."

"I'm not defending her actions, but these people think of each other as a family. In families, you overlook the faults of others. For example, at Craige Castle we have a sheep herder who's a bit touched in the head. He can barely watch the sheep, let alone do any other job, but we make extra time for him." She paused, uncertain how much to say, then added, "Besides, I'm asking you to do this for my sake. The other servants blame me for her dismissal."

John's eyes grew stormy. "It wasn't your fault. I made the decision."

His swift anger in her defense surprised her. "John, please, don't do anything rash. I'm having enough trouble as it is—"

"What kind of trouble?" he demanded.

"It's nothing," she said firmly and would have walked away but he caught her arm.

"What is it, Mallory?"

"I don't fit in here. I sense that people don't like me," she confessed.

The anger eased from the lines of his face. "Mallory, that's nonsense." He placed his hands on her shoulders. "Of course, they all like you."

"No, they don't. I made a mistake and got upset yesterday in the kitchen with Mrs. Irongate and the cook. I acted more like Lady Craige than Mrs. Dawson. It didn't settle well with them."

"And now this incident with Ruth hasn't helped matters," he said, with sudden understanding.

"No, it hasn't," she admitted. "Silly, isn't it? That I should be concerned about what the servants say? I've never worried before."

He gave her shoulders a reassuring squeeze. "We all want to feel like we belong. I'll take care of it." He paused. "But I'd like you to do a favor for me in return."

Mallory went still. She should have known. "What is it you want?"

"Oh, now, I feel your shoulders tensing," he said, removing his hands. "Mallory, you don't know what I'm going to ask you."

"No, but I have an idea."

John flipped her braid over her shoulder. It was an innocent gesture but an intimate one. The sort of thing a man would do unconsciously while talking to his wife. "Come with me to collect the rents today."

His words caught her by surprise. "That's it? That's all you're going to ask?"

His eyes sparkled. "Well, I wouldn't mind sleeping in your bed." He waggled his eyebrows, teasing her.

Mallory smiled, feeling foolish. Had he been teasing last night, too? "I could collect rents with you," she suggested.

She was rewarded with a flash of his dimple, the little one at the corner of his mouth.

"We'll leave shortly after noon, then," he said.

She relaxed, pleased that he had asked her to accompany him. "I'll have your lunch ready when you come by the cottage."

She started to walk away, but again he stopped her. "Wait, pack it in the hamper. We'll have a picnic."

"A picnic? I haven't been on a picnic since I was a child." Years ago, long before her father had taken ill.

"Then we'll go on one today," he said decisively.

For a second, Mallory stared at him. "You're serious, aren't you?"

"Yes. Why would you think I'm not?"

Mallory glanced over at the blacksmith. "Because we both have work to do."

John shook his head. "I'll be finished with him in a few hours. Mallory, Lord Woodruff has ordered me to collect the rents. He didn't say I couldn't enjoy myself while doing it. Come on, let's go on a picnic," he urged her gently. "It will be good for us to get away for an afternoon."

She hesitated, tempted.

His eyes pleaded with her to agree.

She nodded. "I suppose it won't do any harm."

"Of course not," he assured her, bestowing upon her such a dazzling smile, it was as if the sun had suddenly come out from behind a bank of clouds.

His smile made her feel light-hearted, even giddy. She started walking back toward the path, unable to take her eyes off him.

"We'll have a good time," he promised.

"Yes, a good time," Mallory repeated dumbly.

Her feet stumbled over a rock, bringing her to her senses. She turned and hurried on her way.

John watched her until she disappeared out of sight. He felt absurdly pleased with himself for suggesting the picnic. And as for her problems with the other servants, he was more than happy to be her white knight.

John knocked on the cottage door promptly at noon, much earlier than Mallory had expected him. However, she'd had the hamper packed for the last hour.

He hitched the pony to the green and yellow pony cart and soon, with a snap of the driving ribbons, they were on their way toward Tunleah Mews.

Mallory was glad now that she'd said she'd go with him. The day had turned a touch overcast, but a summer breeze promised to send the clouds scattering later. She didn't even fret about her lack of a bonnet, enjoying this moment out in the fresh air. The cart had benches that ran down either side. John sat across from her.

He waited until they were well past Cardiff Hall before saying, "I told Evie that Ruth could come back tomorrow."

"Thank you," Mallory said, her relief genuine. "How did it go with the blacksmith?"

John shook his head. "The horses haven't been taken care of properly for months. I don't understand Woodruff. There is so much work to be done. How can a man completely ignore his responsibilities? I discovered from Evie this morning that he hasn't paid last quarter's wages yet, and we're almost finished with this quarter. I went up to the house to speak to him and see if I could get the money, but he refused to come out of his office. I could hear him inside muttering to himself about his damned book. So I banged on his door, and he talked to me, although he wasn't happy about it at all. I got the wages paid, though."

Mallory heard the echo in John's words of the complaints she'd made less than a week before about him. She wondered if he'd noticed.

As if reading her mind, he said ruefully, "Of course, I suppose I could give lessons on abdicating one's responsibilities."

She surprised herself by quickly jumping to his defense. "You trusted your uncle, John. You thought you were being responsible."

He frowned. "A man has a lot of time to think while he mucks out a barn. I trusted him too much. And I find myself wondering why he betrayed me."

"Greed?"

"I paid him handsomely for his services. Father provided him with a generous allowance, and I doubled it when I took over the estate." He shook his head. "But I can't lay the blame solely on his shoulders. There is no excuse for my not being more attentive to you. I should have come to East Anglia when I returned to London. I should have tried to communicate with you while I was in the military."

Mallory looked over the fields of ripening grain. "I could have written," she admitted quietly. "I did try to communicate to your uncle, but obviously he never passed on my complaints . . . I never went further, John, because I—" She faltered, uncertain how to say it.

"You what?"

She forced herself to look at him. "I knew you didn't want the marriage," she said in a rush of words.

John pulled the pony to a halt. He turned to her. "What if I did want the marriage?"

Mallory could scarcely believe her ears.

He watched her, as if anxious for her answer.

Her heart was beating unusually fast. She didn't know how she felt, or what she wanted—not anymore. The realization startled her.

When had she changed?

She lifted her gaze to meet his. "I don't know that I can answer that right now." Her words sounded as awkward as she felt.

He laughed, the sound almost joyful. "We're making progress, Mallory," he said, as if her answer delighted him. With a flick of the reins, he set the pony in motion. "What do you think of those fields over there? Are they about ready to harvest?"

Mallory blinked, caught off guard by his sudden change of subject. She turned toward where he indicated. "The wheat appears to be about ready."

"That's what I thought," he said, nodding.

"John, are you thinking about harvesting those fields yourself?"

He frowned. "What do you mean?"

"Because if you are," she said matter of factly, "then I should warn you, you can't do all the work involved in cutting the fields with just three women and Terrell."

"What do you suggest?"

She studied him, seeing beyond his good looks. He appeared more relaxed, happier, less jaded than when she'd first found him in London.

The change went beyond his casual attire. He still wore the lawn shirt with lace edges, although the shirt was frayed at the cuffs and collar from repeated washings in the pond with harsh soap. His jacket lay folded on the seat beside him. The breeze ruffled his hair.

But the look in his eyes seemed less intense and foreboding, the lines around his mouth softer.

"You're enjoying this adventure," she accused him.

His lips curved into an easy smile. "I don't enjoy sleeping in the barn."

She ignored that, knowing he was teasing her. Instead, she answered his previous question. "I'd hire a harvest crew for fields this size. Otherwise, it will take you weeks to cut the wheat, and depending on the weather, you won't have that much time."

He drove the pony cart up into a pear orchard by the side of the road. "Will this do for a picnic spot?"

"It will be fine," she answered.

It was more than fine; it was ideal. A stream ran along the far edge of the orchard and the sound of its rushing water carried through the quiet peace of the place.

John jumped from the cart and held his hand out to her. His action was no more than common courtesy dictated, but as Mallory placed her hand in his larger one, she felt a very feminine response to his very alluring masculinity.

He smiled up at her, and Mallory forgot to breathe.

He seemed to be equally affected. For a long minute, they stood looking at each other as if frozen in time.

John moved first, bringing his hand up to brush back a tendril of her hair that had escaped her braid. His fingers lingered on her cheek.

This wasn't the touch of a rake or a man intent on seduction.

It was a lover's touch.

He dropped his hand, the moment's magic gone. "I'll see to the pony while you spread out this blanket." He took it from the cart and handed it to her.

Mallory did as he asked, but her mind was on what had happened between them. It was as if John had awakened this morning a different person.

He joined her on the blanket and took the bread and cheese she offered. "Tell me about these harvest crews."

Mallory poured a glass of cider for him. "They are men and women who travel through the countryside and hire out for the harvest. At Craige Castle, wc worked with the tenants to cut all our fields at once, using the same crew for all the land," she said, relieved to have a safe topic of conversation. "Then afterward, we sponsored the harvest home. We had grand ones at Craige

Castle. Everyone always had a good time, and we always had our pick of the best crews."

"What's the harvest home?" John asked.

"It's a feast to celebrate the end of a good harvest and lots of hard work. We'd have musicians and food, and there was dancing. Everyone was invited, including the children. Even in the leanest times, we've thrown a good harvest home at Craige Castle." A new, sad thought struck her. "I wonder what will happen this year. . . ."

John gently took the cup of cider from her hand. "Mallory, don't worry. I'll see us through this."

She turned to him. She wanted to believe him. Still—

"Tell me, did you enjoy the harvest home?" he asked, wisely changing the subject. "Did you dance all night?"

Mallory self-consciously touched her braid. "No, I didn't dance. Mother and I would make an appearance and welcome everyone. Then we'd quickly leave so the tenants and all could have a good time."

"You didn't dance?" He sounded disappointed.

"I don't dance," she admitted. "Papa was sick for so many years, dancing wasn't a priority. Then after his death, I was a married woman with my husband off at war. It wouldn't have been seemly for everyone to see me kicking up my heels like a grass widow."

As John studied her, she knew he understood far more than she'd given him credit for.

Feeling uncomfortable under his intense scrutiny, Mallory pulled the ledger book out of the woven hamper. She opened it. "The closest tenant is Wadham. He lives off this road perhaps a half mile or so further on."

John popped the last piece of bread in his mouth and hopped to his feet. "Then shall we?" He helped her to her feet and together they cleaned up the remnants of the picnic and went on their way.

Wadham's farm was a collection of stone buildings almost two centuries old, but the grounds appeared neat and tidy. "Well, here I go," John said. He jumped out of the cart and went in search of Mr. Wadham. After a few moments of waiting, Mallory decided to join him. They found Mr. Wadham by the cattle stalls, sitting at a lathe, shaving a new ax handle.

"Hello," John called in greeting.

Without rising, the man glared at John as if daring him to come closer. "I know who you are and what you want. You can tell Lord Woodruff I'll not pay my rent until he drains the field. You tell him that. He'll know what you mean." The man turned his attention back to his task.

John started forward but Mallory placed a cautionary hand on his shoulder. "Tell him you will talk to Lord Woodruff, but you expect a portion of the rent by next Monday," she instructed in a quiet voice. "Then turn on your heel and leave."

To her surprise, John did as she'd suggested. In the pony cart, he gave vent to his anger at the tenant's high-handed treatment.

Mallory shook her head. "Something must be wrong for the tenant to be so dead set against

Lord Woodruff. You said he hasn't been taking care of Cardiff Hall. He may not be honoring his obligations to his tenants, either."

"And how do I find out whether he is or not?"

Mallory shrugged. "Ask him?"

John snorted. However, they met Wadham's rudeness at the next tenant farm and the next.

"I realize no one likes the rent collector," John said, "but these people seem to be carrying it too far." They were driving into Tunleah Mews, a small village with a stone church at one end, an ale house at the other, and a few shops and cottages in between. The cottages were neat and tidy, with flowers blooming in every yard. A small group of women, wearing aprons and mob caps, gossiped in one of the yards. They watched the pony cart drive by with curious and suspicious eyes.

"We're doing something wrong," John said thoughtfully.

"Us? We're not the ones behind in our rent."

"Yes, but we're the ones who have to collect it." He focused over the pony's head, as if turning something over in his mind. "Everyone can be gotten around, Mallory, but first you have to think of how to do it."

"Gotten around?"

"Won over."

She considered his philosophy for a moment and then opened the ledger book on her lap. "Whenever I wanted to take up an unpopular matter with my tenants at Craige Castle, I always went to Savoy Tarleton, who was my largest tenant."

"Who is Lord Woodruff's largest tenant?"

"That's what I'm looking for right now." She ran her finger down the ledger page. One name caught her eye. "Freddie Hanson." She consulted the map in the rent book. "He lives back the other way about two miles behind Cardiff Hall."

"Freddie Hanson," John repeated. "We're going to call on Freddie next. But first, I need to make a stop." He pulled the cart to a halt in front of the cobbler's shop.

"Why are we stopping here?" Mallory asked.

"I promised you shoes, wife," he said with mock authority. He opened the cart's back door and jumped to the ground. "Your shoes were made for ballroom dancing, not trekking through fields," he said, helping her to alight.

"But can we afford it?" Mallory asked.

"I've two gold ones to my name, enough to spend on your feet."

A half hour later, Mallory had been fitted for a new pair of sturdy leather shoes to be ready in three days' time, which was fortunate. Her kid slippers were about worn through.

John then drove the cart to the public house. He went inside, and in a few minutes emerged with a bottle of whiskey.

"What's that for?" she asked.

"Freddie Hanson's favorite brew. He's very well known to the tap man."

"What are you going to do? Bribe him with it to pay his rent?"

"Yes," John said candidly. "Now come, Mallory, we're off to make friends with Freddie Hanson."

Hanson farmed one hundred and ten acres for Lord Woodruff. His house, like so many of the others, was made of yellow stone. Several yards from the house were a few outbuildings beside a deeply rutted road that, according to the map in the rent book, led from Hanson's farm back to Cardiff Hall. Apparently this house had at one time been the steward's home.

A cow lowed a greeting from the small mud-and-stone barn. On either side of the house's front door, butterflies fluttered among purple cone flowers and daisies.

As they pulled up in the cart, Hanson, a big, hearty man, stepped out on his front step, a pipe held in his teeth, his hands fisted at his hips. "I've heard who you are, John Dawson, and you can stop right there. You are not welcome in this house."

John reined in the pony. "Even if I come with a gift from Lord Woodruff?"

The man's eyes narrowed shrewdly. "Lord Woodruff doesn't give gifts. He doesn't even know half of us are alive except to fill his church pews."

John lifted the bottle of whiskey for Hanson to see. Sunlight turned the dark amber liquid to red gold.

Hanson took out his pipe. He wet his lips. "And what business could Lord Woodruff have that he would be offering me a gift? Because I'll not be paying my rent, not until he makes the improvements he promised me."

"Aye, I came to talk to you about the rent," John said, easily falling into the speech habits of a

Sussex man. He opened the door and jumped down from the cart. "I also want to plan the cutting crews for the harvest—"

Hanson made a rude noise. "We do it alone here. We don't need help."

"We help each other now," John said. "And you and I need to talk about the harvest home."

"Harvest home?" Hanson repeated. He came down off his front step. "We haven't had a harvest home since the year before the Duke of Tyndale inherited Cardiff Hall, nigh over ten years ago."

"We're having one now," John said. "Provided the wheat is cut and everyone works hard."

Hanson put his pipe back in his mouth. For a second, he appeared to debate John's words, and then ever so lightly his gaze rested on the bottle in John's hand.

John smiled. "It's a hot day. A man could use a drink."

"Aye, he could." Hanson abruptly made up his mind. "Come in then." He marched back into his house, leaving the white door open.

John shot Mallory a triumphant glance before tying up the pony and helping her down from the cart. His fingers laced in hers, they walked into the house together.

Inside, Hanson waited for them with his wife, Sylvie, and three of their six children. After introductions, Hanson ushered them into the family's sitting room.

The man was prosperous indeed, Mallory noted. His family was well dressed and they had the help of a serving girl. Polished wood floors shone in the rambling rooms and the well-built furniture didn't show signs of wear. Above the stone mantel hung a violin.

John walked over to it. "Do you play?" he asked Hanson.

"My father is the best player in the shire," said Libby, the Hansons' fourteen-year-old daughter.

"Is he now?" John ran a finger over the wood. "I play a bit myself," he said, surprising Mallory—and then she remembered he'd mentioned during their wedding that he played the violin.

Mallory doubted Hanson played the same sort of music John would have learned from music masters as a boy. However, Hanson's whole manner toward them changed, his face becoming a wreath of smiles. He set his pipe aside. "Do you?" he said to John. "Well, take it down. Try her."

John tucked the instrument under his chin, picked up the bow and pulled a chord experimentally from the instrument. "She's sweet," he said to his host.

Hanson nodded. "Belonged to my father and his father before him." He turned to his children. "When I was a lad, when we had the harvest home at that great old barn at Cardiff Hall, the very rafters rang with music."

"What's a harvest home, da?" Libby asked.

Her father launched into the telling of vivid memories while a serving girl appeared with a tray, a pitcher, and glasses.

"Would you care for a drink of cider?" Sylvie asked Mallory.

"I'd enjoy one very much," she said.

Hanson pulled the cork out of the bottle John had set on the table and poured two healthy glassfuls. He took a sip and smacked his lips with satisfaction. "Now, what is this about Woodruff offering the harvest home?"

John didn't answer. Instead he put the bow to the strings and started playing the merry jig Mallory often heard him whistling. Hanson's two youngest children, twin girls, gathered around him. Hanson clicked his fingers in time to the music. Sylvie tapped her toe. A moment later, Mallory watched wide-eyed as the big farmer rose to his feet and proceeded to dance a jig. She'd never seen a man throw aside decorum so freely.

When John finished, Hanson clapped his hands. "Very good, Dawson, very good. Do you know any other tunes?"

"One or two, although I prefer to play the guitar. I learned to play in Portugal."

"What of the mandolin?" Hanson asked.

"Of course I can play it," John answered.

Hanson turned to his wife, his eyes bright with excitement. "Sylvie, doesn't Will Wadham have a mandolin?"

"He has, but he never learned to play it," Sylvie answered.

Hanson slapped the table with his hand. "Libby, fetch your brother out in the barn. Tell him to ride over to Wadham's place and borrow his mandolin. No, better yet, have him bring Wadham and his wife. We have enough for supper, don't we, dearie?" he asked his wife.

"Well, yes," Sylvie answered with mild surprise.

"Fine, then. Tell Wadham to come here, and bring that drum he has, too. And on the way home, have Christopher stop at Bowling's and invite them to join us. Tell Christopher to spread the word. Everyone's invited!"

"Yes, father," Libby said, and ran out of the room, her cheeks turning pink with excitement.

Hanson poured another glass of whiskey and took a gulp before holding his hand out to John for the fiddle. "Do you know 'Leg o' the Lamb'?"

"Never heard it, but play it for me once, and I'll get the tune," John answered, handing the violin to Hanson. A minute later Hanson was fiddling a hand-clapping reel.

Within an hour, and several glasses of whiskey and cider later, many of the tenants John and Mallory had met that afternoon filled the Hansons' sitting room. Even the cobbler arrived carrying a fife.

Furniture was moved back to allow more room to dance. The whiskey disappeared quickly, but jugs of ale and other home brews appeared in its place.

After spending nearly half an hour tuning the instrument, John proved he played the mandolin better than he did the fiddle. Soon, five of the men—the cobbler, Hanson, John, Wadham, and a Jeremy Rawlins—formed a musical group.

The news that a harvest home would be held at Cardiff Hall spread quickly. Mallory heard those words on everyone's lips. The thought of it sent a tremor of excitement through the crowd, making this night special. Food appeared on the table in the dining room, as well as more jugs of ale and cider. Soon, young and old alike lined up for dances, and the floor shook with the stamping of their feet. The air smelled of food, ale, and sweat as the dancers threw themselves into having a good time. Mallory found a place in the corner close to an open window to watch everyone have fun.

She noticed that more than a few women eyed John with obvious interest, but he appeared oblivious to everything save the music. Between songs, he and the other musicians joked among themselves, and the dancers laughed, enjoying their banter.

He fit in easily, Mallory noticed. She envied his ability to blend in with people of different classes, something she had never been able to do even with the people at Craige Castle.

"Hello, Mrs. Dawson." Evie waddled up to her, one hand on the small of her back.

She was delighted to see someone she knew. "Hello, Evie. Did you just arrive?"

"Aye, and I wish I were home. But I wasn't going to let Ruth or my Stephen leave me alone with my mother and the children while they had all the fun." She nodded toward the dancers. Mallory saw Ruth in the arms of a brawny young man who turned and gave Evie a smile.

"Is Ruth still with you, or has her husband taken her back?"

Evie shrugged. "I don't know. Malcolm came by to talk to her earlier, but she hasn't told me she's leaving. He's got a bad temper, and Stephen and I believe she might be better off with us, although I can't say she doesn't try him sorely. She's a flirt, you know, Mrs. Dawson. She has to try her games on every man who is new to the shire. I told her to behave around the new steward, but Ruth doesn't listen well."

"I understand, Evie," Mallory answered, and the young woman appeared visibly relieved.

At that moment, the dance ended. Ruth whirled around with the last step, turned, and noticed Mallory. Her laughing expression turned hostile before she coldly walked off in another direction. Evie had made her way over to a small group of women talking a short distance away, and didn't notice.

Once again Mallory was alone.

"May I have this dance?"

She didn't realized the older gentleman was speaking to her until he repeated his question. He was bald, save for a fuzz of white hair around the side of his head, didn't have many teeth, and was half a head shorter. He probably had trouble finding partners.

"I'm sorry, I don't dance," she admitted regretfully.

"Don't or won't," came Ruth's sharp voice. She'd come up behind the man. "She's too good for us, Tad," she said. "Puts on airs and the like."

"That's not true," Mallory said quietly. She turned to Tad. "I don't know how to dance."

"Then I'll teach you," Tad said with enthusiasm, and did a jig step to show her he could.

Mallory felt the heat of a blush steal up her cheeks. She couldn't go out on the dance floor and make a fool of herself. She shook her head. "That's very nice of you, but I can't."

"See what I mean?" Ruth whispered loudly in Tad's ear. "She's *better* than us. Come, I'll dance with you." She moved off and Tad followed, eager to take his place in the next dance set. Ruth slowed down next to the group of women and said a few words. They, in turn, craned their necks to take a good look at Mallory.

Mallory's place by the wall seemed lonelier than ever. She watched Tad and Ruth dance. After the set, Tad found another partner while Ruth spent her time with a knot of women gossiping by the cider.

By the covert glances sent her way, Mallory knew Ruth was gossiping about her. She turned away, but her gaze met Sylvie Hanson's. The farmer's wife sent her a shy smile, but there was a touch of pity in her eyes.

Mallory pretended it didn't matter. She and John weren't going to be here long, and after all, she was really Lady Craige. But her excuses rang hollow in her ears. She found herself tapping her toe to the music . . . and wishing she could be carefree and confident enough to join them.

She overheard two women whisper something about Mrs. Dawson insisting Ruth be turned out and then the new steward changing his mind and making amends. So, that was how the tale was being mangled, was it? Mallory felt a complete outcast.

After the next song, John set down the mandolin. He said something to Freddie and started across the room toward her.

Mallory panicked. He was smiling, but she could tell by the set of his jaw and the concern in his eyes that he was coming over to check on her.

It surprised her that a man could be so astute. Or perhaps he'd overheard someone gossiping? She didn't want to know.

He was making his way around the dancers now. In a second, he'd be in front of her.

Acting on impulse, Mallory moved swiftly out into the hallway. She had almost made it through the front door when John's hand captured her wrist.

Chapter 12

Adown in the meadows the other day,
Agath'ring flow'rs, both fine and gay,
Agath'ring flowers, both red and blue,
I little thought what love could do.

"O Waly, Waly"

"Where are you going?" John asked.

"I need a breath of fresh air," Mallory answered. She looked down at his hand holding her wrist and back up again, an imperial order to let her go, if John had ever received one.

But he wasn't going to. "If you leave, even for a breath of fresh air, Ruth will think she has run you off. The others will believe what she says. Don't give her that satisfaction."

Mallory pulled on her wrist. "I don't care."

"Oh yes, you do. I was watching, Mallory. You want to be a part of them but you don't know how, do you?"

Without answering, Mallory glowered up at him with mistrustful eyes. John almost smiled.

His wife had ruled Craige Castle for so long, he doubted anyone said nay to her.

"Don't let her chase you off," he said softly. "Come and dance with me."

"I don't know how to." There was an edge of sadness in her words.

"Then let me teach you." His hand moved from her wrist to take her fingers in his.

For a moment, he thought she was going to pull away again. Instead, she said, "John, I'll make a fool of myself."

"Then you'll have company. I don't know half the steps they do in these dances either. But we'll learn together."

"People will laugh at us."

"At the *two* of us . . . and we'll laugh at ourselves. Now, come."

Ever so slowly, Mallory let him draw her back toward the dancing. He tucked her hand in the crook of his arm and found a place for them against the wall where they could watch until the end of the current set.

John whispered in her ear, teaching her the different movements.

Mallory shook her head. "It seems confusing. I haven't danced since before my father took ill, when I was fourteen."

He nodded to the first couple in the line. "All we need to do is exactly what the couple ahead of us does. It's quite simple."

"Not to me. I have no idea of the steps."

John laughed. "But I do, and it's my job to lead my partner through them. If we appear foolish, everyone will blame me."

"You could never look foolish, whatever you did," Mallory whispered under her breath.

John leaned back. "Dear me, did my wife just pay me a compliment?"

She blushed prettily, as if surprised she'd spoken aloud. At that moment the dance finished and the next set started forming. John dragged her out onto the dance floor.

Mallory was digging in her heels. "There won't be room for us."

"As many that wish to dance can dance, Mallory." He let go of her hand and joined the line of men facing the women.

For a second, he feared that Mallory would take flight. Then, after a moment's hesitation, she assumed her place across from him.

"So you've decided to dance, have you, Dawson?" Hanson shouted out, lowering his fiddle.

"I have," John responded good naturedly. "And I'll ask you to play a lively tune. My feet don't move to any other."

"Right you have it," Hanson agreed, and nodded to the other musicians. "Let's do the *Irish Wash Woman* for our friend." He counted the beats and the musicians began to play in quick time.

Everyone else in the line seemed to know the steps. Mallory earnestly studied the feet of the woman next to her, attempting to make hers move in the same way.

John wanted to call out, "Relax, Mallory," but he knew better. The first couple completed their pattern, finishing with a *brisé,* in which the man and woman circled each other quickly before casting off right and left to their respective lines.

It was a simple move, but a frown of concentration formed between Mallory's eyes.

And then it was their turn. Mallory's alarmed gaze met his. John gave her a reassuring smile and danced out in the middle to meet her.

She stood rooted to the floor. He went the necessary steps to grab her hand and drag her out, then, holding both hands, they started skipping sideways between the lines of dancers, as all the couples had before them.

They were halfway to the end of the promenade line before Mallory started to loosen up a bit. Their bodies began moving in step. Her legs brushed against his, her hands clasped his, and she actually smiled.

At the end of the line, they had to perform the *brisé*. They started around each other—and then Mallory stomped on his foot. John had been stepped on by mules that didn't hurt him the way his wife's stomping foot did.

Immediately, she broke the movement of the dance. "I'm so sorry. I didn't mean to—" she said and would have bolted in embarrassment, except that John slipped his arm around her trim waist.

Ignoring his pained foot, he lifted her off the floor, her breasts pressed against his chest, and whirled her around until her feet lifted in the air. Mallory hugged his neck as if she were afraid she would fly away.

The dancers shouted their approval. It was with reluctance that John set her back down. He was starting to cast off to the left and join his line when he realized that Mallory was still rooted to the spot and staring up at him, her expression slightly dazed. He turned her in the right direction and gave her a little push.

Recovering her balance, Mallory hurried to her place and everyone in the room laughed at their little pantomime. They were such a success that the next dancers down the line attempted to outdo them by spinning even longer. The next couple added their own twist, as did the next and the next. Soon, everyone's sides ached with laughter.

The dance ended. John limped over to Mallory and bowed. "You were splendid."

"No, you were. I would have run away the moment I stepped on your foot. How is it?"

"It's nothing," he assured her.

She placed her hand on his arm. "Thank you."

Looking down in her golden brown eyes, John felt like St. George after he'd slain a dragon. "I didn't do anything."

"I would never have attempted it if you hadn't forced me to try." She removed her hand. "Do you think I could do it again?"

"Of course," he agreed, eager to take her back into his arms. He held out his hand, but instead, she turned and searched the crowd.

"Excuse me a moment, John." She left him standing there with his hand outstretched and worked her way around the other couples toward a short, balding older man. She said a few words, and a big smile spread across the man's face. He led her out onto the dance floor.

"Dawson," Hanson called. "Come up here and play for me so I can dance with my wife."

John was happy to do so since he had no desire to dance with anyone but Mallory. Taking Hanson's fiddle from him, he asked, "Who is that man with Mallory?"

Hanson shot a glance in her direction. "Oh, that's Tad Nevins. Loves to dance, our Tad does, but Mallory should look to her feet. He can get a bit carried away." He went off in search of his wife.

John and the other musicians played a reel. Hanson was right, Nevins did stomp on a few of Mallory's toes, but she laughed and stomped right back. John winced. When the dance ended, the blacksmith who had scowled so ferociously at her that morning claimed her for the next set.

Hanson reclaimed his fiddle and John picked up the mandolin. As the evening wore on, he watched fascinated as Mallory blossomed before his eyes. Her careful reserve evaporated. If she made a mistake in the dance pattern, she laughed and attempted to do it better the next time. The other dancers teased her and took time to show her new steps, and she accepted both with equal grace.

When she wasn't dancing, she chatted with Sylvie Hanson and the other ladies. John realized that in the time they'd been together, she'd rarely laughed—at least, not with the freedom she did so now.

He managed another dance with her and this time his toes were safe. They almost moved as one.

All too soon the evening came to an end. John and Mallory were among the first to leave. At the door, they promised the Hansons to meet after church the next day and continue making plans for the harvest. Everyone at the party hailed John as a hero for giving them back the harvest, a role he played to the hilt.

Hanson clapped his hand on John's shoulder. "I may even consider paying my rent."

"I'd appreciate it if you would," John returned good-naturedly, and everyone laughed. John didn't think he'd have any trouble collecting the rents after this night.

They climbed into the pony cart and John drove them home by way of the country lane, through the fields and meadows between the Hansons' and Cardiff Hall. Mallory waved until the Hansons' house was out of sight. Then she fell back on the bench with a satisfied sigh. Her eyes sparkled with her enjoyment of the evening. The air around them smelled of night flowers and ripening fields of grain, a heady combination.

"I've never had such a good time in my life." She reached out, her hand lightly touching his, which were holding the driving ribbons. "Thank you."

Her simple words stirred him. "I didn't do anything."

"You taught me how to fit in. Otherwise, this night would have been like all the other parties I've attended where I've sat with the matrons. Oh, John, you can't imagine how I feel tonight. For once in my life, I feel as if I've been accepted for who I am. I've always felt as if I was the outsider looking in . . . but tonight I was part of the group."

"Mallory, surely you had friends among people of your own class."

"No, no one." She hesitated before confessing, "I was a married woman. I had an obligation to you."

"And so you waited for me?"

"Of course."

John studied her before saying softly, "I'm surprised."

She appeared startled that he would doubt her. "John, I was your wife."

The words hung in the air between them. He didn't know what to say. Her commitment humbled him.

She turned to look over the dark meadow, dangling an arm over the side of the cart. The moon bathed her in silver light and the night songs of crickets and frogs filled the silence between them.

"Aren't the stars beautiful tonight?" she asked. "They appear so close and bright."

"I haven't noticed," John answered.

"Haven't noticed?" Mallory looked at him over her shoulder. "How could you not appreciate such a beautiful evening?"

"Because I'm too busy appreciating a beautiful woman."

Mallory's lips parted. She studied him for a long moment, her expression uncertain, then shook her head. "You're teasing me," she said with a shy smile.

"No, I'm not."

She sat up. "You don't need to say that, John."

"I didn't say it because I needed to, Mallory. I said it because I believe it."

"I think you've had a touch too much whiskey tonight." And she hiccupped, a small, feminine sound.

"And you've had a touch too much cider?"

"Perhaps a touch," she admitted, and then laughed, the full-bodied sound full of joy.

Listening to her, John felt a sense of wonder building inside him. Something was happening to him. He felt light-headed, dizzy, happy—and all because she'd laughed?

No, he realized with a start. It was something more . . . something he'd never anticipated.

It was as if he was seeing Mallory truly for the first time. She'd attracted him from the moment he'd laid eyes on her at Sarah's party, but now there was a new depth to his feelings for her. His gaze lingered on the determined set of her chin, the spirited intelligence in her eyes, the open honesty she wore like a cloak around her. He even admired her freckled nose.

I'm falling in love.

He heard the words in his mind as clearly as if a voice had whispered them in his ear. He was in love with Mallory.

Love. He'd never imagined it before—but how strange it was. It was almost as if he'd been empty inside, a shell of a man, until this very moment, when he'd realized he'd fallen in love . . . and now he felt filled with the most indescribable happiness, simple, pure happiness. He'd never known such an emotion existed—and he'd also discovered that the poets were right. Love was something to celebrate, and to die for, and to sing about.

He stared at the point between the pony's ears, too startled by this new knowledge to truly understand it.

When had it happened? What change had been wrought inside him to turn a man who had once been so cynical into a moon-eyed fool in love?

He felt as if the earth trembled beneath him. His hands shook, his heart beat rapidly. Slowly, he turned and drank in the sight of Mallory as a thirsty man gulps down water.

She shifted, as if sensing his gaze upon her, and looked over her shoulder at him, her expression quizzical. "What is it?" she asked.

John couldn't answer. No words would pass his lips. Here he was, a man who had made love to camp followers, married women, even a foreign countess . . . and he couldn't speak to his own wife!

She smiled and shook her head. "When I met you at Lady Ramsgate's house, I thought you were the most jaded Corinthian in all of England. But look at you now." She reached across to cover his hand with hers. "John, you've given the people of Tunleah Mews something to look forward to. I don't know how you'll persuade Lord Woodruff to sponsor the harvest home, but you'll think of a way."

She squeezed his hand and then stood to climb out the back of the cart. She jumped easily to the ground.

Confused by her actions, John looked around

and realized they'd arrived home. The cart was halted in the barnyard. That was how powerful love was . . . it had robbed him of all sense of time and place.

Mallory took a deep breath of fresh night air and closed her eyes. Spreading her arms, she spun around. "This is a beautiful night," she said again. She opened her eyes and smiled at John. "And a fitting end to a perfect day. Thank you." She lifted the hamper from the cart and ran toward the path, pausing at the edge of the barnyard and waving at him. "Goodnight," she whispered.

John just stared at her—dumbfounded by another new and amazing thought: *She didn't feel what he felt.* He, John Barron, military officer, peer of the realm, and infamous lover, had fallen in love with a woman who didn't love him back.

And she was his wife!

The pony turned and looked at John, then impatiently stamped its foot. Slowly, he climbed out of the cart and settled the animal for the night, all the while talking to himself.

What kind of a man was he to meekly accept a pat on the hand and a whispered good night? She seemed to consider him more a brother or cousin than a husband—and could he blame her? In every confrontation they'd had, she'd ended with the upper hand! Well, the time had come, he told himself, to show her that he wasn't some eunuch to be pacified with dreamy smiles. When he told her she was beautiful, he expected her to believe him and be properly appreciative of the compliment.

Tossing aside the grain bucket, John marched out of the barn and headed down the path toward the cottage. His long legs ate up the ground and he was before the door in no time at all. No candle burned in the window, which further fueled his anger. She'd assumed he knew his *place* and would sleep in the barn.

Well, she'd soon find out differently.

He pounded his fist on the door. He had to knock a second time before he heard her sleepy voice. "Who's there?"

"John."

"Is something wrong?"

"I need to see you, Mallory."

He had to cool his heels a full two minutes before he heard the scrape of the bar being lifted. The door opened. She hadn't lit a candle, but John could see in the moonlight that she stood before him in her brown dress. Her long braid hung over one shoulder, and the expression in her eyes was full of concern. John didn't think she'd ever looked so lovely as she did at this moment bathed in silver light.

She pushed a loose lock of hair from her face. "What is it, John?"

He stared down at her, words escaping him.

"John, are you all right?" She placed her hand against his cheek. "You feel hot and your complexion is slightly flushed. Are you coming down with a summer cold or some other ailment?"

John couldn't answer her. The words he'd rehearsed in the barn would not pass his lips. Instead, he placed a hand on each of her arms, pulled her up to him, and brought his lips down on her mouth.

Caught off guard, she tensed and tried to push him away. John pressed her closer, enjoying the sensation of her body against his.

To his delighted surprise, the back of her dress was unbuttoned, as if she'd hurriedly thrown it on to answer the door. He slid his hand through the opening, his fingers brushing the soft cotton of her undergarments, feeling the curve of her waist beneath them.

Her resistance faded and her lips parted. He was quick to take advantage, stroking her bottom lip with his tongue, urging her to open to him.

With a soft sigh, she submitted to him.

Her arms relaxed and came up around his neck. Her hands pulled his head down to her. But it was her low moan that took him over the edge.

John hugged her even closer, feeling the tight buds of her nipples through the layers of fabric. Kissing her was as natural as breathing. He could lose himself in the feel of her. The stroke of his tongue no longer surprised her. She accepted it, invited it . . . stroked him back. She tasted of sweet cider and woman. Her kisses, timid and shy at first, became more demanding.

And she felt so good in his arms. She was soft where he was hard, submissive to his need to dominate. No longer afraid to let her feel his need for her, he pulled at the layers of her petticoat and skirt and lifted her up off the floor.

But he was caught in a web of his own making. Her legs pressed against either side of his body, cradling him to her. He marveled at her unpracticed response to him.

He wanted to bury himself in her, to take her right now, this moment, in the doorway, on the floor, wherever.

Her heart pounded against his chest. She strained against him, unconsciously begging for more.

It took all the strength in John's character to set her feet down on the ground and break off the kiss. A shudder ran through her. He placed his hands on her shoulder to steady her while she leaned against the door frame.

He looked down into her wide, dazed eyes and said distinctly, "I'm getting tired of sleeping in the barn."

Without another word, he turned on his heel and walked off into the night.

Mallory slid slowly to the floor, her legs too weak to support her. Her head against the door frame, she watched him climb the path to the barn.

Every inch of her flesh quivered with emotions she hadn't known existed. She raised a hand to her face. His whiskers had been rough, burning her skin. Her lips felt swollen; they tingled.

Slowly, she rose to her feet and shut the door. Her dress had slipped off one shoulder. She shrugged and let it fall to the floor. Stumbling like a drunkard, Mallory made her way over to the bed and fell face down on it.

She struggled for common sense, but all she could think about was that incredible kiss. Who would have thought a kiss could have such an effect on a person?

She rolled on her back and stared at the rafters. It was going to be another sleepless night, full of restless dreams and mysterious longings. . . .

I'm getting tired of sleeping in the barn.

His words ran around and around in her head. Would it be so bad if he slept with her? After all, they *were* married.

This evening had been the best night of her life, dancing with John the highlight. She hadn't wanted to admit it to him. She'd tried hard to keep her distance, to ignore his flirtations, and the fluttery way he made her feel. When he'd called her beautiful, it had taken all her willpower to remember that he'd probably said those words to many women.

Mallory flopped over on her stomach and rested her chin on her hands. Wouldn't it be lovely to make believe even for a few moments that John loved her?

The idea stole her breath away . . . and it was then that she realized she'd fallen in love with him.

Mallory sat bolt upright in bed. She spoke the words aloud, testing them: "I've fallen in love with John."

They rang true.

She leaned back in the bed, her mind replaying the events of the last week. When had it happened? At what moment?

And, dear Lord, why?

Hal would be a much better husband to her.

Hal was steady and reliable. He'd even kissed her once . . . but his kiss hadn't turned her inside out.

And then she had the forbidden thought . . .

Before Mallory could question her sanity, she rose from the bed, picked up her dress, tugged it on over her head, and let herself out the door.

Outside, all was still and quiet. Not even a breeze stirred through the trees. John was gone. She could see no sign of him on the path leading to the barn.

Lifting her skirts, she went after him.

She was several yards from the cottage when a dark shadow stepped out from behind a tree into her path. A man's hands came down around her arms.

Mallory gave a scream of alarm.

Then John's distinctive, raspy voice said to her, "What took you so long?"

Without another word, he swung her up in his arms, carried her back to the cottage, and kicked the door shut.

Chapter 13

I kiss'd her lips like rubies red,
Fair maid is a lily, O!
She blush'd; then tenderly she said:
Come to me quietly,
Do not do me injury;
Gently, Johnny, my Jingalo.

"Gently, Johnny, My Jingalo"

The white coverlet on the bed seemed to shine in the silver moonlight streaming in from the window. John let her body slide slowly down his until her feet touched the floor. He kissed her thoroughly and completely, but there was a message in his kiss: he was done with waiting. He wanted his wife.

And Mallory wanted to be his wife. His kiss this time was every bit as potent and demanding as it had been at the door. He tasted of smoky, heady desire.

She loved the feel of his tongue. It pulled deep inside her, rousing feelings in places where she didn't even know she could feel. Oh, but she wanted more as she leaned against him and kissed him back.

His hands pushed her dress down off her shoulders. Her fingers tugged at the material of his shirt, urging it up over his head.

For a moment they had to break apart. He drew off his shirt. Her brown cambric dress fell to her feet.

Their gazes locked. "Take down your hair," he ordered softly.

She obeyed, keeping her eyes on him. Her fingers slipped the ribbon off the end of her braid. Using both hands, she combed the tresses over one shoulder.

"So lovely," he whispered, as he touched a strand of her hair, rubbing it between his fingers. "I've dreamed of touching you with your hair down and around your shoulders." The back of his fingers brushed against her breast covered by her worn cotton chemise. The nipple hardened, proud and erect.

Embarrassed, Mallory moved to cover herself with her arm, but he would have none of it. Instead, he skimmed her hair back over her shoulder and lowered his head to press his lips against her nipple.

The unexpected sensation surprised a gasp from her. Both her breasts tightened, tingling and growing firm and full. The heat of his mouth seared even through the cotton undergarment.

His lips left her too soon. She gave a soft sound of displeasure, but his hand around her waist drew her close and he slowly began moving, taking her with him. Mallory smiled, recognizing the dance steps they'd performed earlier that evening—only this time the tempo was unhurried, their movements more intimate. Nor did they need music.

His legs brushed hers. His hand slid down to the curve of her buttock. She looped her arms around his neck and rubbed her cheek against the silky mat of hair covering his muscular chest, reveling in the texture of his skin. He was warm, hard, satiny, and male.

She could feel his heartbeat. It was as fast as her own.

"Mallory, I'm going to make love to you."

She stopped breathing. "I know."

"I love you, Mallory."

It took a full minute for his words to make sense, and even then she thought her ears were playing tricks. She peered up at his face. "John, did you just declare yourself?"

His face was hidden by darkness. He gave a shaky laugh. "I've never before said those words to a woman, and now that I have, she doesn't believe me."

Before Mallory could answer, he led her over to the bed with its patched white coverlet and sat her down. He dropped to one knee on the floor in front of her.

Taking both her hands in his, he said in a direct, unloverlike fashion, "I said I loved you. And this is the moment when you sigh, appear terribly flattered, and tell me you love me, too."

She tilted her head. "Is that so?"

"Yes, that's so."

"Now let me see . . . what sort of a sigh was that? Like this?" She drew in her breath and let it out in a soft sigh of boredom. "No, that's not it," she quickly answered. "Perhaps it's more one of longing." She sighed again, drawing it out and fluttering her eyelashes dramatically.

He was frowning at her now, his scowl plain.

Mallory decided to be done with teasing. "Or perhaps it would be best if I answered honestly and simply, 'Yes, John Barron, I love you, too.'"

He stared at her blankly for a moment. "You love me?"

"Yes, I do," she admitted.

"You do?"

Mallory reached for his ears, looked him squarely in the eye, and said, "I love you, John Barron, Viscount Craige." She let go of him. "There, *now* do you believe me?"

In answer he gave a loud whoop of joy, picked her up in his arms, and circled round and round the room until she was laughing and dizzy. And then he kissed her. This time, the kiss was hard and demanding, and was full of promise.

John sat on the edge of the bed with Mallory in his lap. He began unlacing the ribbons of her chemise and petticoats.

Mallory's hands covered his. "What are you doing?"

"I'm taking my wife to bed," he answered, intent on his task.

Tiny goosebumps formed on the tender skin he exposed to the night air. He kissed the goosebumps away and didn't hear a word of complaint from his wife.

His lips covered one firm breast, the nipple rising and hardening as he suckled. Mallory buried her fingers in his thick hair, amazed at how her body reacted to his touch.

John undressed her slowly, making her stand between his thighs. The petticoat fell to a puddle at her feet and she wore nothing but her silk stockings. "You're beautiful," he whispered, his voice hoarse. "All ripe and rosy and naked." The modesty that was so much a part of her forced her to try and cover herself, but he wouldn't let her. He pushed her hands aside and ran his hands down over the smooth line of her hips and along the long muscles of her thighs. "Your skin is like the finest satin."

Other women were soft and plump. Mallory's muscles were like those of a dancer. She pleased him; she pleased him very much. He untied the ribbons holding her stockings up and slowly rolled them down her long, lovely legs.

"John . . ." Her voice trailed off.

"John what?" he asked. Now it was his turn to tease. "John, please don't do this?" He rubbed his cheek against the smooth white skin of her belly. A tremor ran through her, and he smiled.

He drew his hands up along the back of her thigh, cupping her buttocks. "Or, John, don't do this?" Ever so slowly, he circled her navel with the tip of his tongue.

"That tickles," she whispered, in a breathy voice.

"It does?" He did it again, this time running his tongue up to the underside of her breasts.

Her knees started to shake and she went to wrap her hands around his head. His touch felt good, too good, like the most exquisite torture. But John wasn't finished with her yet.

He captured her arms and held them in place so that she could not stop him. "Or, John, don't do this?" He lowered his head to the dark triangle of hair between her thighs and nuzzled her gently.

"John, what are you doing . . ." Her words ended a moan as he touched her most sensitive spot with the tip of his tongue.

"You taste of the sweetest honey," he whispered. "And you are so wet, my love." He pressed his mouth closer.

"John! People don't do this—!" Her words ended on a soft cry.

Mallory couldn't stand on her own two feet any longer, but she found herself supported in his arms. He shocked her, amazed her. Her world began spinning in mindless wonder. She heard herself cry out his name over and over. He should stop! He had to stop, but she didn't want him to stop. She felt she was climbing a steep pinnacle, searching for something just out of reach. Then, just when she believed she might find it, John rolled her over onto the bed.

His lips came down to kiss hers and she tasted herself upon him. His tongue stroked her, imitating the movements he'd performed only seconds ago . . . and Mallory answered him with a strange, wild need building inside her.

Her fingers stroked and caressed the strong

muscles of his back. Her legs opened to him. She wanted to feel his weight upon her body—and she was reminded of a time seven years ago when they had been together like this.

Only this time, she would remember what had happened between them.

John pulled away, breaking free of her arms. "I need to finish undressing," he rasped, and it was only then that she realized he still wore his breeches.

She shivered in the night air. She watched his silhouette move in the darkness. One boot hit the floor with a thump, then another. First one button, then another and another was unfastened. John hooked his hands inside the tight doeskin and slid his breeches down his legs.

He stepped into the patch of moonlight and Mallory came up on one elbow, startled by her first sight of aroused male—and John was very aroused. In fact, no stallion in her father's stables had ever looked more ready.

Mallory started to have second thoughts.

Perhaps *she* wasn't quite ready for such an intimate relationship. She started to roll off the bed, but his hand caught her wrist.

They stared into each other's eyes for a long, intense moment. Neither moved. Neither spoke . . . but Mallory knew her thoughts were mirrored on her face—she wanted to stop. Now.

He spoke first. "*Don't* let it frighten you." He inched closer. "I'll stop if you want me to, but Mallory, please—it's the way things are supposed to be between a man and woman. Trust me, darling." He raised her wrist and placed a kiss on the tender pulse point. He nibbled his way up her arm, past the tender flesh in the crook and up her neck.

Her fear ebbed and pleasure returned.

His teeth nibbled on the lobe of her ear and she allowed him to press her back on the bed. His hand still on her wrist, he guided her hand to his erection.

How soft it felt! And hot, but also hard, like iron wrapped in velvet. Except this rod of iron had a life of its own! It quivered beneath her touch . . . but no longer frightened her. She ran one finger up and down the length of him and marveled at his response. "Can you feel this?"

Above her head, John groaned an answer.

She raised her eyes to his. "Is this like what you did to me? Is that how you feel?"

"And if I say yes?"

She slid a sly glance up at him, and then tightened her hold around his shaft.

"Now I've gone and done it," he said with an unsteady grin, even as his hand covered hers and started teaching her how to pleasure him. He kissed her as he did it, his tongue strokes mimicking the motion of her hand.

Mallory groaned against his lips.

She felt his hand move down her body toward the sensitive spot he'd discovered between her legs. With a shiver of anticipation, she attempted to shield herself, but his knee slid up between her legs and held her in place.

"Don't be afraid, love," he said in her ear, and lifting his body, settled himself between her legs.

John pressed against her, testing her. She was

slick and ready for him. He looked down at her beneath him. For a fleeting moment, he remembered another time, another place when they had been like this. But that night, she'd been frightened. Had he overcome her fears this time?

Her eyes appeared wide and luminous in the moonlight. "John?"

"Yes, love."

Her lips curved into a timid smile. "I do trust you."

He pressed her hands into the mattress on either side of her head. She looked at him with expectancy and yearning.

She was his woman.

His wife.

And after tonight, no other man would have her.

With fierce pride, he kissed her, demanding a response, and then, when he felt her lips move against his, when he felt her open to him, inviting him, he entered her with one smooth, probing thrust, tearing the thin protection of her maidenhead.

Mallory's body tensed. She strained up off the mattress. Her fingers clenched his. Any cry she might have made he silenced against his mouth.

John went still, giving her a chance to adjust to the sensation of him inside her. She was so damn tight. His body shook with the need to push forward into her. Sweat dampened his brow. He whispered, "It will be all right, Mallory. The rest will be pleasure. Trust me."

"I trust you." Her muscles gradually relaxed.

Steadily, carefully, John began to move inside

her. "This is the way, Mallory. Ah, you feel so good . . . you're so beautiful. Let yourself come with me . . ."

Her first hesitant movement in response sent his spirit soaring. "Yes, Mallory . . . come with me . . . come." Dear God, he could lose himself in her.

The pain and shock Mallory had felt at his entry subsided. She listened to his words of love and encouragement the way a pupil listens to a favorite teacher. His voice seemed to rumble deep through where they were joined, and it set off little radiating rings of desire.

This was how it was between a man and a woman. This was what she couldn't remember from her wedding night. His breathing was labored and shallow. She squeezed her legs against his sides and felt him groan as his next thrust took him deeper.

This was not mere animal copulation, as she'd been led to believe years ago. This was an act of joining, of becoming one, of uniting.

Mallory clung to him, finding herself again reaching for that elusive pinnacle that had teased her moments before. Only this time, they flew toward it together. John kept taking her higher and higher—and then she reached it, that place she'd never imagined existed. What she found changed her forever. Her body shuddered with her release and then, wave after unrelenting wave of pure, exquisite pleasure rolled through her. It vibrated outward from where their bodies were joined and carried her she knew not where, she cared not where. Her only thought was holding onto the man in her arms.

John heard her startled cry, felt her muscles contract and the warm rush flow through her. With one deep, hard thrust, he filled her with all he had to offer and found his own sweet oblivion.

Neither moved for what seemed like hours. Slowly, the world righted itself and they were brought back to reality.

John rolled over, bringing Mallory with him to lie on his chest. Her arms hung limply over his shoulder. He kissed the top of her head.

"Is it always like that?" she asked.

He hugged her close. "No, it's never been like that before," he answered. He pulled the sheets out from underneath and covered their nakedness.

Mallory started to roll off, but he held her place. He wanted her this close. Her heart beating against his chest matched his own. Running the tips of his fingers down her back, he whispered, "I love you."

She lifted her head to look into his eyes. "I love you, too."

In that moment, John knew his life was complete. Sated, loved, and happy, he fell asleep holding his beloved in his arms.

A pounding on the door woke him. He opened one eye, and then the other. The room was filled with the gray light of dawn. The woman next to him sighed and snuggled deeper under the covers.

Mallory.

John came up on one arm and looked down at her. She appeared more beautiful this morning than she had last night in his arms. He traced the pattern of freckles across her nose. Her nose twitched and she waved him away with her hand. She settled herself closer to him. Instantly aroused, John pressed himself against the curve of her bare bottom. He cupped her breast and bit her ear, teasing her awake.

The pounding on the door began again. John frowned. "Whoever you are, go to the devil!" he commanded, and rolled his sleepy wife over, ready to make satisfying love to her.

"Mr. Dawson!" Mrs. Irongate's voice shouted with authority. "You've overslept! It's almost time for church, and Lord Woodruff is waiting for the coach."

Mallory's brown eyes opened. Her movements still lazy, she rubbed the sleep from them and pushed back the thick hair spilling over her shoulder in a wanton mass. Her nipple hardened against his palm.

"Mr. Dawson!"

"Aye, I hear you, Mrs. Irongate," he answered, his gaze on Mallory, who gave him a sleepy smile. No practiced courtesan had ever seduced him so completely as his wife. "I'll bring the coach around in less than an hour." He leaned down and traced the curve of her ear with his tongue. Her heartbeat beneath his hand on her breast quickened.

Mrs. Irongate's face popped up in the open

window. "Less than *half* an hour," she corrected him. "You're already late."

"Mrs. Irongate, do you think you could give us a bit of privacy?" John snapped, pulling the covers higher.

The housekeeper's shrewd gaze took in the clothes scattered across the floor. "It appears, Mr. Dawson, that the two of you have had privacy enough. Now, up with you! There's no more time for Dickie Diddle. You can lie in bed all afternoon long if you wish, but for now, you'd best be getting the coach up to the house or be looking for a new position."

John made an irritated sound. "It's only shortly past dawn."

"It's halfway through the morning!" she corrected him. "Why else would Lord Woodruff have sent me down here?"

Now she had John's complete attention. He stared at the sky behind her and realized that what he'd thought was the soft light of early morning was actually leaden, overcast skies.

Convinced he now understood the gravity of the situation, the housekeeper said, "We'll see you up at the house in half an hour. And you too, Mrs. Dawson. Don't forget Lord Woodruff likes to see all his servants in church. Terrell usually hitches up the hay wagon for the rest of us." With those words, she marched off.

Mallory had come fully awake by now. She looked over her shoulder at him.

"Dickie Diddle?" he said, with a lift of an eyebrow.

A soft blush stained her cheeks. She looked so incredibly tempting, John decided to wish Lord Woodruff to the devil and pull her under the covers. After all, what did he care about another steward's position?

But Mallory stopped him. "John, we dare not make Lord Woodruff angry. We need his approval to host the harvest home. Everyone is expecting it to be here now. In fact, we should talk to him as soon as possible . . . and hopefully when he's in a good mood."

John studied her, weighing his priorities.

She placed a hand on his chest. "We *must* go."

With a grunt of dissatisfaction, he threw back the covers and bounded out of the bed. He was still fully aroused. Conscious that she was watching him, he gave her a small bow as he picked his breeches up off the floor. "It's my base nature—and the natural response to having such a lovely bed partner," he explained.

"Then we both have base natures," she admitted shyly, and he laughed. She started out of bed, and then grimaced.

"Mallory, did I hurt you?"

"I'm sore in places I didn't know existed. I didn't feel this way after our wedding night."

John climbed into his breeches, a niggling of guilt pulling at his conscience. "I'm sure it'll go away."

She took a few steps around the cottage. "The stiffness is already leaving," she said, but John wasn't listening.

Instead, he was mesmerized by his first sight of

his wife in the light of day. What a beauty he'd married and he silently thanked his father for arranging the match. Her legs were long and incredibly shapely, with slim, muscular thighs and trim calves. The rosy nipples of her breasts peeked out at him from the tangles of her hair.

With the shy expression of an innocent, she smiled at him, and John thought his heart would stop in his chest.

Here was the one woman who loved him for himself. He had no money. The fine houses, horses, and other trappings of power were gone. All that was left was the man.

She stroked his arm lightly. "I love you."

"You have my heart." He brought his lips down over hers, sealing his promise with a kiss.

Her surrender was as sweetly complete as it had been the night before. He would have laid her down upon the bed and taken her right then, except for Mrs. Irongate's sharp voice. "Mr. Dawson, hurry!"

John lifted his head. "Is the damn woman waiting for me outside the door?" he asked rhetorically. He placed a quick kiss on Mallory's nose. "Later, this afternoon," he promised. He slipped on his pants, pulled on his boots, and grabbing his shirt up off the floor, let himself out.

Mrs. Irongate was impatiently waiting for him on the path. "It's about time."

He waved her on, pulled his shirt over his head, and, whistling, headed to the barn to see if Terrell had thought to harness the coach and wagon.

John looked up at the overcast skies and

thought he'd never seen such a beautiful day. With any luck, it would rain and he *could* spend the afternoon making love to his wife.

Terrell did not have the coach hitched. John got him moving with a low growl and then hurried back to the cottage. He needed to shave and make himself presentable for church.

Rapping once on the door to let Mallory know he was coming in, he entered the cottage. "I've been thinking of how we should approach Lord Woodruff on the harvest home—" he started without preamble and stopped when he realized his wife was glaring at him with fire in her eyes. She was dressed and ready to go, her wild hair coaxed and tamed back into its proper braid, but her color was high and her fists were doubled so tight at her sides, she fairly shook with rage.

Alarmed that someone may have tried to hurt her, John rushed to her side. "Mallory, what's wrong? Has something happened?" He was her protector, her defender. No one would dare harm her while she was guarded by his love.

Words seemed to be choked in her throat. She backed away from him as if she abhorred the sight of him.

"Mallory?" He took a step toward her.

"Stop! Don't come near me." Hot, angry tears welled up in her eyes. It broke his heart to see them there.

"What is it? Tell me what's wrong and I'll make it right."

"Make it right?" she repeated, an edge of hysteria in her voice. "I trusted you. You told me you loved me, and I believed you."

"Mallory, what's wrong?"

"There, John." She pointed to the reddish-brown bloodstains on the top of the white coverlet. "There's what's wrong. Did you really believe I was so naive that I wouldn't realize I was a virgin when I saw those stains?"

Chapter 14

Cold blows the wind to my true love.

"Cold Blows the Wind"

John was faced with two choices: lie or admit the truth. There was the devil to pay either way.

So he decided to try and use a bit of each—the truth with a touch of a lie to make it palatable.

"Mallory, it's not what you think," he assured her, but she wasn't interested in being placated.

"I'm right, aren't I?" she demanded impatiently.

She didn't wait for his answer, but crossed her arms against her stomach as if she felt a sudden chill and started walking for the door. He stepped in her path. She turned and walked in the opposite direction, putting space between them.

By the hearth, she confronted him. "Did you or did you not consummate our marriage on our wedding night?"

"Let me explain—"

"You can answer yes or no. It's that simple—"

"No, it's *not* that simple," he ground out.

"You didn't," she said, accepting his refusal to answer for what it really was, an admission of guilt. She drew a deep breath, steadying herself, before saying, "But I saw the blood on the sheets myself. There was more blood than there is now. How did you manage that?"

He held up his thumb with the small scar on it. "It was my blood you saw. I cut my thumb with a pen knife."

She stared in fascinated horror at the scar. "Our marriage was never consummated. For the last seven years that I've spent *waiting* for you, I was never actually married in the eyes of the church or the law. I could have gotten an official annulment and accepted Hal's proposal with a free and clear conscience. I could have married another man and had children by now!"

He moved toward her. "Mallory, you're working yourself into hysterics over nothing. After all, the fact remains, we *are* married." He reached for her arm, wanting to draw her close and reassure her. "There's no harm in what happened between us last night."

"No harm?" She yanked her arm away and moved across the room from him. "You've *lied* to me. All this"—she waved her hand to encompass the cottage—"has fallen on my shoulders because of *my marriage* to you. I could have walked away from the fear of debtor's prison and the enormous debt and being chased through the streets of London like a common criminal. I could have had a home and a family—"

"And I'll give you those things," he swore, "if you will stay by me."

"Stay by you? A man who has so completely debased everything I believe in with his lies?"

He was across the room to her in two long strides. She started to turn away, but he captured her arms. She struggled against him, tossing her head and fighting to be free.

He forced her to look at him. "I love you."

For a second, he saw a softening in her eyes. Then she averted her face from him, the cut going directly to his heart. He struggled with the desire to shake sense into her.

"Do you remember what happened on our wedding night?" he demanded gruffly. "Beyond my walking into the room?"

Staring at the door, she refused to answer. An angry muscle worked in her jaw.

"Stop acting like Joan of Arc," he said. "I love you, Mallory. But that night and what happened afterward has been between us since we first met in London. Let's take it out in the open now . . . and whether you wish to admit it or not, I know the truth."

"What truth? That our whole marriage has been a deception?"

"All right, if that's the way you want it put! But who was deceiving whom? You don't remember anything of our wedding night. The wine you drank was drugged. You passed out in my arms before I could even touch you."

"Let go of me," she ordered coldly.

He did as she'd bidden him.

Mallory stepped back, rubbing the places on her arm where his hands had been.

"I didn't know the wine was drugged," she said at last.

"Did my father have a hand in it?"

She blinked in surprise. "Your father? No, my mother did it. She hadn't meant for me to drink so much, but I was nervous and exhausted. Papa's funeral had taken so much of my time and energy and then planning the wedding on such short notice right afterward—I was not myself, and she was worried about me. Her only purpose in drugging the wine was to relax me. It wasn't meant as an insult." She drew a deep breath. "But if you remembered it all, why didn't you tell me, John? Why have you let me live a lie for so long?"

"Because I believed that was what you wanted." He put his hands on his hips and stared out the window before saying, "If I had confessed that I hadn't consummated the marriage, or if that damn wedding sheet hadn't been stained, Father would have ordered me back from the military. I wasn't going to give up the only freedom I'd known in my life for a mere slip of a girl who was a complete stranger to me. Furthermore, Father had already threatened to throw you and your mother out of Craige Castle unless I went along with the marriage. He told me it was the only way you could save your home." He turned toward her. "And think what you will of me, Mallory, I'm not so cold-blooded that I would take a green girl while she's passed out unconscious!"

"That's not the point, John. You could have told me this story at any moment over our past week together. You could have told me last night!"

"What? And have you leave me?"

"I don't know," she replied candidly.

"There you have it," he said. "So I shall tell you now and beg your forgiveness. Mallory, I didn't consummate our marriage seven years ago, but I did so last night out of love for you. I've never loved a woman before . . . and last night was like no other time before it. You're my wife. I want us to build a marriage. I want to give you the home and family you dream of."

Tears pooled in her eyes. She looked away.

John waited, silently praying she would accept his proposal.

Her head bowed, and he knew she would not. She twisted his wedding ring from her finger. "I trusted you. Without trust, we don't have a marriage."

He took a step forward and stopped when she held up her hand, warning him not to come closer. "Don't say that, Mallory. Don't speak words without considering them thoroughly first."

With a small, sad smile, she shook her head. "You don't understand, do you? For seven years, I trusted you to do the right thing without love—and I paid a price. Last night, I trusted you with all my love . . . and I'm afraid the price is too high." She placed the ring on the table.

"Mallory—"

"No, John." She held up a hand, warding him back. "All I've ever asked from you was your honesty, and that turned out to be too much to give."

Anger flared inside him at the unfairness of her accusation. "And your precious Craige Castle," he reminded her bitterly.

"I don't have that, either, do I?" She walked to the door. She was about to open it when she looked over her shoulder to him. "Do you know, John, sometime between the chase from London and our living together here, Craige Castle ceased to be important. You'd taken its place in my heart. Now, I have nothing."

She opened the door and left the cottage.

Lord Woodruff was not happy to arrive late to church.

John and Mallory stood side by side in the pew behind Lord Woodruff's, along with the other household servants. Ruth, Evie, and Terrell sat in the back with their friends.

If she'd been asked, Mallory would not have been able to say what the reverend had said in his sermon or what readings were given. But she was deeply aware of her husband.

His large hands held the hymnal, and she was all too mindful of what those hands had done to her last night, of the soft moans they'd elicited, of the pleasure they had delivered.

She could barely stand beside him, feeling the heat of his body and smelling the clean scent of Mrs. Irongate's homemade shaving soap, without remembering how well the two of them had fitted together in bed. If she closed her eyes, she could recall the scents and textures of their lovemaking.

She warned herself not to think this way. First, he had abandoned her, and now he'd betrayed her trust in him. She repeated the warning over and over in her mind until it became a litany and wished she could ignore the burning lump in her throat.

Standing beside Mallory, John wished he could read her mind. She appeared so composed and self-possessed . . . while his world was falling apart. The wedding ring resting in his pocket felt as heavy as a millstone. . . .

He would get her damned castle back for her. He'd do whatever was necessary to prove she was wrong about him and make her regret she'd ever removed the ring from her finger.

The church service ended. Lord Woodruff hurried after the vicar to argue a point made during the sermon.

Both John and Mallory were relieved that he did.

No sooner, though, had his lordship left his pew than Freddie Hanson clapped John on the back and said heartily, "Grand time last night, grand time. By the way, why don't you and Mrs. Dawson join us for Sunday dinner? We can make our plans for the harvest home."

John said, "Yes—"

Just as Mallory said, "No."

Without looking at each other, John amended, "No, then," and Mallory agreed readily, "Yes, of course."

Confused, Freddie glanced from one to the other. Then, apparently deciding to choose his own answer, he smiled and said, "Very well, we'll see you both around two."

Actually, supper at the Hansons' was not such a bad idea, Mallory told herself. She and John had driven over in the pony cart in almost unbearable silence.

Well, that wasn't completely correct. He'd attempted conversation several times, but she hadn't answered. Her emotions were still too raw.

Fortunately, the two of them were seated several chairs away from each other at the dining room table with the Hanson children in between. The Reverend Luridge, the rector of St. Michael's Church, was also a guest. He was a tall, thin man with a bald head and gold-framed spectacles on the end of his nose.

Mallory had been surprised to find the vicar there. At Craige Castle, she'd always hosted the rector for the Sunday meal after the service. Apparently, Freddie Hanson, and not Lord Woodruff, assumed that role in Tunleah Mews.

Sylvie Hanson served a leg of mutton and the food was good and plentiful. Mallory noticed that John ate as if he'd never eaten before and managed to avoid answering any questions from the Hanson children about the harvest home.

"Mr. Dawson, I'm surprised to hear that Lord Woodruff has agreed to host the harvest home," the Reverend Luridge said. "In the past, he has not been at all interested in shire activities. My congratulations to you for bringing him in." He took a moment to put a pat of butter on a roll before adding, "I said something to him this morning after the service about how pleased I was to see him taking part in our parish life, but he was so anxious to discuss the particular passage in Luke that I used in the reading today, I don't believe he heard me. Either way, it is good to see him and his benefactor Tyndale more involved." He popped the roll in his mouth.

Mallory looked up the table at John, waiting for him to admit to the vicar and the Hansons that he hadn't secured Lord Woodruff's approval yet.

"Yes," Sylvie chimed in. "Everyone is excited about the harvest home. I don't ever remember an event spawning so much enthusiasm around Tunleah Mews."

"We're putting together a musical band," Freddie said, leaning forward in his chair. "A few fellows and I want to practice a bit before the harvest so we play better than we did last night. You'll join us, won't you?"

Everyone stopped eating and waited for John's answer—especially Mallory. Now was the moment when he should tell all. The Hansons and the Reverend Luridge would understand that approaching Lord Woodruff wasn't easy.

John looked around the table. He took his time before answering. Mallory watched as he smiled at the Hanson children, who listened to the adult conversation with avid interest.

This community had spirit, and it saddened Mallory to realize their spirits were being starved by the lack of leadership a good landowner could provide. But if ever there was a time to admit the truth, it was now. Mallory waited, expecting John to do the right thing.

She's just taken a sip of ale when John said, "Lord Woodruff is excited about the idea."

Mallory choked and had to cover her mouth with her napkin. Sylvie, who had been smiling at John, turned concerned eyes on Mallory. "Are you all right, Mrs. Dawson?"

Reverend Luridge began slapping Mallory firmly on the back. "Something went down the wrong way, eh?"

She held up her hand, begging for him to stop. "I'll . . . be . . . fine," she managed to get out, between the Reverend Luridge's assaults.

She lowered the napkin and glared meaningfully at John. "That's not entirely true about Lord Woodruff, is it, *Mr. Dawson?*" she prompted.

His lips stretched into a benign smile. "Oh, yes, thank you for reminding me, *Mrs. Dawson.* He also offered to supply the kegs of ale."

Hanson slapped his hand down on the table. "Well done!" He laughed with delight. "Who would have thought the old miser would turn out to be so generous? This will be a harvest home like none ever seen in this shire before, right, Reverend?"

The Reverend Luridge, all smiles, rubbed his hands together in anticipation. "You're right. What a good sign this is. If Lord Woodruff is willing to do all this, perhaps we can convince him to be the benefactor of some other parish works that need to be done."

"Such as what?" John asked, his expression one of complete sincerity and interest, enough to make Mallory want to pull out her hair and gnash her teeth like a madwoman!

"Our bell tower is in a sorry state of repair. One bell is cracked, and all of them need new ropes. I've requested several interviews with Lord Woodruff to discuss the matter, but he has unfortunately been busy with his writing."

"Yes, he's very busy with his book," John agreed sympathetically. "Perhaps I can discuss your request with him."

"Oh, would you?" the Reverend Luridge said, his eyes glowing with delight.

Mallory twisted the napkin in her lap into a knot to keep from shouting at her husband. Did the man have no shame?

The rest of the meal passed with Hanson and John making plans for the harvest home and the Reverend Luridge going on and on about his bells.

Mallory couldn't wait to get John alone.

It rained after the midday meal, delaying their departure by an hour or so. By the time they'd said their goodbyes, Mallory was more than ready for a confrontation.

She waited until the pony cart was out of sight of the Hansons' house before exploding with pent-up anger. "I can't believe you are *deceiving* these good people this way!"

His jaw tightened, but he kept his gaze on the mud puddles in the road. "Oh, you've decided to speak to me, hmmm?"

Mallory sat back on the bench, crossing both her arms and legs. "Is that what you were doing?" she asked, feigning enthusiasm. "Telling the Hansons and the Reverend Luridge patent untruths in order to get me to speak to you? How fortunate for you it worked!"

"You are jumping to conclusions. I will secure Lord Woodruff's approval for the harvest home."

"And just how are you going to do that, John? The same way you attempt to charm me—through deceit?"

He turned on her, his blue eyes bright with rising ire. "I *will* convince him to sponsor the harvest home."

She nodded and then checked items off on her fingers: "And provide all the ale, and contribute to the repairs on the bell tower . . . you're going to have a busy week, aren't you?"

"I'll pay for the ale. Peterson probably has the blunt now from the sale of the necklace. I could buy enough ale to keep this village befuddled with drink for a year—"

"Oh, that's a lovely thought," Mallory replied coolly.

"I can also put in the damn bells," he finished, through clenched teeth. He drove the cart over a rut in the road and into a deep puddle. Mallory's bottom bounced on the seat and she was forced to unfold her arms and hold the side. She thought he'd done it on purpose.

"It still doesn't give you the right to stretch the truth, John. You did it to me, and now I've witnessed you doing it to these good people."

"What would you have me do?" he said. "They're excited about the harvest. You heard them. Hanson told me there hasn't been so much goodwill and neighborliness since before Tyndale took over Cardiff Hall. I'll see that Woodruff sponsors the harvest home and that he does it gladly."

She came forward, leaning an arm on her knee. "Are you sure?"

"I'd stake my life on it. There, is that what you wanted?" His eyes bored into hers, and Mallory quite wisely decided to back down. They rode the rest of the way in silence.

A flock of ducks scattered out of their path as the cart pulled into the barnyard. Terrell and the others weren't around, since they had been given Sunday afternoon off.

Mallory didn't wait for John to come to a complete stop before she opened the cart door and hopped out. John jumped easily over the side, right into her path. Their eyes locked. She smiled grimly and whirled around, ready to march off to the cottage like a soldier, when a young man stepped out of the barn. His riding clothes were damp and mud-stained, as if he'd ridden through the summer shower earlier.

He removed his hat. "Lord Craige? I'm Roger Ambrose. Major Peterson sent me."

John glanced over his shoulders to ensure they weren't being watched. "Come, let us go in the barn."

Mallory, not about to be left out, followed the men.

They stopped in the middle of the barn. Roger gave John a letter. Breaking the seal, John moved over to the shaft of light coming in through the door and held the letter up to read. Mallory read over his shoulder.

Craige—

Richards sold the necklace and we've hired men to search for Louis Barron. You were right. He did pay the Runners to track you down and has offered a bounty on your capture. Your Mayfair place and other properties were auctioned off by the Bailiff last Wednesday to pay some of your debts. Richards and I started rumors that you and your wife have fled to Italy or Greece to escape your creditors and this is now the accepted truth among our social circle.

I have done as you asked and have men watching every shop Louis was known to patronize in hopes of learning his whereabouts. I also took the initiative of having men check all the ports. There is no record of his leaving the country. However, there is a record of three Runners leaving Dover for Italy. My source with Bow Street tells me they were paid very handsomely to track you down.

Be careful,
John

He'd underlined the word "careful" three times.

I'll send another message through Roger next Sunday. Don't trust the Post. I delivered Lady Craige's letter to her mother, who wished me to assure her daughter she will do as asked and seek a temporary home with a family friend in East Anglia. Her mother said Lady Craige would know the name. In the meantime, enjoy the carefree life of a farmer, don't let those pigs grow too fat, and here's a bit of the money we earned off the necklace to tide you over.

Peterson

Several crisp pound notes of different denominations were folded in with the letter. John held the notes up to Mallory. "Ale money." There was enough there to do as John had promised—keep the village of Tunleah Mews in drink for a year.

John rubbed his hand against the back of his neck. He turned. "Louis can't have just disappeared."

"Why not?" Mallory asked.

"You don't know him, Mallory. The man is . . . flamboyant. But he's also a creature of habits. He has a card game he plays in every Tuesday night, and he's done so for the last twenty years or more. He patronizes only one coffee shop. His clothes are made by the same tailor, no matter what the style. Even the snuff he uses is a special blend made by the same tobacconist ever since I can remember. For him to disappear . . . ?" He shook his head. "No, he's waiting. I can feel it in my bones. Once he's certain it's safe, he'll come back to London."

"Is there a message you wish to send to Major Peterson, my lord?" Roger asked respectfully.

John tucked the letter in his coat pocket. "Tell Peterson thank you for the good work and that I shall anticipate his next report Sunday."

"Wait, I have a request," Mallory said. The gentlemen turned to her. "Is it possible that Major Peterson could deliver a small note to my mother in East Anglia if I have it ready for you next week?"

"I'm certain he can," Roger answered. "Does he have her address?"

"She's staying with Squire Hal Thomas," Mallory said proudly, knowing full well that John would not like to hear this. "The Post will know how to deliver it."

John tensed at the mention of Hal's name. "I hope you didn't tell her our whereabouts."

Refusing to be cowed, Mallory met his gaze levelly. "I don't plan on it."

"I have another message for Peterson," John said. "Have him send some of the money from the diamonds to Mallory's mother. I want her taken care of."

"Yes, my lord," Roger said. He cast an uncertain glance in first Mallory's direction, then John's. "Is there anything else?"

"No, nothing," John answered, and waved him on. Roger bowed and went to fetch his horse, tethered in one of the stalls. He led it out of the barn, mounted, and rode off across a meadow.

John stood silhouetted in the barn door, his feet spread wide apart. He watched Roger leave, his expression unreadable. When the messenger was out of sight, he brought the pony and cart into the barn.

Watching him unhitch the pony and comb it down, Mallory allowed herself for the first time to contemplate the unthinkable. *What if they were forced to leave the country?* What would happen to her mother?

Tears came unbidden to her eyes.

John turned and saw them. The harsh lines of his face softened. "Mallory, don't worry."

"I'm not," she denied, and pressed a hand against her burning cheeks.

"I'll find Louis—I promise."

"Yes, like all the *other* promises you've made." The words flew out of her before she could stop them.

John went very still. His eyes glittered. Mallory stepped back, suddenly wary—but she was too late.

His hand shot out and he grabbed her by the wrist. "Come." He half-dragged her out of the barn and toward the house.

Mallory twisted her arm, trying to break his hold. Her feet were forced to move at double time to keep up. "Where are we going?"

"To see Lord Woodruff." He stopped and pulled her up to him. "I'm going to prove to you that I do keep my promises."

"All right," she said brightly. "Let's go."

He made a low growl in his throat, but Mallory wasn't intimidated. She was good and angry, too. It became a race to see which one of them arrived at the servants' entrance first.

Mallory nearly won.

"Mrs. Irongate," John said, his voice one of authority as they entered the kitchen. "We need to see Lord Woodruff."

Mrs. Irongate and Mrs. Watkins looked up from their dinners of beef and cabbage. Mrs. Irongate pushed her overlarge mob cap back up her forehead. "I'm sorry, Mr. Dawson, but Lord Woodruff is eating his supper now. This would not be a good time to pay a call on him."

John slapped the table with such force that the plates, silverware, and ladies all jumped. "All the better."

"I beg your pardon?" Mrs. Irongate said.

John leaned toward her. "Ladies, you see before you a man who is like Jason, leader of the Argonauts."

"Argo—who?" Mrs. Watkins asked.

John gave her a secret, sly smile that Mallory knew first-hand could make a woman do anything he wanted. "A hero, Mrs. Watkins. A warrior." He faced the kitchen door. "Now, go announce me to Lord Woodruff."

Mrs. Irongate put down her napkin. "He's serious about this," she said to Mallory. "Bloody serious."

Mallory shrugged. "He's looking for the Golden Fleece."

"Fleece?" Mrs. Watkins asked.

"It's a long story," Mallory assured her.

"Mrs. Irongate . . ." John prodded.

"Very well," the housekeeper said. She set down her fork. "But Lord Woodruff isn't going to like this." She bustled out of the kitchen. John and Mallory followed her through the dining room and into the foyer.

Mallory was starting to have doubts, but John appeared supremely confident. She tugged on the arm he still held by the wrist and whispered, "Perhaps we should wait. After all, the point is not to make him angry. We need him to agree with us."

John cast her an irritated glance. "Getting cold feet?"

"I'm just trying to be wise."

"We're calling on him now," was his resolute reply.

They stopped in front of the door to Lord Woodruff's study. From inside the room, they could hear muttering. Unconcerned, Mrs. Irongate rapped twice.

Lord Woodruff shouted what sounded like, *"Whozzztha!"*

Mrs. Irongate looked over her shoulder at them. "He talks with his mouth full. It is so disgusting. Please wait here." She opened the door and went in.

A moment later, John and Mallory heard Lord Woodruff clearly and distinctly yell, "I don't want to see him!" followed by Mrs. Irongate's well-modulated tone.

Lord Woodruff raised his voice again, but to their surprise, Mrs. Irongate cut him off.

A moment later, she opened the door. "Lord Woodruff will see you now."

Chapter 15

O keep your gold and silver too,
And take it where you're going;
For there is many a rogue and scamp like you,
Has brought young girls to ruin.

"Mowing the Barley"

John had three impossible tasks before him. The first was to win Lord Woodruff's approval for the harvest home. The second was to recover his reputation and the fortune he had carelessly managed. And the last was to earn Mallory's trust and the love he valued above all else.

He entered Lord Woodruff's study ready to accomplish the first task.

Books were once again strewn everywhere around Lord Woodruff's desk, and balls of paper littered the floor. At one side of the room, small stacks of paper had been laid out in rows.

The room could use a good airing, and since the sun had finally decided to shine, sunlight glared off the streaks of dirt covering the windowpanes behind Lord Woodruff's desk. He sat at the desk eating, both elbows on the surface, spearing pieces of cabbage off his plate with a three-pronged fork.

On his head was a green fez, the hat favored by Mediterranean men, with a purple tassel. His hair stuck out in all directions beneath it. Since returning home from church, he'd removed his coat and neck cloth and now sat in a gold brocade dressing robe worn over his shirt. This is how Beelzebub would look, John decided irreverently, and his determination to win this man's sponsorship of the harvest for the good people of Tunleah Mews increased tenfold.

The question was, of course, how to do it.

"Well, what is it?" Lord Woodruff barked. "Have you come to apologize again for making me late for church? I hope you've not come to berate me again for not paying wages. I'm up to date and owe no one!" His beady, black eyes glared at them from under his bushy brows. He didn't wait for John to answer but snapped, "Speak up, damn you, I'm busy."

"I realize that, my lord," John answered, his smile forced.

"If you realize it, why are you here bothering me?"

John struggled with a very strong desire to rub the rude, ill-mannered oaf's face in his plate of cabbage.

And then he felt Mallory's touch. She stood a half-step back, by his side, as would any good country wife, but her hand lightly touched his. He curled his fingers, capturing hers. She gave his hand a reassuring squeeze in return.

"I'm here to see if there's something I can do for you, my lord," John said confidently.

"Do for me?" Lord Woodruff repeated. He made a circling motion with his fork toward all the books stacked on his desk. "Can you finish the verse that eludes me? Hmmmmm? Here I am, on the verge of the most original, brilliant work of my life, and I can't find the words! Can you help me with that?"

Without waiting for an answer he pointed at the stacks of papers on the floor. "Or can you help me with these blasted reports that Tyndale's cursed land agent keeps sending me? Some go back more than five years. Tyndale has ordered me to fill them out or find new quarters. Can't he respect the fact that I am a poet? I'm not a farmer. I don't want to be a farmer."

He pushed back from the desk and stomped over to the table holding a selection of decanters. As he poured a healthy draught of claret, the mouth of the decanter rattled against the glass. "I hate the interruptions that go with farming. And details. All day long, I am forced to think about details, rents, crops, yields, and whatever elses." He drained his glass.

John knew in a flash what he was going to do. Lord Woodruff was no different than any number of complacent, self-centered generals he'd known during the war. These men sat far from the front lines, complaining of hardship, while their men died on the battlefields. John had learned early in his career the trick of maneuvering these senior officers into believing his ideas were their ideas.

The first step was to get the man in a good frame of mind.

"I can help with the reports, my lord."

"You can?" Lord Woodruff asked, looking at him over the rim of his glass.

"Of course, that is what a steward is for."

Lord Woodruff lowered the glass. "Yes, of course." He drew the words out thoughtfully. "That *is* what a steward is for." He slammed his glass down on the table and strode purposefully back toward his desk. With a flip of his dressing robe behind him, he sat in the chair. "Dawson, I want you to complete all those reports on the floor before the end of the month." He sat back in his chair. "There. Now all I have to do is collect the rents and Tyndale will be pleased with me and leave me alone."

"But you *have* collected the rents, my lord," John said.

"I have?"

"Yes, sir. You asked *me* to collect them."

"I did that?"

"Two days ago, my lord," Mallory said, speaking for the first time. "You asked me to take the rent ledger to my husband."

"I did that, did I?" Woodruff's eyebrows shot up in surprise. "And you collected the rents?" he asked John.

"Yes, sir. Most of the tenants will pay next week, if they are able."

"What of those who are not able?"

"They will pay after the harvest, in two weeks' time."

Lord Woodruff steepled his fingers in front of him. "This is good, very good." He spoke more to himself than to John and Mallory. "Tyndale will be pleased and will leave me alone."

"I was also going to suggest," John started and then stopped. He shook his head. "No, I shouldn't. It would be an insult to someone of your talent, my lord. I beg that you excuse me. Come, Mallory, we must not waste any more of Lord Woodruff's time while the light is still good for writing."

He'd taken two steps toward the door before Woodruff's voice stopped him.

"I say, what do you have in mind, Dawson?"

"I hesitate even to suggest it, my lord."

Lord Woodruff waved him forward. "By all means, suggest it."

John paused a moment before saying humbly, "I think there is something poetic about an English harvest."

A rude snort erupted from Lord Woodruff. "What's poetic about *work?*"

"Nothing," John hastened to agree. "But there is something special about the smell of freshly cut sheaves of golden grain standing out in the summer sun to dry." He drew a deep breath as if he were smelling the sheaves.

Lord Woodruff's nostrils flared as he took a sniff, too.

"And have you ever seen the harvesters at work?" John asked.

Lord Woodruff shook his head, his eyebrows coming together with interest.

John took a step toward him, drawing from his memory of what Mallory had told him during their picnic and embellishing it. "Did you ever notice that the fields are never so crowded as they are at harvest time, Lord Woodruff? They're full of all sorts of people. First come the reapers, reaping hooks in hand." He doubled up his fist and swung an imaginary reaping hook through the air. "They cut in wide rows, sir, and as a man cuts, he folds the stalks under his arms until a sheaf is gathered and then lays it upon the ground."

Lord Woodruff's gaze dropped to the floor as if he could see the sheaf.

"Then the women and children come through," John said. "They bind the sheaves and stand them up to dry. By midday, when the men and women break for their lunch, the field is dotted with sheaves of grain drying in the sun. It's a wonderful sight."

Lord Woodruff shuddered. "I've seen the cut fields, but I've never considered them a wonderful sight."

"Ah, but sir, use your imagination." John edged even closer to the man's desk. "The harvest is the very essence of English life. I've seen many a picture painted of the harvesters, but I've never read a poem that captured it."

He had Lord Woodruff's full attention now: he could tell by the shine in the man's beady eyes. John frowned thoughtfully. "It's almost as if no writer is capable of using the King's English to document the joy of the harvest."

Lord Woodruff stroked his chin. "Do you read many poems, Dawson?"

"I've read the ones I was taught in school," John answered with sudden humility. He nodded to the shelves of books against the wall. "Of course, I am not as widely read as you, my lord."

"I've read a poem or two concerning the harvest," Lord Woodruff said, "but nothing on an epic scale."

"Yes, an epic! What a brilliant idea, Lord Woodruff."

"Idea? What idea?"

"To write an epic poem on the harvest. Publishers will be lining up for the privilege of printing such a manuscript."

Lord Woodruff sat back in his chair. For a second he looked off into space, and then muttered to himself, "Yes, it might interest a publisher, mightn't it?"

"Of course it would, sir," John agreed readily. "The public is tired of poems about fables and myths, and they already know enough about heaven and hell to frighten them for an eternity. What would interest the public is something fresh and original. Something charming, like the simple pleasure of the harvest home."

"Harvest home? What is that?" Lord Woodruff said, sitting straighter.

"It's the celebration of the harvest, my lord, a tradition as old as time."

"Never heard of it."

"I'm surprised. After the workers are finished

with the harvest, they hold a great feast with music and dance to rival the pagan ceremonies of old." John stood beside the desk now and used several books to illustrate the placement of what he envisioned for the harvest home. "We'd hold ours in Cardiff Hall's barn, just as they did years and years ago."

"In our barn here?"

"Aye, sir. The musicians will sit here." John used smaller books to show the various areas. "The food and drink will, of course, be set up out in the barnyard. Only dancing will take place inside."

Lord Woodruff reached across the desk and moved one of the small books. "I think it would be better if we kept the food inside and had the dancing outside."

John mulled over his suggestion. "Why can we not have both the food and the dancing inside? After all, the barn is large enough, once we remove the coach and wagons. We can set up the ale keg here." He moved an ink bottle to the "barnyard."

Lord Woodruff considered the ink bottle and nodded.

"Very good, sir," John said. "We shall do it your way." He took a step back. "Now, with your permission, I'll go ahead and make arrangements."

"Arrangements?"

"You want to know the details, don't you, sir?" John said, deliberately misunderstanding Lord Woodruff's question. He turned to Mallory, who watched in wide-eyed wonder, and asked, in the brusque, good humor of a country man, "What do you say, Mrs. Dawson? What shall we feed the people, and how many kegs of ale shall we order?"

Mallory blinked, startled not only to be included in their conversation, but by the whole turn of events. How had John done it? Lord Woodruff waited in anticipation of her answer. She thought quickly. "I believe it would be best, ahmmm, to roast a full pig and a lamb."

John looked down at Lord Woodruff for his opinion. His lordship gave a small shrug. "It sounds fine to me."

With more confidence, she continued. "We should have at least. . . ." She paused and mentally counted the number of guests who had been in attendance at the Hansons' last night and doubled it. "Two large kegs of ale should do. As for side dishes, the women in the parish will prepare those."

"Well, there you have it, Lord Woodruff," John said cheerily. "My wife and I will carry out all your plans. It's as good as done."

Lord Woodruff appeared slightly befuddled by the swift turn of events—but he didn't argue. "Very well. We'll hold the harvest tomorrow, eh?"

"Tomorrow?" John questioned.

"I want to get started. I'm ready to write!"

"I'm sorry, my lord, but the harvest won't be ready for another week, maybe two." John shot a glance at Mallory for verification.

She nodded and added, "And we must arrange for the harvest crew."

"Two weeks?" Lord Woodruff frowned in disappointment. "I'm ready to write now. What shall I do in the meantime?"

John looked over the stack of books on the desk. "Research?"

Lord Woodruff's eyes came alight with purpose. "Ah, yes. Research." He clapped his hands together. "Dawson, organize it all. Spare no expense, and make it a true English harvest. I'm going to immortalize it!"

"Yes, sir. Thank you, sir," John said, taking Mallory's arm and backing toward the door. "We'll make it the best harvest ever."

Lord Woodruff actually tried to smile. "You do that. Now, hurry off with you. I have my research to see to."

John turned the handle of the door and they would have slipped out of the man's presence except that Lord Woodruff called them back. "Dawson, aren't you forgetting something?"

John stopped. "No, my lord, I don't think I am."

"The reports," Lord Woodruff said. He'd picked up his fork to resume his meal and pointed it toward the papers stacked on the floor. "Tyndale's land agent wants them by the first of next month. We should also include any information on this new harvest."

John and Mallory exchanged glances, then suppressed smiles of relief. They hurried across the study and picked up the stacks of papers. Bowing and scraping like the most faithful of servants, they left Lord Woodruff at his desk, running his finger down the page of a reference book while munching on cabbage.

Once outside Cardiff Hall, they burst out laughing. Mallory shifted the heavy stack of reports in her arms. "You have the skill of an actor on the stage," she declared to John.

"No, my persuasive skills come from years of working with senior officers."

"I've never seen the like," she said. They'd reached the barnyard. A hen scurried out of their path and the last golden light of the day stretched long shadows over the yard. "When he asked you what he should do until the harvest and you said research, I could barely keep from laughing out loud. John, you were brilliant."

"Thank you, my lady," he said. "And, if you noticed, I managed to get him to agree to buying the kegs."

"Yes, I did notice, and I thought that was the smoothest trick of all!"

John laughed, and balancing his stack of papers in one arm, he threw his other around her shoulders.

Mallory let it rest there. She was in far too good humor to want to fight with him. "What are you going to do about these reports?"

"I think I'll ask Freddie Hanson to help. He's the only man I've met who will have the answers Tyndale is looking for."

"You're right," Mallory conceded. They walked a few yards further down the path in silence. The closer they came to the cottage, the heavier John's arm on her shoulder felt. At last she could endure it no longer and shrugged him off.

John knew the glow of camaraderie they'd experienced earlier was fading with each step.

For a moment he weighed the idea of offering to take the reports over to Hanson this evening and giving her a chance to be alone, but then he changed his mind. He was determined to win her back. He'd lay siege to her heart, if he had to. He wasn't going to give up, and he wasn't going to make it convenient for her to ignore him.

He placed his arm back around her shoulder and didn't remove it until they arrived at the cottage door. Inside, he set the reports on the table. He held out his hands for the reports Mallory was holding. She'd grown very quiet and seemed to be staring at the coverlet and the faint damning stains. John cursed himself for not thinking ahead and burning the cover before bringing her back to the cottage.

"Mallory, let me have the papers."

She passed them to him, going to a bit of trouble not to touch him.

He stacked the reports neatly while wondering what his next step should be.

"Why don't I cook our supper?" he said, pretending nothing was wrong. He crossed to the hearth, took kindling from the basket, and started arranging a fire.

"I'm not very hungry," Mallory answered.

"Well, I am," he said, with forced cheerfulness. "I could eat a leg of lamb myself."

Mallory didn't answer.

He glanced at her over her shoulder as he reached for the tinder box on the mantel, and then froze. She was pulling the coverlet off the bed. "What are you doing?"

She didn't look at him. "I need to wash this."

"Now? Mallory, it will be dark in another hour. You won't be able to see what you're doing."

She ignored him, gathering the thin white coverlet in her arms. Then, picking up the wooden bucket and a bar of soap, she left the cottage.

John swore softly under his breath and followed her out the door.

Down at the bathing pond, Mallory knelt and began scrubbing at the stains. John came up quietly behind her. "Can I help?"

She didn't answer him or acknowledge his presence.

Placing his heels right beside her, he stretched out on the grassy bank. "I think we should have a truce between us," he said.

Her hands stopped moving and her brows came together. "We already have a truce, remember, John? The bargain we made that you would grant me a divorce if I helped you recover your fortune?"

John felt like a squirming schoolboy when she talked to him in that tone of voice. Why was he married to the one woman with the uncanny ability to make him feel like a complete ass? And she'd done it twice in one day!

Lay siege, he reminded himself.

As she returned to her wash, John cast about for a safe topic of conversation.

"I've been thinking about Uncle Louis," he said, deciding this was one thing she wouldn't ignore. He was right. At the mention of Louis's name, her hands paused a moment in their furious scrubbing.

John continued. "I've been searching my memory for other facts and tidbits of information about him. I didn't see him regularly, even after I returned from the war. The last time I saw him before the war was at our wedding. I remember him being quite taken with Craige Castle. Are there any pieces of information you can remember from your dealings with him?"

As he talked, she picked up a rock and began pounding at the coverlet. The stains were no longer visible to John's eye, yet she pounded and pounded and pounded as if she were attempting to purge herself of something more significant.

John captured her fist around the rock. "Mallory, don't do this. Please forgive me."

She bowed her head, staring at his hand over hers.

John spoke from his heart. "I should have told you the truth about our wedding night. I didn't realize you'd given up your own wishes and dreams to be a wife to me. I didn't think of it that way, Mallory. I only thought of my own selfish desire to make us one . . . and we are one now. No matter how hard you try to pretend it's not true, you know in your heart that we are destined to be together."

He wished she would turn to him so he could see her face. He needed to know if there was some softening in her attitude toward him. Then he felt a single, hot tear land on his hand.

Hope sprang up inside him. She could forgive him. He knew it . . . and then she pulled her hand from his and started pounding away at the cover again.

John sat back. He cursed the fates that he had married such a stubborn, willful woman—but he would have it no other way. Whether she admitted it or not, the armor she wore against him had chinks, and he vowed to work away at those places until she completely opened her heart to him.

Suddenly, she threw the rock to the side with vehemence and broke down in quiet sobbing. He moved to take her in his arms.

Mallory jerked away and came to her feet. She didn't look at him. "I can't let you close, don't you see? I'm the most foolish of all women. I've fallen in love with a man who has betrayed me over and over again."

John rose from the bank. "Mallory, I promise it will never happen again—"

"It has already happened two times too many," she said, whirling on him. "If I let myself believe in you one more time and you use me again, you will destroy me. You're too fickle to trust. It's always what *you* want or what *you* think. I had no role in your life until you decided *you* were ready. Well, what about me? I have to consider my needs now, John, and I can't let you hurt me. Not again."

She lifted her skirts and ran from the pond.

John watched her leave. He'd caused her this pain, and it tore at his very soul. Yet didn't her intense emotion mean that she cared . . . even a little?

He looked down at the cover lying in the water. The first stars of the evening were coming out and he could see no stains. He picked up the coverlet, washed off the mud from where she'd thrown it down, and spread it over the bushes to dry.

Filling the pail with water for the next day, he took it and the slippery bar of soap back to the cottage.

Mallory had left the door open for him and John considered that a very good sign. He told himself it meant that she truly didn't know her own mind anymore . . . that she was weakening.

Resolved not to give up, he marched forward. The inside of the cottage was shadowy and silent. No candle had been lit, and he didn't see Mallory immediately until his gaze turned to the bed. She lay there with the sheets practically pulled up over her head.

"Mallory?"

"I left the door open so you could get what you need to eat or whatever," came her curt voice. She didn't turn over to face him. "I expect you to sleep in the barn."

John closed the door, set the pail down by the door, and placed the bar of soap on the table. His desire to make amends battled with his irritation at her high-handed treatment. He crossed over to the bed. All he could see of her was the top of her toffee-colored hair and the tip of her obstinate little nose. Even though her eyes were closed, feigning sleep, he suspected she was every bit as aware of him as he was of her.

Lay siege. He was her husband, not some lackey. If he wanted to win her back, he could not allow her to subject him to her whims.

He removed his jacket and hung it over the

back of a chair. Returning to the bed, he began removing his shirt, watching her all the while. She didn't stir as he folded it and laid it neatly at the foot of the bed.

He sat down on the bed and began removing his boots. She didn't rouse. He deliberately dropped the boot on the floor.

She flinched.

John smiled. He bent over and pulled off his other boot. He dropped this one on the floor also—but she didn't respond.

That was fine. He knew he had her attention. Pulling off his socks, he threw them down by his boots, stood, and facing her, began unbuttoning his breeches.

First one button, then the second, and he'd started the third when she threw back the sheets and sat up. She wasn't ready for bed at all but still wore her brown cambric dress. "What do you think you're doing?"

"I'm going to bed with my wife." He flicked open the third button.

"Oh, no, you're not!"

"Oh, yes, I am." John pulled down his breeches, unashamed to let her see he was fully aroused and ready for her. He wanted her even now, when she was so angry she was practically spitting with fury.

Mallory scooted closer to the wall on the other side of the bed. "Leave me alone."

But John wasn't going to relent. He couldn't, if he wanted to win her back. He placed his knee on the mattress. "I'm your husband," he said quietly. "I love you. Your place is beside me on this bed."

Mallory scrambled off the mattress. She pushed down her tangled skirts and confronted him. "Never!"

Sitting on the bed, John shook his head. "So dramatic. . . ." He patted the spot next to him. "Now, come to bed, Mallory, and let us set aside our differences for one night. I promise I won't bother you."

She cast a doubtful glance at his already aroused state and crossed her arms. "Now, let me see," she said, angrily tapping one foot. "You expect me to believe that I can spend the night lying next to the most infamous rake in England and not expect him to attempt to seduce me?"

John held his hands up in the air to show her he meant no tricks. "I want only to hold you."

"I'm not that green, John . . . not anymore."

"Very well, we shall not sleep together." He bounced back on the bed and grabbed the sheets to cover his nakedness. "However, *I* am not going to be the one spending another night in the barn. It's your choice, Mallory. You can either join me in bed, sleep on the floor, or toddle off to the barn." Placing his hands behind his head, he stared up at the rafters. His ultimatum was a stroke of genius, and he considered for a moment that winning his wife was like a game of chess . . . and he had just said "checkmate."

He knew Mallory was glaring at him. Her body was radiating heat, she was so angry. But her voice was that of a true aristocrat—cool, calm, and slightly superior. "I shall take the barn, because it is the place furthermost from you."

John gritted his teeth. He didn't want her to

leave. His impulse was either to rise from the bed, grab hold of her and kiss her until she mindlessly confessed that she was madly in love with him . . . or relent and go to the barn himself, letting her have the bed.

He refused to do the latter. He was a man, not a lap dog. He heard the door open. His whole body tensed as he willed himself to stay where he was.

She paused in the doorway. So attuned was he to this woman, he could sense her presence. He heard her take a step out the door and then stop.

Closing his eyes, John wished her to return to the bed—and then she started walking toward him. Her kid slippers were almost soundless as they crossed the hard dirt floor.

Relief ran through him. She was backing down.

He turned to her, ready to make amends and forgive her, when a pailful of cold water splashed right in his face.

Mallory threw the bucket aside and it clattered into the corner. "I hope you enjoy your sleep," she hissed, before storming out of the cottage.

John sat up in the now soaking bed. He wiped his face, chest, and stomach with the already wet sheet. "Siege," he reminded himself as he set his feet on the ground, pulled on his breeches, and chased after his wife.

Chapter 16

Young women they'll run like
hares on a mountain,
If I were a young man,
I'd soon go a hunting,
To my right fol diddle dee.
Young women they'll sing like
birds in the bushes,
If I were a young man,
I'd go bang those bushes,
To my right fol diddle dee.

"Hares on the Mountains"

Mallory ran up to the barn, fearing John might be angry enough to follow her. Perhaps dousing him with the bucket of water hadn't been a prudent action, but oh, she had enjoyed seeing him all wet. Nor would she apologize. Ever.

When she reached the barn, she attempted to close the door, but the hinges were rusty and wouldn't work. She abandoned that idea and ran down the row of stalls to the first one that was empty. She threw herself down on a clean bed of hay.

The swaybacked coach horses were in the stalls on either side. They both nickered a greeting. She shushed them to be quiet.

At that moment, a shadow crossed the barn door. Mallory held her breath.

She strained her ears, listening for movement, but didn't hear anything until he stood in the stall's open entrance. He was wearing his breeches, a damp scowl, and little else. "Here you are."

Mallory sat up, her heart in her throat. "I thought you were going to sleep in the bed."

"It's wet."

"I don't want you here."

"I'm aware of that." He turned and walked away.

Mallory felt a small glimmer of surprise that he would give in so easily.

The next moment, he was back carrying the horse blanket they'd used for their picnic. "Here, lie on this. It will make the hay more comfortable."

He flapped it up in the air and let it drift down to cover the hay.

Warily, Mallory did as he'd suggested. Hay was not as comfortable to lie on as she'd imagined it would be. "Where are you going to sleep?"

"Right here beside you."

Mallory struggled to get up, but John had knelt beside her and placed his hand on her shoulder to keep her in place. "You can leave, Mallory, but it won't make a difference. I'll follow wherever you go. I will sleep beside you tonight."

"And I was told chivalry was dead," she answered, her voice dripping with sarcasm.

John pressed his lips together in a poor attempt to hide a smile.

"I don't want you in my bed." She bit each word out.

"I'm not here to make love to you—"

"Oh, is that why you got yourself naked and ready?"

He grinned at her and Mallory wanted to wipe the grin off his face with her nails. How *dared* he laugh at her when everything inside her was confused and jumbled?

"Mallory, I won't deny I want you . . . although the bucket of water in my face dampened my ardor some." He sat down on the straw, leaving the blanket to her. "But my reaction to you is the natural reaction for a man when he's around the woman he loves."

She clutched handfuls of the blanket, telling herself not to believe him. Last night he had initiated her into passion, and apparently she was a very good student because even now, when she was so dreadfully angry with him, she'd like nothing better than to melt into his embrace.

She hid behind sarcasm. "Oh, John, please. Men are capricious characters. I've been made to understand that they feel an attraction like *that* for every woman who passes in front of them."

He pinned her with his gaze, his expression open and honest. "Mallory, I'm not a rutting animal. I've always had control over myself except when I was around you. I've been this way ever since I saw you standing by the pond with your gorgeous hair down."

"The pond?" she said doubtfully. "You mean the day Ruth was plastered naked against your body?"

His teeth flashed white in the darkness. "Your jealousy gives me hope."

"I'm not jealous. I'm merely pointing out your fickle nature."

He leaned on one elbow. "I'm *not* fickle. I felt nothing for Ruth or any of the others. I love you."

Mallory covered her ears with her hands. "I don't want to hear this. Stop saying it."

Reaching up, he pulled down her hand. "I won't stop saying it, not ever."

"Yes? Well, you'll never be my ideal of a husband."

"That's because I don't know what your ideal is!" John pulled her down on the blanket and on her side to face him. He didn't let go of her hand. "Teach me, Mallory. Talk to me. I've never been a husband. I've only known one married couple who seemed happy in their marriage and that was Peterson and his wife, Liana. It seemed to me the difference between them and other couples, including my parents, was that they considered themselves partners, and Peterson never did anything without talking it over with his wife first. We used to tease him about it. Of course, Liana had a Latin temper. I certainly never wanted to make her angry. But I'm not afraid to face you."

He gave her a gentle squeeze. "I'm laying siege, Mallory, and I won't give up until I win your heart."

"Siege?"

"Yes, siege. It's what we did in the army to capture a city behind high walls. We would camp right next to the city and wait. We wouldn't give up until those walls came down." He leaned toward her until they were almost nose to nose. "I'm not giving up, Mallory, not until I've torn down every wall between us."

In spite of her anger with him, she felt a small trill of excitement at his words. Did he really care so much that he would never give up? *Test him and see,* a small voice said inside her. *Wait and watch.*

"I don't care where you sleep," she said. A fleeting expression that looked like disappointment appeared in his eyes and then vanished. She must have imagined it in the dark. She turned over to her side and surprised herself by falling almost immediately asleep.

John woke her up shortly around dawn, before Terrell and the dairy maids arrived for work. He was already dressed for the day. The cuffs on his fine lawn shirt were frayed beyond repair, and Mallory couldn't help but remember how fashionable he'd appeared that night at Lady Ramsgate's party.

While she was tending to her toilet by the stream beside the cottage, he prepared her tea and hauled fresh water from the bathing pond. She couldn't stop herself from admitting drolly, "I could grow used to being under siege."

He answered with a quick laugh and carried the wet mattress out in the sun to dry.

John headed up to the barn to set the others to work. He surprised Mallory by returning later that morning. She was kneading bread dough when he poked his head in the door.

"I've just learned that Tuesday is market day in Horsham," he said. "Is that where we'll find harvesting crews?"

"Yes, or hear word of who is in the area."

"Good," John said with a smile. "You and I will go to Horsham tomorrow." He didn't wait for an answer but dropped a light kiss on her forehead and disappeared out the door.

Mallory watched him go, a bemused smile on her face. Her whole day seemed suddenly brighter because he had taken the time out to pay a surprise visit. The terrible anger she'd felt against him yesterday morning had abated somewhat.

She'd just set the bread to bake when she had another visitor, Mrs. Irongate. Mallory offered her a cup of tea.

"I say, Mrs. Dawson," the housekeeper said, after they'd talked about several mundane subjects, "is that your bed mattress out in the yard?"

"Yes, it is." Mallory suppressed a smile. Now she understood what had lured the curious housekeeper to the cottage that morning. Mallory knew the other servants must be whispering about the mattress but was sure none would have the courage to ask John.

"Why is it out there?" Mrs. Irongate asked.

"Because it is wet."

Mrs. Irongate's lips formed "oh." "Is there a

leak in the roof? Did the mattress get wet in yesterday's rain?"

"Oh, no," Mallory assured her. She paused, looking over the brim of her cup before some mischievous imp urged her to say, "It got damp because I threw a bucket of water on my husband, who was sitting on the mattress at the time."

Mrs. Irongate's eyes opened as wide as an owl's. "You don't say. Did he deserve the bucket of water?"

"I thought so then."

The housekeeper burst out laughing and slapped her knee. "Oh, this is rich; this is rich, indeed. Wait until I tell the others."

Mallory set down her cup. "Please, Mrs. Irongate, I don't think you should bandy it about—"

"How could I not, Mrs. Dawson? It's so seldom we poor women get the last laugh on our men." She wiped tears of mirth from her eyes. "I'd have paid to've seen the expression on his face." She placed her elbow on the table, getting cozy with her topic. "Sometimes with a man as handsome as your husband, it's good to rattle him up every once in a while. Of course, I imagine the reconciliation for your misdeeds was worth the trouble, right, Mrs. Dawson? We've all been talking about it in the kitchen ever since Ruth reported the mattress in the yard and Evie noticed the coverlet by the pond. You must have had a busy night last night, Mrs. Dawson." She waggled her eyebrows up and down.

Embarrassed to be the subject of such speculation, Mallory didn't know what to say. Fortunately, Mrs. Irongate changed the subject.

"Have you started the plans for the harvest home? Mrs. Watkins and I have some ideas."

Mallory refreshed the tea in their cups. "I'm to meet with Sylvie Hanson this afternoon on that subject. Why don't you come with us?"

"We'd like that very much." The housekeeper reached across the table and patted Mallory's hand. "When I first met you, I said to myself, that woman thinks she is too good for us."

"And what about me made you believe that?" Mallory asked, truly curious.

"Oh, it was the way you carried yourself, all stiff and quiet. Then there was that afternoon in the kitchen when you got so hoity-toity about our doing a bit of teasing. But you're not such a bad sort, after all." She lifted her cup to lips. "Besides, I have to admire any woman can keep a man like Mr. Dawson chained to her side."

Her words startled Mallory. "Chained to my side?"

Mrs. Irongate waved a dismissive hand. "Not actually, but you know what I mean. The man adores you. Everyone's noticed it. They say he picked you up and twirled you around at the Hansons' the other night and made all the other women so jealous, their own men had to do the same. The lads are all grumbling that they got dizzy trying to keep pace with Mr. Dawson."

"Are they, now?" Mallory said thoughtfully.

"Aye, they are. And in church yesterday, the man could barely keep his eyes off you. If I hadn't asked Mr. Dawson myself and found out you've been wed a good seven years, I'd have thought you both newlyweds."

"And why is that?"

"This may come as a surprise to you, my dear, but most husbands don't act the way yours does, not after the first year or two of marriage," Mrs. Irongate confided.

Mallory could well believe that. "And how do most men act?"

"Well, if it is a bad or mediocre marriage, the wife is ignored a good deal of the time. You should consider yourself a lucky woman to be married to a man who still enjoys ripping your clothes off and taking you to bed."

"Mrs. Irongate!" Mallory protested, her cheeks turning hot.

"You can't pretend with me. I saw your clothes thrown all over the floor every which way." She heaved a jealous sigh. "You must have had a wonderful night." With a wink, she added, "I'm surprised you don't have a score of children."

Mallory didn't want to touch that subject. "What is a good marriage, Mrs. Irongate?" she asked instead.

Mrs. Irongate gave a moment's serious thought to the question before replying, "A good marriage is where you and your husband know each other very very well and still like each other in spite of all the flaws. Of course, it helps if you enjoy a little Dickie Diddle every now and then. Smoothes over the bumpy times." She placed her teacup on the table. "I must be off. Thank you for the tea, and Mrs. Watkins will meet you at the barn to ride over to Mrs. Hanson's house."

Mallory thought about what Mrs. Irongate had said while she cleaned out the mugs. When she'd first seen John in London, she couldn't have imagined him as a father . . . but now she could. He'd be a good one.

I'd never condemn a child to the half-life I've lived . . . that was what he'd said when she'd asked if he'd fathered children out of wedlock.

Yes, he would take his responsibilities seriously, just as he took his responsibilities on the farm seriously. Even Hal, who was the very soul of reliability, would not have worked as hard as John had been working.

For a moment, she let herself dream she was pregnant. John's babies would be beautiful, especially if they had his eyes, and they'd be healthy. He was a strong man and she could expect strong children from him.

Of course, the same could be said for Hal—or could it? Her mother had pointed out that all three of Hal's sisters were sickly. Mallory didn't want weak children. She couldn't imagine any pain sharper than the death of a child.

She rose from the chair and set the cups in the cupboard. What nonsense was she thinking? The kind of father John would be and the health of his babies were not of importance to her, particularly since she knew she wasn't pregnant. Her menses had started that morning.

Telling herself not to be a goose, Mallory left for the pond to fetch the coverlet.

However, later, when John came in for the midday meal, Mallory caught herself studying him. She'd always admired his easy grace and long, tapered fingers. Now, while he slathered butter on a slice of her fresh bread and ate it, she noticed he had good teeth, his forehead was the right height, too. She didn't admire men with high foreheads, and she didn't want it for her children.

"Mallory, a shilling for your thoughts."

"What?" She shook her head, coming to her senses.

"You've been wool gathering," he told her, moving to stand by her, next to the hearth. He picked up the heavy iron teapot and poured boiling water into his cup. "You had such a frown on your face, I was afraid you were thinking of me."

He placed one arm against the mantel, his other holding his teacup, and Mallory was surprised by how close he was standing. "My thoughts weren't very interesting."

"I don't believe that. I find everything about you interesting."

For a second, she thought he was going to bend down and kiss her. Then he walked away . . . and she felt a small stab of disappointment.

"Freddie Hanson wants to accompany us tomorrow," John said. "I told him he could. Is that all right with you?"

"What? Oh, yes."

John sipped his tea and nodded at the stack of papers on the table. "We'll take these reports over to him when we pick him up. I discussed them with him this morning and he is actually excited by the prospect of filling them out. He considers them his link to Tyndale. Furthermore, he already has records based upon his crops. If Tyndale is smart, he'll hire Hanson as steward after I'm gone. The man's a bookkeeper as well as a damn good farmer."

"Most good farmers are," Mallory said. She busied herself by putting up the bread and butter, but she couldn't help admiring how long John's legs were, stretched out in front of him, and she had to step over them to cross to the cupboard. She'd want her sons to have long legs.

"Mallory, are you all right?"

She paused. "Of course, why would you think differently?"

"You keep looking at me. I'm starting to feel like a prize horse at Tattersall's and you're the buyer."

"John, that's ridiculous."

He laughed and rose from the chair. Before she realized what he was about, he planted a kiss on her lips, a light, quick one. "I'll see you this evening. Enjoy your afternoon with Sylvie."

Mallory thought about his light kiss all afternoon while she and the women planned the meals to be served during the harvest, when the workers would stop for a midday meal. John's light caresses had more power to slip by her defenses than his hungry, demanding kisses did.

She wasn't sure she liked being under siege—while another part of her liked it all too well!

It took a great deal of organization to feed people during the harvest. However, Mallory discovered, the menus and schedules that used to take her weeks to prepare when she was mistress of Craige Castle took merely hours with the competent help of Sylvie, Mrs. Irongate, and Mrs. Watkins. She enjoyed the work more, too, and wondered why she hadn't asked for assistance from the wives of her tenants at Craige Castle all these years past.

That evening, she and John discussed the plans that had been made. He was interested in every detail. When it came time for bed, he took her hand and with the coverlet and sheets under one arm, led her up to the barn. The mattress was still too damp to sleep on.

He made a bed for them in the same stall they'd used the night before, only this time he lay down on the covers beside her. Mallory considered protesting, but when John rolled over and fell into a sound sleep, she realized how silly her protest would have sounded.

Instead, she closed her eyes and went to sleep.

Freddie Hanson was good company on the way to Horsham. He had John stop beside several wheat fields and the three of them checked the grain heads. Mallory agreed with Hanson's opinion that the fields could be harvested at any time, especially if the good weather held.

In Horsham, amid the activity in the market square, they had very little trouble contacting a harvesting crew. After the price had been negotiated, Hanson ordered the crew to arrive at Cardiff Hall the following Monday. "We'll start with Lord Woodruff's fields first, then cover mine, and then the others."

John agreed.

Having accomplished their goal, John asked Hanson if he'd excuse them for an hour or so while they did a little shopping of their own.

Mallory was surprised by his request, but she was delighted when a few minutes later, John bought three new ribbons for her hair and a straw bonnet.

"I thought you said you liked my freckles," she teased, as she tried on the hat. It had a wide brim and shaded her face perfectly.

"I do," John answered with a lazy smile, "but I also want my wife to feel like a proper lady. In fact, why don't we go in here?" He nodded at a dressmaker's shop.

"Oh, I don't know," she said, suddenly shy. "I'm sure she won't have anything made up."

"Let's ask." He opened the door and a merry tinkle signaled their arrival.

Mallory stepped inside the cluttered little shop. A table in the center of the room held bolts of fabric. Tiny clippings of material littered the floor. The dressmaker sat in a windowseat where the light was good. She was hemming a lovely pale yellow muslin dress with tiny, perfect stitches.

She lay the dress aside and rose to assist them.

"I'm looking for a dress for my wife," John said.

The woman took in their ragged appearance from the toe of John's scuffed boots to the neckline of Mallory's worn out brown dress. "Can you pay?" she demanded rudely.

"Would I be here if I couldn't?" John said.

The woman sniffed her answer. "I may have something that will work. It's secondhand but quite serviceable." She hurried into a back room hidden behind a curtain.

Mallory drifted a finger over the pale yellow muslin, the color of sweet butter cream. She was tempted to lift the dress up to admire its cut, but hesitated.

"The color would be beautiful on you," John said close to her ear. He reached around, picked up the dress, and held it against her. The muslin fell gracefully to the floor at her feet. A green velvet ribbon trimmed the empire waist, and the short sleeves and modest neckline were exactly to Mallory's taste.

"I'd like to see you in this dress," John said.

"The dress is already sold," the dressmaker replied from behind them. "And I'll ask you to set it down."

John and Mallory turned as one. "But I'd like it for my wife," he said reasonably.

"I don't think you can afford it," the dressmaker said bluntly. She'd folded a dress over her arm, which she now shook out. It was a gray cotton printed with small purplish-blue flowers. "This is what I was thinking of. I can let you have it for six shillings, sixpence."

John considered the dress. "Do you like it, Mallory?"

She stepped forward. It was clean, and, as the dressmaker had said, "serviceable." "It's fine."

He smiled. "Good, we'll take the gray dress *and* the yellow dress."

The dressmaker made a sound of impatience. "Sir, the dress is not for sale . . . and even if it were, you would not be able to afford it."

Mallory shifted nervously. She didn't want a scene and tugged gently on John's coat sleeve. "I believe we should go, John."

He didn't budge. "I will give you fifty pounds for the gray and the yellow."

The dressmaker's mouth fell open. "Fifty pounds?"

"Fine," John said, taking the money from his pocket. "I'll give you sixty pounds for it."

"Sixty pounds?" The dressmaker raised a hand to her forehead. "But what shall I tell Lady Elizabeth? She wants this dress for a house party next Thursday."

John started counting out the money. "You can either make a new dress or think of an excuse. Tell her she doesn't look good in yellow."

He offered the money to the woman, who didn't hesitate to take it. "You're right, sir. She looks terrible in yellow. It makes her complexion sallow." Tucking the money in her bodice, she said, "Let me finish the hem and then I'll wrap up both gowns." She disappeared with an armful of clothes into the back room.

Mallory, who'd been watching the bargaining in amazement, found her voice. "John, where am I going to wear a dress like the yellow muslin? It's ridiculous to pay that price for a simple dress."

"You'll wear it to the harvest home. Besides, I've paid three times that amount for dresses before."

"For your mistresses?" she asked archly.

He crossed his arms and leaned against the door frame. "You knew I wasn't a saint." In a hopeful voice, he added, "Jealous?"

Yes. "No."

The dressmaker returned with both dresses

wrapped in paper tied round with string, and John and Mallory left.

Their next stop was the tailor's, where John found a linen shirt like the ones most of the men in Tunleah Mews wore. It was also secondhand.

They were on their way to meet Hanson when John spied an ancient cavalier's hat hanging from a traveling peddler's cart. He grabbed the hat off its hook and plopped it on his head. "Look, Mallory, what do you think?" He struck a pose.

"I think you look a spirited young blood in that hat, sir," she told him dramatically.

"Do you, now?" he said, taking it off. "Do you think my valet would approve?"

"Of course. You shall set a new style," she teased.

John turned to the peddler, waving the hat with a flourish. "My lady admires this hat and I must have it."

The grizzled peddler raised doubtful eyebrows and named an outlandish price. After a bit of haggling, John had a hat to wear for the reasonable price of ten shillings.

Freddie Hanson almost doubled over with guffaws at the sight of John's hat. "You look like a regular lord," he declared. "Lord John, the lord of the harvest feast."

"I knew you would be jealous." John held out a paper cone full of lemon drops they had purchased at a confectioner's. "This is for your children."

"Thank you," Hanson said. He nodded toward Mallory's packages. "I see you've done a bit of shopping. Your hat is charming too," he told her.

She sighed. "Thank you, Mr. Hanson, but I fear that standing next to my husband, I'll go completely unnoticed."

"That would be impossible," John countered. "They would see your lovely smile and the light of laughter in your eyes and wonder how did such a foolish bumpkin like me end up with you on my arm."

Mallory at first thought he was teasing and then realized from the serious expression in his eyes that he wasn't.

Before she was forced to reply, Hanson cut in good-naturedly, "No, Dawson, we'd all assume she's blind."

The three of them laughed and in high spirits headed for home.

On the way, John and Hanson began to discuss politics. Mallory should have warned John that whenever farmers got together there were only three topics of discussion: the crops, the weather, and politics. Actually, Hanson did all the talking and John listened.

"The House of Lords should be abolished. Half those fat and happy lords don't even show up to take their seats during the session. It's a crime we pay for those wastrels while the real work is being done by the common man." Hanson punctuated his words by pounding his fist against the side of the wagon. "Look at Woodruff or Tyndale. They don't care about us. All they want is their rent money."

He talked in that vein until they dropped him off at his door. John waited until they were well away before saying, "What do you think he'd say if he found out I was one of those he'd ranted and raved about?" He shot a sidelong glance at Mallory. "In the six months since I've inherited my seat in the House of Lords, I haven't stepped through the doorway once. I doubt I would know what they were talking about if I did. And I'm not alone. I can't imagine any members of my old set of friends listening to Freddie Hanson and taking his complaints seriously."

"Unfortunately, that's what this country needs," Mallory answered. "I agree with much of what he said. We do need men in power who understand the plight of the farmer and the yeoman. But so few in the House of Lords realize what those needs are."

John grew very quiet after that.

They shared a simple supper. John brought the mattress inside and they made up the bed together. He gave her a few moments of privacy.

Mallory climbed in the bed between the sheets, so tired she anticipated falling asleep before he returned. She was wrong. She lay awake waiting for him, certain that he would stretch out beside her, but uncertain how she'd react.

In the end, she was surprised when he lay down on top of the covers. He pulled her close, draping his arm over her body.

Mallory tensed. She waited.

John didn't move. His relaxed fingers were very close to her breast. If she took a deep breath, she could push herself out to touch him.

But she didn't.

Instead, she held herself rigid, ready to snap in outrage if he should attempt to seduce her—

while another part of her waited in the hopeful anticipation of a bit of seduction.

To confuse her feelings even more, he fell right asleep, as if being this physically close to her didn't bother him at all.

It was a long time before she also fell asleep.

There was much work to do around Cardiff Hall to prepare for the harvest. Each day, after another restless night, Mallory would rise and work by John's side. She learned to value and trust his judgment. She also enjoyed sharing the work with someone who knew how to laugh and lighten the load.

Evening and the very early hours of dawn became her favorite time because that was when they could talk in private. They didn't speak just about the harvest. Mallory questioned him about the war, his school years, and the places he'd traveled.

He asked her about her childhood and remembered enough details to tease her later. She started to look forward to his teasing—and to his touch.

John touched her often. His hand would rest on her waist while they listened to one of the farmers talk about his crop, or would brush loose strands of hair that had escaped her braid from her face, or would take her hand as they walked side by side.

A sense of longing and frustration began building inside her. She caught herself wishing that he wasn't such a gentleman, that he would sweep her off her feet and not give her any choices—and yet she understood that John was leaving the decision concerning the next step in their relationship up to her. Unfortunately, she still feared taking that step.

Sunday was usually a day of rest, but not during a harvest. John gave the other farm servants the afternoon off while he and Mallory prepared for the harvest crew that would arrive in the morning. The crew would live in the barn until all the crops were in.

It was a hot, busy day. Furthermore, they were both disappointed when messages arrived with young Roger. Peterson's message was the same as the week before: Louis Barron still had not been found.

There was also a letter from Mallory's mother and another from Hal.

Her mother was frantic with worry and insisted Mallory leave John immediately:

I have finally come to realize you were right in wishing a divorce from John Barron! It tears at my heart to see our beautiful home in the hands of a stranger. He has let all the servants go, and no one from the village is allowed to work there. They say he wears the strangest clothes and smokes tobacco and takes snuff. I cry when I think of my furniture.

Hal's letter was to the point:

My dear Mallory,

Tell me where you are and I will rescue you. Your

husband is beyond redemption. Save yourself. All that I have is yours. I pray you won't forget the promises we've made to each other.

Fondly,
Hal

She folded both letters and put them in the pocket of her brown dress. "I have no response," she told Roger.

John didn't ask her about the letters, although she was certain he was curious.

That evening they sat on the grassy bank of the bathing pond, watching the fireflies flit in and out of the shadows.

"You've been quiet ever since the messenger left," Mallory said. "Are you thinking about Louis?"

John leaned back in the grass and looked up at the stars. "He's one of the things I'm thinking about."

"What is the other?"

"The letter you received from your lovestruck squire."

She couldn't stop herself from answering as he'd answered her once, "Jealous?"

He glanced at her out of the corner of his eye. "Yes."

His blunt honesty took her aback. Mallory decided to change the subject to one they could agree upon. "I wish I could be more help in finding Louis Barron. We passed letters back and forth for years, but I don't know the man at all."

John leaned upon one elbow. "Please think,

Mallory. Did he ever mention anything personal about himself in any of his letters?"

She thought a moment and then said sadly, "No, it was as I told you. His letters were always vague responses to my questions or complaints. If he ever initiated a letter, it was only to ask questions after some major repair had been performed around the castle. Sometimes, he'd hire workmen who would show up to do things I hadn't authorized or felt were important."

"Such as?"

"Oh, the brick walkway that led to a new grape arbor he had built. Only three months ago, he put in a new pond and had it freshly stocked with trout. Meanwhile, he refused to send a decent allowance for our day-to-day expenses. And anytime I talked about the needs of the farm, he ignored my requests."

John lay back down. He was quiet for several minutes.

She placed her hand on his arm. "John, we'll find him."

"I want to think so, Mallory, but the more time elapses, the stronger my doubts grow." His next words shocked her: "I'm beginning to realize I may not get Craige Castle back for you."

Before she could answer him, he got to his feet. "Come. I'm ready to go back to the cottage." He offered her his hand.

Mallory placed her hand in his and he pulled her up. But he pulled her too hard and the bottoms of her new shoes were slick. Her feet went out from underneath her and John barely caught her in time before she fell into the pond.

He hugged her close and Mallory felt his swift, almost immediate reaction to her. She also discovered an answering response inside herself and pressed closer.

"Do you know what you are doing?" His raspy voice sounded hoarser than usual.

Mallory lifted her gaze to meet his and then had to turn away from the intensity of his too-knowing eyes.

"Do you want me, Mallory?"

Yes. One word, that's all she had to say—but she couldn't say it. She had to be careful. She had to protect herself.

"You still don't know, do you?" he whispered. "I'm beginning to wonder if you'll ever forgive me. Meanwhile, I'd like nothing better than to lay you down on the grass beside the pond and make love to you. I want to take you and fill you until you can think of no other man but me."

His hands gently pushed her away. "But I won't. You must come to me freely."

"You may be asking too much."

The intense light in his eyes faded. "I know."

Without another word, he turned, took her hand, and walked with her back to the cottage.

Mallory wondered if he noticed that her hands were shaking.

Inside the cottage, he pulled the coverlet off the bed. "We can't go on this way, Mallory. I think it would be best if I started sleeping in the barn again." Without waiting for her reply, he left.

She watched him until he'd climbed the path and disappeared into the gathering darkness. Slowly she closed the door and lowered the bar.

She was alone. It had been some time since she'd been alone in the cottage. She stretched. "Well, at least I'll get a good night's sleep." Her voice sounded lonely in the empty room.

Having nothing else to do, she undressed and went to bed . . . but sleep eluded her.

Would she be stupid to give John one more chance? Or would it be even worse if she didn't?

The questions chased around and around each other. It wasn't until past midnight that she finally realized what her heart had been trying to tell her.

She made her choice, and once it was made, fell into a sound, dreamless sleep.

The next morning, before dawn, she woke rested for the first time in weeks. She knew then that she'd made the right decision. She dressed quickly in her gray dress and hurried up to the barn.

John was already too busy organizing the harvest workers to exchange more than a few words of greeting. Mallory went to work. The harvest had begun.

Mallory worked as hard as anyone, but at one point, she managed to slip away. She found the Reverend Luridge sitting with Lord Woodruff in Cardiff Hall's dining room chairs. The chairs and a small table had been set up on a small knoll overlooking the fields. His lordship had brought out ink and paper and was already busily scribbling away.

"Reverend, may have a moment in private with you, please?"

"Why certainly, Mrs. Dawson," he said, coming to his feet.

Mallory led him several feet away from Lord Woodruff. "Reverend, I would like to surprise my husband during the harvest home and I need your help."

Chapter 17

They grew till they reached the church tip top,
When they could grow no higher;
And then they entwined like
a true lover's knot,
For all true lovers to admire.

"Lord Thomas and Fair Ellinor"

Harvesting fields is hard, back-breaking work.

A team of five men could expect to do two acres of fields a day. With the sixty men from the shire and the twenty-five men on the harvesting crew, John hoped to have the harvest done in ten days. Often, the men would break into song to relieve the tedium and strain of using the hand sickle row after endless row.

The women and children worked as hard as the men. Mallory divided her time between helping with the meals to feed such a large crowd and going out in the fields to tie off the sheaves of wheat after they'd been cut and gathered.

Her fingers ached from pulling at the stalks and twisting the ties. Her shoulders were sore from lifting, bending, and carrying. Each night she fell into bed exhausted.

John did not join her in the bed. He slept in the barn with the harvest crew. When the two of them did see each other, they rarely had time or energy to say more than a few words in passing, but no one from Cardiff Hall or the village noticed or made comment of their estrangement. Everyone, including Lord Woodruff, who wrote furiously while sitting at his desk beside the fields every day, was worn out.

Reverend Luridge insisted Sunday should be a day of rest. Most of his parishioners slept through his sermon. Then, that same Sunday afternoon, Evie had her baby. The people of Tunleah Mews considered the birth a good omen. Lord Woodruff practically danced for joy, declaring that the baby would be a harvest metaphor for his great "epic." Many people wondered what he meant.

Roger, the messenger, arrived late in the afternoon. Again, Peterson had nothing new to report and wanted to know what John wished to do. John sent back a message asking him to continue stationing men at all the ports and at the shops and places Louis had been known to patronize.

Mallory thought John might come to her Sunday evening, but he did not.

Finally, by midday of the following Friday, the last field was cut. When John took the last sheaf in his hand and held it high over his head, everyone cheered.

Tears came to Mallory's eyes. John had done

it—but more than the harvest, John had given this village a sense of community which, according to Sylvie Hanson and Mrs. Irongate, had not existed before.

In the middle of all the cheering, John and Mallory's gazes met. He walked over to her and offered her the sheaf of wheat. "We did it," he said.

"No, *you* did it."

"I wouldn't have attempted it without you."

No words of praise had ever sounded sweeter to her. "You're a very special man, John Barron."

"And are you glad you married me?" he prodded.

Mallory just smiled and walked away, pleased at this sign that his heart remained true.

That night the men dug two pits and started roasting the meat. A keg of ale kept them company. Mallory sat at the table beside the cottage window listening to them laugh, joke, and sing.

She was about ready to go to bed when she saw John approaching the cottage. His neck cloth was untied and hanging around his throat. He'd rolled up his sleeves, and he moved with a loose-limbed gait. She hurried to open the door, happy to see him. "John, come in."

He ducked his head under the low threshold and entered. This was the first time he'd been in the cottage since he'd left the night before the harvest. For a second, Mallory was tempted to run her hand across his strong, broad back . . . but then she noticed he was weaving slightly and the expression in his eyes was slightly glazed.

He said her name with a soft sigh. "Mallory."

The fumes on his breath almost knocked her backward. "John, you've been sampling the brew!"

"Someone had to do it," he confessed almost regretfully, as his tall form started to list to the right.

Mallory propped him up and walked them both over to the bed where she sat him down. He grinned up at her, his smile slightly silly. "Are you happy to see me?"

"Yes, very."

With the playfulness of a very large puppy, he put his arms around her waist and fell over onto his back, pulling her with him.

Mallory lay on top of him, held firmly by his iron embrace. It felt good to be this close to him. She rested her head against his chest. His fingers stroked her hair.

John yawned, then whispered, "I missed you, Mallory."

She rubbed his whisker-rough jaw with the back of hand. "I missed you, too."

"Enough to let me be your husband?" he asked, snuggling into the mattress.

"Oh, John, more than enough." She reached up to place a kiss on his lips—and then discovered he'd passed out cold. For a second, she stared, certain he must be playing a trick on her.

When he snored, she knew it was no game.

Smiling, she rose and with a great deal of effort removed his boots and tucked him in under the covers. She then undressed down to her petticoats and crawled happily in beside him.

* * *

The next morning a pounding on the door woke them both. John sat up and immediately groaned, grabbing his head.

Mallory slipped on her brown dress and answered the door. It was Wadham. He nodded a greeting. "We need Mr. Dawson. I arrived this morning to find one ale keg empty. We'll need another for the feast."

Mallory looked over her shoulder at John, whose face was very pale. "John, he says the men have already finished one keg. Would you know anything about it?"

John rose stiffly to his feet, pulled on his boots, and made his way to the door. "I know about it intimately." He pressed a small kiss to her brow and followed Wadham, who was declaring they had to get busy and clean out the barn for the party.

Mallory quickly dressed and joined the men and women cleaning the barn. Even with the help of Mrs. Irongate and the women from the harvesting crew, setting up for the feast required as much hard work as the harvest had. Furthermore, Mallory wanted this day to be extra special.

By four in the afternoon, all was ready and the first families had started to arrive. Every family brought at least one dish of food to share with the others. Soon the buffet tables were filled with every form of vegetable known to a farmer's garden. There were potatoes, cabbages, turnips, and carrots. Blood sausages and cheese were laid out on cutting boards, baskets of bread placed beside them. The highlight of the meal would be the desserts. The children couldn't stop eyeing the cherry and apple pies set out on a separate table. When Mrs. Watkins and Lucy walked in with their contributions, three large puddings and a bowl of rich custard, the children clapped, "oohing" and "ahing" with anticipation.

Mallory smiled at the children's excited expressions. Many had tasted pudding before, but few had sampled a custard. Mrs. Watkins beamed with well-deserved pride.

Lord Woodruff sat at his writing table, engrossed in finding words to describe the children's reaction to the custard. Over the last week, he'd written constantly, and Mallory sensed he seemed happier with his work. Certainly, she reflected, there were fewer wadded-up balls of paper at his feet. Furthermore, the villagers displayed more tolerance for his oddities.

Mallory suddenly realized the feast was about to begin and she wasn't ready. Begging Mrs. Irongate to supervise the carving of the meat, Mallory headed for the cottage at a run.

She practically bowled John over coming around the bend in the path. He caught her by the arms and steadied her. "You're going the wrong way."

She looked up at him and stopped, stunned. John had changed to a clean shirt and donned his jacket. He was also wearing the neck cloth trimmed in lace he'd brought with him from London. He looked the part of a gentleman farmer—a very handsome gentleman farmer. "You shaved," she said inanely.

"And managed to catch a few winks of sleep this afternoon." He ran his hands up and down her arms. "Mallory, I've been a damn fool. I miss you so much—"

"Dawson!" Freddie Hanson's voice shouted over the growing noise of the crowd. "Where's your cavalier's hat? You're the lord of the feast, man, and you must look the part!"

John raised his hand holding the ancient hat with its bedraggled gold plume and placed it on his head. Everyone watching from the barnyard roared with laughter. Mallory took advantage of that moment to slip away.

She hurried down to the cottage and changed from her "serviceable" gray dress to the lovely yellow muslin. Reaching behind her back, she tightened the laces and wished she had a mirror. She brushed her hair until it shone and then pulled it up on top of her head and tied it in place with a piece of green ribbon. The ends of her hair curled down past her shoulders. She knew John would like it this way.

Her stomach felt nervous and fluttery, and she pressed her hand against it. What if John didn't like what she'd planned? Immediately she erased all doubts from her mind. John loved her; she knew that now, just as she knew he was the only man she would ever love.

Realizing it was growing late, she hurried back up to the barn. Everyone was waiting for the feast to begin. The children were running in and out around the tables while the adults stood talking.

The Reverend Luridge appeared at Mallory's side. He took arm and patted her hand. "Are you ready?"

A shiver of anticipation ran through her. "I think so."

"He doesn't know anything?"

She shook her head. "It's going to be a surprise."

The Reverend Luridge led her to the head table, which had been set with Cardiff Hall's china. "Excuse me, everyone," he called in a loud voice. "I need your attention."

Everyone in the crowd shushed each other. When John, standing over by the keg, turned and saw her, his gaze warmed appreciatively. It made her feel very feminine.

"Before I give the blessing on this great feast," the Reverend Luridge was saying, "I've been asked to perform another small ceremony. Mr. Dawson, would you come forward?"

John handed his cavalier hat to Hanson and pushed his way through the crowd to stand by Mallory's side.

"Your wife, Mr. Dawson, has requested that the two of you repeat your wedding vows before we start the feast," Reverend Luridge said.

Mallory felt as nervous as a bride until John, his face lit with surprise and pleasure, took her hand in his. "I would like nothing better," he said.

The Reverend Luridge addressed the gathering. "I won't do a proper service because we're all hungry, but I'm going to say the important words. It's symbolic, you know, on this day of great celebration for our hard labor in the fields, that this couple wishes to renew their vows, because marriage is hard work too. It can be back breaking—"

Many of the men guffawed at this observation.

"It can also be fruitful," he continued, nodding toward a group of children impatient to start eating. "But it is always a challenge—at least, the good ones are." He turned his attention to the couple standing before him and began to recite the words from memory.

"John Dawson, will you have this woman to be your lawfully wedded wife, to live together after God's ordinance in the holy estate of matrimony? Will you love her, comfort her, honor and keep her, in sickness and in health; and, forsaking all others, keep her with you so long as the two of you shall live?"

John didn't hesitate. "I will."

The Reverend Luridge turned to Mallory. "Mallory Dawson, will you have this man to be your wedded husband, to live together in God's ordinance in the holy estate of matrimony? Will you love him, comfort him, obey him—" (John gave her hand a little squeeze on the word "obey") "—honor and keep him, in sickness and in health; and, forsaking all others, keep yourself only unto him, as long as you both shall live."

"I will."

The Reverend Luridge gave them a beatific smile. "Then I pronounce you man and wife." He rubbed his hands together. "Now for the harvest prayer."

"Wait, Reverend," John said. From his pocket, he pulled out her wedding ring. "I want to place this ring on Mallory's finger and I want as many witnesses as possible when I say to this woman, who has taken a vow to *obey* me—" His words were met by several chuckles around the room. "When I tell her," he repeated, "that she shall never remove this ring from her finger again." He slid the sapphire-and-diamond band on the ring finger of her left hand.

"Good heavens," the Reverend Luridge said, startled. "That ring must be worth a fortune!"

"It was my mother's," John answered, his gaze never wavering from Mallory's. And then, ever so slowly, he bent his head and kissed his bride.

After that, the harvest feast became a true celebration. There were few women in the room with dry eyes. Mrs. Irongate and Mrs. Watkins hugged Mallory with tears streaming down their faces, which dried quickly when they saw the ring. They appraised it with knowing eyes.

"First-rate," Mrs. Watkins said.

"It's been a while since I've seen a diamond that fine," Mrs. Irongate agreed.

Finally, everyone sat down to the feast, and a fine meal it was, too. John insisted upon feeding Mallory from his plate, the way any bridegroom would do for his bride.

Lord Woodruff sat beside them. "I say, this is fun. We should do it again next year."

"Yes," John agreed, giving Mallory a conspirator's smile.

Mallory waited until Lord Woodruff had wandered off, who knew where, before she said, "You're going to miss this, aren't you?"

John looked around the room. Most of the children were finished eating and begging their mothers for a slice of pie or a spoonful of custard. The men had gathered in a group around the ale keg while the women formed their own clusters around the children and the food tables.

"Yes, I will. Before coming here, I thought the only thing I was good at was being a soldier, a fighter. But I've now learned it's more rewarding to plant something, even something as simple as an idea, and watch it grow." He leaned toward her. "Thank you, Mallory."

"I did nothing."

"Oh, but you did. There were times during the last week when tempers flared and petty fights started among the workers, when I ached with exhaustion, but I continued on just because I wanted to prove you were wrong to consider me a worthless husband."

"I was wrong," she admitted readily.

Before they could say anything else, the call went out to start the dancing. This time, Mallory didn't hesitate to take part. John had to play with the small band of musicians, but he managed to steal three dances with her. The last was a waltz.

She'd never waltzed before, but she trusted him. He took her in his arms, one hand on her waist, and they joined the other couples twirling and gliding around the barn.

Then John waltzed her out the door into the velvet night.

"Where are we going?" she asked.

"Where we can be alone."

Taking her hand, he led her down the path. They weren't the only ones with the same idea. Other couples strolled along the moonlit path, and a few were even hiding in the bushes.

Inside the cottage, John barred the door and

pulled the shutters closed. He turned and watched Mallory as she lit a candle. Its glow filled the small room.

His wife . . . she was graceful, lovely, serene, intelligent, spirited, and challenging—everything a man could wish for in his life's mate.

He pushed away from the door and walked to her. "I've been wanting to do this since the moment you walked into the barn tonight."

Taking her in his arms, he swooped down and kissed her with urgent hunger. And Mallory kissed him back, her passion matching his own.

John buried his face against her neck and her sweet-smelling hair. He pressed against her until she could feel the strength of his need for her.

"I don't ever want to lose you."

Her arms hugged him fiercely. "You won't. I'm yours, John. I want to be yours."

With a glad cry, he kissed her again and then picked her up and carried her to the bed. Their lips met, her tongue teasing his while his hands unlaced the dress.

He laid her out there. His loins throbbed to possess her, but he wanted to take his time. He wanted this night to be memorable.

Coming down on one knee, he lifted her foot and removed one worn kid slipper. They were the shoes she'd worn when they escaped the bailiff. "I, John Barron, Viscount Craige, take you, Mallory Barron, Viscountess Craige, to be my wedded wife." He slipped her other shoe off her foot and placed it on the floor.

She wore no stockings, and he smiled, remembering the pair with the hole in the toe. He ran his hands along the back of her calves and up her thighs, pushing her skirts up. He pressed a kiss first on the inside of one thigh, then the other.

He looked up at her. The neckline of her dress he'd unlaced now hung wantonly around her shoulders. The bow in her hair ribbon had come loose during the dancing. He reached out and pulled it. Her hair came tumbling down around her shoulders. Nuzzling her collarbone, he pushed her dress lower and lower, but then she stopped him.

She tilted his head up to his. "I, Mallory Barron, Viscountess Craige, take you, John Barron, Viscount Craige, to be my wedded husband." Her voice sounded sure, feminine, possessive.

She pushed his jacket off his shoulders. Her bare thighs on either side of his body hugged him in place when he started to move. Her fingers began untying his neck cloth. "I promise to love you," she said, and tossed the neck cloth aside. She tugged on his shirt. "To comfort you and honor you."

She smiled as she said the words. He reached over and nipped her neck, working his way up to her ear. "You forgot 'obey,'" he reminded her.

She laughed, the sound seductive. "Oh no, my lord. If you are to be obeyed, then first you must *earn* it." She leaned back, pulling his shirt off over his head.

John sat on the edge of the bed beside her and took off his boots, then rose to his feet. "And how do I earn it?"

"By honoring me, and this marriage."

"I worship you." He pulled her up to stand on

the bed in front of him. Greedy now, he pulled down her dress and chemise, while his lips came down on her breast. Her nipple was already hard for him. He took it in his mouth, indulging himself in the sweet taste of her and her small sighs of pleasure. Her fingers curled in his hair and she repeated his name over and over.

John pushed the yellow muslin and cotton petticoats down over her hips and looked into her pleasure-glazed eyes. "I will love you as I have never loved another, and I will comfort you and honor you all the days of my life," he swore earnestly.

Mallory came down on her knees in front of him. Her eyes shone with her love for him, and he could swear he'd never met a more beautiful woman.

Her fingers began unfastening the buttons of his breeches. "And I shall obey you, my husband, because I choose to obey you out of my love and respect for you. I will be by your side wherever you are, and I will always be proud to be your wife."

He hugged her to him. "Dear God, Mallory . . . there is no gift more precious than your love for me. I could never live without you."

Tears ran down her face, but they were tears of joy, and he kissed each and every one of them away, and then kissed her freckles until she was laughing with joy.

His fingers touched her and then slid inside her as he laid her back on the bed and stretched out beside her. Her hips arched.

"John, I want you in me. I need you."

He settled himself over her. "Mallory, this is our wedding night. This is our consummation." He kissed her, and as he did so, he slowly entered her, marveling at the feel of her muscles tightening around him and pulling him deeper.

He took his time making love to her. He wanted to erase any bad memories she might have had of their time before.

But Mallory didn't want to go slowly. The wanton movements of her hips matched his, and soon John didn't know who was the seducer and who was the seduced.

She brought her legs up around him, pulling him still deeper. Sweat dampened their bodies as he increased the tempo, driving into her over and over again, giving her as much as he could. . . .

And then he felt the trembling inside her. She cried out his name, giving herself completely over to that magic moment, the completion, the release.

John, buried inside her, lost himself. There would be no other woman for him. He realized it in his soul, and for the first time in his life, he found a home . . . right here in Mallory's arms.

They lay together for long moments afterward, and when he thought he finally had enough energy to move, he lifted his head and asked, "How do you feel?"

Her dark eyes still glazed with passion, she answered, "Married."

John made love to his wife three more times that night. He couldn't seem to get his fill of her.

When he wasn't making love to her, he held her

in his arms and they talked. They talked about anything and everything.

They wondered what Lord Woodruff would do when they left the area and decided he would be fine if Freddie Hanson agreed to be steward. They shared confidences of things they'd never discussed with anyone else—ever.

They made plans. Her head on his chest, Mallory idly circled his nipple with one finger. "I was afraid of what would happen if we were forced to leave England." She flattened her hand and felt his heart beating beneath it. "I'm not afraid anymore, as long as I'm with you."

He hugged her tight. "It won't come to that."

"But if it does, I no longer fear the future."

John placed a kiss on her forehead and ran the sole of his foot against the back of her calf. "I keep asking myself where is the one place I wouldn't think to look for Louis, because that is where he will be. He's been planning this for years, but he's wrong if he believes I'll let him get away with it."

Mallory rested her chin on his chest. "John, I love you."

When he smiled at her, she laughed.

"What's so funny?" he asked.

"Your dimple. You have a secret dimple that every once in a great while pops out right here." She traced the right corner of his mouth with her tongue.

Her actions excited him again and she squirmed when she felt his arousal pressed against her stomach.

She started to roll over onto her back, but he held her in place. "Let me teach you a new trick," he said softly, and then, lifting her up, seated her upon him.

"Oh, John," Mallory whispered, "I love this trick."

An inner voice woke John in the wee hours of the morning. He started to roll over and return to sleep, but the voice was persistent. It echoed his words spoken earlier: *Where would be the last place you would look for him?*

Mallory's voice intruded into his thoughts. "John, are you awake?"

"Yes." He snuggled her close to him.

"I find myself wondering about the new owner of Craige Castle," Mallory said. "In her letter, Mother said no one has seen him. He stays to himself. I can only hope he takes care of the tenants."

John nodded—and then was struck by her words. "You said the new owner stays to himself."

"Ummm-hmmm." She was already starting to drift back to sleep. "Mother is worried about her furniture. She claims the new owner smokes and takes snuff. She probably fears he will leave burn marks on the tables. We shall have to teach her, John, that there is a good life beyond Craige Castle."

John sat back, stunned by what he was thinking. "No, Louis wouldn't.

"Wouldn't what?" Mallory asked, turning over to look at him.

"Craige Castle," John answered.

"Excuse me?"

John rose from the bed. "Louis is at Craige Castle."

"You can't be serious."

"I am completely serious. In fact, the more I think about it, the more I know I'm right. It's the only place he could be." He lifted Mallory from the bed and gave her a big kiss. "We've solved the mystery, Mallory. We're going to recover our fortune!"

Chapter 18

Then I will stay with you for ever,
If you will not be unkind.
Madam, I have vowed to love you;
Would you have me change my mind?
O No, John! No, John! No, John! No!

"O No John!"

After church that morning, John joined Lord Woodruff in his study and told him they would be leaving that very day. Woodruff did not take the news well.

"What shall I do? Who will take care of me?" he asked, pouring himself a very full glass of wine.

Mallory was struck with the observation that during the harvest, when Lord Woodruff hadn't been hiding away in his study, he'd actually drunk very little wine. Now the man was back to his old habits.

"Who will manage Cardiff Hall?" he continued. "What will I say to Tyndale?"

"The man to manage Cardiff Hall is Freddie

Hanson," John said. "He's living in the steward's quarters as it is and he's finishing the reports for Tyndale. I took the liberty of speaking to him this morning. He'll do the job but expects you to pay him well. I believe he's worth the money. As for Tyndale, you don't need to say anything. He has no idea who I am."

Lord Woodruff scratched his chin with an ink-stained finger. "Then that whole story about your being robbed and all was a hoax?"

"Not exactly," John said grimly, but didn't elaborate.

Mallory found that the hardest people to say farewell to were Mrs. Irongate and Mrs. Watkins. She'd told them their full story.

"A Viscountess!" Mrs. Irongate exclaimed, as she hugged Mallory good-bye.

"Oh, now, dry your tears, Lydia," Mrs. Watkins said. "We should have known something was up the minute we saw the ring he placed on her finger last night."

"Oh, but Emma," Mrs. Irongate said, "think of the things we've said to Mrs. Dawson—I mean, our lady . . ." She covered her mouth with her hands. "Oh no, that's not right."

"The Viscountess," Mrs. Watkins supplied for her.

"Yes," Mrs. Irongate agreed, bobbing a curtsey. "The Viscountess." Fresh tears of joy rolled down her cheeks. "It's so romantic. You looked beautiful, dear, in the yellow gown last night. Just like a true lady."

Mallory left the two women crying and waving

their farewells from the kitchen door. John had received Lord Woodruff's permission to borrow his coach, which was still hitched to the horses after the ride to church, and they'd packed what little clothing and personal items they had in the hamper. Freddie Hanson was going to drive them to Horsham, where they would hire another coach. John was hoping to meet Roger on the road. If not, he would send a message directly to Major Peterson from the Horsham posting inn.

While he was busy, Mallory took a moment to return to the cottage. It looked so forlorn and empty now . . .

She walked through the open front door and stood in the middle of the room. The mattress was bare since she'd returned the sheets and coverlet to Mrs. Irongate. The smoke stains on the white-washed walls were more noticeable now, and she missed the smell of fresh baked bread that had already disappeared from the room.

This cottage had been their first home, and she realized she was going to miss it.

"Are you ready to go?" John said from the doorway. He stepped inside. "Mallory, you're crying. What's wrong?" He wiped several big, fat tears from her eyes with his thumbs.

Mallory threw her arms around him and buried her face against his neck. "I love you so . . . but I'm afraid. What if we leave here and you find you don't love me as much as you've loved me here?"

He pulled her away so that he could look in her eyes. "Mallory, I will always love you. I love your intelligence, your wit, the way you laugh, and the way you cry." He brushed another tear away.

"But most of all, I love your courage . . . and that in my darkest hour, you stood beside me. You're everything any man could ever want in a wife, whether he's living in a small cottage or in a grand castle."

He kissed her then—and by the time he was done, Mallory could barely stand on her own two legs, let alone doubt his love.

Fifteen minutes later, they set out in Lord Woodruff's coach to meet their fate at Craige Castle.

They met Roger on the road outside Cardiff Hall and John sent him back with a message for Major Peterson to meet them in Chelmsford, a point halfway between London and Craige Castle, as soon as he was able.

In Horsham, Hanson bade them godspeed and good luck, then drove the aged coach back to Cardiff Hall. John hired a driver and a sleek, well-sprung coach pulled by a spirited team.

"We might as well travel in style," he told Mallory, as he knocked on the roof, a signal for the driver to start.

"We'll be on the road for days. What shall we do with our time?" Mallory asked, disappointed to be leaving on a Sunday rather than on a day of the week, when the shops were open. She would have appreciated a book or small game of some kind to while away the hours to Craige Castle.

"Oh, I imagine I can think of ways to keep you entertained," John said, with a suggestive smile.

"Entertained? How?" she asked.

John pulled the shade down over the coach

windows and kept her very well entertained, indeed.

They spent the nights at coaching houses. Major Peterson was waiting for them in Chelmsford with five hired men.

Mallory knew John would prefer to be riding with the men, but he stayed in the coach with her. She felt guilty.

"You'd make better time if you rode with Major Peterson and left me behind," she said.

"Louis will be there no matter when we arrive," he told her.

"How can you be so sure?"

"Because he thinks we've left the country . . . and because my uncle obviously believes I'm stupid." John smiled. "I can't wait to see the expression on his face when I walk through the front door."

It took them another day's travel from Chelmsford to East Anglia. Both John and Mallory had grown more quiet, the closer they'd come to their destination.

Mallory stared at the passing scenery, watching it become more and more familiar. Finally, she gathered her courage and turned to her husband. She touched his hand resting on the seat between them. "John, I'd like to see my mother before we go to Craige Castle."

He frowned at her. "She's with your squire, isn't she?"

Mallory slid across the seat to him. "He's no longer *my* squire, but yes, I need to see him, too." She covered his mouth with her fingers to stop the protest he was about to make. "John, do I have any reason to be jealous of other women in your life?"

He leaned away from her as if he knew where this conversation was leading and didn't like it one bit. "Of course not."

"Then you have no need to be jealous of Hal. But I do owe him an explanation, and my mother as well, about what has happened. I must do it now, John. It won't get any easier the longer I wait. Furthermore, Hal is the Magistrate. He can help us, but first I must face him."

He pressed a kiss against her finger and then stuck his head out the window, shouting for the coachman to pull up. "You will need to give the coachman directions to Squire Thomas's home."

They pulled up the drive of Squire Thomas's home several hours before dark.

John was impressed. The rambling country house was larger than Cardiff Hall and showed more signs of prosperity. The cobbles in the drive were fresh and new. A manservant opened the front door to greet the visitors. His eyes went wide when he saw Mallory, and he rushed out to help her from the coach.

A minute later, Lady Craige and a gentleman came hurrying out to greet her.

Mallory squeezed John's hand. "Please, give me a few moments alone with them."

John was not happy, but she didn't wait for his consent. Instead, she walked forward to hug her mother.

Lady Craige was much the way John remembered her. Mallory had told him that her mother had donned black at her father's death and never taken it off. She was a touch shorter than Mallory, and though they had the same coloring and similar features, Lady Craige lacked the alertness and directness in her gaze that John so admired in his wife.

Hal Thomas was a complete surprise.

Far from being a pudgy, balding, self-important squire, the man was almost as tall as John himself. He had the wavy black hair women so often found attractive and that John wanted to dismiss as effeminate. But what was truly disconcerting to John was that Thomas had something that John had envied all his life, a look and air of respectability, of good family and fine breeding. No scandal had ever touched this man's name—and it said a great deal about the depth of Thomas's affection for Mallory that he would be willing to marry a divorced woman.

Thomas ignored John's presence while Lady Craige scowled fiercely at him, then the three of them went into the house. John watched them walk away: Lady Craige in her black, Thomas in his well-cut jacket and shining boots, and Mallory in the lovely yellow dress she'd worn the night of the harvest home. She and Thomas made a handsome couple—and John hated the thought.

After three minutes of waiting, he was tempted to enter the house, throw Mallory over his shoulder, and ride off with her. Instead, he cooled his heels pacing up and down the drive.

Peterson and the other men had watched the homecoming silently. Now Peterson approached him. "I believe we'll travel up the road a bit to a posting house in search of fresh horses. Do you wish to accompany us, or should we bring you back a mount?"

"Bring it back," John said curtly.

Peterson smiled. He tried to cover it with his hand, but John caught sight of it. "What is so amusing?" he growled.

"You," Peterson said. "I never thought I'd see the day you were in love."

John didn't deny it. "She's my life."

Peterson laid a hand on his friend's shoulder. "I'm happy for you."

"Well, let's just hope I can keep her."

"Craige, she's mad for you. No other woman would have gone through what she has the past several weeks if she wasn't in love."

John stared at Thomas's front door. "I believe that, but he can offer her so much more."

"John, don't be a jealous fool. Your lady loves you."

Peterson left with the others. John resumed his pacing.

It seemed like hours before the door opened and Mallory came out. Lady Craige and Thomas followed her, their expressions grim.

John had been leaning against the coach, and he now pushed away. He searched her face, afraid to see some change in her feelings toward him mirrored there.

Mallory crossed the cobblestone drive, and with a reassuring smile, placed her hand in the crook of his elbow. "Mother, you remember John."

"I do." Lady Craige's voice could have frozen the Thames.

"It's good to see you again, my lady," John answered, and made a courteous bow. He knew better than to move closer to her.

"And this is Hal Thomas, who has been a very good friend to my mother and myself."

John could tell from the man's rigid stance that he wasn't any happier about Mallory's choice than Lady Craige was. Therefore, John was surprised when Thomas stepped forward and offered his hand.

"Congratulations, Craige," the squire said.

Releasing Mallory's hold, John took the few steps necessary to shake the man's hand. "Thank you."

Suddenly, the next thing John knew, he was knocked flat to the ground by the power of a left fist.

Stars flashed before his eyes as Mallory cried out in alarm. John shook his head and raised himself up on one elbow. He gingerly moved his jaw back and forth to be sure it wasn't broken.

Mallory had dropped to her knees beside him, but John held up a hand to ward her back. He looked up at Thomas. "You throw a strong left punch."

"So I've been told," came the calm reply. The squire offered his hand to help John up.

Accepting his offered hand, John said, "I suppose that was for Mallory."

"Aye, and for the seven years you left her alone."

"Well, I deserved the punch." He held out his hand.

Thomas took it. "You won this time, but don't ever mistreat her, Craige, for I'll be there to sweep her up if you do. I shouldn't have lost her this time."

"There will be no next time," John promised.

Thomas turned to include the women in their conversation. "Let's go inside then and see what we can do about bringing this uncle of yours to justice."

The plan they made was simple. They formed a party of ten mounted men, which included some of Thomas's servants, and rode straight into the confines of Craige Castle. Mallory was unhappy to be left behind, but neither John or Hal wished to risk her life.

It was a dark, misty night with heavy fog, and no one challenged them until they were inside the old courtyard past the rebuilt stone walls. There, three rough-looking characters were huddled under the eaves, trying to stay dry. They carried rifles.

Without waiting for the others, John dismounted and walked right up them. "Good evening to you, gentlemen."

The largest of the group blocked his path. "We don't like visitors here," the man said in the unmistakable accent of a Thames arkman.

Now John was sure Louis was here. He didn't waste time, but jabbed the man in the gut and then knocked him out cold with a blow to his jaw.

The other two men started for him, but Peterson's voice stopped them in their tracks. "I've got a brace of pistols trained on each of you. You'd best put down your weapons."

The men quickly complied.

While one of Thomas's servants tied them up, the squire said to John, "You don't plant such a bad facer yourself."

"You'd be wise to remember that."

Thomas laughed. "What I don't understand is why you would take on an armed man with nothing but your fists."

"I was gambling his powder wasn't dry," John answered, and then led the way into Craige Castle.

They found Louis Barron dining alone in the great hall. John motioned for the other men to stay back in the shadows while he stepped forward.

"Good evening, Uncle," John said.

His uncle looked up from a stuffed capon and all color drained from his face. Louis had the Barron looks. Like John's father, he was short of stature, with light blue eyes and graying blond hair. He wore a napkin for a bib over his yellow velvet evening jacket. "You're back? You can't be. I sent men to Italy to make you sure you didn't return. They didn't kill you, did they?"

John sat on the edge of the table. "I never left for Italy, Uncle."

"But I saw proof. There were tickets."

"Purchased, but not used." John reached over and untied the napkin. "Why did you do it, Louis?"

Tears pooled in the man's eyes. He looked away and collected himself a moment before saying, "I got damned tired of working for my living—and being poor."

John scoffed at the idea. "You were far from poor."

"You don't know. You didn't have my expenses. You never cared for much in the way of comfort, like I did. And it wasn't fair."

"What wasn't fair?"

"That you inherited. You're a bastard. I'm the real Viscount Craige. This all would have been mine—"

"And so you stole it."

Louis clapped his hands down on the table. "I've just righted an injustice."

For a fleeting second, John felt pity for the man—and just as quickly squashed it. By Louis's own admission, he'd wanted to do more than steal John's money; he wanted to see him dead. But it wasn't fear of his own life that made John angry—it was that Louis had threatened Mallory.

"And I'm here for vengeance," John said grimly.

Louis's eyes opened wide. He shoved the chair back and looked as if he were about to bolt, but instead, fell to his knees at John's feet. "No, John, you can't."

"Yes, I can. Where's the money, Louis?"

His uncle started shaking. "I have some of it, but I lost a great deal."

"Tell me."

"I lost it gambling, John. I got in debt over some heavy play."

"How long has this been going on?"

"Years. My brother wouldn't help me, and it made me angry, because it all should have been mine. But then, I realized I had your money, the funds you had from your mother, and I borrowed some."

"Borrowed?"

"I would have paid it back. I planned to."

John shook his head. "I would have given it to you, but instead, you stole it and forced my wife to go without."

"Oh, John, look around you. The estate is fine," Louis said, but they were the last words he spoke for a few seconds, as John grabbed him by his neck cloth so tightly that the man couldn't breathe.

Peterson came forward and touched John's arm. "Don't murder him, Craige—he's not worth it."

John stood and let Louis drop to the floor, where he gagged and choked, trying to draw breath.

"What about the rest of the money?" John demanded impatiently.

Louis struggled to his feet. "Most of it is gone," he croaked out. "I kept gambling with it, hoping I could recover my losses, and then I was in so deep I had to go the moneylenders. That was years ago. I've been borrowing from them using your name ever since."

"Then when I returned from the war, you decided to leave," John guessed.

"I knew it couldn't go on much longer. I took

what I felt was rightfully mine, Craige Castle, and left London."

John turned on his heel and walked away, afraid he'd strangle the man if he stayed close. At last he exercised enough control over himself to ask, "Is there any of it left?"

"A good amount," Louis said. "It's in a strong-box up in my bedroom."

John nodded to Thomas, who stepped out of the shadows. "This man is Squire Thomas, Louis. He is the local Magistrate. I am remanding you to his custody. Goodbye, Louis. We shall never see each other again."

"But what will happen to me?" Louis asked.

"I'll see you deported," Thomas answered. "Especially after witnessing the confession you've just made."

Mallory paced the floor of Hal's front hall. Her mother was just as nervous. She sat in the drawing room, twisting a handkerchief in her lap.

They both heard the horses on the front drive at the same time. Mallory reached the door first and flung it open.

John sat on a dappled gray horse in front of the door. Behind him, the others dismounted—except for John's uncle. Mallory barely remembered the man from the wedding. With his arms tied behind his back, he sat waiting for one of Thomas's servants to help him down from the animal.

John held out his hand to her. "Mallory, come join me."

Without a backward glance, she went over to him. He reached a hand down, and taking hold of her wrist, pulled her up to sit in front of him. She spread the skirts of the yellow muslin over her legs.

"Wait!" Lady Craige said, starting toward them. "Where are you going?"

"Home," was John's answer, and he put his heels to the horse.

His body shielded her from the mist as he rode down a road she could walk in her sleep, the road to Craige Castle.

"You found him?" she asked.

"Yes."

"And the money?"

"There is some." His jaw tightened a moment in anger and she laid her hand against it.

"We will be fine," she said.

He smiled down at her. "Yes, we will. Peterson told me that most of my debts have been satisfied by the sale of my properties and possessions. They sold everything except Craige Castle. Louis had had papers drawn up that made it appear the castle was his property."

A few minutes later, they trotted through the gates of her beloved home and up to the front door. John dismounted and placed his hands on her waist to help her down, then paused for a moment. "Do you know, Mallory, I can't say that I'm sorry he did any of it."

"You aren't?"

"No." He pulled her from the saddle and cradled her in his arms. "Because if he hadn't stolen my money, I would never know what I know now."

Mallory looped her arms around his neck. "And what is it you know now?" she asked softly.

"That the richest of all men, my dearest love, is a happily married one." He turned the handle of the door and carried her over the threshold. "Welcome home, darling."

Afterword

For now she'll be my bride,
My joy and my dear,
And now she'll walk with me anywhere.

"My Man John"

John and Mallory Barron, Viscount and Viscountess Craige, lived to celebrate fifty-one years of marriage together.

Lord Craige took his seat in the House of Lords and became one of the most respected members of Parliament. He was known for his intelligence and compassion, and especially for his knowledge of issues pertaining to agricultural matters.

When the Duke of Wellington's party came into power, he asked Lord Craige to serve as a member of his cabinet, which Lord Craige did for two years, until 1830. At that time, he was named British Ambassador to Italy and later to the even more difficult position, Ambassador to France.

Many inside the government believed the success of his ambassadorships had much to do with the charm and grace of his wife. Lady Craige could converse comfortably with anyone from the lowest chimney sweep to the highest grand dame, and so great was her influence in society that she almost made freckles fashionable.

The Viscount and Viscountess had five children, four sons and a daughter, all of whom went on to successful positions in society and government.

To this day, Craige Castle remains in the hands of the Barron family.

As a note of general interest to the reader: no works written by Lord Bartholomew Woodruff have been passed down to us today. It is not known whether he ever finished his great epic poem, "The Fields of Harvest," or if publishers found it unpublishable. However, parish records from St. Michael's in Tunleah Mews document several "harvest poetry readings" held by Bartholomew Woodruff, 4th Baron Woodruff, between 1814 and his death in 1827.

The records also show a harvest home has been celebrated in the great barn at Cardiff Hall from 1813 until the present day.

And may its rafters always ring with music, love, and laughter.